DARK WIND RISING

Brenna glanced again at the sky—could she get home before dark?—and at Parker, trying to gauge him. What he might do if she simply got to her feet and left him there.

What could he do? He was stuck on the other side of the creek.

And that's when Druid whined. His fearful whine, the warning whine. Reminding her that while she was out of Parker's reach, the darkness—the rising power—had no such boundaries. "Shhh," she said, even as she dreaded what might happen next. What *did* happen next.

That trickle of breath-sucking fear she'd finally come to recognize. The hair standing up on the back of her neck, goosebumping down her arms. The breeze rising, lifting the strands of her long thick hair, then roaring across the bottom of the pasture like a tornado.

Heading straight for her. . . .

D1051344

BAEN BOOKS
by Doranna Durgin

Dun Lady's Jess
Changespell
Barrenlands

Touched By Magic
Wolf Justice

Wolverine's Daugbhter

Seer's Blood

A Feral Darkness

Other Books
Star Trek: The Next Generation—Tooth and Claw
Earth: Final Conflict—Heritage

A Feral Darkness

Doranna Durgin

A FERAL DARKNESS

This is a work of fiction. All the characters and events portrayed in this book are fictional, and any resemblance to real people or incidents is purely coincidental.

Copyright © 2001 Doranna Durgin

All rights reserved, including the right to reproduce this book or portions thereof in any form.

A Baen Books Original

Baen Publishing Enterprises
P.O. Box 1403
Riverdale, NY 10471
www.baen.com

ISBN: 0-671-31994-9

Cover art by Larry Elmore

First printing, June 2001

Distributed by Simon & Schuster
1230 Avenue of the Americas
New York, NY 10020

Typeset by Brilliant Press
Printed in the United States of America

This is Jag's book

Runes, like our own words, can differ in interpretation depending on context.

With thanks to:

John Forth-Finegan of Canine Specialties, Peter Braggins of the Greece Animal Control, Martyn Miller DVM, Gretchen Wood of the Greece Humane Society, the Anti-Animal Fighting Task Force of Monroe County, Tom Haverly at Colgate Rochester Divinity School, Reverend Marie Sheldon, Donna & Tara Defendorf (who might well recognize the barn), Morgan Ryan, Anne Bishop, my family, Jennifer who put up with my fits of creative angst, and (deep breath) Judith!

Chapter 1

ᚦ

THURISAZ
A Gateway

Always

Forgotten gods fill the layers of heaven. Quiescent, subordinate, long ago superceded. Waiting. And every so often, reminded of their own existence.

Nineteen Years Before Now

She is nine years old, with tears streaming down her face and the intermittent hiccough of a sob jerking her chest. Dressed in the ragged cut-offs and worn T-shirt that have been the choice of a generation of children, she does not wait to hear the rest of her mother's words. She races out of the house, the screen door banging hollowly in her wake, and runs across

1

the soft spring grass of the yard to duck between the first and second strands of the electric fence, feeling the swift zing of electricity run above and below her.

The old hound follows at his leisure, but follow he does, as stubborn in this as ever in following a trail—even though it takes him a moment to rise and his movement is stiff when he does. His tail waves in gentle arcs as he detours to slip between gate and post rather than duck the fence wire. The day is barely warm enough for the shorts that hang on the girl's lanky frame, but he is already panting.

She stops to wait for him. Of course. And one hand slips inside her back pocket to feel the stiff, folded square of paper only recently purloined from her father's magazine. On it is a photo of a sculpture, a simplistically elegant hound—not a treeing hound like her lifelong companion, but a gaze hound, couchant, with a long neck and pointed nose, and a gaze hound's insignificant ears.

He catches up with her, pleased with himself, and lifts his head to look up at her with a hound smile through his panting. Unlike the statue, his ears are long and heavy and the softest things she ever has or ever will feel. But she doesn't care about the differences between her companion and the Lydney Hound. She's not particularly concerned about all the details in the accompanying article that are beyond her ability to digest—cold anthropological facts that even her father doesn't read. She's seen him turning the pages with dirt-encrusted fingers, skipping from one bright glossy photo to another and getting glimpses of places that don't yet pull her own attention away from this small farm. That's all he wants, the glimpses, and when he's had enough he puts the magazine beside his lounge chair and ambles off to see if he can fix whatever mechanical thing has gone wrong now.

This is how she finds the Lydney Hound, and—later, sneaking the magazine into her bedroom—reads about the oddly named god called Mars Nodens who favors hounds, who likes dogs of all sorts. Who has an ancient shrine from olden days so olden she can't even begin to imagine the scope of it and again . . . doesn't care.

What she cares about is that his shrine was a healing shrine. That he favors dogs, that the shrine, even after all this time, is littered with representations of them. And that the right-side pasture has some of the other things she's been able to make sense of in that article—the wide, cold creek that runs deep in all but the driest months, a hill rising on one side of it to hold not only the area's biggest oak, but a tiny spring as well. The tiniest of springs, really, a damp spot that the ground downhill reabsorbs practically before the water has a chance to join the creek, but a spring nonetheless.

She wonders briefly if her own God, her assigned God, will thunderously disapprove of her intent.

But then, He's had His chance, hasn't He? Hasn't she said her prayers to Him, over and over? And did it stop her mother from saying *those* words about her cherished old hound, only moments ago? Or her brother from making fun of the dog's aged movement?

She smears the drying tears from her cheeks and runs her hand down the dog's soft ear. Maybe Mars Nodens will listen. He is not likely to have heard a more heartfelt prayer—now *or* then.

Four Years Before Now

They come in the middle of the night, breaking fences in a final night of tearing up pastures with the knobby tires on their growling ATVs. Drunk, getting drunker, they spin doughnuts in the wet spring turf,

spitting out chunks of sod in their wake. Picking
pastures without stock because they somehow have
sense enough to know that damaging or losing stock
will take them over the line from wild young men
to criminals.

But they are mighty wild.

They pick a spot up against a creek too deep to
cross, heeding a darkened house in the distance. A
young woman lives there, they know, but has been
gone this summer, working several jobs as if the extra
income will somehow be enough to keep her father
alive. She is an odd girl with amazingly long hair, the
one who has an uncanny way with dogs and an
unsettling way of looking through a man as though
he's not even there and it wouldn't matter if he were.
But she is not home, and her pastures belong to
them.

They settle in for a time to swallow the beer
they've brought, shaking the cans, popping the tops
to soak themselves and the hillside beneath the
spreading oak. They don't notice that they trample
the grave markings of the old hound who lived longer
than anyone had ever thought possible. They don't
notice the sudden stillness of the night around them,
or that even as they drink, they often glance over their
shoulders, looking for that which they feel but can-
not see.

Not a benign feeling, for in this place of power
they have not thought to call upon things benign.
Instead they call upon aggression, building the
strength and ego of the one who will shortly present
himself for army basic training. They call upon brag-
gadocio, chest-thumping stories of prowess, and dark
promises of manly revenge for those who have
recently wronged them. They spill beer from can and
bladder, and when they find the struggling remains
of a rabbit they roared over in their ATV frenzy, they
spill blood.

And then they go home, leaving the debris of the night behind them and never suspecting what they have awakened.

At least, not right away.

Now

It begins.

Chapter 2

⟨

KANO
An Opening

"Don't even *think* about it."

The tiny Poodle looked back at Brenna with defiant eyes; it gave another jerk of the paw she had trapped between gentle fingers and added a calculated curl of its lip, revealing age-darkened but still needle-sharp teeth.

What was left of them, anyway.

"Quit," Brenna murmured, deftly clipping between the lilliputian toes. On second thought she briefly rested the flat of the blade against her own cheek. No more than warm. Nothing to complain about. A quick adjustment to the flat nylon grooming noose restricted the Poodle's head movement, and Brenna went back to work. "You're supposed to be one of my *good* customers," she muttered, shifting the animal so she could handle its hind paws.

Not today. *None* of them were good today. The tub room behind her reeked—she couldn't name a single dog who hadn't messed in its crate today—and still bore the effects of the escapee Collie who had torn around the room like someone's little brother, tipping over shampoo, spreading wet towels, and knocking over the tall, standing dryers. The tub walls were covered with shed dog hair—literally blown from the backs of several double-coated dogs whose owners hadn't taken a brush to them for at least a season.

And the noise. Every dog had something to say today. Loudly.

She had put the earplugs in early. And swallowed a couple of aspirins only a few moments ago, washed down by more caffeine than she normally dared. It made her hands shake, and that wasn't something she could afford in a business full of sharp blades and shifting clients. No wonder she had lost her childhood touch with dogs these days.

Flowers the Poodle, thinking herself sly, jerked her paw from Brenna's grasp and made a break for it, darting for freedom—only long enough to hit the edge of the table and the end of the noose at the same time. With an exasperated noise, Brenna scooped her out of midair and plunked her back in place. "Act your considerable age. You're not making my day any easier," she growled, and there was something to that growl that finally got through to the tiny dog.

Or else she was simply humbled by her brief midair experience. Brenna sighed. "Count yourself lucky it wasn't a bungee cord," Brenna said and went back to work, once more thankful that the Pets! grooming room was tucked away from customer eyes and not behind glass as some of the other major pet store chains insisted. Between the clamping adjustment on the noose and the dog's inconsequential weight, she could have hung there for quite some time without dire result, but best if no one saw. Not something a customer would understand.

Or a manager, for that matter.

Especially not the manager who now stood in the doorway, arms crossed. She found him when she circled the table to get a better angle on Flowers' back leg, simultaneously changing to a longer blade without stopping the clippers, a practiced motion of skillful fingers. But when she saw Roger . . . *then* she turned off the clippers. She knew that look, and it never boded well.

Roger was boss, and he knew it. And being boss meant telling people to do the impossible and smiling benignly when they had no choice but to agree. He wasn't a big man, but he had a meaty look to him; he filled out his shirts with a bulk that at one point had been muscle and now wasn't so sure anymore—just as his dull brown hair still held the style that had suited it when it was thick. Now Brenna thought a quick pass or two with her clippers—a nice #4 blade—would be a mercy.

"Busy in here today," he said. "That's the way I like to see it."

"Keeps things interesting." Brenna grabbed the ever-handy broom for a few quick, futile swipes at the growing tumbles of dog hair around her feet. The small room held three height-adjustable grooming tables, but the third table no longer adjusted without several people grunting and hauling and twisting it, so they kept it at the lowest height and used it for the largest dogs. Other than that, it usually held a fishbowl full of tiny handmade bows, with the bows-in-progress beside it. There was a short set of corner shelves and two rolling carts crammed with grooming equipment; the tub room held the shop vac and a plain grooming table where they towel-dried the dogs before popping them into crates to sit before

powerful crate and stand dryers. Three tables but not
quite enough space for three active groomers; they
never had more than two on shift at once, with only
three on the payroll and Brenna as senior.

"Just signed up another one for you," Roger said,
and his voice held that tone, the one he used when
he knew he'd done something to ruin her day but
had done it anyway because it would make a happy
customer. Or so he thought, with the giant assumption that things would turn out his way.

They weren't likely to. Not this time. "I can't fit
in any more dogs today. I can't do any more dogs
than this in one day *ever*, unless you get me experienced help."

"I gave you Katy," he protested, throwing his arms
out wide.

"For two hours in the morning, and she hates it.
She's bad at it, and she doesn't know what she's
doing."

"What do you have to know to bathe a dog?"

"The question," Brenna said, managing to keep her
voice light only because she'd had so much practice,
"is what do you have to know to bathe a dog *correctly*? Or even, say, to get a dog in the tub?"

She shouldn't have said that last; she knew it as
soon as the words were out of her mouth. His face
closed down at the reminder of the time Katy had
needed his help and *neither* of them could get the
seventy pounds of quivering German Shepherd into
the waist-high tub—not by trying to convince her to
walk up the ramp meant for large dogs, nor by tugging or shoving or lifting. Until Brenna walked in from
lunch, expecting to find the animal bathed and drying, and with no more thought than *I don't have time
for this*, slung the dog up into the tub.

Only in retrospect had she seen the look on Roger's
face, now imbedded in her mind's eye. Embarrassment. Resentment. It had at least, she'd hoped, taught

him that he couldn't simply throw just any of the interchangeable floor associates back to work grooming for a day.

She had *hoped*.

"It's just a bath," Roger said. "No clipping. Medium-sized dog, I checked."

Brenna felt something clutch hard in her stomach. She waved toward the tub room. "There's a whole room full of dogs waiting for me, and every one of them is a problem today. I swear, there's something in the air today. I can't do it, Roger. I can't even do what I've already got."

"We don't turn away walk-ins, you know that."

Steadily, her voice as flat as it could be when she had to raise it over the dryers and the barking, she said, *"Then get me help."*

Agreeably, as if he'd never consider asking the unreasonable of her, he said, "I'll grab someone off the floor when the dog comes in," and left the room with the air of a man who has just solved a major problem with much aplomb.

Brenna closed her eyes, momentarily overwhelmed by the impossible.

Then she picked up her clippers and went to work.

Twenty minutes later she presented Flowers to Ginger Delgaria, a pleasant woman who had come to Brenna since Flowers' first puppy cut. Flowers, by this time tucked into the nook of Brenna's elbow with a sulky expression pasted on her face, merely stared at Mrs. Delgaria without bestirring herself to move; Brenna had to hand her over. The woman gave a rueful shake of her head. "I see her mood hasn't improved."

"They're all like that today," Brenna said, absently rubbing her forehead between her eyebrows as she filled out the charge slip for the cashier, already calculating how long it would take to have the Sheltie done; she'd finished dematting before the bath, but the dog had way too much hair for its owners to handle, at least not without a judicious amount of trimming and thinning. Like a woman with just the right makeup . . . no one could see where the work had been done, but people could definitely appreciate the difference.

The Sheltie would take too long, that was the answer. And there was the Cocker in for a cut-down; she hadn't done the dog before and wasn't encouraged by her behavior in the tub. And Roger's new appointment still hadn't shown—

"—feral dog pack," Mrs. Delgaria was saying.

Brenna looked up at her, unable to reconcile the words with the neatly professional woman before her. *No, don't ask. Give her the charge slip and go get the Sheltie.*

She asked. "What did you say?"

"You haven't heard? I'm surprised. It's been in the news since last night." Mrs. Delgaria shifted Flowers into a more protective hold that Brenna didn't think was coincidental. "And you live out toward the lake, don't you? That's where they're supposed to be. If you've got animals out there, you'd better make sure they're put up safely."

Sunny. Numbly, Brenna held out the slip. "I don't listen to the radio much," she said. "Thank you for mentioning it." *Sunny the hound.* Poor dumb Redbone reject would stand there with her tongue hanging out, happily watching the canine visitors approach and never know the mistake until they bowled her over and chewed her into little pieces. She glanced at the clock. Two hours till her shift ended and not even then, if this new dog was other than what Roger said it would be.

Get the Sheltie started. She grabbed the stand dryer and wheeled it over to the table, which she swiftly adjusted to height. Then the tools, ready to hand; she snapped a #7 blade onto the clippers, pulled out her good thinning shears from the locking toolbox where she kept her personal gear, and hunted out the wide-toothed comb and a couple of different brushes. In moments the dog was on the table, losing the last of his matted hair and voicing his displeasure in high-pitched complaints from behind a nylon muzzle. He wasn't nearly as tough as he thought he was, but she was in no mood for the toothy pinches he commonly dealt out.

Definitely one of those days. The if-I-had-my-own-shop days. She wouldn't book this many dogs at once, not without the right kind of help. *And no one allowed to book dogs against my say-so*, she thought grimly, back-brushing the generous tufts of hair between the dog's toes and scissoring them to neat round paws.

But she never approached the thought too seriously. Years of her brother Russell's dismissive comments, of her parents' unintentional discouragement—though now only her mother was left to fill that role. "Let someone else worry about the bills," they'd say, her father with loving protectiveness when he was alive and her mother—now and then—with the assumption that she couldn't handle the load. "Russell will tell you." And Russell would. "Can't see you doing the accounting for your own business," he would tell her, and of course he knew, what with his partnership in the small carpet and flooring store in Brockport. "You haven't got a single class under your belt outside of high school."

True enough. But not how she'd wanted it, either.

She clipped the Sheltie's nails and pulled the muzzle off; just the thinning and a little trimming to go, and he'd be fine with that.

Feral dogs. A pack of them. What was that all about? She worked in a suburb north of Monroe City, but lived fifteen minutes northwest of that, between

Lake Ontario and the city. Definitely rural—but generally tame. A handful of coyotes, not as many stray cats as there used to be, lots of small farms no longer supporting anything but a handful of cows or horses, plenty of farmland owned in modest lots but leased to larger operations. Her own place had taken that role over the years, and even now the old north pasture was in corn for Bob Haskly—the lease paid her winter's heating bills in the old farmhouse. But the right-side pasture, hilly and divided by the creek, had only ever been pasture and still was. Maybe next summer she would get another horse; right now the field was fallow, recovering from some hard grazing from Emily's last batch of cattle.

Plenty going on in her part of Parma Hill, but never had feral dogs been any part of it. Nothing more than your basic random stray, half of whom seemed to find their way to Brenna for feeding and grooming before Brenna passed them along to the local animal advocate group for placement.

"Brenna, you in there?"

Think of Emily, and Emily arrives.

"Be out in a moment," Brenna said, taking one more pass through the Sheltie's thick ruff with the thinning shears and then shaping the result. She stepped back to give him a critical eye, found a tuft she'd missed, and tucked him under her arm to step into the tub room and turn off the last dryer. The Cocker behind it gave her a bright and manic eye. "Best you change your attitude," she told it, and went out to the counter area to stash the Sheltie in one of the two open-wire crates stacked for finished dogs.

"What's up, Emily?" she asked, reaching for the charge slip and doing a quick calculation of the extra time she'd spent on the mats.

"In town for project supplies," Emily said. "As usual. Those girls go through crafts like they were born to sell little-old-lady cutouts for people's front yards. You know, the kind bending over with all their pantaloons showing."

Brenna stopped writing to look up. Emily, with her honey-blond hair drawn back in a hasty ponytail, not a trace of makeup on her slightly too-wide, slightly too-large blue eyes, looked back at her quite seriously, but there was a trace of humor hiding at the corner of her mouth. "Solemnly swear," Brenna said, "that you will never allow that to happen."

"Sheep, then," Emily said. "Lawn sheep."

Brenna gave a firm shake of her head. "Lawn skunks at the most." She finished the charge slip and stuck it in the proper cubby slot behind the counter, noted the date and the Sheltie's new wart on his customer card, and dropped it in with the others to be refiled. "No project supplies in Pets!, unless they're going to build you a cow out of rawhide bones."

"They wanted to see the big lizards," Emily said, and smiled as she glanced through the glass of the counter area to the store proper. The grooming room had its own entrance, right next to the main store entrance; the counter area served as a functional antechamber behind glass. The girls, of course, were out of sight around the corner, where the reptile area boasted several huge snakes and the biggest monitor lizards Brenna had ever seen. At nine and eleven years old, Emily's daughters were fearless and outgoing children, and no one had ever told them that girls don't like that sort of thing. "Say, Bren, have you heard about the dog pack? I'm trying to figure out a way to put the goats up, but you know they're little escape artists—say, who's that?"

Brenna had started back for the Cocker; she looked over her shoulder to see Emily focused on the store entryway, just beyond which stood Roger and a customer, talking.

No, not just a customer. Something more. Roger was nodding with exaggeration and high frequency,

and he had a veneer of pleasant enthusiasm applied
to his face. The man he spoke to took a more casual
stance, his hands stuck into the pockets of his worn
jeans with the thumbs hanging out. He carried himself
in a sort of lounging slouch, and offered the occasional lift of a shoulder, the short nod of his head.
And he looked . . . casually disheveled. It didn't fit.
Not a dog-food rep—they came in with spit-and-shine
polish, just shy of car salesman-slick.

"Niiice," Emily said, watching them talk.

"Do you use that mouth around the girls?"

Emily tossed her ponytail. "If I'm comfortable
expressing myself around them, then maybe when
they're gorgeous teenagers with every single boy in
school whining for them to do the dirty in the back
of a pickup, they'll feel comfortable expressing themselves around *me*."

"Dream on," Brenna muttered, still watching the
byplay between her manager and the man he so
clearly wanted to impress with his affability. A man
who apparently didn't have the wits to discern the
sales job behind Roger's smile. Brenna gave a mental snort. With her luck the man had an entire van
of fully coated English Sheepdogs and Roger was even
now promising them an appointment for today. "Anyway, he's—"

Scruffy. That's how he struck her, which was why
she couldn't figure out Roger's fawning interest. But
then she realized that his clothes were neat enough
despite being far from new, worn jeans and a flannel shirt with cuffs rolled back to mid-forearm. And
he was clean-shaven, and his hair—every bit as dark
as hers—barely licked the collar of his shirt. And
yet . . . scruffy.

"—made you speechless, apparently," Emily teased.

Brenna went back and collected the Cocker, letting the stocky bitch stand on the table while she
hunted up a #5 blade. "It's Roger I'm thinking about.

He's up to something. Look at his expression and tell me he's not." The black Cocker, a badly bred individual with developing skin problems, eyed the floor and gave a wag of her stumpy tail; Brenna put an absent hand on her back and finally found the blade, accomplishing the switch one-handed and popping the new blade home with an expert flick against her thigh.

"You're no fun," Emily said, coming to stand in the doorway.

"Blame Roger for that, too. Did you see how he ran up the schedule today?"

"You need your own place," Emily said, completely unaware of Brenna's thoughts on the subject and not the least deserving of the sudden angry frustration that rose up in Brenna.

She turned her back to hide her glower, and concentrated intently on cutting the dog's nails—not entirely without necessity, since the Cocker had thrown herself back on her haunches and was jerking on the entrapped foot with manic intensity, a low moan in her throat that long experience told Brenna would soon be the sort of scream to draw spectators from two parking lots over. She startled the dog by swapping her end for end while maintaining her hold on the paw and quickly targeted the nails while the Cocker struggled with the notion that she could neither yank the leg forward nor up from that position. "Roger'll yell at you if he sees you behind the counter."

"No he won't," Emily said, somewhat smug. "I'm a customer. He'll do anything for a customer."

"I've taught you well, I see," Brenna said, finishing the nails and exchanging tools, firing up the clippers.

"Well enough so this is one place *I'll* never work," Emily said over the buzz of Brenna at work, smoothly drawing the clippers over the Cocker's dumpy back.

"As if you'd ever let a job take you away from the

family." Not Emily, married right out of her two-year college program and a mother a year later, in love with her good-natured garage mechanic and totally devoted to her girls. Happy, that was Emily. Happy and given to occasional fits of childish rowdiness—the best kind of rowdy, the water hose fights in midsummer, sledding and snowmen in the winter. Brenna envied her kids, and enjoyed being her neighbor.

But sometimes—on days like this—Emily just didn't *get it*. Didn't get that while Brenna was obliging her with light conversation, she was twisted up with the pressure of achieving the impossible in a day with constantly shifting rules. She'd never be done before dark at this rate, never mind at shift's end. And one day she'd just walk right out on Roger, because she'd told him no and he'd ignored her and for once she'd meant *no*.

Hang on. You've got tomorrow off.

"Listen, Em, can you do me a favor? Can you grab Sunny up and stick her in the dog room?"

Emily stopped watching Roger and her self-assigned eye-candy to give Brenna an uncertain look. "I thought you didn't want her in the house because she'll mess."

"Just make sure the door's closed to the main house. Shut her in the dog room. She probably *will* mess, but it's linoleum. And I won't be that late." Not if she could stick to her schedule. Six-thirty to three-thirty, up early and out early, just the way she liked it if you didn't count the Sunday morning shift. Elizabeth joined her mid-morning and worked until eight at night, and with Kelly doubling up on weekends and filling in on their off days, they kept the store covered.

"Dumbest dog I ever met," Emily said of Sunny, a mutter nonetheless meant to be heard.

"That's the consensus," Brenna agreed. "She's an idiot. How do you think she ended up with me?"

"No one else would take her," Emily said. Not even guessing, just flat knowing.

"I'd still rather not have her torn up by that pack. Can you do it?"

"I can try." Emily made a face. "If she's even learned her name well enough to come to it."

"Get the birdseed bucket and rattle it. She loves birdseed."

Emily, bless her heart, managed to hold her tongue on that one. "I'll do my best," she said. "I'm hoping the business about the dog pack is just a rumor gotten out of hand."

"But you're still putting up the goats." Brenna lifted the Cocker's back leg and bent to clear out the hair on her stomach, carefully skimming the sensitive skin. Her own hair fell free of its confinement down the back of her grooming smock and the doubled braid thumped against the table. Dark and thick and wavy and almost impossibly long, just as it had grown in after that summer she was nine years old and had made her silly offering to try to keep her hound alive.

Or maybe not so silly, considering the years she'd had with him, years that had made her parents puzzle—just as they had puzzled over her hair, hair she had been trying so desperately—and mostly unsuccessfully—to grow, and which she'd chopped off with a pocket knife and no explanation whatsoever.

Mars Nodens had liked offerings, her father's article had said. She had given him the only one she'd had. And had not cut her hair again since then—not counting the occasional light fringe of her bangs— though it was neither a rational nor a practical decision.

"Well," Emily said, talking about the goats, "I'll put them up. I don't know that they'll stay that way." She checked her watch. "Enough lizard-time for one day. They've got homework to do, anyway."

"Yeah, better make a run for it. If that straggly

Wheaten Terrier coming this way is my mystery customer, things are going to get real ugly around here, real fast."

Emily needed no more encouragement than that. Brenna crated the partially groomed Cocker and returned to the grooming counter, steeling herself for battle. Wheaten hair was notoriously soft and prone to matting; randomly scheduling Wheaten owners were notorious for not noticing the mats until they all but covered the dog's body, and then squalling at the suggestion of a cut-down. And Wheatens . . .

Wheatens were notorious for their own reasons.

I don't have time for this today. And as she thought it, as she tucked back a tendril of loose hair and prepared her customer-service face for an appointment she suddenly had absolutely no intention of keeping, she was startled to catch a brief glimpse of the man Emily had drooled over, and to discover that he was looking at her. Staring.

Dismissive, she would have said, reacting instantly to that expression with an inward bristling. As if she *needed* to be judged and dismissed by someone who would stand still for Roger's Happy Manager act. And as if she didn't get quite enough of the same from her own brother. She had only an instant, with the Wheaten close enough to give the corner of her counter a preparatory sniff and the owner oblivious enough that she had to preempt the dog's rising leg and welcome the owner at the same time—but that was time enough to return his look with her own cool expression.

And then she went back to work.

Chapter 3

ᚨ

ANZUS
The Messenger

She made it home somewhere between sunset and darkfall, her headlights splashing a long path up the steep, narrow driveway to the farmhouse at the crest of the hill—the same hill that wound away to the south, right of the house and barn, and upon which sat the oak and gravesite she'd managed to keep up even after all these years. Not including that one spring when she'd been so distracted with her father's illness, and someone—some*ones*—had invaded the fallow pasture and wreaked havoc at the oak.

There was no sign of Sunny as Brenna parked in the pole shed that served as a garage; she thought briefly about the dogs, and the unnatural silence of the night made her wish that she had climbed out of the car with her hands wrapped around a base-ball bat instead of the super sub sandwich that would keep her fed for three nights. And then Sunny cut loose from inside the house, a beautiful Redbone bawl that ought to be sounding out in the woods for squirrel and coon—if only the young hound had had the faintest drive to hunt.

With her relief came the realization of how tired she was. Thank goodness there was no livestock waiting—although the knowledge that her unpredictable work life kept her from putting a horse in the old pasture, or even a goat or two to keep down the weeds, created its own resentment. At least she had today's small victory on the scoreboard, a patch of ground she'd won and kept for her own—the Wheaten had gone home with a new appointment for dematting and a bath, the owner's ire assuaged partly by sincere apologies but mostly by the coupon for a steep discount.

Roger had not been pleased. But Roger had been coming off his happy nodding conversation with the dismissive stranger and, occasionally, even Roger seemed to sense when he had pushed Brenna too far.

With deliberate effort, she put that part of her day behind her, and redirected her thoughts to more pleasant things. The sub sandwich and a nice cold soda, and then a long soak in the claw-footed tub that hunkered in the corner of the recently remodeled bathroom. She hadn't had any choice about that, not when a long-undetected leak sent the toilet through the floor and into the basement, but she was glad for the results—fresh, desert rose tile, the resurfaced tub, plenty of shelves, and faucets it was actually possible to turn off.

And despite the upkeep she was glad her brother Russell hadn't wanted the farm, though he had maintained his perceived first claim as son and oldest child even as he passed on it. She needed it more than he, he'd said—he could make his own way.

She'd never been sure why he had thought she couldn't.

Sub. Soda. Soak. She mounted the steps to the half-enclosed front porch—vertical slats below the handrail, open above—making the habitual observation that the third one sank a little too easily beneath her weight and ought to be replaced. With the sub, her coat, the cargo bag that served as a purse and carryall, and her mail jammed under one arm, she reached for the porch door.

Something whined.

Feral dogs. Roaming pack at the boiling point.

Something whined *on the porch.*

Brenna froze, her hand on the door latch. *Yank it open, bolt inside*—but any sudden movement could trigger an angry dog—or worse, a frightened dog, unwittingly trapped in the corner of her porch. *Open the door* slowly *and slip inside*—but any retreat could trigger excited prey instincts. *Turn and face it*—but that could be seen as a challenge.

For pity's sake, just stand here indefinitely, until this sub is so stale you can beat the creature to death with it.

It wasn't a pack of whines, it was a single whine. It wasn't an eager whine, it was a distressed whimper. Intermittent, with no sound of movement, no tick of claw against the hard painted wood.

Brenna turned around.

At first she saw nothing, until, blinking in the darkness, she became convinced that there was nothing to see. That it hadn't been *on* the porch, but under it, and now had fled. And then it whimpered and stirred, and she saw the faint sheen of an eye reflecting the dim night light from the dog room on the other side of the door.

As eyes went, they weren't terribly far from the ground.

"Hey," she said to it, a low-key and noncommittal

response, just to lob the ball back into its court again. But there was no more forthcoming, and she opened the door behind her, snaked her arm around to feel the wall until she hit the light switch, and squinted in anticipation of the bare overhead bulb.

The dog had had no such warning; when the light blazed, it started, jumping into a jerky flight—but losing courage and freezing up instead. Brenna had all the time in the world to look it over—and she still wasn't sure what she'd found.

Ears, that was for sure. Big ears, upright like a German Shepherd's, and just as large as a Shepherd's even though the dog's head wouldn't reach her knee, not even if it had been standing alertly instead of cowering, its short legs spraddled out and its toenails digging into the porch as though at any moment it might go flying off the face of the earth from centrifugal force. She could almost hear its terror, its indecision, a fast babble of *runrunrun* and *which way should I go, whichwaywhichway* and *don't move, don't move, can't be seen if I don't move.*

What it was missing in length of leg it made up in length of body, but other than that the details were completely obscured in the stark chiaroscuro light and shadows of the overhead and the thick, all-encompassing coat of gritty dark mud soaking into the dog's coat.

Cardigan Welsh Corgi, she could tell that much. Nothing else had all that ear and so little leg—with the possible exception of a dock-tailed Pembroke Corgi, the queen's choice of breed—but she could quite clearly see a tail, flung out behind like a rudder, the quiver of it the only movement in the dog's body. Male dog, another glimpse told her.

Brenna didn't move. The dog didn't move. Sunny barked a query, her voice sweet enough to drive a tree hunter to tears, and the dog whimpered again, a sound that seemed to have been torn right out from the depths of his body.

This is starting to get more than silly. He wasn't going to hurt her; she couldn't stand there all night. Her feet hurt, the tub called, and some ill-advised soul had left a rare-breed dog loose to get lost on the turf of a roaming dog pack. "Look," she said to the dog, a matter-of-fact tone on the soothing side, "why don't you just—"

And he screamed—he *screamed*—and somehow flipped his long body around and flung himself over the side of the porch. Even having seen it, Brenna had no idea how he'd managed. "Damn," she said into the darkness, straightening and only then realizing she'd been slightly crouched, and that her back hurt along with the rest of her tired parts.

She didn't even think about going after him. Chase *that*? No point. She would eat, bathe, and go to bed—and in the morning she'd call animal control and report the sighting, so if they were on the alert for a Cardigan, they'd at least know where he'd been.

Sunny greeted her with much happiness and not the least resentment that interesting things had been happening just out of her sight; she cared only for the food that Brenna poured after dumping her own things on the kitchen table beyond the dog room. Sunny wasn't Brenna's dog, not really—never had been. She had arrived a reject, undernourished and severely lacking in intelligence, trail sense, and the potential ever to find another home. She adored Brenna—when she happened to notice her—and spent most of her time sitting in the yard watching the world happen around her, perfectly content that way. For visitors she'd bark a couple of times with a slightly puzzled expression, as if she were trying to remember if barking was what she was supposed to do, and then she'd give up and offer slobbery kisses instead.

Brenna thought it was more like having a pet rock than a dog, but in a strange way Sunny suited her current life perfectly. She didn't miss Brenna, she didn't get into trouble, and she wasn't wasted potential in any category—hunting, tracking, obedience, or agility work. She filled her role in life perfectly by being the sort of dog at which cat owners could point and feel superior.

Brenna gave Sunny's floppy gold-red ears a rub and placed the bowl in front of her big wire crate. This room was large for the mud and laundry room it had once been, and just a tad small for the dog and laundry room it now was. Aside from the old washer and dryer, it held several folded wire crates of various sizes, several nested rubber garbage cans for dog food which she un-nested at need, narrow metal shelves with grooming and medical supplies spilling over the edges, and a discreet stack of clean dishes. Not to mention Sunny's water dish, around which she'd spilled enough water to support the Loch Ness monster. Or the laundry, on which she'd been sleeping instead of the perfectly good dog bed; if it had been dirty before, now it qualified for the heavy-duty cycle.

Dropping her boots by the door, Brenna closed off the mostly unheated dog room and padded into the living room to kick the heat up from its frigid daytime setting. March first it might be, and sometimes warm enough for a vest over a sweatshirt, but on a day with lake clouds the house held a chill with vengeance. Pulling her hair from its doubled braid helped; she scrubbed her fingers through it, massaging her scalp, and let it fall to warm her neck and shoulders and the sides of her face. Then she found her slippers, hopping to put them on as she made her way to the first-floor bedroom, where she made a face at her own absentminded distraction, pulling them back off so she could shed her work pants.

Tired, all right. If she had tried to stay and work that Wheaten, she'd have been too tired to stop for the sub and too tired to eat it, anyway. She'd pay for

pulling the stunt with the discounted rescheduling—
Roger would give her a passive-aggressive cold shoulder for a week—but it had been the right thing to
do. Someday Roger would realize that groomer
injuries happened when the groomers were
exhausted—not quick enough to avoid the unexpected
snap of a jaw, not alert enough to see it coming.

She and her hair were tangled in her Pets! store
shirt, struggling with her bra hook, when Sunny
sounded off. "Nice timing," she grumbled at the
dog—but rushed to disentangle herself all the same.
It was the *stranger* bark, one Sunny seldom used; all
the world was a friend by her definition. Brenna
jammed a nightshirt over her head and a sweatshirt
over that, and stumbled into a pair of excessively well-
worn jeans—one of these days she would put her foot
right through the seat of them—and hopped back
down the hall while slippering her feet.

Sunny stood with her nose shoved up against the
back doorjamb, snuffling noisily enough to inhale all
of outdoors through the narrow crack. The hackles
of her short, slick coat raised a dark line at her
shoulders and down her spine; she didn't even look
up as Brenna entered the cold room, hugging herself and wishing she'd at least taken the time to grab
up her vest. She pulled the sweatshirt sleeves over
her knuckles and peered out onto the porch.

She had forgotten to turn the light off, so all she
saw was the glare of the bare bulb against the shiny
enamel paint and pitch darkness beyond. But Sunny
growled, a low monotone warning that Brenna
couldn't recall ever having heard before. "Shhh," she
said absently, not particularly expecting a response,
but Sunny shushed all right.

"Gone?" Brenna looked down to ask her.

But Sunny cowered at her feet. She whined, and
her eyes showed white, and then she bolted away
from the door and ran circles around the room, her

claws scrabbling in her usual graceless galumphing stride and her tail tucked so tightly to her belly that she didn't even appear to have a tail at all.

"Sunny!" Glancing from the bewildering dog to the starkly empty porch and back again, Brenna would have reached for her, tried to calm her—

But then she felt it herself.

A whisper of dire gibberish in her ear, a cold brush of fear down her neck; she slapped a hand to it, but this was no bug to brush away—it tickled down her spine and curled her toes and made her recently freed breasts feel tight and naked and exposed against the cold T-shirt. Behind her, Sunny crashed into her own crate and dove blindly inside, heading for the corner, where she hid her face and whined.

And Brenna clenched her jaw to keep from doing the same, clenched it till it ached, and still there was nothing on the porch but a pair of old mud boots and the wispy remains of last summer's potted impatiens. She made her arms into an X in front of her chest, and her fingers peeked out of the sweatshirt sleeves to grasp the material at her collarbones, kneading it without thought, her own hands mindlessly seeking to comfort her. *Whispers and tickles and fear and a blind, groping invasion of—*

Of nothing.

It left as abruptly as it had come.

Brenna gave a little laugh, sharp and bitter. "This job is getting to me," she told Sunny, ignoring for the moment that Sunny had no reason to let "this job" drive *her* into a crate and turn her into a whimpering ball of Redbone Hound. "I need more food and less caffeine. Definitely less caffeine." She went in to cut the sub up and pop tonight's portion into the microwave after slathering more of her favorite specialty mustard onto it than she probably should have. By the time the microwave dinged at her, she had a Sprite ready to go and had stuffed a few carrots in her mouth to assuage the inner voice that kept wanting to clamor about vegetables. Heck, there were tomatoes on the sub, weren't there? And onions—those should count for something.

A glance in the dog room showed her that Sunny had not moved, and she squelched the strong impulse to coax the dog out of the crate and soothe her. Sunny wouldn't come out until she was good and ready, and dragging her out would hardly create a soothing effect.

Brenna took her meal into the den—dark paneling left over from the seventies, a sagging couch she'd known all her life, her father's recliner, bought specially for him the year before he died and not something her mother could bear to take along to Sunset Village, the retirement community where she had been invited to stay with her younger sister, Ada . . . it was a room Brenna loved, but not one in which anyone else spent much time. The little television was here, the one that got only two channels no matter how you twiddled the antennae. She flipped it on, found a news-magazine show, and turned most of her attention to the sub.

Too much mustard, all right.

She ate it anyway, with as much—or as little—decorum as Sunny had used to devour her kibble. Then she went and washed the grime of the day from her face, and dusted the insides of her elbows with corn starch powder to get rid of the dog hair that often worked into the skin there. She'd given up on the bath while gathering her wits in the kitchen, not about to sit naked in a tub after feeling so naked and frightened right out there in the dog room. She checked on Sunny—who seemed to have forgotten the entire strange incident, and was hard at work on a bone—and plopped back down in front of the news show. Normally she just opened the back door and gave Sunny the boot until bedtime, but not tonight. Tonight she'd have to rig up something to keep Sunny under control when she went outside. An old longe line from Brenna's childhood horse, maybe, if she could find it.

But for now she settled in for a few moments of important enlightenment. This particular news show segment seemed to have something to do with cruise ships and their chefs. "*. . . and you'll be as surprised as we were to learn who* really *handles the food behind the scenes*," as they cut to a commercial.

"Bet I'm not," Brenna muttered at the television, pulling an old knit afghan off the back of the couch and wrapping it around herself as the commercials droned on. She closed her eyes; at some point the news show returned, diving into its intense scrutiny of shipboard cuisine with a grand display of moral outrage. Brenna drifted away, envisioning those same cameras behind the scenes at Pets!, focusing in tightly on Roger while in the background—

"*—regret to report that there were no survivors found on the farm, another entire family lost to this new rabies.* Shedding rabies *is the common term being used for the mutated virus—*"

Brenna jolted awake, squinting at the screen, frantically trying to refocus her thoughts and her eyes on the information they were presenting. *Rabies? What?* She hadn't heard—

"*Not only were most of the workers we found less qualified than claimed, but our hidden cameras revealed unsanitary work habits—*"

Back to the cruise ship. No, that wasn't *right*, they'd been talking about rabies, she was sure of it. A new kind of rabies. . . .

Yeah, right. Or maybe it was just her imagination, fueled by a pack of loose dogs and one spooky moment in the dog room. Brenna drew the afghan closer, curling into a tighter ball on the couch, letting her hair become a shroud in which she could hide while she thought.

And abruptly decided that she didn't *want* to think. She had things to do, and then she wanted to go to bed. Let Emily tease her about hitting the sack earlier than Emily's two kids; the kids didn't get up as early as she. Holding the afghan around her shoulders, she got a garbage bag and went from room to room, gathering the week's garbage in semidarkness out of sheer laziness when it came to turning on the lights— only to realize, as she reached the kitchen on her way out, that there was no way she was going to put out garbage with the feral dogs running crazed. She left the sack in the corner behind the kitchen door and went through her mail, pulling out the bills and dumping the rest, and then relinquished the afghan long enough to clean up the kitchen sink and table.

She ought to pay some of those bills while the table was clear enough to do it—she had a desk in one of the second-floor rooms, but its main purpose seemed to have evolved into providing a delicate balance of shifting and layered papers—old records, grooming newsletters, and a growing stack of clipped articles on introducing yourself to the computer age, keeping business records, and thrifty advertising methods. She *ought* to pay some of those bills . . . but not tonight.

Tonight she would beat Em's kids to bed; tomorrow she'd deal with the bills and other such things that hadn't been done over the course of this week. Spring grooming season getting into gear . . . it was always like this.

Sunny waited for her, back to snorting at the doorjamb. Brenna couldn't blame her; the dog wasn't used to being confined during the evening. "Let me find you that longe line," she said, and started poking around on the metal shelves. Theoretically this was all dog stuff and not horse stuff—the barn held the old horse gear— but maybe if she was lucky . . . she hadn't sorted the shelves in some time, and that gave her some hope.

"*Whoouh*," Sunny said to her—said to the door, actually, and Brenna jerked to look at her with no little dread—but the dog's hackles were right where they belonged, smooth and slick all the way down her backbone. And her tail swung in an even, happy arc, steady at hip level.

Of course Brenna had to look, even as her hand closed over a tangled skein of flat cotton line. Absently shaking the line out so she could re-loop it around her hand and elbow, she went to the back door. Not so long ago she'd stood here shaking; now there was no menace—only her back door with a light she ought to have turned off burning outside in the cold night.

And there, standing at the top step, was the mud-dipped Cardigan Welsh Corgi. Stone-still, as if he had been that way for hours and would stay that way for hours yet. As she appeared in the doorway, Brenna thought she saw the slight tilt of one of those big ears, but she couldn't be sure; it didn't happen again. Finally she nudged Sunny into her crate and put her hand on the doorknob, slowly turning it.

He heard it, all right. You couldn't get any more alert than *that* pair of ears, radar-scoped at the door. But his expression was entirely different from the first time she'd seen him. Then he had been terrified beyond rational thought; now he stood at attention, his posture suddenly full of anticipation despite the fact that he hadn't truly moved.

Slowly, she pulled the door open. Slowly, she pushed the creaky screen door out.

They stared at one another.

Finally she said, "Would you like to come in?"

He trotted in as if she had been a doorman holding the door to his personal doghouse.

Her eyes widened; that was all. Until she had the door closed behind him, it was the only reaction she could afford. But she needn't have worried. He went to the center of the shallow room and plunked his bottom down, his eyes never leaving her face—and her eyes never leaving his—as she closed and latched the doors. From her crate, Sunny made a noise of protest—she still wanted *out*—but Brenna shook her head. "In a minute," she said, never moving her gaze from the mud-coated Cardigan. She crouched down and patted the floor. "C'mere," she said, an offhand tone.

He came.

He not only came, he rested his muddy face against her leg and gave a sigh of contentment that verged on being an outright groan. Surprised, she hesitated, her hand hovering over his filthy coat—and in the end rested her hand on his shoulder, so damn happy to have him there that she couldn't quite believe herself. *Didn't* believe herself. This was the happiness of a dog long-lost, regained—not the simple relief that she'd pulled a stray in out of reach of trouble. It made no more sense than his flip-flop in behavior.

"Only a little while ago," she murmured, searching for her equilibrium, "you were so terrified of me that you practically did a backflip over the porch rail. Now you think I'm mama?"

Unless he had never been terrified of her at all.

Unless that which had come so soon afterward, that which had so frightened both Brenna and Sunny, had not been their combined imagination at all, and this dog had felt it too.

Something else that made no sense. Brenna shied away from thinking about it.

Sunny's antics in the crate acquired a certain fevered intensity, and Brenna retrieved the longe line, snapped it to Sunny's collar, and tied the end around a porch pillar, all while keeping half an eye on their guest. He sat waiting with all the patience in the world, and when she stuffed her hair down the back of her sweatshirt, grabbed a handful of towels from the top of Sunny's crate, and crouched by him again, he stoically allowed her to sop up what mud she could. That gritty, black mud, as if something had driven him through one of the many local mini-swamps at top speed.

Though she didn't know what it could have been, that wouldn't have *caught* him. Nimble and speedy as the Corgis were—and well they should be, having been bred to herd cattle—those short legs wouldn't outrun anything big enough to be a threat, not in the long haul.

Then again, she hadn't actually seen anything out there tonight, and he had performed Corgi gymnastics to run from *that*.

Quit trying to make it make sense. Sometimes things just didn't. What she knew for sure was that she had a Cardigan Welsh Corgi in her dog room, and that even the generous pile of towels accruing beside her wouldn't do anything but soak up dirty water, leaving the grit in his coat and a bath the only recourse. She couldn't be sure—not in this light, not without someone holding him so she could step back and take a look—but she had the feeling he was a fine dog, lots of good bone and without the exaggeratedly twisted ankles so many of them had. Someone would be missing him. She ran her hands around his neck and finally came up with a narrow nylon strip—not a collar, no more than a tag holder. And the tags, too, clinking dully in their wet and mud-coated state.

She tried to make them out, turning them to catch the light, but the engraving would take a good scrubbing before it became legible. The dog cocked his head at her, a quizzical expression, and it was then that she realized how she'd squinted her face up in her attempts to read the unreadable. Alert, then, and plenty responsive. She could stick pencils up her nose and waggle her fingers in her ears without getting anything but a bland stare from Sunny.

Not that she ever *had*. Ever.

In any case, she'd take him into work tomorrow—stealing a few moments with the tub and dryers was a job benefit for any groomer—scrub him up, clean up the tags, and see what she had to work with. Along with a few phone calls to animal control and the local volunteer adoption group, it would probably be enough to have this fellow home by tomorrow night.

She left the wet collar around his wet neck and pulled out one of the smaller wire crates; a touch too small for him, but for one night he could deal with it. The sharp noise of the shuffled crates put him on edge; his huge ears went from alert to wary as he moved to the far wall, his body hunched and poised for escape—even if there was nowhere to escape *to*, not this time. Still, no point in making it hard for him; she took the crate into the kitchen and assembled it there, flipping the sides into place with practiced ease and snicking the fasteners into place. She had planned to keep him in the kitchen, anyway—he was too wet to stay out in the cold dog room.

Unlike Sunny, who had been outside quite long enough to take care of her needs. Sunny whined and moaned and threw herself at the door if Brenna tried to keep her inside on a cold night; the most she could enforce was the compromise of the dog room.

Brenna tossed a few towels into the bottom of the new crate and went out to reel Sunny in and crate her with an outlandish bone. She'd been intending to use a slip-lead on the Cardi, but when he got a glimpse of the crate, he pushed his way through the partially open door and installed himself in his new quarters.

Brenna put a hand on her hip and made a face at him. "So you're crate-trained. Show-off." She freed her hair from her sweatshirt and debated whether or not to feed him—he'd need it, but she didn't want

to dump food down him when he'd been stressed—
and ended up giving him a scant handful of kibble.
"Make yourself at home," she told him, deciding she
wasn't going to be spooked away from her tub. "I've
been waiting for my own bath all day, and I'm about
to have it."

He met her gaze for a few moments, and then
deliberately turned to the kibble, nuzzling it first and
finally settling in to eat with a catlike finickiness.

"I guess I know when *I'm* dismissed," she said, but
couldn't help but linger to watch him, so at home in
her own kitchen, the very picture of a content dog.
It was almost enough to make her forget the strange
circumstances of his arrival.

But not quite.

Chapter 4

ᛈ

PERTH
An Initiation

Early afternoon in the Pets! parking lot, a shared lot in a strip mall that no longer held the sparkle of fresh construction but hadn't quite descended into rattiness. Bills paid, laundry done, and she'd even found some old boards in the barn to lay over the mud hole between the house and the car shed. The Cardigan had jumped readily into her pickup and sat quietly on the towel she'd laid over the seat, happy enough to be in the car, happy enough to keep her company. Happy enough to hop out again, onto the warm asphalt of a spring day that had actually chosen to be sunny.

Which left Brenna entirely unprepared when he took one look at the Pets! storefront and screamed like a panicked child.

He tried to bolt, couldn't, and flopped at the end of the leash like an enraged fish out of water, issuing bloodcurdling screams, foaming at the mouth—and *whew*, there he went—blowing his anal glands on top of it all. Of course, he could hardly pitch a protest of these proportions and *not* release his anal glands.

In a way, Brenna supposed she was lucky. *They* were lucky. He was in an empty parking space, and not in the path of careless parking lot traffic. And unlike the average dog owner, she'd seen this kind of thing before. She'd had dogs squirt out of the tub, screaming in outrage; she'd had cats ping-pong across the wall like something out of *The Exorcist*. She'd dealt with pets in all stages of temper tantrum and protest. So now she held the end of the leash and rolled her eyes and tried to figure out what had set him off while she waited for it to end.

Not that he hadn't been through enough. The night hadn't been easy on either of them. She had emerged from the tub to find him sleepy and satisfied, and he'd even, after some hesitation, accepted the longe line rigging for his outs before bed. But—dry now, if still muddy—he hadn't been so happy about returning to the crate. Once inside, he had given her a look, a *this isn't the way it's supposed to be* look, and she'd almost let him out.

Almost. But a second look at his dry but no less grimy state brought her up short, and she murmured an apology and took herself to bed—not quite as soon as Emily's children despite her intentions, and exhausted to the bone. Maybe she'd even sleep in, despite her body's natural greet-the-dawn inclinations; she'd certainly sleep hard.

Or maybe not. Maybe it was the dog's fussing that woke her; maybe it was something else. But this time, when she went to the kitchen to check him, she couldn't harden herself to the plea in his eyes. She

let him out and grabbed one of the towels; he seemed
glad to follow her to the den, and just as glad to settle
on the towel she spread before the couch—although
he didn't truly relax until she plopped herself down
in the worn cushions and drew the afghan over
herself. Eventually, she let one hand fall to rest on
his shoulders, and they dozed that way.

But not for long.

She didn't know what brought her to alert, just that
the dog had sensed it, too. He was a tight bundle
of muscles anchored to her touch, and she felt his
fear creep right up her arm and curl around her
heart. It was the only thing she could hear, her
heart—the rest of the house was utter silence, and
yet there was a pressure in her ears as if a giant black
fist squeezed the house and everything in it. And the
moments pounded on and she thought surely the fear
would ease, her heart would slow, but it never did.

It stopped as suddenly as it had begun, and only
then did she start shaking. Only then did the Cardigan let a whine slip out. She reacted automatically,
and for both of them. She forgot about his grubby
state and she lifted the afghan in silent invitation. He
jumped up without hesitation and snuggled in next
to her, water-bottle warm and smelling just like the
swampy mud he'd run through. She turned to her
side, giving him more room, and then lay awake
feeling the rise and fall of his ribs against hers and
the puff of his breath on her forearm. Somebody's
pet, all right.

Why did he seem to think he was hers?

And why, she wondered grimly in the Pets! parking lot the next day, couldn't he just remember how
he had trusted her the night before? And just how
damn long could he keep this up, anyway?

A woman with a Shih Tzu waddling along beside
her hesitated for a horrified look at the Cardigan's
antics; Brenna gave her a forbearing smile and a little

shrug. A few moments after that, the dog eased off into wary cease-fire, panting, attractive little bubbles of spit on his lips.

"Are we done?" Brenna asked him, as sardonically as she could muster. And with much relief, because someone else was approaching from behind, and she didn't think she could pull off another forbearing smile. "Look, dog, I'm already giving up my day off for you—"

"Trouble?"

She didn't recognize the voice, but a glance showed her trouble, all right. The dog must have thought so, too, for as the glazed look left his eyes and he focused on the new arrival, he went into instant action, shrieking and flopping, thirty-five pounds of idiot at the end of the leash. Brenna felt an odd moment of disorientation, a *wrongness*, and for a moment her world teetered with him. And then she caught herself. She looked at the man—Roger's friend from the day before, with a cell phone in one hand, a gym bag in the other, a pager visible on his belt through the gaping front zipper of his leather jacket and a reasonably solicitous look on his face.

"Why, no," she said, with an edge of sarcasm so fine he might or might not perceive it. Trouble? As if it weren't obvious, and as if he'd taken for granted she couldn't handle *trouble* on her own.

He shifted the gym bag in his grip, easing back on one leg to narrow his eyes at her—eyes easily as blue as hers, hair easily as dark, glinting with nearly hidden chestnut in the spring sun. And as recognition came into those eyes, the solicitous expression faded. "You're one of the groomers."

"And you're the man who was talking to Roger yesterday." She didn't mention the look he'd given her; he knew he'd done it. And though she was tempted, it would take her just a little closer to *bitchy* than she liked.

And who wouldn't be, with a manic dog jerking her arm around—though he was once again settling—spooky things ruining her sleep, a day off slipping away, and Mr. Scruffy adding his presence on top of it all? It was his hair, she decided—a nice style but ready for a trim—or maybe that he evidently hadn't shaved today.

And he grinned at her words, but it wasn't in apology, it was . . . it was . . .

She didn't know *what* it was. Acknowledgment of some sort?

"Good luck with the dog," he said, clearly abdicating the unspoken offer of help. He nodded at the dog. "Interesting kind of storm for Winnal's Day, I suppose." And without explaining either comment, he turned on his heel and left, heading for a pale blue SUV with some sort of logo on its side.

She didn't have a chance to note just which logo it was, because the instant he moved, the Cardigan blew his wits again, catching her up in another moment of inexplicable *wrongness* before she recovered. Poofing her bangs out of her eyes with an exaggerated sigh, she decided she wasn't going to gain anything by waiting for the dog to work through whatever kept triggering him and headed for the store, thankful enough that he was a Cardigan instead of a seventy-pound Lab as he flailed along behind her.

"Oooh, that's special." Elizabeth, the second-shift groomer who caught Brenna's early shift on Brenna's off days, leaned over the counter to admire Brenna's acquisition. "What do you call that breed, the Freaking Mudball?" She looked closer, and reconsidered. "Freaking Mudball with Ears."

But now that they were inside, the dog settled again, clearly exhausted. His tongue hung long from his mouth, and his sturdy front legs spread wide.

"Doomed Mudball," Brenna pronounced; Elizabeth knew a Cardigan when she saw one. "Is the tub free?"

"Only if you clean it when you're through with *that*," Elizabeth said without hesitation. "I'm done with my baths for the day."

Brenna did an automatic glance-about before saying darkly, "Don't worry. Roger will schedule you something."

"No way." Elizabeth popped a thin mint into her mouth from her perpetual stash behind the counter—like Brenna, she rarely had time to eat a full lunch. "I've got two minutes to do paperwork while my first finishes drying, and then I'm clipping for the rest of the afternoon."

"Take a look at the schedule," Brenna said, nodding at the desk. "See that dog he tried to sneak in yesterday? It was a matted Wheaten."

Elizabeth made a face. She was a tall young woman, very blond, with generous features that seemed a little too big for her face; when she twisted them up, she got impressive results. Brenna grinned at her and headed for the tub room.

The Cardigan followed her like a gentleman, tired but amenable. He stood quietly in the tub—three shampooings it took before the mud didn't run off him anymore—he let her blow the water from his coat with the high-velocity dryer, and he went quietly from her arms into a second-tier crate to sit under the stand dryers while she scrubbed his collar and tags and cleaned up the tub area.

Finally, she turned to the collar, blotting it dry and taking her first good look at the tags. Rabies tag, though it didn't look quite right to her eye and she couldn't say why; it had the vet clinic—*her* vet clinic—stamped on the tag, along with Rabies I/II and the serial number. But here was something useful—a round ID tag, phone number and all. She took the collar out to the grooming room and dangled it up before Elizabeth, who was trying to get a smooth clipping line on a perpetual-motion

Springer. Not her strength—Brenna specialized in the exacting breed clips. But Elizabeth could take any odd hairy breed and turn it cute or handsome, so she didn't begrudge Brenna her breed certifications.

Brenna grinned at her from behind the collar. "Score!"

"What's the deal with him, anyway? That's not a breed you see very often."

"Showed up on my porch last night," Brenna said. "But he ought to be home tonight." She caught up the receiver from the wall phone, stabbed an unlit outgoing line button, and dialed the number, twirling the collar around her finger as the line rang.

"I'm sorry, but that number is not in this service area. Please check the number you are dialing and try again."

"Huh." Brenna frowned at the phone, hanging it up with much less flare. She looked at the tag again. "Number doesn't exist, according to them. But who'd keep a tag with the wrong number on it?"

"What's the address?"

Brenna shook her head, running her thumb over the engraving. "There isn't one. Just the phone. Dumb."

"Well, it'd be fine if the phone *worked*." Elizabeth's voice came out muffled; her head was in the vicinity of the dog's flank as she fought for control over its foot. Giving up, she straightened and glared into the Springer's eye long enough to bellow in a startlingly loud voice, *"Straighten up!"*

Astonished, the dog stood stock still, watching Elizabeth with wide eyes as she quickly went back to work. "Sometimes it gets 'em, sometimes it doesn't," she said. "I give it three feet."

"Mmmm," Brenna said in agreement, staring at the other side of the ID tag. "Champion Nuadha's Silver Druid."

Elizabeth snorted. "Yeah, there's a name for you. It'd make more sense if he was blue merle. What was that, *New-AHD-ja*?"

"*NWUH-dja*," she said absently, looking at the name and thinking Elizabeth was right. Silver could describe merle, but not a black, white, and brown tricolor. Elizabeth grabbed the collar to look with vast uncertainty at the tag.

"Noowahja?" she said, coming close. "Do you think?"

Counterintuitive as the pronunciation was, Brenna didn't doubt it—although as she retrieved the collar, she gave it her own thoughtful look. She *ought* to doubt it.

But she didn't.

So she tucked the question away to think about later, and stuck her head in the tub room to offer an experimental, "Hey, Druid!"

From behind the wind of the dryers, he got to his feet, cocking his head at her. No mistaking that. "Never mind," she told him, and retreated to the grooming room. "Druid for a call name, that's not too bad. But you'd think anyone with a champion would make it easier to return him!"

"No kidding. All right, Springer, you've had your last chance," Elizabeth said with some exasperation, as her fourth attempt to trim under the dog's tail was met with a spinning tactic. "At least I got all the feet done," she said, shortening the noose and using a second noose to secure the dog to the front of the grooming elbow. "If these people would just *handle* their dogs—"

"Yeah, yeah, you're preaching to the choir here." But Brenna slid Druid's collar down her arm and let it dangle at her elbow while she went to the Springer's head and distracted her with kissy-kissy noises. Fortunately, the dog was fundamentally sweet, if uncivilized, and she was glad enough to squint her eyes with happiness at Brenna's attentions—although the tail-wagging didn't necessarily make things much easier for Elizabeth.

Elizabeth moved on to the dog's head and ears, and Brenna went back to check the Cardigan, flipping off the dryers and rolling them out of the way. She laughed, then, at the somewhat stunned look on his face; he'd had all the dryers on him, and his coat was as flyaway as it could get. Except for his haunches, which of course he'd been sitting on.

She considered the temperature—nice for early March, mid-fifties—and decided against taking him out in it without some spot-drying. A few moments on one of the tables was all it took, and then she stepped back to consider her new charge.

"He's got a lot more white on him than I thought," Elizabeth admitted, pausing in her own work.

Or than Brenna had thought. No way, under the mud, to see how broad his blaze was, how symmetrically it encompassed his muzzle, narrowed just enough to miss his eyes, and broadened again at his forehead. Or to see the dark freckles on the bridge of his nose, or how richly his brown cheek patches stood out against the black on the rest of his head. He had a white bib and undercarriage and—except for brown points, a white tail tip, and a jagged white collar—the rest of him was sleek black. Black, aside from his ears. The interior of one was stark white; the other light brown. But it was the backs of those huge ears that were so beguiling, mostly white with thick brown freckles. Utterly unexpected, utterly charming.

And his eyes. Coming from a clean face, they looked softer, more open. Big *love-me* eyes that followed her every movement.

He's somebody else's dog.

Brenna gave a sudden sharp shake of her head. "Gotta figure out who owns him."

"Yeah," Elizabeth said, her voice knowing. "Better do it fast, too."

Brenna made a face at her, absently fingering the collar and its tags. No actual license; that didn't surprise her. An ID tag was what got a dog home again, and a license cost money to replace. Sunny didn't carry her license either, just the rabies and ID tags. She looked again at the rabies tag, still not quite sure what wasn't right about it, and the Lakeridge clinic name caught her eye. If the clinic kept track of which dog had what vaccine serial number, then . . .

The Cardigan—Champion Nuadha's Silver Druid with no silver—decided she wasn't going to fuss with him anymore and eased his bottom down on the table. She kept an eye on him as she called the clinic, picking the number out from the emergency list by the phone. "Hi," she said when Donna, the receptionist, picked up the phone and identified herself. "Listen, I've got a stray here with one of your rabies tags. Can you identify the owner from the number?"

"If the tag isn't outdated. What's the number?"

Brenna gave Elizabeth a thumbs-up as the other groomer looked up from her work to eavesdrop, and held the tag so the engraving showed clearly in the light, reading off a five-digit number and waiting expectantly for the sound of Donna's fingers at the keyboard.

But Donna said, "You're missing one. There should be six numbers."

Brenna frowned. "Only five. They're all very clear; the tag looks practically new." *Now that it's been cleaned.* "And it's a young dog; he's probably on his first three-year shot." He was, she thought, at least that old—past the first six months when they didn't give rabies, and then the year after the first rabies, which was only a one-year shot. But she wouldn't put him at much beyond a couple of years. His teeth were still white and strong, and his carriage that of a young dog. All the same, he was a well-developed adult, with masculine features and all his parts intact.

A show dog loaded with identification, and none of it could lead her to his owner.

Donna said, "I suppose you could bring the tag in; maybe one of the vet techs could make some sense of it. Unless you've got six numbers, I can't be of much help."

Brenna sighed. "Maybe I will," she said, but knew she wouldn't. If the tag was defective, there was no point. What was she going to do, ask them to search record by record? Or— "Can you search your clients by breed?" she asked. "This is a Cardigan Welsh Corgi. You can't have many of those."

"We don't have any," Donna said. "We haven't, for several years. And we haven't done that kind of search before, but it might be possible. Tell you what—leave your name and number, and let me get back to you. I'm going to have to sneak this into my schedule. And you said it was a young dog?"

"Male, young adult, tricolor," Brenna said, and gave Donna her name and home number. "He's in good shape—he hasn't been on his own very long. And he's tagged as Champion Nuadha's Silver Druid. Have you ever heard of them?"

"You might search the Web," the woman said. "If you can find the kennel, the breeder should know who owns the dog now."

"Good idea," Brenna said, but upon hanging up she slumped back against the wall and stared at Druid. "You're not making this very easy." Search the Web . . . as if she had a computer, or even knew how to use one!

Emily.

Of course, Emily. Or to be more precise, Emily's daughters, who shared a computer and whose on-line time had been a subject of much discourse in the Brecken household, drawing even Emily's workaholic husband Sam into the fray.

"I can't tell if you're stumped, or if you've got bad answers," Elizabeth said.

"Stumped," Brenna said. "I'm going to make a few more calls from here, then go on back home. No point in spending my whole day on this." She'd call PePP, the local rescue group that showcased their adoptions at Pets! during the weekend, and the local animal control—that way if anyone started calling around *looking* for the dog, they'd be directed to Brenna. And she would hope that Roger didn't come in and catch her making personal phone calls from the store phone.

Druid watched—he had settled into a couchant posture, with his short legs curled in front of his chest like a cat's, curved wrists gracefully meeting in the middle—as the rescue group representative offered to take him in. "Oh, no," she told them in an off-hand and casual tone. "He's fine at my place, and he's been through enough change already." The animal control officer was out, as usual—he must be especially busy with the dog pack situation—but she left a message. And when she hung up the phone the final time she looked at Druid and said, "I hope you appreciate this."

Elizabeth snorted. She had traded the Springer for a Lhasa mix that bore a typically snubbed face and sausage body, and a nasty temper to boot. Elizabeth had the cat muzzle ready and waiting. "Yeah, right," she said. "As if they ever do. All they want is more food and a place under the covers." She gave Brenna a pointed look as she reached for the clippers to rough out the scissors cut. "And you better be careful not to give him any more than the food. I can see that look in your eye already."

Too late, Brenna thought, thinking of the night on the couch, of how contentedly he'd snuggled beside her. Of course, those circumstances had been special. She wasn't quite sure just what those circumstances *were*, other than strange and frightening, but they had certainly been out of the ordinary. The Cardi would sleep in the crate tonight. Or at the least, on the floor by the bed. "This is my *not-enough-sleep* look, nothing else," she said. *Not* a getting-attached-to-someone-else's-dog look. "And have you heard anything more about the feral dogs? Has animal control been able to break up the pack?"

Elizabeth shrugged. "I didn't see the news. Customers seem to think the dogs have been pretty active. That guy who's been around talking to Roger—he seemed to know a lot about it, but he's not exactly what I'd call chatty."

"Or even friendly," Brenna said. "Although he was nice enough out in the parking lot until he realized I was a groomer."

"Can't make sense of *that*."

"Maybe it's just his nature," Brenna said. "Whatever. If you can get anything out of him, do it, okay? I'm right smack in the middle of the pack action, and I'd really like to know just how worried I should be." Come to think of it, it might be time to clean up her grandfather's old .22 and take a few test shots into the hill that followed the creek.

"What makes you think he'll talk to me?"

Brenna thought of the exchange in the parking lot and gave Elizabeth a wry smile. "Maybe he won't. But I'm pretty sure he won't be talking to *me*."

Chapter 5

ᛚ

LAGUZ
Water, That Which Conducts

Thnnck!

The .22-long bullet buried itself in the damp soil of the hill just to the right of her target, abruptly reminding Brenna that the sights on the old rifle were slightly off and she'd need to adjust for them. Which she did, and promptly shattered the bit of a stick she'd jammed into the ground as a target.

Not that she was far away from it, certainly not far enough to crow about her marksmanship. But if she ended up firing this thing, it would be at close range. And the real point to the exercise was to trigger the years of target plunking she'd done in her teens, to reengage her handling and safety practices.

Besides, although she counted herself lucky to have

avoided Roger during her time at the store bathing Druid, she was happy enough to imagine him here on the hill in a Manager Effigy. She pumped the old shell out of the chamber and the new one in, and settled the rifle to her shoulder. *Thnnck!*

She found a certain satisfaction in solitary target shooting, especially with the relatively quiet .22. No big kick, no rendingly explosive noise, just sighting, shooting, and working the smooth pump for another round. The creek burbled behind her, glinting in the sun; the hill blocked out the rest of the world before her, and the breeze that played in her bangs could almost—with some imagination—be called warm.

But she couldn't stay here forever. Aside from the fact that she had just run out of shells, there was a lost dog waiting to go home, and she didn't imagine he was terribly happy to be crated while she was gone. She needed to get him and walk on over to Emily's—not close but the next house north, a newer home built on the edge of the Calkins' recently sold farmland lots. A quick phone call had put the girls onto the computer search, and with any luck they'd have the information she needed by evening.

She double-checked to make sure there was no shell in the chamber, pointed the gun at the ground, headed for the hill—and stopped short. The old shrine, her hound's gravesite . . . she hadn't been there since the final snow had melted. So she walked along the hill instead, further out from the house, following the whimsical creek bed until the great oak loomed above her. Her tattered sneakers gave her perfect purchase in the grassy sod; twenty-four hours ago it would have been just the other side of muddy out here, but now she had nothing more than pleasantly soft ground beneath her feet. Up the hill she went, straight to the grave, where she set down the rifle and knelt, reminded of the first time she'd been allowed to shoot, and how the old hound had hung by her legs, always touching her, bumping her . . . worried about her, as if the loud noise might harm her.

He'd been shot once; X-rays later in life had shown the birdshot still buried in his haunch. So he had had good reason to worry—or so he must have felt.

She had loved him for it then. She loved him for it now. She shoved back the long sleeves of her hooded sweatshirt and tenderly straightened the site marker, an arrangement of rocks chosen for their size and shape and which, at the time, she had put a great deal of effort into creating. They were just plain old rocks, nothing more, but it didn't really matter. All that mattered was that seeing them helped her to remember him.

Rocks straightened, she let her sleeves slip back down over the heels of her hands—a hand-me-down from Russell, this one was—and placed one palm flat on the earth, remembering those years. And the years after them, when she had seemed practically able to speak to any dog that wandered by, to intuit their needs and the meanings of their slightest body language. Or that's how it had seemed at the time. At almost twenty-nine, she had a more jaded view of the world, and didn't particularly trust that things had been as she remembered them.

And all the same, she wished she could experience life on that level again. Simple. Not fraught with daily struggles just to make sure she could do her job safely and professionally. Being with dogs to *be* with them, and not ending up in adversarial relationships with animals who spent the afternoon with her now and then and didn't want to be there at all.

"I love you, old hound," she told the gravesite, and pushed herself to her feet, brushing off her damp knees, thinking of that terrible year when she had found the place desecrated, when her father had died and horror seemed to hang over this area for the rest

of the year. Which didn't mean that the tiny trickle
of a spring couldn't use a cleaning; it generally did.
Leaves settled there, and the grasses grew long and
bent over into it. Brenna moved over to tend it and
stopped short, eyes narrowing.

Not a leaf, not a stick, not a single stray stem . . . she
couldn't remember ever having seen it so . . . tidy. It
looked as though someone had put giant lips to the
spring from the other side and given a mighty puff,
clearing away every stray bit of everything.

It made the tracks at the spring stand out rather
starkly. Far too starkly for Brenna to miss. And after
a youth spent tracking this critter and that on the
farm just for the fun of it, far too starkly to mistake for the newly encroaching coyotes or, even less
likely, fox.

Dog.

But not dog running across the area, or dog hanging around for a drink and making a mishmash of
prints. Dog tracks coming from the spring, deep-set
and clear in ground that was now dry enough to hold
them that way, and heading for the creek. Digging
deeply into the ground just at the spring, the way
anything does when it's bolting into instant speed.

She followed them to the creek—they weren't as
clear where the grass thickened, just a tuft or two
of sod out of place along the way—where two deep
prints showed how the dog had launched itself into
the wide, relatively deep water. Not water over her
head, but certainly over the top of any boots she
might choose to wear, so she stopped there.

Dog on the run. Dog full of fear. Dog with
Cardigan-sized prints.

Brenna went back to consider the spring.

Dog out of nowhere.

After a time she quit looking for answers where
there weren't any, collected the gun, and returned

to the house. There she had the middle section of the sub for dinner, fed the dogs, let Sunny hang out at the end of the longe line long enough to finish the dishes of the past few days, and then put Druid on a leash for the walk over to Emily's. The girls, she rightly thought, would love his silly long-bodied shape and his expressive ears, and until she had a better understanding of his puzzling responses, she'd rather have him with her than crated alone in her house.

The strong light of the day was finally fading when she presented herself at Emily's door and said, "What computer wonders have you wrought?" as Jill, the youngest, answered the door.

In response, Jill said, "Oh, he's so *cuuute*. But what happened to his legs?"

"That's how they're supposed to be," Brenna said, but she might as well not have bothered, as Jill leaned back and bellowed, "Marilee! Come and see Brenna's new dog!" Druid quailed at the sound, but then, so did Brenna.

"He's not my—" she started, and gave up, because Marilee had arrived and both girls were on their knees, petting and kissing and making gooey admiring noises. "Here," she said, and handed them the leash. "Don't frighten him, d'you hear? He's been through a lot in the past few days."

Whatever it might have been.

Emily, a sheaf of papers in hand, leaned against the kitchen archway and nodded at her daughters. "They're okay with him?"

"Even if he has one of his ... *moments*, he's not going to do anything to hurt them," Brenna said, repeating the reassurance she'd given Emily on the phone. "If he was going to bite, he'd have nailed me by now." Given what she'd put him through, and how frightened he'd been at moments. Definitely not a fear-biter. Fear-freaker, now ... *that* label, she'd paste on him. "I'd be more concerned about what two little girls could do to *him*—if they weren't yours."

"Okay, you get points for that last bit," Emily said. "Come sit down. Want some soda?"

"Anything decaf," Brenna said. It was, after all, her day off. She took a seat at the table, in a kitchen that was the antithesis of her own—too new to carry the hint of generations past, bright and open and airy. And peach-colored. Every time she came here, Brenna left with an impulse to paint her own kitchen, but when she got home she would realize again just how many other things needed attention, too—a new sink would have been outstanding—and so never got around to any of it. "What'd you find out?"

"A whole lot of nothing, I'm afraid," Emily said, pulling a one-liter bottle of Sprite out of the refrigerator and hunting through the freezer for ice cube trays that actually held ice. "The girls were delighted to play detective for you, but they couldn't find any kennel with the name of Nuadha, no matter what the breed. They did find the Web site for the national Cardigan club, and emailed the contact person. You gotta love email—they got an answer just a few moments ago." She set a glass in front of Brenna, but her expression didn't hold any triumph. She sat across from Brenna and pulled the coated elastic band from her ponytail, only to regather her shoulder-length hair and confine it again.

"Don't tell me," Brenna said, and felt all of her hopes for an easy resolution to Druid's fate fade to nothingness. "They haven't heard of any such kennel, either."

"They suggested that it was a fanciful call name as opposed to the dog's actual kennel name."

"With *champion* at the front of it?"

Emily shrugged. "Don't ask me. I don't know anything about this sort of thing. Now, if you want to talk cross-stitch—"

Brenna waved her to silence and Emily smirked. Any time Brenna became too full of jargon in her talk of dogs, Emily—who cross-stitched like a fiend and regularly sold patterns to stitchwork magazines—interrupted with chatter of her own specialty. "Well, the point is that we aren't going to locate the owner through them. Or even through the Web, it seems."

"You really ought to get yourself a computer," Emily said. "You could keep business records on it—"

"*What* business records?" Brenna snorted.

"—*if* you had your own business, and you'd be surprised what kind of resource the Web can be. You know the girls would be glad to show you how to use it, or you could go to the library—they run little classes on using the Internet all the time."

"Yeah, yeah," Brenna said, by way of saying, *you're right but we both know I'm not going to rush out and do anything about it*. "Let me get this dog squared away first."

"Looks like that could be a while." Emily sipped her own soda, and raised an eyebrow at Brenna.

"Don't remind me. I'm going to be in trouble with this one, Em."

Emily shook her head. "I don't know why you keep breaking your heart, taking these dogs in. If you're going to do it, hand them straight over to animal control, why don't you? Quit pouring yourself into them and fixing all their woes only to have to give them up."

"If I didn't fix their woes, half of them wouldn't be able to find new homes. And the other half would be dead through animal control if I didn't hang on to them as long as I do, waiting for their owners."

"So you always say. But we both know animal control does a pretty good job, if the owners care enough to check around. I think you just like the excuse."

Brenna, at a loss for any cogent argument, stuck out her tongue. Things hadn't changed much, it seemed; that had always been her answer to Russell, also. Russell, older and teasing her about her useless mutts, about how he did things that mattered—at the time, earning a letter on the school math team, already heading for his part-time job at the carpet store he had eventually bought out and expanded.

Not so many years between them, but a seemingly unbridgeable gap that had widened beyond repair the day he had found her with a new dog, a large, starving adolescent with a short, ruddy coat, handsome head, and what she'd immediately thought of as a permanent bad hair day because of the roughened hair on its back. He'd been more thoughtful, then, hadn't ribbed her or made fun of the animal, ugly in its emaciation despite its solid build and the injuries it had sustained. Injuries from human hands, which made her decide against looking for its former owners. In fact, after she had the dog fed up and responding happily to humankind again, he had casually mentioned he knew of a good home. She'd talked with the man, concurred, and placed the dog.

A year later, she had seen news of the dog's big win in a regional dog show. A Rhodesian Ridgeback, it was, and apparently quite a handsome one. But Brenna knew it couldn't be the dog the man claimed it to be, with the parentage and breeding behind it that he spoke of so glowingly in the printed interview. And Russell had just laughed. "His own dog got hit by a car," he said. "Yours was a perfect ringer. And where do you think I got the money for the junior prom? If you'd been more careful about reading the local weekly, you'd have known he lost the dog and could have had the money for yourself."

Her mother knew, if only she had been willing to see. And if her father had realized, he'd have done something, she was sure—but she couldn't bring herself to tell him and see it hurt him. So that was when she'd started reading up on breeds, a subject which hadn't truly mattered to someone who rescued dogs in whatever size, shape, and color they came to her. And that was when she stopped truly trusting her brother, who never understood her ire. "I never did anything wrong," he had told her. "I just sold him the dog. Not my business what he did with it."

No wonder she spent more time here than with her brother's family in town, and knew Emily's girls better than Russell's two boys.

The girls came clattering down the stairs and into the kitchen, Druid at their heels—leashless—and looking attentive and interested in all the little-girl things he'd been exposed to. Fashion dolls and stuffed animals . . . his fascinated expression led Brenna to decide on the spot that he hadn't been in a family with children, at least not girl children.

Nine-year-old Jill, perpetually chubby, freckled, and heading toward braces, held a brush in one hand and a comb in the other; Marilee—equally freckled but beginning to trade her baby fat for height—carried a surfeit of hair goodies, combs and elastics and a few things that Brenna couldn't even identify.

"Time for the ritual torture," Emily said. "It's what you deserve for coming over here and flaunting that hair in front of two little girls with short hair imposed upon them by their wicked mother."

"It's on my *head*, is all," Brenna said, but smiled. Emily's girls had no monopoly on their attentiveness; little girls too young to have been fully socialized often reached out to touch her hair in the store, usually with soft exclamations of delight.

"Hide it under a hat the next time," Emily responded, unruffled. "Go get her, my little hair stylists."

Already they were behind her, releasing her hair from its braid and finger combing it, as gentle as always.

"I just learned a new way to braid," Marilee said
with enthusiasm. "It'll look so cool with hair this long.
It's called a fishtail braid."

"Now *that* sounds attractive," Brenna said, but she
slid down in the chair so she could relax, the groomer
being groomed. If only half her own canine clients
could learn to enjoy the tug and massage of the
process.

Of course, she wasn't sure she'd enjoy it nearly as
much if she, too, had mats. But without them she
enjoyed it well enough to drift away in thought, Druid
dozing by her feet. At least, until the voices started
up.

They came to her in a murmur, as though she
were stuck in a verbal collage. Male and female,
none of them familiar, expressing themselves in
incomplete sentences as though they came from a
low-volume television with someone hopping through
channels. Druid twitched against her feet, dreaming, but her awareness of it didn't distract her from
the voices. *Authorities have labeled it shedding
rabies,* said a male voice, and *another man found
dead in the city* said a woman. *Vaccine* and *too late*
and then an official-sounding voice that said *take
your dog out and back again, please.* A few jumbled
commands—things like *stay, Druid, it's only for a
little while* and *Druid, no!* And oddly, in a voice that
seemed familiar, . . . *local groomer Brenna Lynn
Fallon succumbed today*—

Brenna jerked alert, barely aware of the girls'
exclamations that they hadn't *thought* they'd pulled
her hair. *What the hell was*—

And Druid jerked awake, looking dazed and disoriented. And then he looked at Brenna, and he
screamed—a human sound no dog should ever voice.
He flung himself backward, and even as Brenna would
have grabbed for him, a dizzying vertigo clutched her;
in the instant it took for solid ground to return, he

was gone, and all three of the Brecken women, youngest to oldest, were staring wide-eyed at his wake.

"Oh-*kaay*," Emily said, turning both her gaze and her expertly raised eyebrow on Brenna.

"What the hell—" Brenna said, out loud this time, and then realized she was in the presence of young ears. "You guys didn't hear that." She grabbed an elastic from the table and brought her hair around. The fishtail braid was indeed cool, but apparently tedious in execution, for it was only a third of the way down her back. She overrode the girls' protests and fastened it where they had stopped.

"Do me a favor," she told them, talking over them, and her words hushed them fast enough. "Help me find him. He's probably hiding behind or under something. Don't try to get close to him. He's too afraid right now, and it wouldn't be kind to him."

Young women on a mission, they rushed from the kitchen.

Emily caught Brenna's eye and shook her head. "You told me he was strange, but . . . Brenna, just what is it you think you can do with that dog?"

Brenna had no doubt that if Druid had been on a leash, they would all have been treated to another incident of flailing and foaming and shrieking, and she sighed, meeting Emily's gaze long enough for an honest shrug. "I don't know. But you saw him . . . when he's normal, he's a charismatic and well-behaved dog. If I can only figure out what's causing the behavior—"

"*The behavior*," Emily said, and laughed without humor. "The *behavior*! Brenna, the dog is hallucinating! He's the doggy equivalent of a homeless man who's not sane and won't take his drugs!"

Brenna could only stare off in the direction of Druid's flight, bemused. *Local groomer Brenna Lynn Fallon succumbed today* . . .

Just how crazy did that make *her*?

❖   ❖   ❖

Crazy enough to go back to work. On Saturday, no less, a day Brenna was used to working but one that always lasted several hours longer than she was actually scheduled, even double-teaming with Elizabeth and with someone pulled off the floor to wash the dogs.

Not someone who actually knew what they were doing, of course. One of the guys from the back of the store, whom Roger must have figured was large enough to handle the big ones. And who obviously loved dogs.

If only he'd ever washed one.

Brenna, swooping in to get her next clip job and crossing mental fingers that the dog was actually dry, found Deryl towel-drying a Collie-mutt and spotted the tell-tale slick of fur at a glance.

"He's still got soap in his hair," she told him, shouting out of necessity; all the dryers were going, all the crates full.

He gave a look of disbelief, clearly not able to comprehend that he'd missed some soapy spots or, more likely, that he'd missed them and *she'd* been able to see them. "But I've already got him half dry."

As if that was relevant. "Doesn't matter," she said, gesturing at the tub with her chin, her arms already full of West Highland Terrier. "Put him back in and rinse him again. If you don't get the soap out, he'll itch and we'll rightly get blamed for it." She freed an arm from the Westie, balancing the dog in her grip just long enough to point. "There. And there. Get those spots rinsed enough to make your fingers squeak."

And still the doubt.

"Just do it!" she said in exasperation. "You're getting paid by the hour, not by the dog!"

He frowned, hesitated, and thought better of it. When she left the room he was reinserting the unhappy dog into the tub.

Elizabeth was hard at work on a Samoyed who

apparently hadn't been brushed all winter. "It's no wonder they hate us," she muttered to Brenna as she used the razor-sharp blades of a mat comb on the dog's haunches; it tried to whirl and snap, but she had it well secured.

Brenna didn't even bother to respond; it was a rhetorical grumble they perfected each spring. Instead she cranked the table up, deposited the Westie, and got to work. "And how are you today, Miss Daisy?" she said, and presented her face for licking.

"No fair," Elizabeth said, still grumbling. "You got to do Daisy last time she was in."

"Gotta be quick!" Brenna told her, grinning. Daisy came on a regular schedule, had a lovely coat, a sweet temperament, and solid conformation . . . good breeding, shining through. Grooming her always made Brenna remember what had attracted her to the job in the first place. Not just working with the dogs, but working with them in a way that they both enjoyed. Not just cleaning them up and putting them through a clipper assembly line, but turning it into an art of sorts, taking handsome little dogs like Daisy and putting a smart breed clip on them so they'd want to strut out of the shop.

And the hardest thing about Daisy was that although she knew to stand, she kept trying to give kisses. With a comb attachment, a little stripping work and thinning sheers, Brenna had Daisy spiffed up with a perky Westie breed cut and a tiny pink bow at the base of each ear. "You're too cute!" she told the dog, and escorted her to one of the front crates. Just in time; her owner would be along in fifteen minutes for pick-up.

By which time Brenna would be snacking on carrots and granola bars. "Everything else is still drying," she told Elizabeth, pulling off her grooming smock. "I'm going for lunch, and maybe even that break I worked through this morning."

"Fine by me," Elizabeth said, discarding a slicker brush's worth of hair on the floor. "I'll no doubt still be working on this dog when you get back. I hope you warned the owners that there would be matting charges."

"Oh, yes," Brenna said. "We had the *my dog's not matted conversation.* I provided visual aids and won the day." What she had done was to stick several wide-toothed combs into the dog's hair—where they stayed upright, quite securely anchored by the mats.

They kept combs on the front counter expressly for that purpose.

But she didn't have to think of that now. She could grab her lunch, her current paperback thriller, and let the rest of her brain take a deep, restful breath in the employee break room, where the biggest challenge was resisting the beguiling whisper of the snack pastries in the vending machine.

Which was where she was when Roger's new buddy sauntered in and poured himself a cup of coffee, a sheaf of photocopies tucked under his arm. She didn't look up from her book; peripheral vision identified him easily enough, although he wasn't moving with the same facility she had already associated with him. And he took no special note of her, not until he carefully eased into one of the folding metal chairs across the table from her and came out of his pre-occupation long enough to recognize her. "How's that dog?" he asked, but his voice didn't sound especially solicitous. Making conversation.

She hesitated, tempted to pretend she was so absorbed by her reading that she didn't hear him and trying to pin down the faint accent in his words— not English, but too elusive to identify. He wasn't dissuaded; she felt his gaze through the book between them and finally she lowered the book to the table, careful to miss the remains of her lunch. "He's strange," she said noncommittally. "He's about the strangest dog I've ever dealt with, if you want to know. But I suppose somehow I'll manage."

"If you decide you want help, give me a call." He took a card from his shirt pocket and shoved it across the table at her.

"You know," Brenna said, feeling her mouth take over and knowing that she would probably regret it later, "if I was going to ask someone for help, it sure wouldn't be someone who makes that . . . *face* at me."

"Which face would that be?" he said, and she could swear she heard amusement. Not outright humor, just . . .

She couldn't tell, and it frustrated her. "The one you're probably making right now—" she said, finally and fully looking away from the book, and then cutting herself short. Whatever his expression, this was certainly the first time he'd had a couple of stitches in one eyebrow and dark purple bruising all the way down the side of his face . . . as if a heavy fist had skidded up from jaw to brow and come to an abrupt stop there. "Well, okay," she said, finding it odd to meet his gaze and those same clear, deep blue eyes as her own—familiar eyes in an unfamiliar framework. "Probably not that exact face. But under all the colors, pretty much identical." She imitated it for him. "Anyway, working with dogs is what I do."

Undeterred by her response, he nudged the business card toward her. Thanks to the stickiness of the table—there was a definite cabal of employees who thought a magic fairy would descend from the ceiling to clean up their mess once they'd gone, but it never seemed to happen—the card didn't go far, but Brenna reached for it anyway. She recognized the logo from his SUV right away, a generic dog silhouette circled by words. *Gil Masera*, it said. *Dog Obedience and Behavior Specialist*.

As she looked up from the card he shrugged and said, "Sometimes it's good to have a backup."

Obedience trainer? Talking to Roger, hanging around the store? Great—it was a probably a professional thing, then, that look. That judgment. Trainer techniques looking down on groomer techniques. She put the card back down where she'd gotten it, in the middle of the table, struck by a sudden bad feeling. "What is it you're you doing here?"

"Having coffee. Listening to you get straight to the point."

"It's better that way—I don't get a very long break." She flashed an annoyed look at him. "Why," she repeated, "are you having coffee *here*? Why does your presence make Roger deliriously happy? And why did do you look at me the way you do—" for he'd done it in the parking lot, too, more or less, "—and don't deny it."

He withstood the barrage with no change of expression, aside from one barely discernable wince when the coffee touched his split lip.

Maybe it would leave a scar, she thought, and gave it some hope.

He leaned back in the rickety chair, wincing again, but ignoring her blatant scrutiny of his physical woes. "I'm having coffee here because I'm *here*. I'm *here* because I'm trying to arrange the necessary layout to hold obedience classes in this store. Roger's happy because he thinks the classes will increase the customer base, and because he didn't think he'd talk me into signing on since I don't need *his* customer base."

"Then why did you? Sign on, I mean." Straight to the point, why not. "And don't think I didn't notice you didn't answer my last question."

"The church I used to work out of not only raised their rates, they kept taking my class space at the last minute." Straight to the point, right back at her. And there was something in his voice that let her know he answered because he chose to, and not necessarily just because she'd asked. "Roger made me a better offer."

No doubt. Brenna had gotten one of those herself, luring her away from her last job. And she'd questioned Roger carefully about her professional concerns, all of which he had assured her would never happen—and every one of which now occurred on a daily or weekly basis.

But let Gil Masera find that out for himself.

"The *faces*," Masera said bluntly, "are because I don't like big commercial grooming setups. I've seen the way the dogs are handled in those situations. I've even picked up the pieces."

Brenna's composure slipped. "You've never even seen me work! And you've *probably* picked up the pieces of what happens when a dog doesn't even see a brush until it's so matted that the owners drop off the mess for someone else to deal with, all while demanding that the dog's coat be saved."

"I've seen enough," he said, not narrowing his eyes so much as lowering the lids in a way that might have made someone else look sleepy but just made him look like a big cat waiting to pounce.

"You come work in the tub room for a week if you want to say anything like that about *this* grooming room," Brenna said, her bangs sliding into her face with her emphatic words. She brushed at them in an automatic gesture and poofed them away for good measure, sitting back in the folding chair. "Are you always this abrasive?"

"It's a gift," he said, watching her. "Sometimes it suits me."

She quite definitely didn't know what to make of him. Under Russell's expectant stare she often kept silent, promising herself she'd do things her way as soon as he looked away—which never took long. But now . . . there was some unspoken challenge in Masera's scrutiny, and she gave him an even look in return. Standing behind what she'd said, the good and the bad of it both.

Still, it came as a relief when the door swung open,
interrupting their temporarily silent exchange. Sammi
Grozny of the People Placing Pets rescue group came
in, hunting down a soda. PePP held weekly adoption
days out of Pets!, during which the volunteers juggled
various cats and dogs, made sure unsupervised kids
didn't poke Fido's eyes out, diplomatically discour-
aged the people who wanted simply to walk away with
a new pet, and encouraged the owner-prospects to
fill out the initial questionnaire in the process of adoption. Saints, in other words, or so Brenna had always
thought.

But not perfect ones. Sammi, who weighed enough
that Brenna worried about her health and who never
seemed to catch her breath, nonetheless used that
breath on endless streams of verbal worrying.
"Brenna!" she said, as though Masera weren't even
in the room. "I wondered why I didn't see you out
front. Have you heard about that dog pack? You're
right in their territory, aren't you?"

Before Brenna had a chance to answer, Masera
said, "No one's seen a single member of that pack."

Sammi ignored him, making her soda selection
automatically enough that it was obvious she knew
this machine well. "I hope you're being careful."

"Sunny's crated," Brenna said, but she glanced at
Masera and realized right away that his own words
had been deceptively offhand in delivery; his eyes
were watching every nuance of the conversation.
"Hold on," she said, balling up the plastic wrap that
had held her peanut butter and jelly sandwich and
twisting to toss it out. "I'll walk back up front with
you."

"Finish your lunch," Masera said, nodding at the
remaining baggie of carrot sticks as he swallowed the
last of his coffee; Brenna winced at the thought of
how hot it must have been. "I'm through here."

It stopped her short, her hand in the act of stuffing

the carrots into her *Warrior Princess* lunch box. He didn't wait for her response, but stood—or tried to. It seemed to take him by surprise, as though his attention had been so diverted that he'd forgotten his battered status. But he pushed himself to his feet, straightened with effort, and tossed his coffee cup at the giant bin in the corner of the room, gathering up his papers.

"Don't forget to come spend some time in the tub room," she said, and gave him a dare-you smile. People forgot she could do that; she had one of those whole-some faces, the kind that take on *cheerful* as their default expression. Her eyes even tipped up a tiny bit, as if they were always smiling. Sometimes she stood in front of the mirror and tried for *sultry*, but couldn't ever pull it off. Not with that chin—strong, in a strong jaw, and with a definite cleft. Or with those lips, which had a little uplift in each corner and, just like her eyes, always seemed to imply a smile even when just in repose. And her nose . . . just hopeless. Not that it didn't suit her face, but maybe that was the problem. It wasn't quite what you would call perky, not with that subtle bump on the bridge of it, but it was darn close.

Taken together, her features made people assume certain things of her. Because of her face, they thought her to be incessantly cheerful, and possibly just a little naive. Because she was tall and lean unto gawkiness, with big hands and bony shoulders and a body that, although it had decent dimensions, couldn't seem to assemble itself gracefully, they somehow thought her to be unsophisticated in a charming way, perhaps even someone to be protected, as her father always had.

But she wasn't. She could meet a challenge as well as anyone, and stand up for herself along the way. And that's what her smile said to Masera, a smile she'd startled herself with because she never bothered to use it on people who couldn't manage to perceive it, and here it was. Some part of her had realized the truth before her thinking brain...that he *could* see beyond her features, beyond her appearance.

The hard smile surprised him briefly, much as she'd meant it to—but it didn't seem to put him off, also as she'd meant it to. There was something about him that intensified, leaping to meet that look; something in those hooded eyes.

"Wait till you heal up from whoever kicked the tar out of you," she told him. "You don't want to have to call me in to lift a dog for you."

"Like you did for Roger," Sammi said with a wicked little grin—right on cue, her eyes lighting at the thought. Like all the PePP volunteers, Sammi was grateful for the adoption days allowed by Pets!—but it didn't make her blind to the way Roger managed his people.

"You see," Brenna said. "People hear about these things here. We watch out for one another."

"We do," Sammi said, quite aware that she was playing a role in a larger conversation that she didn't understand, but willing to team with Brenna to do it.

Again, amusement flickered across Gil's face, settling at one side of his mouth. The side with the split lip. "I'll keep that in mind," he said, and left the room—but somehow left some trace of his attitude behind.

It kept Sammi silent and thoughtful. Brenna gave it an internal scowl and jumped up to prowl the offerings of the snack machine, thinking hard about chocolate. She was still prowling when Sammi spoke up. "Who *was* that? Why don't you like him?"

"Because he doesn't like me," Brenna said, which was indeed what it basically boiled down to. Judging her and Elizabeth simply because of the way they might—or might not, given that he'd never seen them—handle dogs.

"Something didn't like *him*," Sammi said. "Car accident?"

"Fight, I'm betting," Brenna said, thinking of how similar Russell had looked and moved the time several high school rivals had teamed up to put some hurt on him. Not truly to damage him . . . just to make a point.

A very hard point.

Brenna sat on the corner of the table, struggling with the cellophane on the brownie she had just rescued from the depths of the machine. "Anyway, I *am* being careful about the dog pack. Not even going out at night. At least I don't have anyone leasing the barn right now . . . though I ought to try to get someone in there this spring." She broke off a piece of brownie, popped it into her mouth, and spoke around it. "Is it true? That no one's actually seen any of the dogs?"

Sammi hesitated, long enough for Brenna to sift through her own recollection of news briefs heard on the radio going to and from work. Someone had found a mauled cat on the edge of their property and the wounds were determined to be dog-inflicted. Someone else had found a small mutt dead in the woods edging a farmer's field. But had anyone seen the pack? Had anyone seen even a single dog?

Gil Masera knew something, that was for sure.

Or he thought he knew something.

"No," Sammi finally said, picking at the tab opener of her soda. She looked up at Brenna. "But plenty of people have seen what they've *done*. We've got PePP members out in your area right now—someone found another dead dog last night, a little Jack Russell mix. Some of us volunteered to look for signs of the pack. And Janean is at Lakeridge right now with a second dog—this one's alive. It's hurt, but alive. It'll go through quarantine, and if the owner hasn't shown up, we'll take it on till it heals and place it." She gave

Brenna a dark look. "It *used* to be a real pretty little Sheltie mix. So don't tell me those dogs aren't out there somewhere. And don't *you* get careless about them."

Brenna held up both hands. "Like I said, Sunny's crated." Never mind explaining Druid, who was crated right along with the hound but had disdained the bone Brenna had left him; his stare had bored into her back as she'd left the house, sending the certain message that he was supposed to be coming with her, regardless of where she was headed. "And I'm not going out after dark, at least not until this whole dog pack thing is sorted out or broken up or whatever."

"Well, good," Sammi said, mollified. She took a swig of her soda while Brenna chewed the brownie— mostly cardboard, but her body seemed to think it was getting chocolate—and said, "Tell me again who that was?"

It took Brenna a moment, since she hadn't said anything on the subject in the first place. "Gil Masera, you mean? Says he's a trainer. Looks like he's going to be working out of Pets! For a while, anyway."

Sammi waggled her eyebrows at Brenna, no part of subtle. "Bet he cleans up nice."

Brenna laughed at her—Sammi was at all times an earthy delight—but her reply was sober and certain. "And I'm betting he won't be here long enough to find out. Guy with an attitude like that? Roger won't be able to hang on to him."

But he knew something. And before he went, she wanted to know what.

Chapter 6

ᚺ

HAGALZ
Disruption Born of Human Need

Brenna set the rifle against the barn and pulled her target paper off the ancient hay bales she had stacked high, two deep and three wide behind the barn—a nice, broad buffer. Just in case. So far she'd been shooting with a surprising accuracy, considering how long it had been—but then, she'd always had a feel for this old .22.

On the other hand, she'd never pointed it at a moving target. Or a *living* one, for that matter. And she fervently hoped she would never have to.

She stuck the shredded target between two bales and decided against shooting another round; a glance at her watch—five-thirty—told her she had only forty-five minutes until the sun went down, and she still wanted to take Druid on a walk around the pastures.

Pastures, hell. She wanted to take him to the spring. To match his footprints against those that appeared from nowhere. And . . . some part of her wanted to see how he reacted to being there at all, although the rest of her didn't want to admit it, simply because it all didn't quite make enough sense.

She reloaded the rifle, double-checking that she hadn't accidentally chambered a round, and then left the chamber open and the rifle on the porch. Inside the dog room, Sunny beat her tail against the side of the crate in greeting; Druid merely gave Brenna a dignified and offended look at having been left behind. Brenna shrugged her vest on over her black hooded sweatshirt, made sure Sunny saw her fill her pockets with broken biscuits, and then turned the Redbone loose as she leashed Druid. Sunny wasn't reliable on *come*, but as long as Brenna had biscuits, she wouldn't go far.

On the porch, Brenna hesitated, then reached for the rifle. Never in her life had she walked the pastures with a firearm for self-protection. It felt distinctly different—*strange*—from when she walked out for target shooting. "Better safe than sorry," she told Druid in melodramatic solemnity.

Druid was unimpressed, and much more interested in the prospect of a walk. He capered before her, never quite pulling on the lead—a gentleman, he was—but as happily carefree as she'd yet seen him, this silly dog who often whined while chewing his bones, all the important thoughts slipping out. Sunny slid under the gate that Druid navigated without so much as ducking, and they both waited impatiently for Brenna to use the boring human method of open-and-close.

Once out in the pasture, Sunny ran giant circles around them, so pleased with her freedom that

Brenna began to doubt the decision to let her stretch her legs. But when Brenna patted her pockets Sunny came charging to her side, so she relaxed. Chill spring, early evening, and she was out of the grooming room and here in her own little corner of the world. Druid settled to a steady trot beside her, his short legs flashing to keep up with her naturally long stride; together they went down the steep, short bank and then followed the creek to the spring.

The cigarette butt caught her eye first thing.

It lay directly down the hill from the spring; shocked, she stared at it in dismay. Not only had someone been here in this place that meant so much to her, he'd flung his trash down and left it, a harsh visual curse for her to trip over. And so stung was she by its presence and all it implied that she didn't attend Druid's sudden worried whine, the series of small jerks against the lead—he who had capered at the end of it in careful compliance and respect of its length.

Sudden memory hit her; the spring she had found the gravesite scattered, the spring defiled. She sprinted up the hill to it, Druid hanging back, protesting—

Druid, no!

Brenna stopped short. Someone else's voice, someone else's fear. And the strange sensation struck her again, the feel of her world folding in on itself. *Druid, no!* Fear and grief and desperation and a great flash of light, and then Druid screamed and threw himself back on the leash, flopping and fighting and pulling Brenna back to the cool air against her cheek, the diffuse light of a clear, crystal-edged spring night reclaiming her vision.

"Druid!" she snapped, having had quite enough of the little fits and everything that came with them. "Druid, that's enough!" She put her foot on the leash close to his collar, restricting his fit, and it didn't slow him in the least. Nor did it slow him or even seem to reach him when she crouched close, her foot still on the leash, and said in the most matter-of-fact tone she could manage, "Druid, no. No. No."

When he did stop, his eyes wild and foamy spit on his lips, it was only because he was exhausted; there was no intelligence in his eyes, no response to her quiet words. As soon as something moved, as soon as he got his wind back, he'd start again—she had no doubt. So with coordination that surprised even herself, she set the rifle down, pulled her foot from the leash, grabbed him up, and bounded to the bottom of the hill, where she placed him on the ground.

He stood in disheveled shock, panting, but his eyes no longer wild. After a moment he shook himself off, put his bottom on the ground, and looked up at her as if to say, "Well! Wasn't *that* something!" Brenna took a deep breath and let it out in a sigh of relief. Straightening, she fished for the flopping end of her braid and stuck it in her pocket.

A throat cleared. A masculine sound.

Brenna jerked her attention to the creek, to the other side of it. He stood there, looking back at her, meeting her startled gaze evenly. "Interesting dog you've got there."

"Looks that way," Brenna said shortly, thinking with sinking stomach of the rifle out of her reach. But the creek was between them, running cold between two steep banks, and loud enough to discourage casual conversation. "The fence is there for a reason. This is private property."

He shrugged, not the least affected by the news, and rolled an unlit cigarette between his fingers. No doubt it matched the stubby filter she'd spotted upon arrival. Otherwise, he was not so different from her— dressed in jeans and a vest over a light jacket, hiking boots on his feet. And not a big man, no bigger than she, though with more meat on his bones. His hair, a bright blond, matched a neat but full mustache with glints of gold in it; both were clean and trimmed. Nothing about him to make her wary, aside from her initial resentment of both his presence and his littering.

He gave her that time to look him over and nodded at the .22, up on the hill. "Do you always carry a gun?"

"It's a rifle," Brenna said. "I was target shooting."

"Earlier. Yes, I heard."

"I usually have it," she said, answering his first question—perhaps not with the strict truth, but following sudden instinct.

"I know I'm trespassing," he said suddenly, taking a step closer to the bank as he stuck the cigarette in his mouth and dug in his front pocket for what she presumed was a lighter.

"Don't light it unless you plan on taking it with you," she said, with a pointed look back at the butt on the ground behind her.

Startled, he stopped with the flickering lighter halfway to the end of the cigarette, and then let it go out. "I can wait," he said mildly. "I didn't have to come back when I saw you, you know. If I hadn't wanted you to know I'd been here."

Again, she looked back at the cigarette butt.

He grinned at that. "If I hadn't wanted you to know it was *me*."

She shrugged, an acknowledgment of sorts. Behind him, the southwestern sky deepened, a cerulean warning of impending twilight.

He said, "The place means something to me, is all. I was here with some friends, once. Last time I saw one of them before he died. And the other one . . . buried him a couple of months ago. So the place calls to me, I guess."

Brenna hesitated. She didn't recognize him, which

was odd enough; she didn't know all of the names of her most recent neighbors in the divvied-up farm-land near Emily, but she knew their faces well enough. And yet he was charming enough. Not her type, but she had no doubt that smile got him plenty of attention. No reason, aside from the discomfiting circumstances of their meeting, to heap rudeness on him. "If I couldn't tell you'd been here," she said, careful with her words, "I might not care."

"Thanks," he said, and bestowed his smile upon her.

"Don't take it as an invitation," she said.

"I'll take it for what it is," he told her, and ducked his head to light the cigarette, glancing up at her as he drew a deep draught of it. She thought it was his parting comment, but as he turned away he added, "Best get inside. I hear there's a pack of dogs run-ning wild in the area."

You don't look so worried. And he didn't, walking away through the winter-mashed grass with a distinct lack of purpose in his stride.

But she tied Druid to a sapling on the bank and went up to retrieve the rifle, hesitating only long enough to check his footprints in the dimming light, the old against the fainter, newer imprints, mostly obscured by the disturbed turf from his little fit. Long enough to decide that they could have come from the same dog, not long enough—and not enough light—to say for sure.

"Sunny!" she called, her best pasture-spanning bellow. "Suuun-ny!" She slapped her pocket a few times, making the biscuits rattle. Druid made an interested noise, in case she'd forgotten he was there and perfectly willing to relieve her of the burden of carrying all those terribly heavy biscuits. "In a minute," she told him, and switched to escalating tactics. "Co-ookies!"

Sunny might never learn her name, but she knew

cookies down cold. In moments she galloped up, a clump of last fall's burrs stuck to her neck, her tongue hanging long, and her expression eager. Brenna murmured, "Silly," and tossed her a biscuit, which the hound snatched out of midair. She tossed one to Druid, too, but it boinked off his forehead as he made no attempt either to catch it or to get out of its way. Once it hit the ground he snatched it up fast enough.

"*That*," Brenna said, "is something you'll have to learn if you want to hang around with me."

He's somebody else's dog.

"Yeah, yeah," she muttered to her warning inner voice. Somebody else's *strange* dog. But he was here for now.

Here in her life, along with strange black moods in the night, a stranger at her spring, dog packs roaming the rural woods and farmland, and one really annoying dog trainer.

For now.

After that, Brenna made daily visits to the spring area, checking for signs of trespass. But since the weather remained dry and the unwelcome visitor had been warned about his cigarette droppings, she couldn't be sure if he'd been there. There were signs of disturbance by the footbridge that crossed the creek a little way to the west—without question, the way he was getting from one side to the other—but raccoons and coyotes tended to hang out there, anyway.

Well, there was a wet weather system on its way in; she'd have a better indication after that.

She caught glimpses of Gil Masera and his healing bruises at the store, and even saw the periphery of one of his rare afternoon classes—a beginners' class from the look of it, with young dogs sproinging off in all directions, owners looking exasperated, and

Masera with a new and different expression, something softer than his habitual judgmental preoccupation. He was enjoying himself, she realized. He enjoyed the dogs being dogs, he didn't get uptight at the frustration of the owners. And to judge by his reputation—for she checked, in those days after he'd shoved his card at her—eventually those clownish and clueless wonders from his beginners' class would settle down into respectful canine companions.

And in those days after the encounter at the spring, Druid stayed quiet and normal, and graduated to sleeping on her bed. She began to hope that his fits had been spurred by the trauma of his time spent lost and frightened; he even accompanied her to work several times without reaction.

No one called for him. The vet's office couldn't match the rabies tag partial up with any of the Cardigans in their service. No one placed an ad in the paper. The days added up to a week since his arrival, then two . . . and even three.

"I just can't imagine someone *not* looking for a dog like this," Brenna told Emily one Sunday evening over soda at the Brecken table, with Emily's husband Sam puttering happily in the basement and the girls watching a movie while they tickled, scratched, and otherwise adored Druid.

Emily looked up from her latest cross-stitch; Brenna had long been accustomed to the fact that Emily could carry on a conversation and handle complex needlework at the same time. "Not everyone feels the same way you do about dogs, Bren."

"No," Brenna agreed, "but anyone who bothers to own a champion quality rare-breed dog usually does."

"Maybe he's not," Emily said, and shrugged. "You know what that woman at the Cardigan club said. Maybe the owners just made up that name for him."

"I need to find out more about the breed, see if

I can get someone to look at him," Brenna said. "Maybe send a photo to the club. But I'm betting he *is* a champion. When you see puppy-mill pets day after day, you *know* when quality walks in." She craned her neck to get a glimpse of Druid through the kitchen-to-living-room archway; he sprawled on his back with his white-and-freckled legs spread-eagled to the four winds. In the background, Sam's footsteps sounded on the wood-plank stairs. "I'm trying to convince him quality is as quality does. Maybe it's worked—he hasn't freaked since the day I saw that man at the spring."

Sam appeared in the narrow doorway behind Emily, flicking the light switch off as he gave Brenna an alert look, the eavesdropper drawn out. "What man? On your property?"

Emily glanced back at her husband, a short man with a beefy build; one look and it was obvious that the girls took after their slim-boned mother. Round in the face, scant of hair—he at least had the sense to crop what remained short instead of going for a comb-over—Sam had a face that spoke his every thought. Normally Brenna found that reassuring; she always knew where she stood, and half the time Sam was simply emoting his happiness with Emily and life in general. But at the moment he was guarded and halfway to alarmed. Emily took note, stuck her needle into the hoop-stretched needlework, and twisted to look more closely at him. "I thought I'd mentioned that."

"I'd remember it if you had," Sam said. "Because I suspect I know who it was."

"Who?" Brenna asked immediately. Sam owned a local garage, and if there were a male equivalent of beauty salon gossip, he worked in the midst of it.

"Rob Parker. You ought to remember him, Brenna. He's younger than you—you would have been out of high school before he started up—but his family's lived around here for a long time. Used to run with a disrespectful bunch, Toby Ellis and Gary Rawlins, mainly."

Emily, whom he'd met at the community college in business classes and who had grown up on the other side of the city, just shrugged at him. "Must have been before you lured me here to live with you in the great white north."

"She's never forgiven me for putting her in the path of yet *more* snow," Sam said, giving the statement a grave face as he moved up behind Emily and gave her shoulder a squeeze. North of Monroe City received considerably more lake-effect snow than south of it, no doubt about that.

"It was a significant sin," Brenna said, trying to look stern.

Emily said, affecting much primness, "You could have opened up a garage *anywhere*."

"The good school district was here," Sam said.

"Foo," Emily sighed. "I can't argue with that."

Sam grinned briefly, then sobered. "But Brenna, seriously. You might not recall; they got into the worst of their trouble about the time your dad took ill. Then Toby joined the army; word is he was nothing but trouble—eventually went AWOL from basic, got himself killed thumbing a ride home—dark night, bad weather, stupid choices. Driver never even saw him. Gary'd started a good construction job, could have gone places—but he quit it right after. No one really understood what came over him. He never worked steady after that—but always had plenty of money, if you catch my drift. And Rob took off, went to Ohio somewhere, spent time in auto assembly."

"He said he'd lost a friend right after the last time he'd been at the spring," Brenna said. "Toby, maybe? And another friend not long ago?"

Sam nodded. "Gary. Couple of months ago. You

ought to have seen it in the paper—they followed the story pretty closely for a couple of weeks. Unsolved homicide. He brought it on himself, if you really want to know. Just like Toby. Stupid choices. Good riddance."

"Sam!" Emily said, truly shocked.

Sam shook his head, unrepentant. "I mean it, Em. He was bad news, and he carried it around with him. He might have been lost in Monroe, but this community's too small for someone like him. I'm glad he's not carrying on his smarmy deals anywhere near our girls. And I'm not so happy that Parker came back."

"It's been years," Emily said. "And he hasn't been anywhere near his bad-luck friends. He might not be anything like them."

"Those kind make their own bad luck."

Emily tipped her head to stare at him, evidently no more used than Brenna to hearing such harsh statements from Sam, but he didn't give; he just shook his head once. "See if I'm not right."

"People change," Brenna said cautiously. Though *she* hadn't. Just the same now as she ever had been, except maybe a little less patient, a little more tired, and a lot more aware of what people did to their dogs in the name of ignorance. Still in her parents' house, the same house she'd been in when Toby died, Gary led his short and seamy life, and Rob had years of life elsewhere. With Dad dead and Mom living with Aunt Ada in Sunset Village, playing bingo, going on bus trips and fancy restaurant trips and tours of the wine country in the southern part of the state. Russell had married, found a partner and bought out the small flooring company where he'd worked since he was sixteen, and been to the community college along the way.

And Brenna was still waiting to remodel the second floor of the farmhouse into the loftlike master bedroom she'd envisioned when she was thirteen years old.

"Some people do change," Sam said, and she realized he was responding to her comment of moments before. "But this one'll have to prove it by me if he has."

Chapter 7

ᚾ

PERTH
A Secret Matter

Brenna glanced at the clock as she plunked a hyperactive Westie into the tub and slipped the tub noose around his neck, her fingers automatically adjusting it to fit. Good thing she had extra time for this bath; the dog, a new customer, was actively uncooperative and had a bite or two lurking behind the frenetic look in his eye. He was the last of a long string of morning baths for which she'd stuck Druid in the corner on a towel with a fresh shank bone, jammed foam plugs in her ears to filter out the roar of the dryers and the barking dogs, and gone into bathing mode. Bathing mode . . . zoned out, her body hard at work while her mind wandered off to focus on other things.

Other things, like Rob Parker at her spring—she'd
found his footprints the day before—and the fact that
although random victims of the dog pack kept showing
up, Masera-the-trainer had been right—no one had
yet actually seen the dogs. Besides which, dog packs
composed of local pets and castoffs tended to form
around a bitch in heat, and to break up afterward.
By now, the pack members should have been peeling away, returning home, getting caught, or wandering off on their solitary journeys.

More *other things*, like the argument she'd wit-
nessed in the doorway to the stockroom when she'd
gone back to clock in and hang her coat—Masera and
Mickey, one of the stockboys. It had been a real
argument, too, low and intense and the look in
Mickey's eyes surpassing resentment.

What would Masera and Mickey even have to *talk*
about, never mind argue over?

And you'd think Masera would lay off the arguments for a while, considering that he still sported
the fading bruises from the last one he'd been in.

She splashed the gentle shower of water against
her wrist, checking the temp, and wet down the dog's
legs—giving her instant cause for thanks that the zen
bathing-state left her reflexes not only unimpeded,
but faster than any conscious reaction. Cursing a
terrier streak, the Westie snapped for the hand holding the nozzle, falling short only because she snatched
a hind leg with the other hand and jerked him back.

Ah-*ha*. So that's the way it was going to be. No
wonder these people had come all the way from the
other side of the city for this appointment.

They'd already used up the patience of all the
more-convenient groomers.

The bellowing treatment wouldn't work for this
one; nor would a good shake. Not with the shining
intent in his round black eyes, or the instantaneous
way he'd reacted to the water. Holding him stretched

against the noose so he couldn't whip around and nail
her, Brenna fumbled at the shelves behind the retain-
ing wall at the foot of the tub, searching blindly for
the muzzles. They came out in a clump, and she
shook them until only the medium-small remained.

The dog complained endlessly about the water
running around his toes, snapping repeatedly at the
only thing he could reach—empty air. Druid, recog-
nizing the threat as different from the mindless noise
of the crated dogs, barked sharply in warning. Brenna
sighed—a moment ago she couldn't have imagined
intensifying the chaos—and stuck the muzzle strap
between her front teeth so she could size it up with
her one free hand.

That, of course, was when Masera walked in.
Masera, who had already made disparaging remarks
about her professional techniques. Masera-the-trainer,
who didn't think much of the way she handled dogs.

The Westie snarled at *him*, too.

But though he looked momentarily bemused by the
turmoil, Masera didn't react to the sights and sounds
before him. He just stood there, waiting for Brenna
to sort things out—to snag the dog's face with the
muzzle in expert efficiency and tighten it down, to
turn the dryers to their lower, quieter settings, and
to stand by the tub so the dog didn't act on his
posture-signaled intent to attempt some noose-
slipping. To lean back against the tub, actually, and
cross her arms over her wet smock. She felt the bump
of her braid against the back of her thigh—it wasn't
doubled today, but hung at full length—and absently
tugged it up to stuff in her back jeans pocket under
the smock.

"So that's what you were hiding under all that
mud," he said.

Brenna shook her head. "Excuse me?"

"The dog," Masera said, nodding at Druid, who was
noticeably uneasy at Masera's entrance.

"Close the door, will you?" Brenna said. "I don't need him to go walkabout, especially if you left the grooming room door open."

"Closed," he said, and stepped into the tub room so that door could swing closed as well. "Nice dog. I'm between dogs now, but I'm thinking of a Cardigan for the next one. Do you show him?"

"Someone seems to have," Brenna said. Unless, of course, they had made it up along with the name, as the Cardi national club suggested.

Masera cocked his head at her, frowning, and she realized suddenly how little sense that had made to someone who didn't know her history with Druid.

"He's a stray," she said, slipping it in between barks. "I found him the night before you saw him in the parking lot. Can't track down his owners."

He glanced at Druid in surprise—Druid's huge and expressive ears tilted back slightly. Wary. Noting that he was being noticed—and then Masera's expression changed to realization. "So when I saw you—"

"I'd had my hands on him for less than twelve hours," Brenna confirmed. "I had no idea he'd behave that way."

"How is he now?"

It seemed like a genuine question, but Brenna didn't quite get it—or his presence here. He didn't seem apologetic *or* abrasive. More like . . . questing. So she shrugged in response to his question about Druid, crossing her fingers where he could see and not bothering to vocalize above the renewed spate of barking from the Husky in the bottom crate. The dog that would take the longest to dry, of course—fate decreed that those were the noisiest. When the dog paused for breath and perhaps to see if he'd impressed anyone, she said, "Can I do something for you? I've got to get Mr. Congeniality bathed so I can get that Dobie out of here. Her mom's coming in twenty-five minutes."

"Let me do the Westie," he suggested.

She raised both eyebrows high in astonishment, then laughed, short and loud and not quite truly amused. "A week, I said, Mr. Masera. Not one little Westie."

"You did. But I don't have a week, and I never will. I *do* have the time to do the Westie, though— and it looks to me like you could use the help." There it was again, that tease of an accent.

"That's the understatement of the year," Brenna muttered, assuming he wouldn't hear it and surprised when he responded.

"Things change this time of year," he said.

"You a fortune-teller?"

"You want the help?" He nodded at the Westie.

"Yes," she said, and indicated the smock hanging on the corner of the metal shelves. "There's an extra, if you want it."

He gave it a look—at least it was basic black, and not blinding pink as some of the excessively perky smocks often were—and shook his head. She wasn't surprised; it was cut for a medium woman; on her the sleeves fell short and the hem barely covered her thighs where they hit the table edge, leaving the shorn hair a chance to work its way into her jeans. And while Masera wasn't huge—not the beefy type, but somewhere between that and whipcord, with legs as long as her own—the smock would probably be more annoying than protective.

"Call me Gil," he said. "Or Masera. *Mr. Masera* is reserved for Boy Scouts." He rolled up the cuffs on his ubiquitous flannel shirt. Blue today.

Gil. It didn't suit him somehow; she wasn't sure why. And she knew she should tell him to call her Brenna, but when her mouth opened, nothing came out. By the wall, Druid sat wary and watchful, and Brenna suddenly realized that, for some reason, she felt exactly the same way. Wary. So instead she reached for the correct squeeze bottle of diluted shampoo, and tipped it at him like a drink. "This is what he needs," she said, stepping out of the way. And then, though she wanted to hover and supervise, she got a grooming noose from the hook by the door and went to the Dobie's crate. Sweet Sara Dobie with her extreme overbite and her worried eyes; Brenna always tried to get her done first. Druid, who had quickly learned the patterns of activity here, already waited by the door.

When she glanced at the tub, she discovered that Masera had removed the muzzle. Of course. "You'll want that," she told him, turning off all the dryers for a moment of respite and easier conversation.

He looked at the muzzle and said, "Does Mickey ever help out back here?"

"Mickey?" she said. "Why would he? He's in stock. If I've talked to him twice, I don't remember the second time. And really. You need the muzzle."

He said mildly, "I don't."

"You know what?" she said, discovering that she just didn't care enough to be angry or annoyed, not with the dogs waiting to be done and Sara shifting nervously by her side. "Yes, you do. Because no matter how good you are, no matter how many dogs you've trained, you're not going to train that one out of biting in the tub *and* bathe it within the next fifteen minutes. And that's what it's all about in here, you know? Not training them, not civilizing them, not trying to socialize them in the few moments every three months that I might have my hands on them, and *not* getting bitten. Cleaning them up, making them as comfortable as possible so they can get through another season—*that's* what it's about. And doing as many as possible in one day, and getting them done when we've told their owners we will. So if you're not going to use that muzzle, tell me now— because I can bathe that dog and have it dry by the time you even get it near a crate. We don't *train* them. We *handle* them as best we can without getting hurt. Do you get that now?"

For a moment he looked unaffected; she waited for his gaze to grow lidded and hard. Instead his eyebrows drew together to pinch the high, thin bridge of his nose—just for a moment. Then the expression smoothed and he said, "This is killing you, you know. You care too much."

Her eyes widened; deep inside something twisted, and in that moment she hated him. "What an astonishingly personal thing to say," she told him, her own voice as hard as she'd expected from him. Sara the Doberman gave her hand a nudge with a cold nose and offered a whisper of a whine; she put an absent and soothing hand on the dog's head. "Are you going to put that muzzle back on, or should I put Sara back in the crate and do the bath myself?"

"I'll use the muzzle," he said, still mild, and had it back on the dog almost before he'd finished speaking.

She didn't know what to say then—*thank you* might have been good, but she couldn't bring herself to say it. Not when she didn't entirely understand why he was here in the first place, or why he was making this peace overture when he'd also made it so clear how he felt about groomers. Or how quickly, when he wanted to, he could nail down things she knew better even than to think about. *You care too much.* "He'll try to slip the noose," she muttered, and flipped the dryers on in quick succession so that if he had anything else to say, maybe he wouldn't.

He didn't.

He bathed the dog, toweled it off, and had it drying in the crate by the time she worked out the bulk of Sara's fine, shedding winter coat—even Dobies hid an amazing amount of insulation on their thin-skinned bodies—filled out the paperwork, and returned to the tub room. She found him tossing used towels into the hamper, and she spent a studious few moments adjusting the dryers on each dog—there were never enough, it seemed, especially not with that Husky in the lineup—and finally couldn't avoid turning to him.

"Thank you," she said, looking at his wet knees instead of his face. "That makes my day easier."

"A little shorter, maybe." He shrugged, and she looked up to see a fleeting smile. "Probably not actually *easier*." He tossed a final towel into the hamper and headed for the door, where he turned long enough to add, "Though I *meant* for it to."

And left her thinking about it while the door closed in his wake.

Or *not* thinking about it. She was, she determined right then, far too busy to think about any of it for the rest of the day. She felt a gentle pressure on her leg and looked down to find Druid sitting up on his haunches, one paw cocked up and the other barely touching her—for her attention or for balance or out of concern, she wasn't sure. But he got a big hug all the same.

And then she went on with her day.

Brenna left Pets! feeling more upbeat than seemed reasonable after the way the day had started. But Elizabeth had come in early, and they had taken a moment to present a united front to Roger, armed with enough commonsense arguments to earn themselves a permanent bather for the season. No more grabbing whoever was convenient, no more wasting time training a new temp bather every week.

Assuming that DeNise, the cheerful young woman who'd enthusiastically agreed to work with the dogs, didn't quit before the summer was over. Brenna suspected that DeNise had no idea just how much crate cleaning the grooming work entailed. But she seemed sensible enough, and sturdy enough to deal with the physical part of the work. Most importantly, her nails were already neatly trimmed and she wouldn't spend half of her time trying to protect them.

But when Brenna stepped into the parking lot with Druid on a pleasant heel beside her, her arms full of her coat and her purchases for the day—more bones to keep Sunny happy in the crate and please, God, let the danger from the dog pack pass soon— that upbeat mood blew away with the strong spring breeze at the sight of Masera, almost around the corner of the building with his SUV, tailgate open and down, handing off a wad of money and taking two young pit bulls in exchange. Stout and already muscular despite their early age, probably actually some mix of American Pit Bull and American Staffordshire Terrier; people called both breeds "pit bull" and most didn't distinguish between them.

In between dogs, was he? Looking at a Cardi for his next, was he? That would have made sense, too— Cardigans were a herding breed, highly suited to obedience and agility competition, and a good showcase for his training business. But pit bulls? And was that Mickey from the stockroom standing with his back to her, looking sullen even from that perspective?

He'd lied to her.

He'd come in and made nice and lied to her.

And damn, it bothered her.

She wasn't sure she liked him, but she'd respected him for coming to the grooming room, for offering to bathe the Westie—and for doing it her way. But he'd lied, and now he had his hands on a pair of pit bulls in a back-lot transaction that didn't make her think of anything good.

"Maybe he's rescuing them," she told Druid, watching Masera hoist the dogs into the SUV and crate them. But she didn't convince even herself with that one.

So go ask him.

She'd have to run for it, Druid and packages and all, bellowing his name across the parking lot, and he was already climbing into the driver's seat. In the time it took for that thought, she missed her chance; he was pulling away from the building. *Damn.* Druid whined, looking up at her, and she shifted her grip on the slipping coat and packages, heading for her pickup. "As if I care."

She didn't convince herself with that, either.

Chapter 8

ᚾ

NAUTHAZ
Restriction & Pain

A quick stop at the video store netted Brenna a light romantic film she had missed in the theaters, and she splurged on a big bag of malted milk balls from the bulk section in the supermarket when she ran through to scoop up groceries for the week. She grabbed some seedling flats while she was at it; tomorrow was supposed to be fine and sunny, she had the day off, and she looked forward to a day of puttering. Put the little tomatoes in big pots so she could bring them in if they got a late frost, clear out the leaf mulch she'd had protecting her chrysanthemums, do a little target shooting and give the rifle a good cleaning, let Sunny have a good run...

Puttering. And tonight, malted milk balls, a

sentimental happy-ending movie, and maybe if she got her second wind she'd even clean the bathroom. Alone again, of course. Too fixed on her own course, too strong in who she was—for good or bad—to suit anyone else for long.

Besides, she *liked* movie rental nights and puttering days.

By the time she got home it was twilight—even her early hours couldn't make up for a slow grocery cash-out line—so she put Sunny out on the cable run she'd constructed several days earlier and threw a pot on the stove for pasta. They all ate together—even Sunny, who had graduated to strictly supervised moments in the kitchen—and Brenna tossed Sunny back into the crate with a new bone. "Poor hound," she said fondly at Sunny's forlorn look. Sunny was a creature of sinew and long legs and the need to romp, and the crating routine had gone on for far too long— especially considering that there had been no sightings of the pack. Brenna would give her a few extra moments on the run later on. For now, she was ready to settle in to the old couch in the den, a comforter on her shoulders and a Cardi in her lap. By the time she finished the video she'd be lucky to make it from the couch to the bed, despite the early hour—but that was the norm for her lark's schedule.

"Ready for the movie?" she asked Druid, who cocked his ears to their most alert angle, tipping his head to the side as if at any moment he would burst into spoken commentary—or maybe she'd start talking in dogspeak. Between the ears and the bright white symmetrical blaze, he was probably close to illegally cute. "Never mind," she said, when he couldn't place her words into his vocabulary. "How about this one— want to come up on the couch?"

Fast learner, that dog. He was waiting by the couch by the time she scooped up the video and followed him into the den. He waited just long enough for her to settle into the corner of the couch—a quick procedure, given the extent of the dip that many years of use had formed there—and open her arms to him, and then sprang into her lap to curl into a pleasantly boneless cuddle. His nose twitched at the malted milk balls, but he'd quickly learned there was no point to outright begging. A subtle gleam of drool formed on his lips as he heaved a great sigh and resigned himself to sleep.

Brenna gave herself up to the movie, forgiving all of its weak parts so she could enjoy the clever bits. She smiled with the characters, got drawn up enough in the story to sniffle in all the right places, and noted that the hero character didn't lie to the heroine character.

If he didn't somehow matter, you wouldn't be so mad.

Never mind that. Watch the movie.

The first time Druid shifted uneasily in her lap, she thought he'd just become uncomfortable. The second time, he also whined softly, and she put a hand on the dome of his head. "Shhh."

The third time, she turned off the movie and muted the television volume. They sat in the dimly lit room together, the dog tense in her arms and Brenna puzzling at the night, not hearing anything but the rhythmic grate of Sunny's teeth against bone.

Until it struck, an astonishing intensity of dark spirit clenching down on them all, driving the air from Brenna's lungs like a bad fall.

Brenna barely had time to gasp before Druid sprang from her lap, digging his nails into her thigh and arm and leaping away. But her reflexes were well-trained; some thinking part of her brain realized he was headed not for the floor but up the back of the couch and aiming for the shelves behind it, the very shelves full of breakable mementoes. She snatched Druid out of midair despite his sturdy heft.

Panicked, he turned on her, snapping and screaming. She felt his teeth sink into her hand and reacted instantly, grabbing his scruff and yanking him away, letting gravity do the rest; he fell to the floor, still in her grip.

The darkness let go of her but Druid was lost to it, flipping and struggling in her grip. And while a little voice in her head said *let go, you idiot*, she didn't; the last thing she wanted to do was to offer him success—his freedom—in return for this behavior. Even dazed and bitten and scraped raw by emotional darkness, her long-ingrained instincts held true. On her knees on the floor, her worn jeans torn and her hand throbbing, she eventually got the right angle on the scruff-hold to push his face to the floor and hold him there . . . and by then, he was coming out of it, distressed and exhausted.

And appalled, for even in his wild flight, some part of him knew what he had done.

Bitten her.

When she released him to cradle her hand—and it didn't look so bad, not as bad as it could have been, just throbbing from the force of his jaws but barely bleeding although the swelling was coming up fast—he crawled to her with his ears flat and his tail tucked. Beyond woeful. Looking for a way to apologize for the unforgivable.

"Don't even try," Brenna said, and burst into tears, hot but short-lived. Grouchy, ill-mannered grooming customers were one thing, but *her* dogs? Her dogs didn't bite her. Not since she was young and proved herself to have a special way with them, the girl who could take in any dog and turn it sweet and happy, the girl who could handle the worst of them simply because they gave their hearts to her so quickly.

When had she lost that?

And then she heard her own thoughts. *Her* dog. Somewhere along the way she'd made that decision, letting herself believe that Druid's owner would never appear—and admitting how quickly he'd made himself part of her.

Not a biter.

For the first time in memory, she was in over her head. Not objective enough to form a strategy for dealing with Druid, and not ever faced with a puzzle on this level before. So much of her response to dogs was instinct, and not knowledge.

She needed knowledge.

She cleared her throat, smeared her face dry, and disentangled her hair from where it was trapped between her thigh and calf. When she went to the kitchen to run cold water over the heel of her hand and the base of her thumb, her gaze fell on the business card she had eventually taken from the break room table and then dropped on the counter when she'd cleaned out her pockets the same evening.

Gil Masera, Dog Obedience and Behavior Specialist.

She immediately rejected the impulse to call him. She didn't trust him. He'd lied. And the circumstances under which he'd taken those pit bulls . . .

But she didn't have to like him to learn from him.

And she didn't know any of the other local trainers, hadn't spoken to them. Couldn't call them cold at half past eight in the evening.

She kept her hand under the faucet and reached for the card—turning it in her fingers, glancing at the clock, nibbling the edge of the card in indecision. In the background, Sunny had gone back to chewing her bone, her jaws tireless. Druid clung to the wall between the kitchen and den, drawn to her and yet too mortified to slink the rest of the way to her feet. A spot of blood marred the pristine whiteness of his muzzle.

Her blood.

Brenna felt the decision click into place. She snapped the business card to the table like a poker hand being dealt and turned off the water, gingerly dabbing the hand dry. Darned good thing she had the following day off—she'd never be able to work with *this* hand. And maybe not the day after, either; she'd call Roger tomorrow and give him a heads-up.

She looked at Druid, meeting his gaze directly this time. He sank a little lower to the ground. She sighed. "C'mere, then." Slink-walking, he approached her. She gave him a sad pat, which brought his ears up a little, and directed him toward the crate. "Kennel up, then."

Oh, unhappy dog. The picture of dejection, he entered the crate, turning as she closed the door but making no attempt to push his way out.

Sunny was harder to handle; exuberant as always, more than ready for some time outside, once released from the crate she bounded around the small enclosed porch room, whacking Brenna with her tail and singing Redbone joy to anyone who could hear her half-barked, half-howled excitement. Finally Brenna snagged her collar and, with a clumsy, fumbling hand, snapped the run cable in place. Only then did she open the door that had been closed on it, releasing Sunny into the yard.

Then she returned to the kitchen to reassure herself that Masera could let his machine pick up if he didn't want to answer the business line at this time of night, and nabbed the portable phone from its cradle. She dialed quickly, before she could think too hard about it or change her mind.

And he answered quickly, too. Whatever he was doing this evening, the phone was close by. "Gil Masera."

And she hesitated, suddenly not sure how to start or even what she wanted to call him. Enough of a hesitation so he said, "Hello?"

"Yes," she said quickly, so he wouldn't hang up. "It's . . . this is Brenna Fallon—"

It was his turn to be silent a moment. "Sorry," he said. "I wasn't expecting to hear from you."

"I wasn't expecting to call," she said, putting the conversation back on more familiar footing with that edge of antagonism. "I hope it's not too late."

"I wouldn't have answered the phone if it were too late." But he didn't make it easy for her, didn't ask what he could do for her or why she was calling or if everything was all right.

Brenna had the sudden impulse to hang up, to go back to her movie and her malted milk balls and pretend her hand didn't hurt. Or her heart, which Druid had bitten just as hard as her hand. But she closed her eyes and tightened her grip on the phone, and didn't. Instead she managed to say, "You said to call, if I . . . if things got hard with the Cardi. And I could use an objective opinion. On what to do next, I mean."

"What happened?" he asked, as if he knew she would never call him unless something had.

She hesitated, uncertain how to say it. "He had another one of those . . . fear fits. And . . ." Her throat suddenly constricted, as if she were about to say something that should never be said—and in truth, she supposed it was. She shoved the words out. "He bit me."

"Ah," he said, but it was an understanding sound. As if he knew she wouldn't be upset about a snap-bite, a bite that was more a comment than an offensive, and the likes of which she fended off every day. That if she said he'd bitten her, it was more than broken skin and insult, it was jaws and teeth and power.

"The thing is . . . I think I know how to trigger a fit—there's a place on my property that seems to do it." The spring, of course. She'd bet on it. "I was wondering if I could hire you to come out here and help me get him through it. Help *me* deal with it."

Another silence, though a short one. "You said he was a stray."

"He can't stay that way forever," Brenna said.

"No." There was a pause, and she heard background noise—the pages of a book being closed, cushions crunching gently as he got up. "Let me check my book."

Outside, Sunny gave an inquisitive hound hello—*aowhuff?* Druid whined from inside the crate, circling within its confines. She touched the wire with her toe, distracting him; it worked for a moment. Then Masera came back to the phone; she heard him flipping through the pages of his schedule book, a sound long familiar to her ears. "When's the best time for you?"

"I get off work in late afternoon," she said. "Or my days off—Fridays and Mondays, so I have tomorrow—"

Druid barked sharply.

"No," Brenna told Druid, barely considering it an interruption in the conversation as she returned to Masera, "though I can't imagine you'd have time on such short notice."

"Not tomorrow," Masera said, hesitating at the noise of Druid moving restlessly in the crate, the wire shifting, his toenails clacking—noises any trainer would know.

And a look on Druid's face Brenna was beginning to recognize. "I hate to say it, but I think—" and she gasped in surprise as the cold dark hit her body again, and Druid erupted into a frenzy, flinging himself against the wire, snapping and tugging and tearing at it with his teeth and nails. Brenna couldn't find the breath to speak, not to Masera on the other end of the phone or to Druid or to—

Sunny!

Outside, Sunny let off a quick volley of barks, sharp and utterly unlike her.

And then she screamed.

Over and over, she screamed.

Brenna finally found her own breath and threw herself free of the clenching hold on her soul and right out the kitchen door, into the dog room and yelling for her copper-red hound, her sweet-natured, joy-hunting Redbone, slamming up against a storm door that somehow wouldn't open. Senseless—foolish—she hurled herself against it, gaining a few inches and so startled by the bone-chilling cold that poured in through that gap that she staggered back when the door slammed closed, given life of its own by a strong wind.

But there was no wind.

And suddenly there was no sound, nothing but the final scream in her raw throat and her own ragged breathing. Silence from Druid.

Silence from Sunny.

The door swung outward with a familiar creak of hinge, unimpeded.

After the briefest of hesitations, Brenna stuck her head out. She reached for the porch light, then thought better and grabbed the flashlight sitting on the washing machine. The overhead bulb would light up only the porch while blinding her to what was beyond; useless for this purpose.

The flashlight beam quivered along with her hand, splashing shadows across the clumpy grass, steadying enough to find the tree at the other end of the run and from there the run cable itself. She took a step out onto the porch. "Sunny?"

There was no sign of her.

Nothing, until the light created unfamiliar shadows in the middle of the yard, and she stopped scanning the grass to settle on it, her heart beating wildly in her chest. A disc, gleaming dully. It didn't belong.

A few more steps—down the porch stairs, onto the

stepping-stone sidewalk—and light and shadow
resolved into something recognizable. Sunny's collar.
A turquoise nylon collar, looking darker than it should.
Another few steps from there and she could reach
for it, slowly dropping to a crouch to first touch it,
then pick it up. Her swollen hand was stiff and
fumbly, the fingers not sure of what they felt.

"Sunny?" she said, a tentative call into the darkness as she stood. "Sunny?"

She couldn't not look. She couldn't stop herself
from going to the barn, from walking the old rail
fences of the barn paddocks, calling Sunny's name in
a voice that refused to shout, her fingers clenched
around the collar, feeling more and more dazed as
the moments went by and she slowly realized how
little sense it made. Any of it.

She was crazy. Overworked. Imagining things.

Clenching dark cold that stole the breath from her
lungs, air pressure slamming the door back on a clear,
still night. Sunny's cable to the run broken at the
collar, the collar abandoned nearby. *If she'd slipped
it . . .* If she'd slipped it, she'd have left it dangling
on the cable. No way for a dog to slip a collar without
some force being applied to the collar itself.

The flashlight lowered to point at the ground,
seemingly of its own accord, and this time the call
came out in a whisper. "Sunny . . ."

She probably should think about what to do next,
about checking on Druid or cleaning her hand or
calling animal control to leave a message about her
dog, somehow on the loose. But she just stood there.
And then those decisions were taken away from her
as an unfamiliar vehicle made the sharp turn into her
driveway at some speed and charged the hill up to
the house, painting her in a bright halogen light and
driving her shadow up the side of the barn. The man
who got out of it was nothing but a harshly limned
shadow in the night.

"Brenna? Brenna, are you all right? What's going on?"

"What's going on?" she repeated slowly, realizing that Gil Masera was here, that the phone was somewhere shattered on the kitchen floor. "I don't even know how you found my house, never mind what's going on—" And she gestured half-heartedly with the collar, bringing it up into the headlights he'd left on.

Blood.

Blood soaked the collar, and dripped from her fingers; it smeared across her hand.

She stared stupidly at it. *This isn't happening.* But her mouth seemed to know better, for it said, "Oh my God," though the words came out faintly.

"Is that blood yours?" he said, his words as edged as usual. No, not as usual. Edged, but different somehow.

But not to be ignored, as her hand started shaking again. With one hand grasping at the fencepost, she sank to the ground, to her knees in the dry grass. "No, I—"

If not hers, whose? Sunny's?

In a few long strides he reached her, tucked an arm around her waist and drew her back up. "Inside," he said. "You can sit down inside."

Inside, where the blood would be bright and unmistakable. "Oh God," she said again.

But that would leave— "No! I've got to find her. She's here somewhere. She's hurt—"

"Brenna," he said sharply, getting her attention. "You've got another dog inside who needs you. Let me look for Sunny." When she just stared stupidly at him, he said patiently, "I've got my headlights and I'll take your flashlight. Druid needs you."

Druid.

He took her up the porch and in through the dog room, past Druid on his side in the crate, and flipped a kitchen chair around. She sat, only then truly seeing

Druid and the flecks of blood around the crate. Blood from his lips, his teeth, his paws—injuries self-inflicted in his frenzy. He lifted his head to look at her, his eyes as glazed as hers felt.

She wanted to dive into the crate with him and cuddle him up. But that was what *she* wanted, and not what he needed; she'd wait until he had some intelligence gleaming from those eyes again. Wordlessly, Masera returned to the backyard; she heard him bellowing Sunny's name, his voice growing more distant as he expanded his search. Waiting, strangely dazed, she sat beside Druid, her hand pulsing with pain and her mind still too befuddled to hold a coherent thought—still unable to understand what had kept the storm door closed against her considerable efforts, or what could possibly have separated Sunny from both the run cable and her collar.

She glanced down at the collar, the turquoise that had been so pretty against Sunny's burnished red coat—and wished she hadn't.

It wasn't turquoise any more.

Suddenly she couldn't stand it anymore; she couldn't just sit here and wait for Masera to return; she hadn't heard his voice in many moments, though she could swear she'd heard him rummage briefly in the barn. There was another flashlight in the cupboard over the stove, and she got up to reach for it—

Masera returned.

A glance outside showed the headlights turned off; he'd darkened the flashlight as well. But he was alone.

"I'm not giving up that easily," she said, and took the flashlight from his unresisting grip. "She's out there somewhere—"

"I didn't give up," he said.

She took a step back from him, suddenly noticing the starkly pale nature of his normally Mediterranean complexion, the hollow look of his eyes. And then took another step back, and another, until she

was back in the kitchen chair. "No," she said. And
then, immediately standing once more, determined
all over again, "Take me to her."

He didn't try to soften his words. "I already buried her."

Stunned all over again, Brenna said, "You *what*?
What do you mean, you buried her? Without letting
me say good-bye? Without asking me *where* I wanted
her buried?" She didn't know whether to scream in
grief or smite Masera on the spot.

"I'm sorry," he said, and it was the undertone of
comprehension in his voice and on his face that
stopped her from doing either. He understood what
he'd done . . . and he'd done it anyway. She looked
up at him, puzzled, utterly unable to figure it out,
and still only a breath away from bolting out to find
where he'd left her dog. He said, "I know it probably wasn't right. I don't . . . I don't know what got
her. But there was no way in hell I was going to let
you see it."

"I—" she said, and stopped, shaking her head. She
would have wanted to see her dog. To say good-bye.
"It wouldn't have mattered—"

"It was my weakness, then," he said. "You think
of her the way you last saw her, not—" He stopped,
closed his eyes—looking away from her as though she
might somehow pluck the reflection of what he'd seen
out of his eyes, and he couldn't chance even that. And
as she struggled to deal with that, he looked back at
her and said, "Please."

Please don't ask me.

Coward that she was, she didn't. She sat with tears
running down her face and her entire body clenched
so tightly that it ached, the collar cutting into the
fingers of her throbbing hand. Beside her, Druid
stirred in the crate, looking up at her to whine, barely
audible.

"We'll look at him in a moment," Masera said, his

hand on her shoulder; only then did she realize that, unthinking, she'd been about to rise, to go to the crate. "Let's see about you, first." He pried the collar from her grasp, and she gave a hiss of pain as her fingers finally came to life, another noise of protest as he took Sunny's collar away and put it in her sink. He brought back her dishcloth, pulled out another chair for himself, and put her hand over his knee so he could wipe off the blood and inspect it—with some relief, she thought in hazy realization, to have something else besides Sunny on which to concentrate.

She let him tend to her, using the time to come back to herself, to sharpen up her thoughts. She found the phone—on the floor by the crate, and in several pieces, all right—and saw that Druid was indeed recovering, no longer flat on his side but lying upright. What had scared him so much? What had taken her Sunny-hound so horribly, so violently?

Masera made a satisfied noise and returned her hand to her. "No doubt you've had a recent tetanus," he said, "so I won't bother to ask. What I *want* to know—hell, what happened here tonight?"

She probably shouldn't have laughed, but she did. Short and bitter and then a little thick, as she looked down at her hand and thought about the answer—the many answers—to that question. Gingerly, she flexed her hand, and finally met his gaze. Seeing the scruffy version again, definite stubble lining his jaw, his hair forgetting where he'd had it parted earlier in the day. Dark blue eyes reflecting her kitchen light back at her. Concerned and frankly puzzled eyes, still hiding what he'd seen.

She looked down at her hand and frowned. "How'd you find my house?"

He sat back in the chair. "I don't live far from here. I've heard about the groomer who lives in the old farm up on the hill."

She gave him a skeptical look.

He shrugged. "Okay, I'm looking for a place of my own and I was curious about the property. I asked around."

"It's not for sale."

And he just looked at her, because he hadn't asked and neither the words nor the tone she'd used to say them were fair. And she should have been contrite, she supposed, but she was too miserable for that; she just looked away and answered his question from moments before. "I don't really know what happened. I mean, I can tell you what I saw, but—"

"It's a good place to start," he told her, leaning back in the kitchen chair. He quickly perceived that he had chosen the wobbly one and shifted to a position that didn't depend so much on the integrity of the chair seat connection to the back.

She looked at the phone, still on the floor. "I was talking to you, and Druid started up." She hesitated then, uncertain whether to mention the strange feeling she always got when the Cardigan lost it, equally uncertain whether that feeling came from the Cardigan or whether something else existed that they perceived as individuals. No, she decided. If *she* couldn't even figure it out, she wasn't going to muddle up this already confusing evening with trying to explain it, especially when it hardly seemed relevant. "I don't know how much you heard—I mean, I don't know when I—"

"Threw the phone?" he said for her, a dark kind of amusement showing on his face.

"Threw the phone," she affirmed. "But Sunny started barking. And then she screamed, and it was the most awful—"

The amusement disappeared, leaving only darkness. "I heard it."

"She just kept screaming, and I couldn't get out there, the door . . ." She hesitated again, then said firmly, "The door wouldn't open. And then . . . she just stopped. All I could find was the collar, snapped off the end of the run cable."

"The cable snapped?" he asked, surprised, as if he hadn't had the chance to put that together yet.

"It's new, too," she said ruefully, and then realized that it didn't matter, that she wouldn't need a cable for Sunny anymore, and she felt a rush of grief and bolted to the bathroom.

Privacy, she just needed a little privacy, and *what was going on and what had happened to her dog and why to such a sweet dog, never hurt anyone and what was he doing here anyway?* Brenna leaned against the bathroom door and pulled the cuffs of her long-sleeved T-shirt over her hands and then put her hands over her eyes and face, blotting the tears as quickly as they came, until they finally stopped coming.

She took a deep breath, hiccoughed, and waited in a moment of stillness to see if there'd be more.

Apparently not.

At which point she glanced in the mirror on the back of the door and blinked at the sight. Jeans torn across her thigh, her T-shirt ripped over her stomach, a long, clawed welt across her neck and climbing to her ear—Druid had done a lot more than bite her. And now her eyes were red and swollen, and her skin so flushed she wondered if it would ever fade away.

She splashed some cool water on her face just for the soothing feel of it and then decided that as long as she was here, she'd take advantage of the facilities. Whereupon she discovered more bright blood and had a quick moment of panic until her brain started functioning again and dryly informed her that it was *time* for that to happen, had she forgotten? So she took care of that, too, and came out of the bathroom no less bedraggled in appearance but beginning to get a grip on her spirit.

Masera was on the floor with Druid—so strange
to see the man there in her kitchen—checking the
dog's mouth while Druid rolled his eyes unhappily
but submitted to the inspection. Masera looked up
at her and released the Cardi; he immediately trotted to Brenna, unsteady and limping, and looking up
at her with the most abject, the most worried face,
his whole posture full of submission and uncertainty.

She knelt to let him climb up on the sloped plat-
form of her thighs and bury his head under her arm.

"He looks fine," Masera said. "Some split nails,
some cuts on his lips and gums . . . but no broken
teeth."

She kissed the back of his head—all she could
reach—in relief. And then she looked at Masera and
said, "Just because I'm upset doesn't mean I can't take
care of myself."

He seemed to be given to studying such statements,
for he didn't react immediately, didn't strike back as
she might have expected, or walk out with wounded
pride. "Well, no," he agreed finally. "But wouldn't it
be easier with help?"

"You didn't have to come. I'm not sure why you
did."

"I was worried," he said flatly. "You wouldn't have
called me unless you felt you had no choice."

"No," she said, and that one came out more as a
whisper.

"And I *heard* those screams, Brenna. Whatever you
may think of me, my heart's not that cold."

I never said it was. But she kissed Druid's head
again and didn't say it out loud, because they'd had
more than enough between them, unspoken and
spoken, for him to know that she hadn't forgiven him
for the way he'd judged her before they'd even met.
Not that he *deserved* to be forgiven for such rude
arrogance—

You care too much, he'd said to her.

Maybe *he* cared, too.

But when she looked up after that insight, he'd gotten to his feet and was looking thoughtfully out the kitchen door, through its glass pane to the dog room and beyond. "It was confusing from my end, but . . . I never did hear anything other than you, the Cardigan, and your . . . other dog."

"Sunny," Brenna said quietly. "She was a Redbone Hound. Not a single brain cell in her body, but—" *But a good dog.*

He nodded as if he'd heard the last. "Did *you* hear anything?"

"Besides Sunny?" And in between her own screaming?

He nodded again, looking away from the door to return his scrutiny to her. Druid sank into a couchant position beside her, keeping himself within petting distance. "Besides Sunny," he said. "Other dogs?"

She considered it for a moment, but still remembered her own astonishment at the soundless wind. And if she'd noticed that the wind wasn't making any noise, surely she'd have noticed if other dogs *were*. So she shook her head, climbing stiffly to her feet to stand awkwardly in the middle of the kitchen, her arms looking for something to do and finally crossing themselves over her partially exposed midriff.

He frowned, and she was about to repeat the negation out loud, cross at being doubted, when she realized he wasn't doubting at all . . . just confused by what she'd said.

Of course confused. Given her words, how *not* confused? But there was more to that frown—more than just a man confronted with a puzzle. More like a man confronted with other than what he thought he'd hear.

"You were expecting something," she said suddenly. "Something in particular—something *else*. That's why you came over here so quickly. What do you know that I don't?"

"Nothing," he said, but there was a subtle note to his voice that she hadn't heard before. And a distraction to his expression as he looked at the sink and the bloody token that was left of Sunny, then glanced at his watch, told himself, "Ucher," as if *that* were a word, and shook his head. He leaned over the kitchen sink to catch a glimpse of the moon out the big window, heavily waning and still high in the sky. "Medusa Moon," he muttered, and frowned.

"*What* moon?"

He'd been lost in thought; the look he gave her was surprised. "Nothing," he said. "What it means depends on who you are. But *this*—" and he reached into the sink; she heard the clink of Sunny's ID tag moving against the old porcelain.

Brenna cleared her throat sharply. "Still think there's no dog pack?"

He dropped the collar and abruptly ran cold water over it, watching the blood swirl away. "I never said that."

"You did," she told him. "You said it to Sammi. Maybe not in so many words, but that's what you meant."

He grimaced. "No," he said. "I don't think it was a feral dog pack."

She tilted her head at him; one hand found her braid and drew it up to play with its end. "You say a lot," she told him, "in what you don't say."

"Then I suppose I'll have to stop saying anything at all." He turned the collar under the uneven stream of water—stronger when the well pump ran, weaker in between as the water pressure ran down enough to kick off the pump again. "In any event, the day might shed some light on what happened here tonight."

"I doubt it," Brenna muttered.

He gave her a quick grin, that dark expression he'd

so perfected. "You know what? So do I. But we've got to look."

"We?" she said, lowering her head to give him an even stare from beneath her brows.

Blue met blue. "Or not. Your call."

She fiddled with the end of her braid, considering. She knew this property. She knew what was out of place from day to day, and she'd grown up playing trailing games. She didn't know what he thought he could add to that.

Just being there, maybe. In case she didn't want to mourn her dog alone.

But no, he had an interest here. He wanted to know as badly as she, for all he was willing to walk out and leave her to it.

"You said you wanted to work with Druid," he offered. "This would be a chance to get that in."

"I thought you said you were busy tomorrow."

"I am. Sometimes I change my priorities. But you need to make up your mind now, because I've got calls to make if you want to do it."

Work with Druid. Have someone else there as she scoured the yard for signs of Sunny or of Sunny's flight. And did she *really* want to be alone if she found anything? She stuffed her braid into her back pocket and gave him a nod. "Okay then. It's supposed to rain, though."

"Drizzle. And I won't melt. In case you hadn't noticed, I'm not made of sugar."

"Actually," she said, feeling some of her strength come back now that the morrow didn't loom so empty before her, "I *had* noticed."

"Just as well," he said. "It won't come as any great shock later on." And his grin this time was genuine if self-knowing. He turned off the water, shook off his hands, and made a visible decision not to use the towel hanging off the stove. "Call me when you're up and ready to go. I'll be there."

That was it? He had arrived suddenly, swooping in to survey the wreckage, and just as suddenly he was going? And then she'd be alone, with Sunny's collar in the sink and her hand throbbing and her grief lurking.

Well, she'd said it. She could take care of herself. "I'm an early riser," she said.

"Fine by me." But he hesitated by the door, his hand on the knob, his gaze first on the sink, then on Druid, then on her. And this time, she knew what she looked like. "Listen," he said. "Do you have someone you can call, so you're not alone tonight? Family?"

She snorted without even thinking about it. Call who, her mother? Rhona Fallon was already firmly convinced that her daughter couldn't handle the life she'd chosen. Or Russell? Then she'd get to hear about his latest success and hey, at least it hadn't been a child, lost in the night. No, better to be here by herself, even if it meant tears in a quiet house, or dreading the return of the horrifying darkness that had somehow descended upon her and Druid both.

"Listen," he said again, watching her face intently enough that she suddenly knew how much it revealed. "I've got a sleeping bag and an air mat." As her eyes widened, he held up a still-damp hand and said, "I'm not up to anything. I'll sleep out there," and he nodded back at the dog room, "if you like. I just—"

"The floor in the den," she said in a rush of words, and looked down at her feet for a long moment. Not that Masera could do a thing about the inexplicable intrusions into her life.

Not a thing but keep her from facing them alone.

He nodded. "I'll get my stuff, then."

"What about your dogs?" she blurted. "Will they be okay?"

In the moment of silence between them, he searched her face, asking and answering his own questions and coming to the obvious conclusion that she'd seen them or been told of them. "I have a housemate," he said. "They'll be fine. If you've got a phone that's not broken, I'll give him a quick call when I get back in."

By the time he reappeared with the rolled sleeping bag and air mat tucked into one arm and an overnight kit dangling from that hand, Brenna had retrieved the bedroom phone—she never used it except to answer late-evening phone calls from a family that couldn't seem to remember her schedule—and replaced the broken phone. Not a portable, but she'd have to save up to get another one of those. She handed him the slimline receiver and he dialed the number with his thumb, shoving the phone up under his chin for a quick conversation in a language that totally baffled her.

"There," he said, letting the phone slide down into his hand and replacing it on the cradle. "Taken care of." And then, because he must have been used to the question forming on her lips, he said, "Euskotar. It was Basque."

"He only speaks Basque?" she said, a little confounded by how difficult it would be to find translations and services to accommodate that language here in the States.

"No," he said, more like his usual self. Well, his usual self as judged by a few moments in the break room.

Fine, then, he'd just wanted a private conversation. Whatever. She wasn't up for a rejoinder right now, though she rather crossly thought that he could have simply asked for privacy; she could have gone to ready the den.

Not that there was much to ready. The floor space was adequate even if the carpet was worn, the light switches were self-evident, and all she had to do was find the television remote. She'd forgotten it was on all this time, silently flickering patterns of light across the empty room. She'd forgotten all about the half-finished movie.

"That wasn't a bad flick," he said, catching sight of the video case on the floor by the couch.

"I didn't finish it," she said. "I mean, I liked it, I just got . . . interrupted."

"Watch it now," he suggested, unrolling the air mat with a practiced flick and release.

"That doesn't seem . . ." *Right*. It didn't seem right somehow. But the alternative was to go to bed and stare at the ceiling, thinking of Sunny and darkness and terror, and the kind of screams no one should ever hear.

She sat down on the couch and picked up the remote.

Chapter 9

INGUZ
Beginnings

The smell of brewing coffee woke Brenna. Disoriented, she lay quietly, adding up clues. The sagging, comforting cushions of the couch enfolded her; not unusual circumstances. Druid lay tucked up under her arm; also not unusual for this past week or so, though her hand throbbed and must be stuck in an awkward position. But the light seemed brighter than it ought, and who'd made coffee?

She cracked open her eyes and peered through wispy bangs at the room around her, discovering that the VCR clock proclaimed it an hour later than her natural rising time of half past five and that the rolled sleeping bag proclaimed she wasn't alone.

In case the coffee wasn't enough of a clue.

Ah, yes. Masera. And then, a kick in the gut. *Sunny.*

And her hand hurt not because she had slept on it, but because Druid had *bitten* it.

Well, *that* made kicking him out of bed a whole lot easier. Even so, she remembered that he, too, would be sore, and eased his transition to the floor with a hand to his chest. Then she sat up, grumbling at the stiffness of her welted and bitten parts. And she'd fallen asleep on the couch, with Masera right here in the same room. That didn't seem right somehow, she thought, giving a little wiggle of her shoulders to shed the odd feeling. Clutching the afghan around herself, she got up and headed straight for the bathroom, dumping the afghan outside the door and dumping her clothes just inside it. A quick shower would make her feel human again.

Of course, she hadn't thought ahead—too used to living alone and running from room to room wearing whatever she darn well pleased—or *didn't*—and had to stick an arm out the door and feel around for the afghan so she could make a mad dash to her bedroom and clean clothes.

When she reappeared in the kitchen, her face sported a nasty bruise around the welt but the rest of Druid's nail marks were covered by jeans and a sweatshirt with a drawing of a foolishly grinning dog and the slogan *All of my clients are animals.* Her hair still swung free and her stomach growled, but she was awake and ready to go.

Somewhat to her surprise, despite Masera's internal application of coffee, he still looked bleary-eyed, his naturally unpretentious appearance given over to a downright rumpled version—finger-combed hair, lots of stubble, one collar wing inside out.

"Oh, Lord," he groaned upon seeing her—however well that was. She'd found his contact case in the bathroom. "You're a morning person. I let the dog out."

"Thanks," she said, and grinned at his attempt to string complete sentences together. "I left towels out for you in the bathroom, if you want to shower." She helped herself to the coffee; a cautious sip confirmed that he made it much stronger than she was wont, and she added milk. "It's decaf, by the way."

"I was afraid of that," he said, shoving away from the table and the magazine through which he had been flipping—not one of hers; he must have brought it in from the SUV. "Even more reason to take that shower."

While he was gone, she took stock of her hand and decided it wouldn't be doing any grooming for a few days. Glancing dog bites meant scuffed skin and surface bruising; full contact bites meant deep swelling and tissue damage—and while she'd had worse, Druid had definitely nailed her a good one. But the call to Pets! was easy; no one was picking up the phones yet and she left a message for Roger. He'd fume—lost groomer hours on a Saturday drove him crazy—but then, it wasn't like she *wanted* to be hurt. And Sunday was a day off; by Monday she hoped to be two-handed again. Well, it would hurt, but grooming was pretty much like football—you played rough, worked hard, and pretended not to notice the injuries unless the affected body part simply refused to function.

Too bad the pay was a hell of a lot less.

Brenna toasted a bagel and got another one out and ready to go for Masera. Then she sat down in his chair—*her* chair—and looked at the magazine he'd left behind. *Sporting Dog Journal.* Not one she'd heard of. He'd been looking through the ads in the back, which seemed to be chock full of supplement and medical supply offers, as well as some equipment that she simply couldn't place at first glance. Cheesy ads, with lots of superlatives. *The best! Results guaranteed!* She made no real effort to figure it out, her

thoughts drifting to the reasons he was here in the
first place.

Inexplicable horrors, Sunny gone . . . Brenna suddenly felt like her whole world was flying off-balance,
and she fought the impulse to clutch the table just
to keep herself from flying off with it. Poor Sunny . . .

She pressed her fingers over her eyes. *No*. She had
things to do. Things that would require her concentration.

Which was when Masera, looking a lot zippier but
as of yet unshaven, returned for his coffee cup. "Ah,"
he said. "Didn't mean to leave things lying around,"
and snagged the magazine, tubing it and shoving it
in the center of his sleeping-bag roll.

Brenna shrugged as he hesitated on the way back
down the hall, presumably to shave, her equilibrium
reestablished. She had learned long ago that non-
morning people were not to be taken too seriously
before their eyes truly opened. "Would you like a
bagel? I have black cherry butter or plain old fake
grape jelly."

"Your choice," he said, and disappeared again.

She ought to stick him with fake grape, a squeeze
bottle from the store. But she pulled out the same
black cherry butter she'd used on her bagel and stood
by the toaster oven, waiting for the *ding* to signal the
pull-out-bagel, blow-on-fingers game.

He returned just as she slid his plate into place
across the table—same clothes but cleaner self, and
looking like he was just about ready to face the world.
"Thanks," he said, referring either to the shower or
the bagel, she wasn't sure, and going on to refill his
coffee cup. "Maybe if I pretend it's caffeinated . . . ?"

Brenna grinned, flipped her hair out of the way
and sat, crossing her ankles under the chair. He came
up behind her, hesitating; she *felt* more than saw the
hand that hovered over her hair, almost touching.

But not.

She suppressed a smile. *Just like Emily's kids.*
But . . . not.

He sat gingerly—testing the chair and finding it
to be one of the sturdy ones—and took the kind of
generous bite from the bagel that men were inclined
to take. Big bites, big chewing, big swallows. "Your
hair is beautiful," he said, having devoured half the
bagel. "Why do you—" But he stopped, as if he
realized there was no polite way to ask the question
she'd heard so many times before.

"Because I'm a groomer," she said, which was the
answer she gave most people. *Gotta have something
to groom* was the follow-up, but this time she hesitated, and instead told him the lightest version of the
truth. "Because once upon a time I asked for a favor,
and it was granted. You could say that I keep it long
in remembrance of that day."

Not that she had any real indication that the old
hound's extra years were any more than coincidence—
any more than it was coincidence that her hair, the
hair she'd once tried so hard to grow and then sacrificed to Mars Nodens as her father's magazine had
suggested, had suddenly grown fast and thick.

But my, hadn't there been a fuss when she'd
walked back into the house with her ragged new
haircut, accomplished with the same pocketknife
tucked into her jeans at this very moment. She smiled
at the memory, though it had hardly been a fond one
at the time. Then, it had been disaster. Now she
thought of it as the first time she had defied her
parents by going after something important to her and
invisible to them.

She found him looking at her, his assault on the
bagel interrupted. As if he realized just how much
she'd told him in those quick, light words, even if
he didn't yet realize what, exactly, it was.

And then he finished his breakfast—big bites, big
chewing . . .

Brenna grinned to herself and ran her finger up the outside drip on the black cherry butter jar, thinking *men* as she licked it clean. Though at least he'd asked, and listened. Russell wouldn't have given her even that.

For that she let him finish his coffee in peace. Druid needed to be fed, and Sun—

Not Sunny. Sadly, she put Sunny's bowl in the sink. The collar was missing and she discovered it, as clean as it was ever likely to be, sitting on top of the big crate. She thought about breaking the crate down and then couldn't bring herself to do it. Not with so much mystery still surrounding the Redbone's death. By a silent dog pack, by Druid's mysterious force in the night, or—and she laughed silently at herself, but she left it in her mental list—by whatever Masera seemed to have been expecting. She wasn't even tempted to call animal control and report the incident—how would she explain it? *A wild darkness fell over the house and when it lifted, the dog was gone.* No. Not likely.

Masera came out, sleeping bag once more tucked under his arm. "Ready?"

"Um," she said. "Gotta go groom myself. It'll only take a couple of minutes." Damp hair, swift fingers, a couple of thick hair bands and she was out of the bathroom again, tucking the end of the braid in her pocket and reaching for her vest, Sunny's collar, and Druid's leash. Masera waited out by the SUV, under a grey sky with roiling puffs of lighter grey beneath, all of which promised the drizzles mentioned in the forecast.

"Okay," she said, zipping up the vest and reaching for the pebble-palmed knit gloves she always kept in the pockets and gingerly working one over her sore hand. She slid Sunny's collar around her wrist like a giant bracelet, but it wouldn't stay and she ended up catching it in the crook of her sore fingers. "Might as well put us on the clock and see what you can do with this dog."

Something about that amused him, but he didn't say what as she leashed Druid. He just followed along as she went through the gate and into the pasture behind the barn—not, she saw, missing the significance of her target-shooting setup.

But he didn't mention it. He turned to the business at hand. "Bring me up to speed," he said. "Under what circumstances does he start up with the behavior?"

Brenna waved a gloved hand in a vague and expansive gesture. "Any time he feels like it!" At his sharp glance, she added, "Seriously. You saw him acting up in the parking lot. Sometimes he does that, sometimes he doesn't. He hadn't done it in the house until last night, when he did it twice—the first time when he bit me, the second in the crate."

"Then where are we going now?"

"A place where I found his tracks and where I'm pretty sure something scared him silly before he actually showed up at my place. He freaked the one time we went there, and I'm guessing he'll do it again. It's as likely as anything else we can do to trigger him."

"He's calm enough now," Masera said, looking down at Druid between them.

And he was. Trotting along at a happy heel despite his sore paws, tail held at an assertive angle, ears up and sharply intent on the myriad little noises he could hear and they couldn't. "This is what he's like for the most part," Brenna said. *When he wasn't talking to himself.* "That, and what you saw of him yesterday evening."

"Sleeping with you," Masera said, and smiled, though he wasn't looking at her when he did it and she had the impression he was remembering Druid snugly under the afghan. "You're in for heartbreak if his owners show up."

"Oh, they're another mystery." Brenna stopped short suddenly, right before the crest of the hill down to the creek. "Look." And in quick succession, she gave Druid the hand signals for *down* and *sit* and *down* again, then put him on heel, got an automatic sit upon halting, took him through a figure eight, slowed her pace down to a crawl, sped up . . .

Druid took it like a happy game, and gave her a hopeful wag when Brenna stopped, looking at Masera; she raised her arms and dropped them to slap against her sides in a giant shrug. "He's trained."

"And nicely done," Masera commented. "He enjoys it."

"And apparently he's got his championship—"

"You said that last time, too. *Apparently*."

"That's because for all the care someone took with him, there's no record of him anywhere. His rabies tag won't match up, the phone number on his ID isn't in service, the Cardi Club has no record of him—"

"That can't be," Masera interrupted. "Not if he's been shown."

"No kidding," Brenna said, not caring for the interruption. "But he's been shown. Put yourself in handler mode and take him in a triangle, then ask him to stack. See what happens."

"I'll take your word for it. He's a mystery dog, all right. But they say some women like that."

She stared at him for an agog moment. "Was that a joke? Did you actually just make a *joke* with me?"

"A little one," he said, excessively somber of face. "Mark it on your calendar. The Kalends of April today—appropriate enough."

"The Kalends—"

"April Fool's day," he said, not waiting for her to finish.

Then why not say so? She snorted and led him down the hill, along the spring-deep and loudly burbling creek, past the footbridge and to a spot below the spring. There, she handed him Druid's lead. "Hang on a minute, okay? There's something I need to do, first. I'll be right back down."

He didn't understand; that was clear enough from his expression—a little impatient, but not particularly curious. Well, he'd just have to deal with it. Brenna walked the steep incline to the spring some fifty feet above him. By the time she reached it, the expected drizzle had started, but it stayed light and she ignored it. She knelt by the gravesite and carefully placed Sunny's collar among the rocks, wedging it into place. After a while the collar would wear and fade and maybe blow free, but by then maybe she wouldn't need it there anymore. *God*, she thought, *if you're watching out for my dogs, please welcome Sunny. You always had a special fondness for children.* And Sunny had never been anything more than a puppy at heart. She looked at the shrine a moment, trying to sort out, again, how her beliefs fit into one another, and how she could feel comfortable speaking to the God she'd been raised to respect and worship in one moment, and to another culture's ancient god in the next.

As a child it had been easy. The God she knew hadn't responded to her prayers, so she'd tried someone else. It had been her secret, a deep and longlasting one, and in her heart she'd always believed she'd been heard, that Mars Nodens had touched her life. In her practical life—even as recently as this morning—she avoided the issue, thought lightly of coincidence, and rarely turned her inner self to any sort of prayer. Too caught up in life. Probably a big mistake, she thought wryly. Look where it had gotten her—overworked groomer struggling with herself, not knowing how to fix her life, and now caught smack in the middle of . . .

Something.

"I don't know," she said finally, looking up at the

big bare oak; too early in the season for leaves or even buds. "Maybe you just use Mars Nodens as another of your faces, and maybe it's easier to hear about dogs and healing with those ears. Or maybe I'm just fooling myself, and I'm a blaspheming idiot." *Whatever. But I think Druid and I could use some help. I think we're in trouble.*

The problem was, she didn't know just what *kind* of trouble. "Even a clue," she told the oak, and everything it and the spring represented at this moment. "Even a clue would help."

And though it would have been nice for the oak branches to rustle reassuringly in the breezeless air, or the spring, which was never really more than an ooze of water, to burble for an enthusiastic moment, Brenna wasn't really expecting either of those things. Nor, as she got to her feet, was she expecting to be hit by a light dizziness, quickly come and gone—and which in previous days had somehow presaged reaction from Druid, their unlikely connection.

But Druid did nothing. He sat at the bottom of the hill and looked up at her, ears big and forward, head cocked.

Brenna went back down the hill.

"Are you pagan?" Masera asked, and his eyes had narrowed, taking on that hooded look.

Brenna managed to keep her surprise from running away with her mouth. "Presbyterian," she said. "Why on earth do you ask?"

"*Why on earth* is an appropriate way to put it," he said dryly, though his challenging expression eased. "I asked because—" and he almost said something, but stopped on it, and completed the thought as, "because between the oak and the spring and the shrine, it looks like a pagan sort of place."

"It does?" She considered it. "It's a Lydney sort of place," she said. "That's all I know about it. And it pretty much came this way, except that I buried a childhood dog up there, and it's important to me. Why, are *you* pagan?"

He smiled, a mere crook at one corner of his mouth, and shook his head. "Lapsed Catholic."

"Well, that pretty much settles that, then," Brenna said. "Do you want to take him up there? Or do you want me to do it?"

"You go ahead," Masera said, and handed her the lead; he seemed to be paying no more attention to the drizzle than she was. "I want to see what happens, and what you do about it."

"Oh, great," Brenna muttered. "A test."

He laughed out loud at that, short but with true amusement, and when he responded, he was still grinning. "I just need to see where we're starting out."

"Well, prepare yourself, then," Brenna said. "Though keep in mind I said he wasn't consistent."

She needn't have worried. Perfectly happy at the bottom of the hill, Druid had no intention of getting any closer to the spring. He hung behind her for a few steps, whined for a few more steps, and then flung himself backward with enough force that without the leash, he'd have gone tumbling backward down the hill. For once Brenna was ready for him. Acutely aware of Masera's scrutiny, she let the dog struggle for a few moments, then stepped on the leash, walking on it until she had it pinned to the ground close to his collar. "No," she told him sternly. "Druid, *no.*"

And had a sudden flash echo of someone else's voice in her head, saying those words but edged with sheer terror-stricken panic—*Druid, no!*—and she touched the damp earth on the slope above her, suddenly doubting her own sanity as much as Druid's.

He quit, then, panting harshly, one of the cuts on his lip reopened and bleeding.

"Bring him down a few feet," Masera said quietly. "To a spot where he was okay."

When she had him settled there, Masera came up

and joined them. "He warned you about that one," he said. "But you said that's not typical."

"He usually gets out a whine or two," Brenna said. "It's just never clear *why*, so I don't know till after he's started up that it was a warning. Because sometimes he thinks to himself, too. Like when he's chewing a bone—it's just this whine, like he's thinking really hard and some of the thoughts escape. I don't even think he knows he's making noise. It's pretty adorable, actually," she admitted, scratching the side of her nose with a pebble-gloved finger.

Masera gave Druid a rub behind the ears and a gentle thump on the ribs. "I wish I had more to tell you," he said. "You're basically doing the right thing—not making a big deal of it, giving him a chance to stop, and escalating in a low-key way when he doesn't. If he's predictable about the spring, I'd bring him up here frequently. Take him right to the edge of his fear—the last step before he loses it. And sit there a while, giving him lots of love. Give him a chance to think about that. Then take him up, because unfortunately, he's got to learn to work through this fear and to respond to you or you won't have any chance of getting through to him when he flips out under unpredictable circumstances. The instant he stops the fear behavior, no matter how surprised or upset you are, you need to be a little more responsive with praise and petting. Love the hell out of him, if you really want to know. He needs that contrast, so it becomes clear to him—if he's freaking out, there's no love in the offing, but when he quits, he becomes a hero."

"And the biting?"

He shook his head. "There's no easy answer. You're going to have to decide how important it is to you. He's an outstanding dog with a serious quirk, and any time you grab him while he's flipping, there's the chance he'll bite."

Brenna bit her lip and looked away. "It was my own fault. I should have paid attention when he whined. Then he wouldn't have been in my lap when it happened. I guess I was just hoping that he'd adjusted, that he was through with that crap."

He reached to touch her arm but, as in the kitchen, let his hand fall away before it quite reached her. "Hindsight's a bitch."

He had such a wry tone in his voice that she looked at him and laughed. He shrugged, looking back out at the pasture. "This is a nice spot. I can see why you chose it for your dog, way back when."

"He liked to sit at the top of the hill and watch the horses, when we had them here." She crouched next to Druid and bent to kiss his furry head, now surface-damp with the cold drizzle, and looked out over the view with fresh eyes. The creek cut deeply through the pasture, its banks lined with sumac and less identifiable, barely budding brush; some of the low plants were greening, taking advantage of the early sun before the brush turned into thick shadow. Beyond, the pasture stretched to the road, new grass just beginning to shove green blades above the pale remnants of last summer's flattened growth. To their left, the creek curved around and the trees that lined it broke away to form a windbreak between two pasture sections; even in winter, it was hard to see beyond that. Brenna pointed off to the right. "In the summer, wild spearmint grows over there. Just walking through the field is like taking a bath in it. And there it's always shady and cool, and there—" she pointed to a spot just left of the footbridge, which was between them and the spearmint area, "—*there*, the poison ivy has taken over. Doesn't bother me, but most people can't get near it. Maybe," she said in muttered afterthought, "Rob Parker will walk through it one of these days."

Until that moment, Masera had been at ease,

following along in her little travelogue, standing just
downhill of her with his hands relaxed on his hips.
Now he turned back to look at her and said, *"Rob
Parker?"*

And she stared back at him, startled by his vehemence. Then she said slowly, "Rob Parker. I take it
you know him?"

"I've heard of him." Masera looked out over the
pasture with new interest, her *back off* cues apparently
gone to waste. Brenna suspected he'd only now realized that they'd changed direction in walking to the
spring, and no longer faced the same road that ran
down the hill from her house. "He lives around here?"

"I'm not sure that he does. His family has some
old property off that way." She gave a hazy wave.

She'd seen bird dogs home in slower on a close
covey. He searched the line of woods in that direction, as if there'd be some clue to the location of the
Parker Homestead.

"Oh, here," she said, getting up and starting down
the hill. "I'll show you."

He hesitated, but she wasn't sure why. Surprise at
the offer? *Or maybe he just doesn't want to go there
with you in tow.* Ooh, that last one made her wince;
uncharacteristically bitchy of her, it was. Not fair.
Especially after he'd disrupted his whole day so she
wouldn't be alone after losing Sunny to . . . whatever,
and to be here today to work with Druid. "It's what
you want, isn't it? It might be for sale, and it's probably good kennel grounds. Maybe a little marshy in
spots, but all the land around here tends to that."

And at that he turned to look at her again, and
to regard her without haste. "Yes," he said. "I *would*
like to see the land."

So why did it sound like that moment in the kitchen
last night, when she'd asked him what he'd been
expecting and he'd had that unusual tone in his voice?
Not lying, she thought. But not telling her everything.

Well, it's not like he owed her anything. No reason for him to lay his business out before her. So she said, "Come on, then," and continued down to the creek, Druid quite willingly at her heels.

This part of the creek split around a small, flat island; when she was a child it had held an important and impregnable fortress of She-Ra, but Brenna didn't suppose Masera needed to know that. All that mattered today was that it was a shortcut, and that because she felt the sting of his not-lying despite her own rationalizations, she was pleased enough to make him work for his little tour. She knew the rocks that would get her across this shallow fording spot, and she took them, hoisting Druid in her arms so he wouldn't get soaked. Like a child, he curled gently into her hold, making the task easier . . . and like a child, he weighed a lot more than it seemed he should. Short he might be, but at thirty-five pounds, he was not an insubstantial dog.

Masera followed. Once she reached the island he not only followed, he forged ahead, crossing the other branch of the creek before her, and offering a hand when she faced the steep bank with her arms full of dog.

She took the easy way out; she gently launched Druid to the top of the bank, then climbed it herself, murmuring, "That's okay," at his hand. What did he think she did when she was out here on her own?

Cold darkness, landing hard enough to make her stumble and gasp, wringing out her lungs and skipping onward. Brenna found that she had clutched Masera's hand after all, and that Druid braced himself, white-eyed, at the end of the leash. But he relaxed, cautious but under control, and she straightened, disengaging herself from Masera and ignoring the somewhat startled expression on his face—a more open look than usually resided there, as though for once he'd been caught off guard. She blew her bangs out of her eyes and stepped out strongly, with no intention of explaining the inexplicable.

Whatever he thought, he said nothing. He kept pace with her long-legged strides, avoided the tinted early growth of poison ivy before she pointed it out to him, and seemed to have returned to thoughts that were far from her pasture or Druid's quirks or any conversation they might have made.

When they reached the woods line she followed it, taking him to the road, where they had to navigate the marshy ditch that ran alongside the asphalt. Brenna tossed Druid across and made the leap herself, and this time it was she who waited for Masera, and held the dead wire of the old multistrand electric fence so he could climb through. Once they were at the edge of the road, she pointed down the length of it. "See that break in the trees? That's the head of the old driveway. They don't even have a mailbox there anymore; I don't know where Rob Parker's living, but it's not there. It's a long lane back to where the farmhouse used to be. I'm not sure what's still standing, at this point."

"Guess I'll find out," Masera said, and headed off. When Brenna kept step with him, Druid coming along at a fast marching trot, he gave her a surprised glance. "If you've got something you'd rather do . . ."

Yeah, go home and wash Sunny's bowl. Brenna shook her head. "I suppose I should let animal control know what happened, in case it *is* connected to a dog pack—"

Masera snorted.

"What then?" Brenna demanded, wanting to kick him for that feeling she got from him, that *I know something* feeling. Or more because of the other impression he gave off, the *I'm not telling you* part of it. "You don't think it was the infamous feral dog pack, then what *do* you think it was? Something tore that dog from her run and then ripped her right out of her collar. Do you suppose we've suddenly got an insane *bear* on our hands that no one's managed to sight?"

"A bear," he said. "Wonder how fast that one would spread if you started it? Maybe we should have looked for tracks."

"You can be a real pain in the ass," Brenna told him, jumping past annoyance and into real anger.

"Yeah," he said. "I know."

It was only as they approached the driveway—a cleared lane, really, with two rutted wheel tracks running down it—that she realized he'd never answered her question. He'd made her mad, but he hadn't answered her. There were a lot of things he didn't answer, things he held close to himself. Things you learned from talking to most people that he never volunteered in casual conversation.

He doesn't owe you anything.

And he didn't.

Besides, she supposed they'd hardly had what she'd call a casual conversation. Disagreements and challenges, yes. Last night, when he'd really hardly said anything at all; he'd just been there. And then today— dog talk. Or bits of herself that she somehow found herself sharing with him.

Well, keep yourself to yourself, then.

"Recent tracks," she said, which seemed reasonably safe, subject-wise. Surface talk. Not that there was any missing the tracks; someone had been going in and out long enough to stir the mud up pretty well, and there were even a couple of shovels of fresh gravel dumped into the worst of the spots. "Looks like Rob's been spending time here, whatever his plans for the place. Might be there now, if you want to talk to him."

"Even if he's not, it's a chance to look things over."

So why did he sound like he'd prefer it if Rob *weren't* around?

She didn't bother to ask. He wouldn't answer if she did. At that, she had to wonder why she *was* coming along. She didn't have to wash Sunny's dish. There were other things she could do with this day—walk over to Emily's, for instance, and cry on her friend's shoulder. Or she hadn't been to visit her mother for a while, and she could take some of the little fried apple pies she'd made a few days ago; her mother always loved those, and never bothered to make them. Or she could read the big fat book she had waiting in the kitchen, or target shoot, or kick around in the barn—maybe she'd fix the broken doors and advertise for a horse tenant.

Face it, Brenna Lynn. You're too curious to walk away. Curious about what Rob Parker might be up to, sudden neighbor that he was. And curious about Gil Masera, which was his own fault. If he'd answer short and sharp instead of *not* answering short and sharp, she wouldn't have anything about which to be curious.

So she turned down the lane with him, offering a quick, oblivious smile when he gave her another glance.

The branches snared their sleeves, barely leaving enough room to walk abreast. They must scrape along the sides of any vehicle on the lane—more evidence of Rob Parker's long absence. She wondered why he'd come back now . . . why *now*, this moment, he'd suddenly seemed so drawn to her property. Turnabout seemed fair enough—and reason enough to give if he was here and found them.

If she made it there at all. Druid hung back suddenly, giving what was fast becoming a familiar whine, a staccato *whine-whine-whine* with a sharp edge to it. Masera hesitated as she did, looking almost relieved—but Brenna didn't have time to think that through, because Druid had had enough, and *again*, after so many days of quiescence, *again* he threw himself back and shrieked and gibbered and cursed. And again, when Brenna would have handled it, she staggered herself, slapped by a massive whirl of strength and breath-stealing fear, a black cloud on her vision and tight chills up her spine.

She didn't resist when strong fingers clamped down on her arm and dragged her back down the lane a short distance, then further yet, to the road, when Druid didn't calm—although by then she had her own wits back, enough to step on the leash and crouch and speak sharply to Druid—and then to praise him when he stopped, looking as dazed as he ever did. But he did what he had never done; he responded to her praise, taking a hesitant step and pushing his solid head against her thigh.

Only until Masera's hand once more closed on her arm, pulling her upright so abruptly she was too startled to bristle. His voice was low, but it didn't need to be any louder, not as close as he'd pulled her to himself. "What was that?"

"Druid—" she started.

"Not Druid. You felt it, too—just like at the spring. Brenna Lynn, what *was that*?"

"You felt it?" she repeated, still shaken—but not so much that she didn't hear the inanity of her own words. Of course he'd felt it. *He'd felt it.* And at the creek, too. She wasn't crazy, she wasn't imagining things—she wasn't even ill or overworked. *What would he have seen and felt if he'd been there when Sunny disappeared*? And had he felt what she felt at the spring? She had the feeling *yes* and she opened her mouth to ask him about it, but then—

Then her brain started to work again and inside her chest she went as cold as the bounding darkness had ever left her. *Brenna Lynn.* He'd called her Brenna Lynn.

Her mother called her Brenna Lynn. And Emily sometimes, and Sam.

No one else.

Just as she hadn't told him the phone number he'd rattled off to his Basque friend, or how to get to her house. *Masera battered from a fight. Masera buying pit bulls. Masera checking up on her.* She stepped back from him, nearly tripping over Druid; he scrambled out of her way.

"Just what are you up to on that hill?" Masera asked, closing in on her again, somehow using the scant difference in their heights to look down at her. "What did you *do*?"

His words were nonsense; all that mattered was that he had his hand on her arm again and without thinking, she shoved him back, shoved him hard. Made him stagger, and the surprise on his face only fed her anger. "Back off!" she snarled at him. "*Brenna Lynn!* I never told you that!"

For an instant, his surprise turned nonplussed, his startled reaction far too easy to believe. "I must have heard it at work."

"Nice try," she said, her voice still raised with anger, all but yelling into the silent spring woods. No one around; no one driving by on the country back road. She took another step away from him, but she wasn't frightened yet. "*They* don't know."

"I heard it *somewhere*," he said, exasperation showing through. He didn't try to close the distance between them.

"You didn't," she said coldly, anger banking down. "Did you think I wouldn't notice you knew my phone number? Or that you bought two pit bulls only hours after you told me you were between dogs for a while?"

"Ah," he murmured. "I thought I saw someone in the parking lot." He ducked his head, pressing a finger between his brows as if it would somehow help him think his way out of this. "Brenna—"

"You know what?" she interrupted. "For a while

I thought, you know, it didn't matter if I don't particularly like you. It didn't matter if I didn't even really trust you—what mattered was that you're good with dogs. You might be able to help Druid, that's what counted. But that only goes so far. *Only so far.*" *This* far. The end. She drew the Cardigan into a heel position, unthinking protectiveness. "Send me your bill, Masera. And stay out of my way."

"Brenna—" He held out his arms in a helpless, beseeching kind of gesture. No doubt he couldn't find the words—because no doubt there *weren't* any.

He didn't really get the chance to try. A third voice broke in on their confrontation, distant but getting closer by the word. "Hey! This is private property!"

Druid growled when Brenna started, lowering his head and slanting his ears back suspiciously. When she saw the man who approached them, she felt like doing the same. Tall and skinny with a watch cap covering all traces of his hair and leaving a scabby goatee trying to make up the difference, he came at them with a cocky walk, a stride with excessive arm and hand movement. Excessive confidence, too.

"We," Masera said, his eyes getting that heavy-lidded look, "happen to be on the shoulder. Of the very public road." Which they were. At the moment, anyway, and Brenna was willing to bet the man hadn't seen them anywhere else, but had come in response to Druid's screaming.

If he had, he didn't mention it. He looked disappointed, as though he'd hoped to catch them with their toes over some sort of invisible line. "That don't change the facts. This is private property."

Brenna snorted. "Of course it is. It's *all* private property around here. Maybe your buddy would do well to keep that in mind."

He frowned at her. "That's supposed to make sense?"

"It'll make sense to Rob, if you tell him. Or don't.

I don't care." Brenna gathered up the leash and stalked back down the road, Druid at her heels and grabbing wary looks over his shoulder.

"I wouldn't," Masera said to the man. "Doubt he'd like you making a scene like this." In a few quick strides he'd caught up with her—or nearly caught up with her, because she wasn't having any of it and poor Druid's short little legs flew to keep her pace.

She wanted to ask him what *that* was supposed to have meant, but she didn't. She didn't say anything at all, not until they'd gone through the fence, across the pasture and back up the hill, and were heading for the barn gate. Even then, she didn't look at him when she said, "Send me a bill."

"Call it a favor," he said.

"No." Favors like that always cost her, somehow. One way or another, she'd pay. She'd owe him.

She still didn't look at him, but she heard the shrug in his voice when he said, "I didn't think so. See you around, Brenna. Stay inside at night."

Brenna shuddered, and slammed the porch door closed behind her.

Chapter 10

Ո

URUZ
Assertion

Brenna spent the rest of Friday doing what her hand would allow of her, and was glad enough to learn it included target practice. She made mental effigies out of the targets and put Masera in there along with Roger.

She aimed for the spot assigned to tender portions of their anatomies.

She called her mother and told her Sunny was gone, her mother told her brother, her brother called her. Somehow he made it sound like he thought she'd be better off in town so she wouldn't have to deal with such things, instead of that he was sorry for her loss. She cried, and she called Emily, and Emily insisted that she come over for a picnic in the

Brecken family room, where they all discovered that Druid, in the presence of little girls exclaiming, "Can I give him a potato chip, *pleasepleaseplease*" was quite capable of sitting up on his haunches. Unlike a dog with longer limbs, his short front legs didn't fold neatly at his chest, but stuck out to make him look like a child reaching to be picked up.

Upon returning home she went straight to bed, and refused to think about the strange jumble of events that her life had suddenly become.

When she woke up on Saturday, it was with the already formed intent to return to the Parker homestead—and first thing, while she was at her best and everyone else was barely waking up. After all, Rob Parker owed her a look around after making himself so at home on her own property. And if that wasn't enough, Masera's intense curiosity about the place *was*.

After all, he'd also been curious about *her*.

Which meant the more she knew about him, the better.

So she ate, still stiff-handed and with only a twinge of guilt over not going in to work. Just because she could dress herself didn't mean she had any business waving sharp-edged instruments around people's pets. Or had the strength to act quickly and decisively if something else decided to bite her. She stuck her head outside, discovered the day was overcast— standard operating procedure just south of the lake— but had a warmth to it that inspired her to put nothing but the vest over her deep green, long-sleeved waffle shirt as she went out the door.

Druid, she left behind.

The birds weren't as enthusiastic in proclaiming their newly established seasonal territories as they'd been when she woke, but it was early enough that the vireos and robins were still going at it; as she walked the tree line dividing the pastures she heard a scarlet tanager at work. In the woods across the road a thrush serenaded her oh-so-casual stroll along the shoulder, which was about when she thought, out of the blue, *Basque*. Something so obvious that it made her realize just how upset she'd been two nights before, or she wouldn't have missed it then. Basque, and the elusive accent. Masera had been brought up speaking the language, at least at first, she'd bet. And he apparently had friends who still spoke it more naturally than English—the person he'd spoken to two evenings before.

Which meant he had family living with him, or that he lived with family. People she might be able to talk to, if they spoke English at all.

It was a line of reasoning that stopped her short, to see how quickly she'd come to such certain conclusions. She laughed out loud, startling the birds to silence. Since when had she developed deductive powers of any note? Since when, *Brenna Lynn*.

He spoke the Basque language. So did someone else currently in his residence. That's all she knew, all she *really* knew.

Well, no. She also knew that she'd reached the lane, and that suddenly she wished she'd had some excuse to bring the rifle along. Tucked under her arm, casual . . . a nice visual statement of confidence.

Stupid. Like she would ever even point a rifle at someone else. Even an *empty* one. She knew she wouldn't, couldn't; she could well recall the one time she'd done so accidentally, and the horror that had engulfed her as she jerked the empty weapon down to bear at the ground. She wasn't even sure she could bring herself to shoot a marauding feral dog, not even one that was headed her way with toothy intent.

Which left her staring down the driveway, the birds going about their business and an unusually bold Red Squirrel stopping to take a good look at her. She sighed, jammed her hands into her vest pockets, and hunted for the resolve she'd had not so long ago. And found it without too much difficulty . . . of all the unknowns whirling around her, this didn't have to stay one of them.

She took a deep breath and started up the lane.

It must have been a good quarter mile before the barn came into view; no wonder it had taken Mr. Cocky some time to reach them after Druid first sounded off. The lane curved, first one way, then the other, and dumped her from close woods into the old barnyard without much warning. To her left, the barn stood long and low—an old dairy barn, she thought, its long row of windows long broken-out and a cavernous working barn stuck on one end for hay and machinery. Before her, the old house foundation peeked above the weeds—some crumbling stone here, half a chimney there, and one strange series of steps that led to nowhere—old porch steps, she thought.

Beneath her feet and circling through what had once been small, square barn paddocks—she could still see the remains of the board fencing and curling loops of cattle-wire—the tire tracks were deep and fresh. There wasn't any place to live, and there wasn't any evident activity or construction, but Rob and his friends were finding plenty of reason to spend time here.

Slowly, Brenna walked around the barn, trying to puzzle it out. Of what had Mr. Cocky been so protective? What could they have been doing here, other than some equivalent of smoking cigarettes out behind the barn? She skirted rusty old equipment—not worth anything by the time the elder Parkers had died, no doubt, although if Rob bothered to clean it up, he might well snare some antiquers with it—and an old claw-footed bathtub that she instantly coveted for a watering trough. Stacks of weathered old stove-split wood and greyed slat wood, an old tractor tire . . . nothing here that she couldn't find at just about any barn of this vintage.

Until she walked out back, and ran into a diminutive horse walker. No, too small to be a horse walker. Part of an old playset? She puzzled at it, nibbling at a rough spot at her cuticle. Winter was tough on a groomer's hands, though the splits at the ends of her fingers would heal faster if she'd leave them alone. Nibble, nibble, but the strange contraption didn't give up any secrets. Except—was that blood on the ground? Dried blood, worn and kicked up but enough of it left to show. And . . . what was that *smell*? She caught another whiff of it, but no more; she couldn't track it down. So she left the contraption and walked around to the working end of the barn, where there was a people-sized door with glassed windows.

She peered through a pane—or tried to. Dirt grimed them inside and out. So she knocked lightly—not expecting anyone but taking all the right steps just in case—and tried the doorknob. It didn't turn, but the door swung in anyway—closed, it was, and even locked, but not latched. From the way it moved on the hinges, Brenna doubted it *could* latch.

Dim and oppressive, the tiny office was crammed with junk old and new. Old desk, old file cabinet, old chair—each bearing the same layers of grime as the windows. Stacks of ancient, yellowed newspapers in the corner, a block of wood holding up one of the desk legs. In the layers of dirt on the board floor, recently applied footsteps carved a trail from the outer door to an inner door, and from each door to the desk.

On the desk, though, there were new layers. Magazines, but hidden under a folded newspaper, so all she could see was their spines and one title. *Sporting Dog Journal* . . . the same one Masera had been reading? A glance would tell her so much . . . but she wasn't about to disturb the contents of the desk. Not yet, anyway.

On a set of low metal shelves beneath the room's

one high window, sloppy jumbles of supplies caught
her eye. It didn't look so much different from her
own dog room shelves, actually—some basic medical supplies, some syringes, a tangle of leashes, har-
nesses, and thick, wide, double-ply leather collars.
Some big plastic jars of bulk supplements, one of
which she'd used for Sunny when the starving hound
had first staggered into Brenna's life.

Dogs. It added up to dogs, but Brenna hadn't seen
a single one. Hadn't even heard one. And as she
puzzled over it, as she got up the nerve to nudge the
magazines with a finger so she could see the covers,
a man came barreling through the door with no more
idea of Brenna's presence than she'd had of his
approach. She snatched her finger back as he recoiled
in surprise, and before he could say the words piling up in his mouth—angry words, even mean ones—
she smiled and gave him *Brenna the Naif*. The one
that went with her features.

"Oh, good," she said, gushing with apparent relief
at having found someone there. "I'm looking for Rob,
have you seen him? He was over at my place the
other day, visiting, you know, and I thought it would
be neighborly—"

"He's not here," the man said abruptly. This wasn't
Mr. Cocky; this man wore anger like a second skin,
letting it surface in a handful of tattoos and the heavy
studs of a doubly pierced brow. Mr. Mean. Young,
muscles showing under his tight T-shirt and the open
black shell jacket over top it. And big. Big enough
he didn't *have* to be cocky to get his point across.
"Stupid of you to come nosing around where you
don't belong."

Oh, Lordy, that was more than a threat. But
Brenna the Naif didn't know enough to respond to
threats, and Brenna the Naif she stayed. Masera, she'd
meet head-on. This man . . . this man she played, and
for all she was worth. "Oh," she said, faltering, "I'm

sorry. It's just that Rob was so friendly when we talked, I thought—"

From within the barn, far within the barn, a dog barked; several others took up the cry. Profound, ringing chop barks, quickly silenced. That answered one question—whatever the breed, it was big.

Mr. Mean frowned at her, a frown that went deep; his quickly sparked anger seemed to be fading to annoyance, but Brenna wasn't sure. He said, "You have any idea what the hell time it is, lady? Not visiting hours, that's for sure."

She shrugged, but it felt weak even to her. "I'm always up at this hour. I figured, if he's here, he's here—and if not, no harm done. Just a little bit of a longer walk than usual, you know? Besides, I was wondering if Rob might want to sell that bathtub—"

"Shit," he said, with feeling, and she couldn't interpret that at all. "Look, Rob doesn't want any visitors, you got that?" His voice rose with each word, until he was shouting at her, closing the distance between them as she backed up, backed until the edge of the open door jammed into her back and stopped her short. "He doesn't want to talk nice to the neighbors and he sure as hell doesn't want 'em poking around his private things at some fucking hour of the morning when normal people don't even have their pants on!"

Her eyes widened; she couldn't help it. It didn't matter—even Brenna the Naif would know this was trouble. Hell, the Naif was already running screaming down the lane, leaving just plain Brenna to deal with this all on her own. "I really didn't mean—" she started, but stumbled and tried again right on top of it, "I thought he said—I thought he *meant*—I mean, people around here, if they say they'd like to talk again sometime—"

He looked at her with those annoyed but thoughtful eyes, and shook his head. "Shit," he said again. "I don't want to have to deal with you." He looked her up and down, assessing her anew, scowling hard. "You got the idea now? The part where you were goddam wrong to have come around here?"

Brenna nodded, quick and emphatic. "Going," she said, hearing the babble even in that one word. "I'm just going now. And staying away." She waved her hands out at waist level, just as emphatic as her nodding. "Definitely staying away." She inched around the edge of the door, feeling her braid catch in the latch that prodded her hip, fumbling behind herself to free it.

"And you know what else?" Mr. Mean said, coming up close before she could break away, close enough that she froze with her hands awkwardly behind herself, pulling her head back as far as she could as he bent to stare directly into her eyes, putting his hand on the edge of the door above her head. He'd had a drink already, she could tell, but it wasn't enough to make up for his unbrushed morning mouth.

Brenna shook her head, hardly daring to do so.

"If we hear a lot of stray talk about the Parker place, we're going to know where it started. And that," he said, so close now that his nose almost touched hers, "*that* wouldn't be good for you at all. You got that?"

Brenna whispered, "Yes."

It was a squeaky whisper, barely there at all, but it seemed to satisfy him. He jerked the door open wider and gestured sharply at freedom. "Get lost."

Brenna got.

Were she wise, she would have simply stayed at home after that. What had she learned, after all? That Parker's buddies were just as rough as Sam had suggested. That they were up to something. That they had big dogs. Probably guarding a huge cache of drugs or enslaved Asian women or . . . whatever.

Nothing she was ready to suggest to anyone else—
friend or local cop or even 911. Not until she got
the chill of Mr. Mean's warning from her system.

Were she wise, she'd stay right there at home.
Nursing her hand and her spirit, considering more
fully the repairs necessary to the barn in order to
house a horse or two. Taking care of business.

But she looked at her life, and the strange factors
suddenly intruding into her days, and made the
decision to be not-wise. In fact, sitting at the kitchen
table, worrying the edges of Masera's business card,
thinking of him eating there, thinking of the muzzy
look on his face first thing in the morning, Brenna
decided she'd had enough of forces acting on her life.
Time for her to be a force herself, to act instead of
react. Right now, these things *were* business.

Masera knew where she lived. Turnabout, she
thought, was extremely fair play.

She figured it wouldn't be far, not with an address
in the same small rural area, and it wasn't. A small
ranch house on the other side of the compact town
of Parma Hill itself, it sat back from the road a
generous distance, without much in the way of trees
to create privacy. A few bushes around the hanging
sign—she would have mistaken it for a realty sign if
she weren't looking—identifying the place as belong-
ing to Gil Masera, dog trainer extraordinaire. White
siding, deep teal shutters, a few more bushes to pass
as landscaping around the house. It didn't look like
the sort of place he'd live in, didn't reflect anything
of him.

As if you know him so well.

There were trees in back, and a fenced-in yard.
Nothing that looked like rows of kennels or outbuild-
ings, although her view was almost completely
obscured by the house itself and the one strategically
placed evergreen at the back corner of the house. She

wouldn't get a better look in the back without sneaking around, and she'd had enough of that for one day.

This time, she would walk right up to the front door. Pound on it, if necessary.

She had the feeling it wouldn't be. He'd called someone, fully expected whoever it was to be here. And since there was a vehicle in the driveway—a sporty little miniature Jeep kind of vehicle, not Masera's SUV at all—Brenna pretty much expected that whoever-it-was was there right now.

So she pulled in the long driveway and marched up the walk and reached out to stab the doorbell—and stopped, following a wicked little impulse to make sure her hair ran under her vest and stuffing the end into her jeans at the small of her back. The most identifiable thing about her, hidden. *Then* she rang the doorbell.

She heard footsteps within the house almost right away, but no barking. No young pit bulls gamboling around in *this* house. Maybe there were kennels out back after all.

The door opened, and she knew right away she was looking at Masera's brother through the storm door between them. His younger brother. Not as tall as Masera, he had the same features in different proportions. Masera had a sharply defined nose, vaguely hawklike, with distinct planes at the high bridge—side, top, side. This man had that . . . and more of it. And his jaw, although it followed the same straight line, didn't have the same amount of chin to balance it. But his eyes were a familiar deep, clear blue, and his lips, though thinner than his brother's, had the same built-in wry quirk at the corners of his mouth. "*Egun on,*" he said, and then, "Help you?" as though it had been an entire sentence.

"I hope so," Brenna said. "I saw Mr. Masera at the pet store, and I wanted to talk to him about private work with my dog. He's big, and lately he's been growling . . . I'm getting worried. But I haven't been able to get an answer on the phone number on his card." She waved it briefly and repocketed it with a shrug. "I was in the area, so I decided to stop by instead."

The man made a face, the exaggerated face of someone communicating in a second language he doesn't quite know. "Forgot the battery. Again. Very busy most days, Iban is." *Ee-BAHN*, he said, and for a moment Brenna didn't realize he was referring to Masera at all; she just gave him a puzzled stare. And then as she realized he referred to Masera, that this was another name for Masera and it fit so much better than *Gil* to her ear, it was the man who gave a laugh at himself and, still grinning, said, "Gil, I mean. Iban is his first name, but here in the States he uses the Gil name, his second name. Easier, he says."

"In the States?" Brenna said, and then, although she already suspected, added, "As opposed to . . . ?"

"Euskal Herria," the man said. "You know, the Basque?"

All that guessing she'd done . . . not so far off the mark after all. Masera was Basque, his brother lived here, and he barely spoke English. She smiled. "I don't know much, I'm afraid. Though I never would have guessed that Mr. Masera's first language wasn't English." Not quite true.

The brother shrugged. "Him and I, we are different. Older brother, younger brother, you know? I am Eztebe. Steven, you would say in *Ingelesez*, but I prefer Eztebe. And I'll answer you what I can."

She didn't even try to repeat his name. His was a slippery accent, never coming down hard on any of the syllables, just skimming over them like touch and go. "About my dog," she said. "I was wondering if Mr. Masera could take him, maybe evaluate him here. Do you have kennel facilities?"

"Small," he said, holding up three fingers. "Full,

right now. Gil knows if there will be room soon; I do not."

"Do you suppose I could see them?"

He gave a rueful shake of his head. "Best for Iban to show you. I know too little. When I visit, I feed them, I try not to like them too much. I have his list of classes—maybe you want that, so you can find him at the store? What, *Pets!* is the name, I think? Like calling a garden store *Tree!*, you think?"

She did, she decided, like Masera's brother Eztebe quite a bit more than Masera himself. "I've always thought so," she agreed. "If I want an exclamation point after a word, I put it there myself. They've got lots of good supplies there, but if I want my dog groomed, I'll do *that* myself, too." An opening, big and juicy.

He took it. More or less. "Iban says—" and then he stopped, as if realizing sudden discretion. "He says they are very busy, and to think about this when choosing where to go. Some people want a quieter place for their dogs, yes?"

Well, whatever he'd been *about* to say, what he'd actually said wasn't anything but the truth.

"He says go to the woman Brenna if you go there," Eztebe added. "He says she cares."

Well, huh. "Thanks," she said, realizing she'd taken this about as far as she could. "I guess I'd like one of those class lists." More to avoid Masera than to find him.

Eztebe nodded, and left the door open while he fumbled in some papers on a small secretary not far from the door. She had the chance to look through the neat house and right out the back window of the small kitchen—yellow, wasn't everybody's kitchen yellow?—to the greening backyard. She'd only managed to sort out the edges of some kennel runs from the visual jumble when Eztebe filled the doorway again. "I'm kind of surprised," she told him. "I thought a trainer would have his own dogs running around the place."

"He lost the old one not long before," Eztebe said, and then corrected himself. "Not long *ago*. No new one yet. Maybe one of the little Welsh herding dogs, he told me."

Well, double-huh. More truth from Masera. But what about those pit bulls? She was willing to bet that two of those three kennel runs were occupied by the pits, and not by customer dogs. He'd as much as admitted he had them.

Eztebe rustled the papers he held out, looking for her attention.

"Sorry," she said. "Just thinking about my dog. Worried, you know?"

"Talk to Iban," Eztebe said, and then gave her a sudden grin. "But don't tell him I told you that name, okay?" He held the papers out again, and this time she took them. He said, "Class list, price list. You can't find him at the store, use that phone number. Tonight, I put it in the charger myself."

She smiled at him and thanked him and folded the papers up to stuff in her back pocket on the way to her truck. So much for that.

She wasn't sure she'd learned much, at least not much of true relevance. Masera's houseguest was his brother, and his brother didn't know much about much when it came to the dogs. Didn't seem to consider the pit bulls to be Masera's even though Brenna was just as sure they were there behind the house; didn't seem to be so tight-lipped he wouldn't have said if he *did* consider the dogs to be Masera's. After all, he'd told her Masera's secret first name, and more or less told her that their family was Basque, but that they'd had very different upbringings. And that Masera was very busy, but she'd known that. Though she winced at the recollection of her glimpse of his private fee list; she'd had no idea he charged $75 an hour when she'd called him, or when she'd insisted that he bill her. Maybe he wouldn't.

Eztebe *hadn't* said, *My idiot brother is obsessed with a woman who lives on a hill, he gets beat up on a regular basis, he knows something about Rob Parker that you don't know, and here's what he's hiding from you.* For he was hiding something, of that she was sure.

All the same, as she started the truck and backed it down the drive, she found herself smiling. As little as it was, she probably knew just about as much of Masera's life as he knew of hers. It was a start. And with any luck, this was as far as it would go.

Any of it.

The phone pealed inside as Brenna headed for the house from the pole shed garage, muffled but definite enough so she ran for it, throwing herself through both doors and across the kitchen counter to grab it just as the machine kicked in. "Hold on, hold," she said breathlessly, waiting for the machine to realize someone had picked up. Finally her recorded voice and its blasé message clicked off and she was able to say, "Hello?"

She didn't have to ask who it was. The dogs barking in the background gave Elizabeth away before she even had a chance to open her mouth. "Brenna," she said, sounding just as breathless as Brenna had been. "How's your hand?"

"I sense ulterior motives," Brenna said, infusing her voice with high suspicion and stretching to toe the kitchen door closed.

Elizabeth laughed, but there was a hysterical edge to it. "Brenna. Seriously. I'm talking tomorrow. We shifted half of today's dogs to tomorrow, and when I called to ask Kelly if she could work a couple of extra hours, she . . . well, she—"

Brenna had seen this one coming. Kelly had her

own small shop at home, and worked at Pets! for the assured income—for Pets! groomers, unlike most, were paid by the hour. Not paid *enough* by the hour, but the lower salary was a trade-off. Brenna had secure winter hours no matter how many dogs were scheduled, when most groomers worked slow bookings and racked up credit card debt during the off season. Now that spring grooming had hit them, it was inevitable that Kelly would get sick enough of Pets! management to—

"She quit," Brenna said flatly, interrupting Elizabeth as a mercy.

"Yes," Elizabeth said, relieved to have the news said. "Roger doesn't know yet. I figured if I at least got tomorrow covered before I told him . . ."

"It's his own damn fault," Brenna said, lashing out not at Elizabeth but at Roger, and instantly backing off when she realized what she'd done. "Sorry. It's just that—"

"I know," Elizabeth said. "Between the two of us, you'd think we'd have convinced him what it takes to run a good shop. But if he hasn't learned by now— oh, damn, he's coming this way. Can you cover, Brenna? Work a ten to six? I'll be here from eight to four, and we're supposed to have a bather until two—"

Brenna flexed her hand. Ow. Dammit, this was going to hurt. "Yeah," she said, and told the clench in her stomach that this was for Elizabeth, not Roger. "Tell him I'll be there. But tell him I want the bather till three. I don't want this hand trying to hold on to soapy wet dogs."

"Oh, smooch!" Elizabeth said. "I'll bring you some peanut butter cookies. Gotta go!"

Brenna spent some time wondering where Elizabeth would find the energy to make cookies after a Saturday's grooming, but she needn't have. When she arrived at work the next day, thinking dire thoughts about who they'd have as a bather—for DeNise was off on Sundays—and just how many times she'd have to get her hand wet to handle situations the bather couldn't, a paper-towel-covered paper plate of bakery cookies waited for her under the front counter.

"The one with a bite out of it is mine!" Elizabeth sang out from the back. A crate clanged closed and she came out to the counter area. "Ooh, check it out," she said of Brenna's hand, which was barely swollen anymore but which Brenna had creatively wrapped in colorful Vetrap—a flexible, coated gauze that stuck to itself and that couldn't be missed.

Brenna did an automatic scan of the sales floor and lowered her voice anyway. "It's for Roger more than anything," she said. "I plan to wave it in front of his face if he tries to book any more dogs today."

"Good plan," Elizabeth said, and reached under the counter. "Here. Start the day with a cookie and I'll bring you up to date on our customers." She reached for the 4x6 index cards and started flipping through them, dishing out quick information on their status—two almost done, three started, a handful more on their way in. "And three to come in early this afternoon—those are all yours. Well, and this fourth, which is just a Dal in for a bath. José should be able to handle her."

A Dalmatian? Brenna snared the card from Elizabeth and said around a big bite of cookie, "José? Handle Darcy Dalmatian? That'll be the day. She'll lick him to death and then make her great escape when he's lulled to complacency."

"Probably," Elizabeth said, cheerfully enough.

And why not—*she'd* be gone by the time the Dal arrived. Brenna made a face at her, and Elizabeth shoved another cookie at her. "Here," she said. "That should cheer you up for awhile."

Brenna followed her into the grooming room, slipping her arms through the sleeves of her smock.

"I could have had really important plans for the day, you know," she said, unsnapping the lock to her personal equipment toolbox, the expensive shears that tended to walk away for use in the small animal section. "I could have had a hot date."

"Yeah, or you *could* have been washing your hair. That takes about a day, doesn't it?" Elizabeth gave Brenna's doubled braid a tweak on her way by with a sullen-looking Lhasa Apso.

"*Hey,*" Brenna said, aggrieved. "It could happen, you know. The date thing, I mean."

"Uh-huh," Elizabeth said, entirely unconvinced as she selected and set aside a cat muzzle that would fit the snub-nosed dog if he followed up on his expression. "Most guys like a bit of sweet-talking, Brenna. We'll have to practice that sometime."

Brenna grumbled something not at all sweet, and Elizabeth grinned, unaffected. "Why don't you check on that Newfie mix? We've got most the day to dry him, but if José didn't use the high-velocity dryer on him before crating him, even that won't be enough."

Wonder of wonders, José had indeed used the high-velocity, and the Newfoundland mix was drying as quickly as could ever be expected of a dog with that much hair. Brenna found several crates missing, and chalked them up to PePP; the group would be setting up for pet adoption day on the sales floor right about now, right by the inevitable aproned dog food rep trying to give away samples. The Schnauzer wasn't quite dry enough to clip—that one had gone a while without visiting a groomer, that was for sure—so she opened the crate holding a half-dry Shepherd mix and invited the dog out. Might as well get the nails done, and trim up the only long-haired features the dog possessed—several exceedingly silly wisps of hair coming from its ears. He could dry when she was done.

She returned to the grooming room and hoisted

the dog onto a low table, thoroughly dampening herself in the process and spotting Sammi from PePP in the doorway to the counter area as she straightened. "Hey," she said. "I hope you're not here for another crate, because we can't spare 'em today."

"I know, I saw the appointment book," Sammi said. But she stood there, hesitating, her plump face a strange combination of paled skin with brightly flushed cheek patches.

Brenna hesitated, the big nail clippers in hand. "Are you all right? Do you feel all right? Maybe you should sit down." Sammi's breath seemed to be coming a little fast, but that wasn't unusual for her. What was unusual was that she hadn't said anything other than the one acknowledgment, and hadn't come bursting into the grooming room with a freshly soiled young dog who needed a quick bath to be presentable to the families who would flock around the PePP area as soon as church let out. No, Sammi was alone, bringing only a strange look on her face.

Sammi took Brenna's suggestion and sat on the folding chair just inside the door, ignoring the tufts of hair already residing there. Brenna, as concerned as she was for Sammi, let her questions rest while she worked through three feet before reaching the fourth. The Shepherd mix whined as soon as she picked it up. "Oooh," Brenna said. "Is this your *favorite* foot?" *Clip, clip*, big chunks of overlong nails went flying through the room, and the dog made a pathetic sound and yanked on her foot. A series of gooey-lovey noises distracted her long enough to get the other two toes and the dew claw, and then Brenna took a moment while hunting up her thinning shears really to pay attention to Sammi.

Sammi looked back at her and said quietly, "One of our members died this morning."

That got Elizabeth, too; she looked up sharply from the Lhasa, turning her clippers off.

"*Who?*" Brenna said.

"Janean. You probably haven't seen her. Takes in the hardest cases, but doesn't do the adoption day stuff. Too shy."

But Brenna *had* seen her, in to buy supplies with one of the PePP dogs at her side, an old dog that PePP was having a hard time placing. A young black woman, lots of amazing hair, quiet features, quiet manner. "Janean," she said numbly, and shook her head. "A car accident?"

Sammi shook her head. "Rabies."

"Shit," Elizabeth said in shock. "*Rabies?*"

"They're *sure?*" Brenna said, right on top of her. She'd meant to tackle the dog's waving, wispy ear hair . . . but she couldn't bring herself to move. *Rabies.* And in her mind, a sudden jumble of voices, things that had come to her in the past weeks, voices she'd ignored because they'd made no sense, because they didn't belong in her head. Voices that usually presaged distress from Druid. *No survivors found on the farm . . . another entire family lost to this new rabies. Shedding Rabies is the common term being used for the mutated virus . . . local groomer Brenna Lynn Fallon succumbed today—*

She jerked herself away from the voices and back to the grooming room, clenching her jaw tight for a moment and picking up a brisk pace with the dog before her. Thinning shears applied to the ear hair, just so, just enough to take them down and yet keep them natural—

"*How?*" Elizabeth asked. She, too, was trying to work again, but her heart wasn't in it and the Lhasa was sprawled on his plump bottom, neatly—and deliberately—sitting on the legs Elizabeth needed to trim. "Not from one of the rescue animals!"

Sammi nodded tightly. "No one knows what else it could be. But the ones that came from families had a history of rabies shots, and the ones we took in from the street all went through quarantine at Lakeridge. If it *was* one of them, we have no idea which."

"Oh, God," Elizabeth said. "It could be one that was adopted out, you mean?"

"Are they ever like that?" Brenna said sharply, finding a cute place for a little bow just below the dog's ear, and for the first time running into trouble with her injured hand as she tried to apply it, wrapping a tiny rubber band around a tinier tuft of hair. She tossed the ruined bow on the floor with the morning's accumulation of hair and groped in the bow jar for a bigger one. "Like Typhoid Mary? Carrying the disease around and spreading it, but not showing it?"

"They can carry it," Sammi said, answering with such certainty that Brenna knew she'd started gathering information as soon as she'd heard the news. "But they can't pass it along until it reaches an active state in their systems, and they always become symptomatic within a few days after that. There's never—*never*—been a documented case of rabies passed on by a dog who went through quarantine. Once they start shedding the virus, they become sick within days."

Brenna turned on Sammi with vehemence. "*What did you say?*"

Startled, Sammi couldn't answer, clearly at a loss to know which of her words would provoke such a reaction. She sat on the chair with her mouth half-open, looking for a response.

"The shedding," Brenna said. "What did you say about the shedding?"

"Why, that's what they call it, I guess. When the dog has the virus in its saliva, and can pass it on. They say the virus is in its 'shedding' phase."

"So it does shed? The rabies we know about sheds?" Barely paying attention to the dog, Brenna eased it down from the table, having given up on the bow.

"There's only one rabies, the one we know about," Sammi said, looking completely baffled. "Brenna, are *you* all right?"

Brenna realized that Elizabeth, too, was staring at her, and that the Shepherd mix was squirming to get away from the tight grip she had on the noose leash. She felt her face flush, and she said, "I'm okay. Just . . . just upset, is all. Thinking about how often we get careless about checking for rabies tags when we're just clipping nails on a walk-in, you know?" Not the truth, but *a* truth. And pertinent enough.

Elizabeth slid her hand under the Lhasa and stood it on all four legs, pulling its hind legs out behind it slightly when it instantly tipped its rear to sit again. "You're right," she said. "We do. We'd better be more careful. Do all the right things. Even if we both *are* inoculated." One thing Pets! did right.

Sammi heaved herself to her feet, not a sign of her usual humor hidden anywhere on her face as she said, most pointedly, "*Janean* did all the right things."

The PePP news spread through the store as fast as any news, leaving the employees somber and the early customers baffled by the black bows that spread—thanks to Elizabeth and some oddball black dog bow ribbon—on the PePP and sales floor associates' collars and buttons. Roger put a moratorium on all talk of rabies on store grounds, and worried to Brenna about a drop in bookings should cautious pet owners keep their animals at home. But a local death caused by rabies was newsworthy enough that by the time grooming work hit a short lull and Elizabeth and José grabbed the chance to eat, the customers came in looking for details.

"I don't have any real details," Brenna told the owners of Snifter the Brittany when they dropped him off for his bath and trim—not that a Brittany had a breed cut *per se*, but Snifter was gifted with a wild profusion of wispy hair on his back, head and ears, the sort that was best stripped off instead of clipped. "In fact," she added, "you probably know more. I haven't heard a single news report about it. Just what's hit the grapevine."

"They can't figure out how it happened. I have a friend who thinks it started with the dog pack somehow," Snifter's mother said. "But on the radio they say that PePP has logs for all their animals, and that they keep strict track of the shots and quarantines."

"That's true," Brenna said, and gave them a pickup time for the happy but chronically overenergized Snifter. José would be plenty wet by the time he washed the Brittany—and Brenna, with her hand, wasn't even going to try. She took the dog in the tub room and put him in one of the big bottom crates, and then just stood there, staring at him without even seeing the astonishingly hopeful look on his face as he shoved it into the upper corner, somehow expecting that instead of a bath they'd just have a good romp.

Of course they couldn't figure out how it had happened. *Because it shouldn't have happened.* It shouldn't have been possible.

Just like all the other things currently in her life that shouldn't be possible. Weird black hole moods that bounded in like Tigger from *Winnie the Pooh*, a stray with multiple ID tags—all of which led to nonexistent records of one kind or another—startling visions—no, not visions, for she'd only ever *heard* them. Someone else's memories of words about death and shedding rabies. *Why* shedding *rabies, instead of just* rabies?

And Gil Masera mixed up in it all, with his halftruths, his interest in a property newly reoccupied by men who might well be called thugs, his frighteningly complete knowledge of her. *His careful hands checking Druid the night Sunny died. His quiet words on*

the hill as Brenna sought to deal with Druid's fear.
His recognition of what she'd felt along with Druid
in the lane. The demand that had so angered her,
when he'd stepped over the line to grab her arm.
What did you do? he'd said.

Maybe none of it was related. Maybe she was going
crazy, and Masera just happened to stumble into it,
to add to it. Brenna found herself at the tub, her
forehead resting on her crossed wrists atop the cool
porcelain. *God, how am I supposed to sort it all out?*

And that, she realized suddenly, was more than a
frustrated inner cry. It was a prayer, as true a prayer
as she'd ever said.

Except she had no idea which god she was talking to. The God she'd grown up with, the one she'd
been raised to believe in as the only god? Or the
ancient, forgotten god who once seemed to have
answered a heartfelt child's plea, and whom she
thought of as dwelling at the very spring where
Druid's weird tracks appeared?

She didn't know. *Brenna Lynn, good little Christian girl, and she didn't know.* The wrath of God
strike her down or not, she *didn't know.*

And if she didn't know *that*, how could she know
anything?

Chapter 11

ᛋ

SOWELU
Guiding Forces

The busy days usually went quickly, but not this one. This one passed in a strange timelessness, and even when things got hectic—a dog on the table, the phone tucked under her chin, a customer waiting at the counter and Elizabeth gone for the day—Brenna operated in a strangely dissociated way, as though her soul were dazed and nothing else could touch her.

She managed time for a phone call to the church she hadn't attended for several years, the small but healthy little church in which she'd grown up. The one her mother still made a point to attend on Easter and Christmas, although she spent her other Sunday mornings in the barely denominational services provided by Sunset Village. Yes, the pastor would be there in the late afternoon, keeping office hours before the evening youth group. Yes, he'd see her.

"Brenna Fallon," he said, when she walked down the center aisle of the square sanctuary, plain but for one set of astonishing stained glass windows above the pulpit. He wore street-casual clothes, a soft grey sweater over slacks, and his hair had completed the journey to silvery white since she'd last seen him. How many years ago? The year she'd graduated from high school and watched most of her friends journey away to one college or another?

"Reverend Dayne," she said, and then, because there didn't seem to be any other way to start, added the expected. "It's been a long time."

"Too long," he said, as though he were finishing some secret code exchange necessary before they could discuss anything else. He rearranged the candles on the table set before the pulpit, and she realized that it must have been a communion Sunday. That somehow made her long absence worse. And then he smiled, and said, "But I can't imagine you called me after all this time just to make small talk."

"No," she said, and jammed her hands into her pockets. "Though I have to admit it makes it easier to sneak up on what I've really got on my mind."

His smile this time seemed more genuine; he gestured at the front pew. Square backed, barely padded seats . . . she'd never understood why they weren't more comfortable. "To keep people awake," Russell had told her once when they were children, and received instant admonishment. Now, with years of perspective behind her, Brenna couldn't help but wonder if he'd been right.

She didn't need any help staying awake through this conversation. But she sat anyway.

"You look tired," the pastor said, sitting next to her but far enough away that they could turn toward one another, carry on a conversation without bumping knees. "I heard about the young woman who died. You knew her, I imagine. Is that why you're here?"

"No," Brenna said, but then stopped. Without Janean's death, would her thoughts have reached this point? "Maybe," she amended. "More like . . . the last straw." She took a moment to arrange her thoughts, and found she wasn't any more sure of her starting place than before. Slowly, she said, "We both know I haven't been here for years. And I know that a faith is more active when you stay joined with a community, but just because you're not going to church doesn't mean it's not *there*." She hesitated, waiting for some reaction on his part. Any sign of judgment at this early point, and she sure wasn't going any further.

But he gave her none of that. Instead he gave her a faint smile, and a nod. "People take their faith to them in different ways," he said. "Some people aren't as comfortable with group worship. I happen to think it offers a necessary support. Now, if I were a Catholic priest, you can imagine that my response would be quite different."

"It's a good thing I was brought up Presbyterian, then, isn't it?" Brenna said, acerbically enough to raise his eyebrows. She gave a chagrined shrug and let it go. "The point is . . . the reason I'm here . . . is that lately I've been looking at some of the other major religions—non-Christian religions. Non-Yahweh, even. And if you go beyond the god-ness of it, the philosophies seem to have as many good things to say as Jesus in any red-line Bible."

"Ah," Reverend Dayne said, sitting to put his arm along the back of the pew, relaxing a little now that he knew the gist of the issue. "I feel obliged to say, Brenna, that this is just the kind of subject we discuss in our women's religious study group."

"There's a women's religious study group?" Brenna said, surprised and unable to remember any such thing.

Amused, he said, "Things do change. And as we've noted, it *has*—"

"—been a long time," Brenna finished. "And that's why I'm here. Now. Asking you." A women's study group might actually hold some interest for her, but it wouldn't help her *now*.

"What is it, exactly, that you're asking?"

"I guess . . . what I'm wondering . . . is how does the church look at these other religions? If I take on Hindu philosophies for my own, does that mean I'm, well, damned? What about Muslim, or Buddhist? *The Tao of Pooh?* *What if I dance naked in the moonlight by the spring beneath the oak with my hair loose to the wind and flower petals scattered around?* "My faiths, the things I was taught here at this church, are a very deep part of me. They're *important* to me. But right now I'm also finding it important to look at other faiths." Pagan faiths, which she wasn't ready to say. Not when so many people equated pagan with evil. Brenna herself would have to visit the library to understand truly what fell into the definition of a pagan faith, and she wasn't even sure it mattered right now. Not with a veritable shrine to Mars Nodens in her backyard. "I guess I'm worried about crossing some sort of line. The kind you can't come back from."

"Ohh," Reverend Dayne said, a drawl easing into his voice. "There are very few of those, for someone in your position." He crossed his ankle over his knee and rested a hand on that leg, looking very much at home with himself. She hadn't shocked him, then. She hadn't said anything to worry him. She'd just been slotted into one of his past sermons. "Adult faith isn't stagnant, Brenna. An exploration and study of other faiths is an excellent way to confirm our own beliefs. The important thing is to make those explorations in a thoughtful way. Not—to use an extreme example— to dive into a cult situation just because we're trying to fulfill something lacking in our lives."

There wasn't anything lacking in my life when all this came up, Brenna thought automatically, and then suddenly knew how wrong that internal commentary had been. There'd been plenty lacking in her life. Family support and interaction. Career satisfaction. Someone who liked dogs and the farm and movie nights as much as she did.

Someone with whom to share her baths.

She was just so used to dealing with those empty spots that she never saw them any more. But that wasn't the conversation she was having with him. Not this time. "So you don't think it's possible to *add* religions," she said. She found a dog treat in her vest pocket and worried it between her fingers. "To truly believe in more than one thing."

He regarded her for a moment, somber for the first time in the discussion. "Brenna, many of those outside Christianity believe that Jesus existed, and even that he was a great prophet. They just don't happen to believe that he's *the one* Son of God. Here, that's what we do. It may not be entirely expedient—how much easier it would be if we could mix and match religions, or decide what inconvenient part of our faith we'll simply set aside to suit our needs of the moment. No. Yahweh is the one God. And in our faith, the Holy Trinity comprises that God. That's what it is to be Christian."

Of course it was. Brenna suddenly didn't even know what she was doing here. What kind of answer had she *expected*? An arrangement to believe in God on the odd days and Mars Nodens on the even? No, it was a choice. One or the other.

And she had a feeling that the *other* had set up presence in her pasture.

"I'm sorry, Brenna," Reverend Dayne said. "I can see I haven't eased your mind particularly. Is there any other question? Some specifics, perhaps, that I can address for you?"

"No, thank you," she said, standing. The dog treat had disintegrated into annoying crumbs in her pocket sometime during his final comments. "I have some things to think about. I hope . . . I hope I'm welcome to call on you again."

"Anytime, Brenna," he said, warmly enough that she really believed him. He, too, stood, and held out his hand. She removed hers from her pocket, swiped it off on her jeans, and wondered what he thought about biscuit crumbs as she shook his hand. Then, a little too tired to be anything but hazy, her most focused thought relating more to the leftover peanut butter cookies in her truck than spiritual matters, she headed for the exit at the back of the sanctuary.

The next day at work Brenna posted HELP WANTED signs on all the grooming area and store entrances, and stored a pile of applications beneath the grooming counter. She submitted an ad to Roger, who for once had goals that coincided with hers—get a new groomer, and get one fast. It would not, she knew, be as easy as he thought. They'd get applicants who thought that "likes to work with dogs," was adequate preparation for the exacting and demanding work of grooming, and far too few people who'd actually been through any sort of vocational schooling.

At least they had DeNise—short, round, cheerful smile, and the darkest skin Brenna had ever seen— five days a week, and she was picking up the details of her job quickly. She'd even made herself a small step stool so her elbows didn't bang the insides of the tub, which Brenna viewed as a relieving sign of both her initiative and her intent to stay with the work.

Before she left the store, Brenna found a red marker and penned a bold reminder to all of them. *Get Customer Rabies Info!* it said, and she underlined it before taping it to the back edge of the counter where the customers couldn't see it. *And practice what you preach*, she told herself, locking up her equipment for the day. Far too easy to grab a walk-in nail-clipping client without question, especially during the rush periods.

On the way home she pulled into the church parking lot, and stared at the church for a while. The day had turned balmy for early May—shirtsleeve weather, with the interior of the truck too warm to sit in the sun for long. Just long enough to look at the unimposing exterior of the church—not even a bell tower, and the stained glass was at the back of the building—and decide against going in. The pastor might be there, and before she spoke to him again, she wanted to have found some answers of her own.

This wasn't the place to look for them.

The spring. That's where she'd go. Where she could think.

Of course she took Druid, and the rifle to boot. Gossip about the feral dogs was dying down, although at work today she'd heard more talk from people wanting to link them to the rabies despite the utter lack of evidence. Masera, she realized, was right—regardless of the warnings, regardless of what had happened to Sunny, no one had ever seen a member of the oft-discussed pack.

But something was out here. *Something* had ripped Sunny from her collar. And while Brenna was no longer certain it was anything that could be stopped by a rifle, she had a grim appreciation of the weapon's heft in her hand.

What did you do? Masera had demanded, making it crystal clear that the darkness had touched him as well, that he recognized, somehow, something special about her place by the spring. The Mars Nodens place. The place of power.

What *had* she done? Nothing in that magazine

article, so long ago, had hinted that Mars Nodens had a darker side. Maybe it was something else. Maybe her actions as a young girl had nothing to do with the things that were happening to her now.

Which brought her right back to where she'd started these thoughts, to why she felt so driven to visit the spring in the first place. How could she believe both in her one God and in the existence of Mars Nodens?

One thing she knew. She'd never figure out the nature of the darkness while she struggled over how to acknowledge its existence. Or *if* she even believed in anything other than her own internal faltering. Maybe she ought to be calling her doctor, not camping out by a spring.

But Masera felt it too.

If she was crazy, then *he* was crazy.

Given how little she trusted him right now, she didn't find the thought particularly reassuring.

She sat with Druid on the side of the hill for a while, taking him up as close to the spring as she could without triggering him and enjoying the warmth of the lowering sun. Not particularly thinking about anything, but taking advantage of the way the babble of creek water filled her mind so she could *stop* thinking. Early T-shirt weather, all right, despite the bright red hooded sweatshirt dumped carelessly on the ground beside her. And then, because it seemed right and because she so seldom did so, she pulled the hair bands off her doubled braid and finger-combed her hair so it settled over both her and Druid, a procedure he found interesting enough to take his mind off the close proximity of the spring. He sniffed it thoroughly and got strands of it caught in his whiskers, and ended up giving a mighty sneeze. When she laughed, he looked up with a doggy smile, panting as his black coat soaked up the sun, the corners of his mouth relaxed and happy. It was then she decided not to take him any closer to the spring. Not tonight. They both needed a happy moment, and they'd found one. No point in ruining it.

She took him downhill, instead, and tied him off to a tree so she could visit the spring herself. "I bet you'd do a grand sit-stay," she said at his affronted expression, "but I don't want to worry about you right now."

Back up the hill, as always, she paused by the grave site. "Hello, old hound," she said, still full of affection every time she spoke to his memory. "Watch for me these days, will you?" He would, if he were here. He'd be sitting at the crest of the hill, under the oak, scanning the pasture. "And you," she said to Sunny's collar, feeling a sudden fierce ache in her throat. "I miss you more than either of us would have expected, I think. I'm still not sure what happened, but I haven't given up trying to figure it out."

She turned to the spring, sweeping her hair around and into the lap she created by kneeling. "And *you*," she said, more quietly, all the tenderness gone from her voice. "I don't know what's going on here, but I wish you'd give me some clue. *Whoever* you are. There's no need to be so damn mysterious, pardon my language. I need all the help I can get—" Shoot, if it could even help her figure out *Masera*. "And right now, you're just making it worse." And then, deciding that maybe she'd gone over the line with that one, she added, "Well, it *feels* like you're making it worse. I suppose I should allow for some all-knowing plan."

No wonder she hadn't gone into the church. This wasn't a conversation she could have there.

The last time she'd muttered at this spring, an unexpected wave of . . . *something* had washed through her, practically taking her off her feet. This time, she half hoped for some similar response, but there was nothing, so she sat a few more moments, then leaned forward to brush away the several dull-rusty leaves that had settled in the spring area since the last time she'd visited. *Nothing*.

Well, she supposed if a being of power got too predictable, people would start taking it for granted. Couldn't have that.

Druid gave a sharp bark, jolting Brenna from her thoughts—and then another, sounding like less of a statement and more of a warning. Brenna twisted around to scan the pasture. Her property, her special place. She didn't know why it felt like it had somehow become a community meeting hall.

Rob Parker, heading for the footbridge. She'd rather he stayed on the other side of the creek. But he didn't, and Druid moved out to stand, as best he could while tied, between the two humans.

His own human came down the hill with rifle in one hand, the sweatshirt in the other, suddenly realizing she'd worn one of her older, tighter T-shirts, the pink one with the bold flowers across the front and the tear and flap right about over her belly button. A shirt that would not survive her mother's next cleaning sweep though the old farmhouse that still had Rhona's name on the papers.

Not unless Brenna hid it again.

And the other human, of a size with Brenna and in the same jeans and T-shirt, but bulkier, more muscled. Male. With his cigarette burning at the corner of his mouth, and his strides loose and casual as if Brenna weren't watching his every step, and as if the Cardigan's low growl hadn't become a constant grumble.

Brenna loosed the leash and then without thinking—something she'd never have consciously opted to do—she unhooked the snap and let Druid go free. So he could get away if he needed to, she realized, and then couldn't find a way to make the impulse make much sense. *Too much time spent letting your mind empty itself into that spring.*

"Haven't seen you for a bit," Parker said.

"It's my busy season," Brenna said, opting for distantly cordial.

"Never seen you at *all* with your hair down."

So that's the only language he could speak. Probably thought he could get away with anything, if he threw the right combination of attractive grins—and they *were*—and offhand charm in her direction. She could speak that language, too. She could even say *no* in it. She held her hair out from her side and let the thick handful of hair slide from her grasp bit by bit. "Then take a look. Be a while before it happens again, I'd say." Making a point. *It's not for you*.

He pretty much ignored her unspoken meaning, but mused onward. "I didn't know it would draw me up here like this."

She gave him a sharp look. "What, my *hair*?" she said, letting her hand fall abruptly back to her side.

He snorted, shook his head; his eyes were on the hill. "This area. Toby spoke of it, in his letters from boot camp. I swear, it's half the reason he went AWOL. And Gary never would come join me in Marysville, making Hondas for damn fine wages. Had to stay here, he said. Just had to. I understand, now. . . . Now that it's my turn. Poor Toby never had a chance to figure it out, and Gary barely got it. But me, I understand."

"Can't say as *I* do," Brenna said, letting her hands fall to the flare of her hips. "Or how you think this kind of thing works—you come on to my place anytime you want, but don't seem to think that sort of neighborly treatment goes both ways."

He jerked his head away from the hillside and looked at her, looked close. Her and the gun and her hair and the expression on her face. "*It was you* back a couple of days ago, that Clay scared off my folks' old place."

And Brenna finally put the timing together, realizing

just when Parker and his two boy pals had first found themselves this spring. The year her father died. The year it took days to repair the damaged fences, stomp down the gouged turf, remove the pitiful rabbit from the skewer on which it had died . . . she'd even washed down the area, carting buckets to sluice down what she'd considered the defiled area. "*It was you*," she said, "*you*, back years ago, who tore this place up like a battleground."

"Ah," he said, looking caught but not concerned, and ducking his head in a calculated way. "I was younger then. Wilder. Boys will be boys and all that."

"That's a miserable excuse," Brenna said, biting off the words.

"It is. But it's the only one I've got." He looked right at her, the gold glinting in his mustache, his mouth just touching a smile at either side, an expression he no doubt counted on to charm women.

It might have, had she met him in the street. Had she not started to see beneath those effective mannerisms. "It makes me think twice about having you on my land. Especially after the treatment I got from your friend."

"Didn't make a good impression, huh? He's zealous. I tell him, 'Let me know who comes around,' and he twists it into, 'Don't let anyone come around.' It's so run-down, is all. Once we get the place fixed up, there'll be something there worth your time to see." And he smiled again, lowering the cigarette to his side and flicking it with his ring finger, dropping ash.

Brenna was not charmed. But she wasn't as angry any more, and for that she supposed she'd have to count herself as successfully manipulated. Besides, it was evident enough that he didn't intend to let himself be drawn into an argument. "No," she said, "he didn't make a good impression. So you blame it on him that I'm giving you the boot, just like he gave me. When you're ready for the casual attitude about property lines to go both ways, you let me know." She nodded behind him. *Time to go back where you came from.*

His dismay seemed real enough. "Brenna, honey, let's talk about this—"

Brenna, honey? She dropped the fists from her hips and picked up the rifle that had been leaning against her leg. Not with purpose; she kept it pointed well at the ground. But it made its point. "Women hate that, Rob. That *honey* stuff. They really hate that. Keep it in mind the next time you want to get your way."

He gave her a hard look through the gathering twilight. "Real ballbreaker, aren't you?" Druid barked sharply, skittering sideways, and then trotted off toward the house in a purposeful way, hesitating once to look at Brenna and then making up his mind for good. He'd have triggered if he'd been on a leash, she realized—a quick thought that didn't distract her from Parker's expression, or the way he said, "I've got other means to get my way." He let that sink in a moment, exhaling slow smoke through his nose, and added, "If I want to," leaving her to take the implication that if she was smart, she'd stay on his good side. Keep him feeling benevolent about her.

Brenna didn't feel particularly smart. "Whatever," she said, as unimpressed as she could be, wondering if he could spot her heart beating right through the tight T-shirt. Not likely, not in this light. "But right now, you're leaving."

He shrugged elaborately, flicked the cigarette again. Waited just long enough so Brenna wondered if he would go at all, if he was so willing to scorn her authority on her own land. To her face, anyway, because she was certain he'd be back when he thought he could get away with it. She forced herself to stand still, to look unconcerned.

Not to shift her grip on the rifle the way her hand itched to do.

After a moment, he flicked his cigarette to the ground and toed it down flat. And left, sauntering off with as much assurance as he'd had when he arrived.

Brenna waited until he was out of sight. Sam had warned her, that day at Emily's, to stay clear of Parker. Now she knew why.

Or maybe not precisely *why*, but at least the flavor of it. The specifics were as much a mystery as anything else in her life right now. She didn't know what Parker was up to at the barn, and she didn't know what he'd meant by *other means*. He could get what he wanted from her simply by coming around when she wasn't here. What was the point of threatening beyond that point?

Because he could.

Brenna climbed the hill and sat under the oak until the sun was down and only the barest hint of twilight remained. Watching the pasture—and wondering if Parker would be so bold as to come back that very night.

Wondering, too, what drew him to the spring so strongly in the first place. It wasn't *his* dog buried under those stones. Wasn't *his* family's land, the place where he'd grown up and the very hills where he'd found his first stray, trained his first dog, felt the first stirrings of an innate ability to interact with dogs on their own level. Those were all her claims to this spot.

All Parker had was one wild night of carousing, destruction, and a nostalgic memory of two dead friends.

Didn't seem like that was enough.

She stood, wiping off the seat of her jeans with a hand that was still sore and stiffening up from the day's work. She gave it the sweatshirt to hold and carried the rifle in the other, double-checking that the safety was on for her walk in the new-moon darkness.

Not that she didn't know where she was going, or had any concern for getting there. She knew this land day *or* night, and as nights went, this one wasn't as black as some. She was more worried about Druid than about her navigation. Unlike Sunny, he wasn't used to roaming the property on his own, or even hanging around the house. She didn't even know if he had a good sense of direction. Some dogs that hadn't been out on their own didn't, and he'd already proven he was perfectly capable of losing his way. So it was Druid that her eyes strained to find as she returned to the house—some glimpse of his white muzzle and blaze or the waving white tip of his tail and four sturdy, well-boned legs flashing along in his trot.

What she found, as she slipped through the barn gate and rounded the corner of the barn to the driveway, was the pale hulk of Masera's SUV sitting in her driveway.

She stopped short, rapidly cycling through reactions. From *shit!* and annoyance through sudden, overwhelming fatigue and straight through to a resigned place where she didn't really care why he was there or what he wanted. She was ready for a bowl of popcorn and a few chapters of her book followed by plenty of sleep before another day of grooming.

Settled within herself, she came around the SUV and discovered Masera sitting on her porch, Druid at his side. She walked slowly up to the porch and stopped some feet away, just standing there, waiting. He was the one who'd shown up at her place— again—without invitation. Let him take the burden of any conversation.

He didn't, not at first. At first he simply looked at her, making her suddenly aware of herself from the outside in. The chill of the April air across the exposed strip of skin at her navel, the waterfall feel of her hair against her back and swirling behind her knees.

Because, abruptly, she knew that's just what he was looking at—*staring* at, his gaze as tangible as the cold breeze that brought goosebumps up on her arms.

He stood, and took a couple of swift steps to stop short only inches from her, close enough to block the breeze, for her to feel the warmth of his body replace it.

That was when her world swirled and she knew Sammi had been right, that day in the break room a month ago. Whatever Masera thought about grooming and groomers, whatever else he was up to . . . right now, he *wanted*. Enough to forget why he'd come here, to forget that she'd never welcomed him, to forget that they'd last parted ways on hard terms.

Not things Brenna could ignore. Nor could she ignore the tension between them, or the way his hand drifted up to her hair by her neck, hovering but not touching.

The way she could feel it anyway.

So she took control. She ended the moment, looking up and into his eyes as she lingered over a single word. "Iban."

It startled him just as much as she'd meant it to. Enough so his hand fell away and he stared at her with all his intensity fled. She waited for his anger.

He laughed.

A guffaw, really—short and genuine. And then he backed up and made himself at home on her front porch step. "Brenna Lynn," he said, but even in the darkness she caught the quirk of his mouth.

"Iban," she said again, this time as an acknowledgment. And a demand, which he caught. *How do you know what you know?*

"Roger's not careful with his files," Masera said, and now his subtle inflections made sense to her; they fit onto Eztebe's like a shadow template. "I was hunting for something else, I ran across yours, I peeked."

Brenna crossed her arms, silent. Not quite a demand, but certainly expectant. It sounded too much like just enough truth to get by.

He got the point, shrugged, and said, "I *was* hunting for something else. But I didn't know it wasn't in your file until I looked there." Fessing up, yes. Looking guilty, no. He'd been checking her out. And had he been checking her out, somehow, that day he'd come to the tub room to wash the Westie?

"Oh, I do feel better," Brenna said, suddenly sure of it. "Not only do you sneak around behind my back, you sneak around behind Roger's. That certainly makes it all right."

He winced. "Brenna—"

"I could say I never even asked you to call me that, but Ms. Fallon doesn't suit me as well so you might as well."

"Do you suppose you could put that rifle up?" he asked, and that made her smile, because they both knew he was in no danger whatsoever. From the rifle.

"If I want to hit you—"

"—again," he quickly interposed.

"If I want to hit you *again*," though she recalled it as more of a shove, "I wouldn't use my grandfather's .22."

"No, you'd do fine with your own two fists," he said. "Or more likely your wits. Roger really has no idea what he's up against."

Brenna pumped the chamber open and left it that way, empty, and reached beyond him to lean the rifle in a temporary resting spot on the porch. She snorted at the thought of her manager and said, "I think he knows well enough by now. He just tolerates me because I run a good grooming room, and it's hard to find anyone with that much experience who doesn't already have their own shop. I'm sure you saw plenty of remarks in my file."

"I saw enough to know that the reason you run a

good grooming room is that you won't back down to him." He watched as she knelt to hug Druid; the dog's tail wagged wildly, and he rubbed his cheek on her leg. Claiming her, and "purring" as only a dog can purr, with deep breathing patterns verging on happy groans. He waited until she'd finished murmuring to him before adding, "I don't understand why you don't have your own—"

As if she wanted to talk about *that*. "It doesn't matter. It's not why you're here, is it?" She gave Druid an abrupt final pat and stood, aware that the dog continued to lean against her leg in a sprawling sit, watching Masera just as much as she did. "To talk about my work?"

Silence. A long silence.

"No," he said. "It's not. I came for myself, I suppose. To try to understand what's going on here—and there *is* something. With the spring, the lane . . . maybe even your dog. Not *this* one, though there's no particular reason to leave him out, not with the way he acts."

"You were only here for one night," Brenna said. "What do you know about what's *going on here*?"

"What I observed in that one night. And morning."

"Hard to believe you could observe *anything* in the morning," she said pointedly.

"You'd be surprised."

Druid shifted against her and did a whisker inspection of her leg. Up as far as he could reach, down all the way to where her ankle met sneaker. He never kissed or licked, but the frequency of his whisker inspections was high. And this time, as often, he whined softly under his breath. Talking to himself.

"No," Masera said, watching Druid inspect and whine, "there's definitely no reason to leave him out."

"I have to wonder if you're really here because you want to pump me for information about Rob Parker, and you think I won't notice."

After a moment of looking away from her, Masera said, "Rob Parker is another conversation."

"Maybe." Brenna shrugged, found that her hair was no longer enough to keep her warm, and drew her sweatshirt on, tugging the sleeves up to leave her hands free. They fell down again a moment later, of course. One of Russell's hand-me-downs, this one was. If she wanted to, she could withdraw her hands inside the sleeves altogether and let them flop around at the ends of her arms.

Sometimes, entertaining Sunny, she'd done that. This time, she shoved the sleeves back up again. "Maybe," she said again. "Though considering how interested Parker is in my spring, maybe not."

"Is he?" Masera said, surprised. He rubbed his index finger against the bridge of his nose, then— carefully—his eyes. "Extended-wear contacts," he said wearily. "Don't mess with 'em."

"I'll remember that," Brenna said. "Masera, it's dark. I need to eat something. So does Druid. And I have to get ready for work in the morning."

"I know. I'm sorry," he said, sounding it, and spent a moment looking for words, his mouth twitching as he discarded this one and that. She finally sat cross-legged in the grass before the porch, which delighted Druid. He draped himself over her ankles and commenced a whisker inspection of her calves. Masera gave a little grin; it seemed to get him started. "The Basque provinces haven't been exposed to Christianity or even God for as long as most of Europe. You could say that we're a little closer to our roots than the rest of you. And some of us have a family history that puts us closer than others. It gives me a different perspective on things."

"Have you even *been* to Basque?"

"To Euskal Herria? Don't let my English fool you. I spent my childhood there—all except the first four years. Those, I spent here. And I came back when I was able. My brother—"

"Eztebe," Brenna said, and then smiled sweetly. The smile everyone expected from this face. The one that wiser souls knew not to take at face value. "Or Steven, but he prefers Eztebe."

He shook his head—not disagreeing, but perhaps in lieu of throwing up his hands. "Yes. He was born in Alsasua. And he wasn't old enough to really understand the way things were before—" He stopped short, as if he'd stumbled somewhere he didn't want to go. It gave Brenna the chance to let her own thoughts stray, to wonder why she was sitting out here in the dark. Listening. And wanting to hear more.

Maybe because she, as much as he—*more* than he—wondered what was going on in her life.

"My mother," he said finally, "is euskotar. Ethnic Basque. My father is Spanish, and he didn't truly understand her ties to her land. He brought her here; she was miserable. Nothing here spoke to her like it did in her homeland. She was Catholic, and she tried very hard to be a good one. But she was also *sorgin*."

"Of course she was," Brenna said, in no way interested in making this easy for him—and at the same time fascinated. On the one hand, he was as he'd always been to her—with something else going on beneath the surface, something he didn't share with anyone, but that seemed to drive him—and drive him right over anyone who got in the way.

She wondered if he knew that some people would politely step *out* of his way if they had the chance.

She wondered if it made him as lonely as it sometimes made her. To be so uncompromising of self.

"Sorgin," he said, and when he looked up, enough light caught his face so she could see that his eyebrows had gone to trying to pinch the bridge of his nose. "I don't want to use the word *witch*, although that's the literal translation . . . it's more than that, and not the things people think of when they think of a witch."

"That's why you asked if I were pagan," she said, smoothing Druid's ears flat to his skull as he fell asleep—and then stilling as she felt a bloom of anger. She lifted her eyes to glare at him. "You said *you* weren't. But you *are*, aren't you? Is it so easy for you to lie to me? You're probably sorgin yourself!"

"No," he said quietly. In the darkness, she thought she saw him wince. Good. "No, it's not so easy to lie to you. I didn't say I wasn't pagan. I said I was lapsed Catholic—and that's true."

"You deceived me," she said steadily, not backing off. Druid woke to give her an uneasy look. "It comes to the same thing."

"I didn't—" he hesitated, shook his head in frustration. "All right, I *did*. I didn't want to get into it then. It's a complicated issue—there are as many different kinds of paganism as there are Christianity, and none of them are really what people assume they are." He met her gaze in the darkness and repeated, "I didn't want to get into it. I didn't think it would come up again."

"You were wrong on both counts then, weren't you?" Brenna said, surprising herself with the faint tremor in her voice. *It shouldn't matter.* "Why should I bother to talk to you at all, if I never know when to believe you?"

He rubbed his forehead, as if it pained him. "That's up to you, I guess. My assurances that I've never lied to you probably won't mean much. And just because you ask a question doesn't mean I'm going to answer it."

And she still had too many unknowns orbiting around her. Too many to spurn anything—any*one*— that could help her fill them in.

She'd have to pay closer attention to the questions he didn't quite answer.

Like the one she'd asked him moments ago. "*Are* you?" she said. "Sorgin?"

He laughed, a quiet sound. "No. I'm nosy, and I'm a hardass, but I'm not sorgin. I just know what I see and what I feel. Better than most, I suppose."

"Then just what was it that you saw and felt, and that put you on my porch without so much as a phone call?"

"I did call," he said. "You didn't answer. I left a message—go check it."

"In a moment. Let's have an answer to this one first." She leaned back on the heels of her hands and looked up at him, careful not to pull her own hair as it puddled on the ground around her.

He hesitated for so long she thought he was just going to get up and leave—there was a moment she thought he was on his way. Touch and go. Then he sighed, and said, "Power. And presence. More than one. The kind of thing that doesn't show up unless it's called. Or at least spoken to, and from the right place. The oak, the spring, the creek . . ."

"More than one *what*?" Brenna demanded, not about to be the first person to say *a god*. She'd see where he went with this on his own.

But Masera shook his head, the slightest of movements, not taking his eyes from her. "If I had all the facts, I wouldn't be here. You're the one who's got them. And that worries me, because part of what I felt was a dark power. The kind of power you don't want anything to do with."

"As if you know me so well," she said, bitingly sarcastic. From fear, maybe . . . and maybe because she didn't really want to think about what he was saying. What it meant. How it fit into the events of her life.

He let his breath hiss out through his teeth, a thoughtful sound rather than impatient. "I know you're unexpected," he said, as if it were some profound thing. And maybe, from the look he was giving her, it was.

"And we're having this conversation so I can reassure you that I'm not sacrificing small animals to a dark power?"

"Among other things."

"I'll leave that to Rob Parker." She stabbed the words at him with the anger she felt at Rob—anger she was only coming into, having so recently realized that he was the one who had wreaked such destruction at her private place. "He seems to have the knack."

He stiffened at that. "*Akelarre*," he said, to himself as much as to her, and then shook his head at her, rubbing that spot between his eyes with a finger. "I don't have a translation. Please. Tell me about the spring. *All* about it. You know damned well what I mean."

From a sincere request to a demand within words. He was trying, she realized. Trying to keep the edge out of his voice, trying to be less of a . . . well, a hardass. That he failed so miserably gave her the feeling that she wasn't the only one having trouble—that he wasn't as in control as he liked to think.

Not in a conversation about witches and unnamed powers in her pasture.

"When I was nine," she said, carefully choosing her words, "I read about an ancient god named Mars Nodens."

"One of the jainko," he said.

"You know of him, then?"

"Not specifically. I know the nature of those gods. Their names . . . they each had so many names. I doubt anyone today knows them all."

"Well, I read that he was a god of healing, and one with a special liking for dogs. Ever heard of the Lydney Hound?"

Wordlessly, he shook his head. Not daring to use words, now, in case the interruption made her change her mind about this conversation.

"Doesn't matter. I wanted something, and I went to ask Mars Nodens for it. Like you said—the oak, the spring; they were in this article I read. I didn't know that they were sacred pagan things in general—I didn't know anything about it. I asked for what I wanted, and I left something important to me in return."

"Your hair," he murmured.

She looked at him askance, glad the night was bright enough so he'd see it. "Do you forget *any*thing you hear?"

"Not the important things. Did you get what you wanted?"

"I suppose I did. And more. That's when the strays started showing up on our doorstep. It seems like back then, I always knew what to do for them. How to talk to them. That sucks something rotten, you know? When I was a girl, I would have known what to do for Druid."

"You *did* know what to do for him," Masera said. "You just needed someone to tell you so."

Maybe so.

"That's it, then?" he said when she didn't respond out loud. "All you did with the spring?"

"Kinda looks like it was enough, doesn't it?"

He shook his head decisively. "Not entirely. The akelarre. What about Parker?"

"Oh, that." Brenna scowled with the anger of it. "Four years ago, Parker and two of his buddies made a mess of the whole spring area. They had ATVs; they tore the place up. Made a fire, left their beer cans everywhere. And a dead rabbit. Just left it impaled on a stick, jammed it into the ground. It was sickening. I only just figured out it was him." *The jerk*.

She wasn't sure, but she thought his eyes had gone hooded—his *beware* face. But not at her. "Who were the others?"

She shifted in the grass, making Druid stir and sigh

and mutter to himself. "Toby Ellis and Gary Rawlins. Both dead. Toby, shortly after that night. And Gary right before Parker came back to this area." She recalled the moments of sitting under the oak, wondering if Parker would return, would really make trouble. "I don't understand why the place is so important to him. He goes there nearly as often as I do, as far as I can tell. He said it draws him. But I'm not sure what I believe of anything he says, anymore."

"I think you can believe that," Masera said in a low voice. He came off the porch, crouched before her. His hand rested on Druid's shoulder, his fingers brushing her ankle. "Brenna, listen. I don't know Mars Nodens, but I know what you did. You turned that spring into a sacred place. A powerful place. You made it a connection between you and him."

"You're messing with my Christian philosophy of life," she said, trying to make it light and hating the shaky note in her voice. The one that said how much it mattered to her.

He shook his head, short and sharp. "They're not mutually exclusive. And that's not the point right now. The point is, you made a place of power and you kept it up."

"I was keeping up *my dog's grave*," she said, feeling stubborn again, and crowded.

"It doesn't *matter*, Brenna—you kept it up. You went there and you maintained your connection with the place. With the power. You kept it living."

"And that's *bad*?"

"What's bad is that Parker and his friends went to a place of power and performed—no matter how inadvertently—the equivalent of akelarre. They threw raw emotion around the place, they sacrificed an animal. They created something of their own. They were angry, out-of-control young men. What do *you* suppose they created?"

She gave him a defiant stare; at this range she could hardly fail to meet his eyes, even in the darkness. And she didn't squirm back, didn't put any more distance between them. To do that would mean that his closeness mattered. "A *mess*, that's what they created."

He smacked his hand against the ground, making her jump; Druid sprang upright and warily inspected the area, only slowly relaxing; his ears stayed canted back at Masera's tone. "*Stop* it, dammit! This isn't about you and me, this is about something dark and dangerous that formed in the very place of power you created!"

For an instant she was furious, and glared it at him. "If you're in my face, then it's about you and me!"

He blinked, seemed to realize she had a point, and eased back to sit on one heel. He took a deep breath and let it out slowly, and it was his effort to regain composure that got to her, let her know just how important he considered this conversation. Much more quietly, he said, "Parker may not know what's dogging him, but he's going to figure it out soon enough. It'll use him, like it probably used his friends before him. And pretty soon he's going to figure out how to use *it*. Or he'll *think* he has—but that kind of thing never truly belongs to anyone. It goes feral the moment it's made."

"Okay," she said slowly. "Okay." It occurred to her that a month ago she would have thought he was, if not nuts, at least full of crap. That she would have meant something entirely different when she said *okay*, something more like *it's a free country, believe what you like*. But here, now, with weeks of weird episodes and weird feelings behind her, with an inexplicable dog by her side and someone else's memories occasionally intruding upon her thoughts . . .

She was inclined to take him seriously.

"Okay," he repeated, and relaxed a little. "Good."

He stood, unfolding in a way that took a certain amount of grace and strength but mainly had to do with the way he was built. He held out a hand to her, a hand she didn't need.

Truce.

She took it.

And, on her feet and wiping off the seat of her jeans, sighing and wondering what, after all of that, they'd truly accomplished, she said, "What now, then? If what you've said is true . . ."

"It's true enough," he told her. "But I can't tell you *what now*. I may have an understanding of what's happened . . . but how to deal with it? Not even my sorgin mother ever came up against *this*. But it strikes me that it would be a good thing to learn all you can about Mars Nodens. If we're going to get help, that's where it'll come from."

She nodded; that made sense. And she shivered, suddenly and unexpectedly, for the first time struck with the reality of what she'd done. Brenna Lynn, nine years old and not ready to let go of an old canine friend, accompanied by both chance and determination, had touched a . . .

She wouldn't think *god*. She wasn't ready for that. A *force*. A force that had made her what she was today—someone who'd always sheltered herself from her own lifelong sense of *differentness*. Different from other girls . . . different from what her family wanted of her. Devoted to dogs. And somehow now stuck in a job where if she and the dogs weren't at odds, she and her manager were at odds over the dogs' best interests—and her own health and safety.

Somewhere along there, she'd taken a wrong turn.

"What are you thinking?" Masera asked suddenly. Quietly. Close to her again.

She shook her head, wondering when she'd gotten so tired. "Nothing," she said. "Or maybe something, but enough's enough." She put her hands over her face—the sweatshirt sleeves had fallen down again, and she pressed the soft material to her eyes—trying to straighten her thoughts out a little, to bring them to some conclusion. "What about Parker?" she said, sliding her hands down just enough to look over the tops of her fingers.

That's when he went away—from her, from the conversation. When he drew within himself to the place where he knew things he wasn't sharing. "Never mind about Parker. Stay clear of him."

She didn't let it go this time. "You know something you're not telling me."

Caught, he hesitated, and gave a short nod. "Yes."

Back to where they'd started, days ago. She could trust parts of him . . . and other parts of him, the parts that had been interested in Rob Parker all along, had been beaten up, had bought two pit bulls in a back-lot transaction . . .

Those parts, she didn't trust in the least.

Chapter 12

ᚺ

HAGALZ
Destructive Forces

Brenna grabbed a few minutes at the end of the day to look at the half-dozen groomer applications they'd received, sorting swiftly and setting all but one aside—and knowing that one was likely wishful thinking. Well. At least they'd *had* this many applications so quickly, although most of them were from high school students who wanted a quick summer job and thought that fooling with dogs was a great thing for which to get paid.

"No good, huh?" DeNise said, taking a noisy and well-earned slurp of her soda; she too was overdue to go off shift. Elizabeth was already working in the back, with enough dogs left to finish so she'd be lucky even to grab a snack from the undercounter stash.

Like Brenna, DeNise still wore her smock, but hers came down to her knees and looked pretty much soaked through from her shift of heavy bathing. From the neck up she was impeccable, with a complexly molded hairstyle that only African-American hair could accomplish.

That was the secret behind their easy amiability, Brenna had always thought—upon first introduction, DeNise had said, "Your hair is awesome!" and Brenna had said, "How do you *do* that?" and despite the difference in their ages—DeNise would still be in high school, if she hadn't qualified for early graduation and was now saving up tuition for the community college—and backgrounds, they'd formed an immediate connection.

Brenna fanned the applications in the air. "No good," she confirmed. "You've got more qualifications to groom than any of 'em." She gave an automatic glance around the storefront and said, "Don't tell Roger I said that. He'll decide I should train you, as if I can do that *and* carry a full grooming load."

"No worries," said DeNise. "No offense, but I got plans."

Brenna gave her a wistful look. "Smart you."

DeNise shrugged. "Hey, girl, it's not too late."

Brenna made a quick scrawl of a note on the borderline application. "Yeah, well," she said, as if that were saying anything at all. She let the pen drop into the plastic mug pen holder with a decisive clink. "I'm going to get while the getting's good." Half an hour over her shift as it was, but that was hardly worth noting. She shed the smock and tossed it on a hook in the grooming room; Elizabeth came breezing out of the tub room and followed her back out. She went straight to the schedule, flipping through it with a frown. "Gonna be even tighter tomorrow," she said. "Maybe I'll see if Roger'll let me clock in half an hour early."

"Be a good idea if you can handle it," Brenna agreed, leaning against the door into the store proper and bumping the push bar with the small of her back. She spotted a woman with a small carrier—cat or rabbit, had to be—on her way in from the parking lot, and lifted her chin to alert Elizabeth. "Nails, I'll bet. Nothing on the schedule that would fit in that one."

"Shit, it's a mess back there," Elizabeth said, and hastily cleared the upper level of the counter. Which was what they did when things got too booked and a small animal came in for nail clipping, as long as the animal in question was a quiet one, and even though it wasn't the best arrangement in the world by far. Brenna hung by the door, halfway between curious and lacking the inertia to move.

The young woman breezed in along with a waft of expensive perfume, resting long, blunt-cut and manicured nails on the counter. "I'm a little late—is Brenna Fallon still here? I'd like to have her cut my cat's nails, please."

Behind her, Brenna widened her eyes at Elizabeth, pleading. *No!* And since her name badge was on the rolled up smock, she might as well not be. DeNise, still sipping her soda, pressed her lips firmly together over the straw, trying not to smile. Without skipping a beat, Elizabeth said, "She's not on right now, but I'm Elizabeth and I'd be glad to take care of you. How does your cat feel about nail clipping? And are you up-to-date on rabies?"

"Her tag is on her collar," the woman said. "She's always been just fine about clipping, I just can't bring myself to do it. I can't stand the thought of cutting too close and making her bleed. I heard the other woman was good with cats."

Hmmm. No more or less than any other groomer, not when it came to cats. Brenna gave Elizabeth a silent *who knows?* shrug. But someone, at some time, must have left the store happy enough to spread the word.

"She *is* good, though we're all experienced," Elizabeth said, though as she came around the counter, clippers in hand, she took advantage of the woman's attentiveness to her cat to make a face at Brenna.

Brenna returned it in full. She waited just long enough for Elizabeth to draw the cat out of the carrier and to see that the animal was docile enough; then she escaped through the door, heading down the main aisle past the bays of dog, cat, fish, and small animal supplies, once more thankful that the grooming room wasn't wired to the constant broadcast of tropical jungle noises that filled the rest of the store.

Halfway to the break room—and the time clock— a familiar wash of cold fear struck her, so fleetingly quick she wondered if she'd imagined it. But she hesitated, and something made her look back toward the grooming room. Something made her turn around and take a few steps back the way she'd come, almost colliding with a customer in the doing of it. Nothing amiss there. Nothing but the woman holding her cat's collar while Elizabeth started on what must have been the last foot, carefully pressing each toe to express the nail, her lips moving in a murmur of private conversation with the creature.

"Excuse me, can you tell me where the collars are?"

Brenna glanced away from the grooming counter— an instant, that's all it was, an instant—and the screaming started. The screaming and the cold dark fear and the whirl of the world around her—bright packaging and toys and giant rawhides and *screaming*—and the clutch of someone's fingers on her arm, inadvertently bringing her back to reality. The customer, a middle-aged woman, gripping her arm in horror, staring at that of which Brenna was only now making sense.

Elizabeth, screaming at the cat, the two of them locked in a whirlwind of battle, blood spraying across the glass, the cat screaming back at Elizabeth, both of them moving too fast to see the detail of it, and a voice in Brenna's head chanting the *wrongness* of it. *Wrong, wrong, wrong* for a cat to attack and maul so viciously. Wrong for it to have been *Elizabeth*—

And then it was over, and Elizabeth somehow had a grip on the cat's scruff. The woman who owned it had fled outside and stood pressed against the door, her mouth open in shock; DeNise huddled in the corner behind the counter. Dazed and wounded, Elizabeth looked up and met Brenna's eyes, somehow finding her halfway across the store—holding the cat in one hand, her other hand up and dripping blood, blood streaming down both arms to collect in the folds of her smock arms and dribble off her elbow, her face crumpling.

Suddenly Brenna could move again. No one else stirred, no one else knew where to start. Brenna, suddenly awake again, ran.

And still she wasn't the first one there.

Masera.

Masera beat her to the door and whipped himself through it, stopping there to speak low words to Elizabeth, and to move slowly—not upsetting either of them. Brenna hesitated in the open door, unwilling to upset the balance with her entrance. The cat hung quiescent, defeated; it might as well have been dead for the fuss it put up as Masera pried it from Elizabeth's battered fingers and stuffed it back into its carrier, slick with her blood.

As soon as he jammed the carrier door into place, Brenna threw herself into the room. "Call for a manager," she told Masera, squeezing past him to reach Elizabeth. Elizabeth stood with her hands held as though they were foreign objects on the ends of her arms, and even as Brenna reached her, she started to shake. With a hand at her back, Brenna guided her through the grooming room and into the noisy roar of the tub room, muttering soothing nonsense as she grabbed a clean white towel from the laundry service and flung it over her shoulder.

"It's all right," she said, hearing Masera's voice over the intercom system in the background, knowing it would get someone's attention—who was on today, an assistant manager?—if they'd somehow managed to miss the excitement on their own. "It's all right," she said again as Elizabeth stifled a sob, thinking to herself *how the hell can it be all right* and wondering if Elizabeth would even have full use of her hands again as she turned the tub faucet to cold and propped the sprayer at an angle to waterfall across the tub. "Here you go," she said, but a glance at Elizabeth's white face told her the woman was in no shape to offer even that much initiative, and Brenna eased her hands under the water.

She didn't know what a doctor would have had her do. All she could think of was dirty cat teeth—dirtier than a dog mouth, inclined to inflict easily infected puncture wounds. And of getting a look at the damage, though as she carefully removed Elizabeth's smock and returned her hands to the tub, she realized she wasn't sure she wanted to know.

Outside the tub room, DeNise's voice rose in shrill anger, mixing with the owner's in argument. Masera came in, the cat carrier in tow; he flipped off all the dryers and came up behind them, his hand landing on Brenna's shoulder. "How's it look?"

"It's hard to tell," Brenna muttered, as though Elizabeth weren't there—and in truth, Brenna doubted that she actually heard them. "Still bleeding too much."

"Best that it does," Masera said. He glanced out

toward the counter. "Gary just came on shift. I don't know where the hell he is—he's got to know what happened by now. Half the store is gawking in through the glass."

"Probably soothing the customers," Brenna said, anger spurting its way out of her voice as she moved Elizabeth's hands within the shower of cold water, rinsing, rinsing, never seeming to get to the end of it. "Priorities, you know."

"I'll call the police and animal control," Masera said, not responding directly to her comment with anything but an anger that matched hers.

Brenna shook her head. "Gary won't like that."

"Then he should be here to take care of it himself. This cat's not going anywhere but into custody for the next ten days." Masera left, creating a cold place at her back. With the dryers off and the grooming room door open, Brenna could hear the background conversation well enough. The woman, upset and teary, fearful for her cat, demanding its return. DeNise, standing her ground. And Masera, almost offhand, breaking in to say shortly, "The cat is fine. She's in the crate in a quiet room, and that's what's best for her. You won't get her back until she's been through a holding period with animal control. And for your sake, I damn well hope you don't have children at home. Not if you plan to take that cat back."

The woman's high-pitched protests were incomprehensible, but there was no mistaking her distress. Damned pity she loved the beast.

Maybe it's not a beast. What would that dark, cold fear do to a cat? *Maybe it's as much a victim as Elizabeth.*

And maybe it was supposed to have been Brenna. The one the woman had asked for in the first place.

"It doesn't hurt," Elizabeth said in a wondering voice. "Shouldn't it hurt?"

It will, Brenna thought, but kept it to herself, feeling the relief of having Masera out there as her voice, saying things she could never say and keep her job. "It's all right," she told Elizabeth. The blood was thinning, and Brenna turned off the water, taking the towel from her shoulder to enfold Elizabeth's hands gently in it—the only field dressing she could produce on short notice. There were no chairs in the tub room; she led Elizabeth to the useless ramp the store had bought them—as if the average large dog would get any closer to a strange ramp than it would to a tub—and sat her on it, steadying her.

"I don't even want to look," Elizabeth whispered, regaining some of herself to look directly at Brenna again.

"It'll be okay," Brenna said firmly, and thought if she never had to say those words again it would be too soon.

Gary stuck his upper body through the door. Younger than Roger, not as authoritative if easier to talk to, he was the first assistant manager, and he rarely interacted with Brenna on shift. "Everything under control in here?" he asked. "Because I've got a customer—"

"No," Brenna interrupted, sharper than she was wise to be. "You know what? The customer's going to have to wait this time. Elizabeth needs to go to emergency; she needs someone to call her boyfriend to meet her there. Don't you dare walk out of here without making sure she's taken care of."

DeNise had been coming for the door behind him; she stopped short, her already spooked eyes widening further; Brenna had never seen her dark lips look so pale, or that pasty color half-mooning under her eyes. Gary, too, jerked to a halt, stopping his planned withdrawal from the room. Instead he straightened, bringing the rest of his body into the doorway. He eyed her a moment, probably

wondering whether he should call her on her tone
or simply appease her as necessary. Finally he gave
the slightest of shrugs and said, "What would you
like me to do?"

"You're our *manager*," she said, still pushing it and
having been pushed too hard herself to care. "Get
someone on the phone to cancel the appointments
for the rest of the day, for starters."

"Why can't you do—"

But he stopped short, for she'd turned on him
the way she'd take on a snarling dog, and he'd never
seen it in her before. The moment hung between
them like something waiting to explode, and then
Brenna said, very clearly, very carefully, "This would
not have happened if you and Roger and Celine
didn't ignore every plea we ever made for safety and
scheduling limits. Now that it *has*, you'll have to deal
with it. I'm supposed to be off shift. Please sign me
out as of right now. I'll take Elizabeth to the hospital. Before I go, I'll mark which dogs from the
next few days of scheduling need to be canceled.
You'll have to find someone to call them, to clean
up the grooming areas, and to clean up Elizabeth's
blood."

"We don't have anyone to spare," Gary protested.

"You know what? I don't care." And she didn't. "If
I come in here tomorrow and have to deal with any
of it, I'm gone."

"Don't say things you don't mean," he said. "Watch
yourself, Brenna."

"That's exactly what I'm finally doing." Brenna felt
Elizabeth tremble beside her and said, "Are you even
listening to yourself? How long has this woman
worked for you? How many times has she stayed over
hours, or skipped lunch, or faced dogs you wouldn't
even get *near*? Have you even asked how she *is*?"

No, of course he hadn't. But Gary wasn't Roger;
Roger would have bluffed it out. Gary simply hadn't

thought it through past the inconvenience to the store. Once her words hit him, once he looked, truly *looked*, at Elizabeth hunched over her wrapped hands, his face changed. "Okay," he said, quietly enough so she could barely hear him. "I'll clock you out. Mark the schedule for me and we'll call the customers."

Brenna nodded and looked to DeNise behind him; she still hadn't moved—afraid of attracting notice, no doubt, whether she stayed or fled. "DeNise," she said, blowing the young woman's cover as Gary glanced behind himself, "would you come sit with Elizabeth a moment?"

DeNise looked at Gary and seemed to gather herself. "Got to wait for the police to get here anyway," she said. "They want to talk to anyone, they'll want me."

True enough. Brenna exchanged a wan smile with her and put a hand on Elizabeth's shoulder. "I'll be right back," she said, letting her fingers trail down her friend's arm as she made way for DeNise. She would have slipped past Gary but he turned and led the way.

"If the cops are on their way, I've got my own calls to make," he said as the seriousness of the situation seemed to settle on him.

Finally.

Cat attacks were nasty, nastier than most people ever suspected or even wanted to believe. And this cat . . . this cat had been astonishingly vicious. At the best, Elizabeth had weeks of recovery before her. At the worst, she'd lose enough dexterity to affect her life and career. *We are not interchangeable and replaceable commodities*, Brenna thought at his back. *We're* not.

Which made her wonder why she had to convince even herself.

Gary left the grooming room for the back office,

and Brenna slid in behind the counter where Masera was still on the phone—animal control, maybe. Someone he knew, but he was using a reasonably formal voice, short and to the point as ever.

The counter itself was a mess, both levels of it covered with the remains of DeNise's soda and plenty of blood. They'd need a new schedule book, that was for sure, and replacements for the day's customer cards. Brenna made a quick assessment of the next several days of bookings, marked them, and scrawled a note instructing the caller to tell today's half-finished customers that a rescheduled grooming would be on the house. She pulled her wallet from her purse— a minimalist affair she could easily shove in her sweatshirt pocket—and stuffed the purse itself in behind her locked toolbox in the grooming room.

When she returned to the counter to hunt up Elizabeth's bulky monster of a purse—one of those cargo carry-everything bags—she found not only the cat's owner, but Mickey from the stockroom, standing behind her and looking oddly protective. Masera, still on the phone, gave Brenna a wary look, a strange kind of warning look, as Brenna shrugged her sweatshirt on and bent to yank Elizabeth's things from the lower shelf.

"I want to use the phone," the woman said. "I want to call my boyfriend. You can't take that cat from me. I've got rights."

Brenna couldn't decide if they were an unrelated string of statements or were somehow supposed to fit together. She reminded herself again that the cat was a beloved pet, taking a deep breath as she straightened with the cargo bag. "I'm sorry for your inconvenience. We all wish this hadn't happened. But it did, and now we have to deal with it. You'll have to wait for the police and animal control. Meanwhile, I'm sure Mickey can take you to a phone."

"*You're* Brenna Fallon," she said accusingly, while

Brenna looked at Mickey. *Mickey*. He who argued with Masera, who sold him dogs. The woman was oblivious. "You were right *there*. Why didn't *you* clip her nails? This wouldn't have happened."

"I expect it would have," Brenna said, and suddenly she *knew* it. "It just would have happened to *me*."

"You were right *there*," the woman repeated, not willing to let it go, not even though Brenna was already turning away.

"*You*," Brenna said, pinning a swift glare on her, "*let go* of the cat." And she headed for the back with the woman's gasp following her, knowing she'd been cruel and not caring. Not with the mental image of Elizabeth's blood on the walls.

By the time she reached the tub room, she'd decided to take Elizabeth's sedan—her own truck didn't have a back seat or an easy ride—and found the keys to it clipped inside a small front pocket of the cargo bag. DeNise slid away from the table to meet her and say in a low voice, "Did you see? It looks bad, girl," and shudder.

Brenna didn't respond directly, but she kept her voice just as low. "Don't let Gary talk you into making the phone calls unless you really want to. You've put in your hours for the day." She waited for DeNise to nod and, a little louder, she said, "I'll be back for my truck as soon as I can break away. DeNise, I've got Emily Brecken down on my contact sheet. Would you give her a call and ask her to let Druid out for me? And my mom—tell her I won't make dinner tonight." Then she slung the bag over her shoulder and went to Elizabeth. Elizabeth, taller than Brenna and a sturdily built woman, seemed oddly small inside the curve of Brenna's arm. But she wasn't as shaky as she'd been, and her face was no longer ghastly pale. "Ready to go?"

"*Now* it hurts," Elizabeth said. "I don't even want to look."

"Then don't," Brenna said, matter-of-factly. But for all of that, she needed a moment, herself. Just to close her eyes and sit against the wet towels on the grooming table and take a deep breath. Remind herself which of the city's hospitals was closest, and how to get there. Try to rid her ears of the sound of screaming, and the way her very soul had felt the fear of that bounding dark.

At that moment she felt an arm around her own shoulders, and the squeeze of a man's hand on the side of her neck, a touch against her temple—the side of his face.

And then it was gone, and she opened her eyes and took Elizabeth out to her car.

Brenna stayed at the hospital long enough to make sure Elizabeth's boyfriend was on the way, and then until they took her into the back room. She'd seen Elizabeth's hands by then, and wished she hadn't. The cat had bitten her again and again, puncturing her nails, leaving her fingers grotesquely swollen and badly mauled. All Brenna could think of was the wrongness of it—that it had happened to Elizabeth, that it had happened at all. She drove the unfamiliar car back along darkening streets, glad for the abundance of lights in the Pets! parking lot, and for the fact that although there were few cars in evidence, the store wasn't yet closed.

She pulled the sedan into the parking space next to her truck and sat there with her head resting on the wheel, debating whether to go inside and see if they'd cleaned up, to get her purse. To face the people there, and answer all their questions about Elizabeth.

But the walk suddenly seemed too long. And if anyone wanted to steal a purse with an old brush and a for-emergency-use tampon, they could have it. She climbed out of the car and hesitated over the unfamiliar electronic locks, finally settling for shoving down the physical locks and leaving it at that. Then she turned to her truck.

That was when she saw the tires were slashed.

She stared for a stupefied moment, taking in all the implications of it. Not just flat, slashed. Not just one tire, which she could change and be on her way, but two.

She'd have to go into the store after all. Call Triple A, hang around the parking lot for an hour or so until they showed up.

Masera's shadow preceded him, driven by the lights inside the store. "Well, hell," he said, when he realized what she was looking at.

"Are you *everywhere*?" she asked wearily. At her house after Sunny disappeared. At the store when the cat attacked. Sitting on her porch in the dark. His arm—it had been *his* arm—around her in the grooming room.

"I try to be," he said, humor in his voice, in the easy stance of his shadow next to hers.

"I can't decide if this makes you good luck or bad," Brenna muttered. And she couldn't. Every time she thought she knew or understood him, he did something that changed her mind. When he acted from his heart, it spoke to her in some way she couldn't understand. And when he shuttered his eyes and put evasions between them, it made her more wary than she'd ever felt about anyone else.

As if everything he said or did mattered more than it ought to, for good or for bad—and that made her wary, too.

"Let me drop you off at home," he said, and nodded at the auto club sticker in her back cab window. "You can call Triple A tomorrow once you get to work."

Brenna didn't respond right away. And when she did, she found herself saying not, *Okay, thanks* or

That makes sense, but, "That wasn't right. Nothing about that was right."

"No," he said.

"A cat wants to get away, it nails you and runs." Brenna hid her hands in her sleeves, and covered her eyes with them. "It might bite, it might claw, but it *runs*. This cat . . . This cat wanted to maul her."

"I saw," he said, and there was agreement in the way his shadow inclined its head toward her, a gesture she barely caught as she pulled her hands down just enough to look over them. "And," he added more sharply, looking at her, "I felt it."

She sighed, and eventually said, "So did I. But I don't know what it means or what to do about it."

"For starters," Masera said, and his voice had turned grim, "I don't think it's a coincidence that the cat's owner is Rob Parker's girlfriend."

"Oh," Brenna said, and groaned. "Oh, shit."

"Looks like you got his attention."

One more thing connecting Parker to the darkness. Not that Brenna had been left with much doubt. Although ordinary human hands wielding an ordinary knife had done the tire-slashing. *Mickey*, she thought suddenly, and then winced at the assumption. Just because he'd been standing by the woman, by Parker's girlfriend, like he knew her and felt some need to protect her.

No, not *just because*. Mickey, who'd argued with Masera and who'd sold him two pit bulls. And now he was connected somehow to Parker, who had a barn with dogs in it, plenty of supplements and medical supplies, a weird contraption out in the back—

The question popped out of her mouth before she even realized she'd formulated it. "Are you going to fight those pit bulls you bought?"

A blunt question in a quiet moment. He might refuse to answer it, but he couldn't misdirect or evade her.

He didn't do any of those. Without hesitation, he said, "No, I'm not."

She quit watching his parking light shadow and looked directly at him, searching his face to confirm the directness of his response. The realness of it. If he'd tried to convince her, if he'd piled words on top of that simple statement, she'd have lost the wire-thin connection he'd made with his answer.

But he didn't do that, either. He gave her the slightest of shrugs and the suggestion of a smile. An understanding smile, one that said *I know you're having a hard time believing in me* but leaving her to make up her own mind.

"Parker is, I think," she said. "I ought to call animal control, tip them off—"

"Animal control knows about the situation," he said, cutting her off short and hard, and his easiness from the moment before vanished. Brenna felt that wire of trust break and backlash as he turned to face her with a real anger. "You went there," he said. "After we got chased off by one of Parker's boys, you went back there."

"Didn't *you*?" she said, lashing back at him and taking a stab at more truth while she was at it.

"That's not the—" and he stopped short, and Brenna realized with astonishment that they were words he hadn't meant to happen, that he'd slipped and given her a real answer when he'd meant to be evasive.

It was a lot more revealing than he'd ever meant it to be, and he knew it, standing there with his eyebrows crowding the bridge of his nose. *That's not the point.* He *had* gone back, that's what it meant. And she'd gotten through to him at last, that's also what it meant. But he had himself back, now, and he said, "Let me drive you home; I'll bring you back in the morning. You don't really want to hang around here waiting for Triple A, not alone. Parker isn't one to take lightly."

Why? she wanted to ask him. *What do you know?* But she didn't push him any more. Enough for one night, and she was suddenly so tired she could hardly see straight. So she said, "Do you have any idea what time I have to be at work?"

He gave her a cocky grin. "I had to *sneak* to find the file, and I managed that. Your schedule's right there on the wall." Fishing his keys from his pocket, he jiggled them in his hand and nodded toward the SUV. "It doesn't matter. I've cancelled a lot of work in the past few days, and starting the day early will give me a chance to catch up. Eztebe is taking the flack, answering the phone at home—I think he's about to walk out on me. Which reminds me—do you still have my business card?"

Brenna hunted her wallet out of her pocket and pulled out the card, not caring what he might think about the fact that she not only had the card, she had it *on* her; her mind lingered on the way he said his brother's name, the way his tongue handled the unusual phonetics and then jumped right back to plain old boring English with only that hint of foreignness about it. Two different worlds, one man. Somehow it summed him up quite neatly.

"Here," he was saying, as he scribbled on the back of the card. "This is the home phone. Call it if you need anything and you can't get me on the cell."

Brenna gave it a glance as he returned the card. "Does it come with a secret code word, too?"

He snorted. "I'll make one up for you if you want it. Just don't hesitate to call. You ready?"

Home. Brenna did a quick mental inventory of her freezer, pessimistic about her chances of finding a frozen dinner there. If she'd eaten with her mother at the retirement community as was her habit a couple of times a month, it would have been Chicken Kiev and cheesecake for dessert.

Ah, well.

She followed Masera to his vehicle and climbed in, managing to avoid any expression of outright envy at the nifty interior features—lights here, cup holders there, and a CD player that he thumbed off as she entered so she didn't have a chance to catch anything but a few notes of something that sounded classical. He waited for her to buckle up and pulled smoothly out of the parking lot—and straight into the Burger King across the four-lane road.

"I haven't eaten," he said, when she looked at him. "And I don't imagine you have, either. Unless you got something seriously nasty from the hospital vending machine."

She shook her head, sinking into a sudden deep fatigue, and numbly offered up a food order when they reached the buzzy and incomprehensible speaker. She didn't argue when he paid for it, and she sat with their dinners warming her lap until he pulled up the long hill of her driveway fifteen minutes later. Emily had left the porch light on for her, bless her.

He pulled his burgers—two of them, and large fries to boot—from the bag and looked at where she sat gazing stupidly out the window. "Brenna," he said, "I'm not *everywhere*. Just where I want to be."

And that, she knew, should probably have some significance to her, something more than just the words themselves. But she clutched the bag and slid down to the ground from the high vehicle, muttering her thanks.

He smiled a crooked smile at her, suddenly looking just as tired as she felt. "Get some sleep. I'll pick you up tomorrow morning."

She woke up late the next day, alarm unset. She had just enough time to brush her hair out and rebraid it, using a surfeit of hair bands to double it up where she'd gotten sloppy, and to slap a toothbrush around in her mouth. She threw an apple and

some crackers into an old lunch tote, spilled food into
Druid's dish, and leashed him up to come along even
as he ate—he wouldn't have enough outside time to
follow it up with an entire day in the crate. She then
made the mistake of donning her vest with the tote
handles clenched in her teeth and the leash in one
hand, and managed to get her hair caught in both
the leash and the vest. As Masera's SUV pulled up
the driveway, she hopped out to meet it on one foot,
still pulling her sneaker on the other and leaving
Druid in a quandary over how to heel to such a gait.

Masera was still not a morning person.

That was fine; she didn't feel much like talking,
either. She ate her apple and gave Druid the core,
which he seemed to find a novel experience and
worth much extra drooling and excessive chewing. The
Pets! parking lot was empty aside from her truck—
not unusual for the managers to push the opening
to the limit, never seeming to understand that she
needed time to prep for the day's work *before* the
first customer got there—but she thanked Masera and
bailed out anyway, glad enough for the time to walk
Druid along the grassy fringes of the parking lot. He
didn't show any signs of flipping out against the lead;
he'd been unconcerned about the parking lot since
that first day.

Soon enough she was wishing she'd grabbed her
sweatshirt, too, for the clear day wasn't nearly as warm
as it looked. And looking at the truck, canted sideways with both driver's-side tires slashed, she felt less
and less confident about being here alone. So she
jogged up and down the edge of the building until
Roger finally pulled into the lot, and fell in behind
him as he fumbled with his impressive set of keys
and eventually got the door open, saying nothing
much to her at all.

Roger was not a morning person, either.

Then, suddenly wary of what she might find,

Brenna hesitated before the grooming room. The glass was clean; not even a smear where yesterday it had been splattered and dripping. But then, all the managers had always insisted on impeccable glass at the storefront. Brenna had spent many a slow winter day cleaning the double set of airlocked doors.

She pushed her way inside, and had to concede that at first glance, someone had tried, truly tried, to clean and neaten. Nothing to be done about the mess of a schedule book; she grabbed a sheet of notepaper, also stained but serviceable, and started the list of clean-up chores. *New schedual*—darn, and cross out—*new schedule book*. When she looked up, her first customer was on his way in. Chubby little Bichon Frise—*Bitchin' Frizzy* she and Elizabeth called the crabby members of the breed, of which there fortunately weren't many—and Brenna could tell at a glance that no matter what the owner wanted, there were too many mats in that soft coat to do anything but a cut-down.

Well, he'd dry fast.

DeNise came in an hour after Brenna arrived, looking tired, glancing as carefully around as Brenna herself had done. "Not too bad," she said, although Brenna was already discovering sneaky stray blots and spatters—on the phone, along the edge of the counter. Inevitable, she supposed; they'd probably be discovering the widely strewn blood evidence of the attack for weeks.

"Glad you think so," Brenna said. "Two baths waiting for you, and the Bichon should be ready to lose the dryers."

DeNise took a deep breath. "Here goes," she said, and disappeared into the tub room.

Here goes just about set the tone for the day. Nonstop. Barely enough time for Brenna to call Elizabeth's cohabitating boyfriend and learn that Elizabeth was sleeping off painkillers but that the doctors were worried only about her thumb, which had been bitten into the joint, and that while she'd be off grooming for several weeks, she could come man the counter a week or so earlier. After that it seemed like just about everyone in the store had time to drift through the grooming room and ask about the incident. Roger stopped by to ask a few pertinent questions, but Brenna gathered that he'd shown up the day before while the police were there, and pretty much knew the details.

If he called to ask about Elizabeth, she didn't know about it. He didn't ask *her*, that's all she knew.

Near the end of her shift, she remembered what else she'd meant to do the day before, which was to call Emily and sic her and the girls on Mars Nodens through the Internet.

Which is what she was doing when Sammi came into the store, her face grim for the second time Brenna had ever seen; Brenna put the phone to her shoulder and said a wary "What?" by way of greeting.

"It's not on the news yet," Sammi said. "They're keeping it out until they can learn more."

"*What?*" Brenna said, not willing to wait even the moment it took Sammi to frame her next words.

"Rabies." Breathing even more heavily than normal in her upset, she repeated, "Rabies. The man who took one of the dogs Janean rescued. He's dead."

Brenna didn't even ask. Of course the dog had been through quarantine or had its shots on record. Of course this shouldn't have happened.

And then, with Sammi waiting on the other side of the counter and Emily tucked away on her shoulder, her phone-remote voice saying *what do you mean, rabies?*, Brenna knelt to where Druid sat at her feet and ran her finger around his collar until she found the tag she'd cleaned what seemed like ages ago. *Rabies I/II*, it said.

Druid whined uneasily, looking at her with earnest

love-me eyes, his speckle-backed ears dropped back against his head in worry and in acceptance of her hands. A second whine, a thinking-too-hard whine, and Brenna's world whirled slightly, with someone else's words in her head.

Shedding rabies.

Chapter 13

THURISAZ
Foreseeing

If Roger had had his way, Brenna wouldn't have gotten days off at all. But for now, she had considerable power with Pets!—if she walked, the store would be without a groomer. If she left on bad terms, she could worsen the already tenuous reputation Pets! had in the grooming community. So today she was out and about, decompressing. Not working.

Most groomers preferred the uncertain hours and higher wages per hour to the Pets! unusual retail schedule structure. Most preferred having more control over how they charged for their extra work, or for hazard duty with rough animals. Brenna had once opted for the health insurance that a Pets! position provided, and now found herself staying through inertia.

Or misguided loyalty.

Be loyal to Brenna, she thought, jamming her backpack full of books outside the Parma Hill library. Paperbacks, mostly, because she could fit in more of them in one trip, but one hardcover thriller she'd snatched from the *new* rack and couldn't resist. As if she needed any more thrills in her life right now. This one was a Robin Cook, too—but he was writing about organ conspiracies again, and not plagues or rabies.

The day—not her usual day off but nothing was *usual* of late—had been too gorgeous to waste. After an early trip to the spring with Druid, some target practice and a little much-needed, old-fashioned rug beating—a token nod to the spring cleaning to which she ought to be subjecting the house—Brenna pulled her bike out of the barn, topped off the air in the tires, and headed the handful of miles into town. She had books to return, but mostly it was just for the ride. The sun on her shoulders, the breeze in her face, the pleasant burn of active muscles in her legs. Of course, with her hair bundled up to avoid the bicycle spokes, her jeans taped with duct tape to stay out of the chain, her vented helmet, and the dorky sunglasses she found that fit her and the helmet both, she was also the ultimate in biking geekery.

As a glance at her ghostly reflection in the slightly smoked library glass door panels confirmed. *You've definitely got it*, she told herself in mock solemnity, but refrained from giving herself a thumbs-up. That would be too weird.

And there were already enough weird things going on in her life.

She swung a leg over the bike and wove her way through small-town traffic, flipping to a higher gear once she reached the shoulder of a more open road. The later part of the afternoon was ahead of her . . . maybe she'd get to some of those cleaning

chores yet. Or maybe she'd finally put that new dryer
vent hose in place. Or what the heck, maybe she'd
sit down in the hammock with a good heavy quilt and
read a book.

A crossroad presented itself; a different way home,
but not much longer. On an impulse, she cruised
around the corner.

Or maybe not much of an impulse after all. For
there, bright white in the sunshine, the church cried
out for her attention. And she thought of what Masera
had once said, that the Christian philosophy wasn't
contradictory to the idea that Mars Nodens lived in
her backyard. Well, maybe that's not exactly what he'd
said. Something about them not being mutually exclusive. Brenna stopped pedaling, straightening, leaving
the bike to follow the road on its own.

Reverend Dayne's car sat in the incomplete spring
shade of the single mature tree at the edge of the
parking lot. There'd been more, lots more, before the
ice storm of the early nineties, but now all they had
was one scarred maple and a scattering of staked
saplings.

Brenna's bike seemed to make the decision for her,
wobbling slightly in its trajectory. She leaned over the
handlebars and swooped into the parking lot, leaving the bike unlocked and the backpack leaning by
the front wheel with her helmet propped against it.

She found Dayne in his office, absorbed in nota-
tions. *Writing his sermon*, she thought with guilt,
knowing she was interrupting, suddenly not so sure
this was a good idea anyway. And then he flipped a
page and she realized he was looking at a television
guide. Perversely, the discovery took away her nerves;
she stifled a grin and cleared her throat, leaning in
the doorway. Abruptly aware that her dorky sunglasses
hung from her fingers, she jammed the earpiece into
her back pocket.

Her presence startled him, which she hadn't

expected, either, especially since she hadn't been particularly stealthy. He touched his ear—*a hearing aid?*—and that, too made him seem more human. More approachable.

"Brenna," he said. "I'm surprised to see you." Then he must have realized how it sounded, for he smiled. "Glad, of course. But after a gap of so many years, I expected more time to pass before our next encounter."

"I've been thinking," she said, and she had, too—furiously, these past several minutes, about just the right way to ask this. And still she hunted for words.

"I can see that you have," he said, after a moment of struggling silence. "I didn't mean to take your presence lightly."

"If a culture hadn't been exposed to Christianity yet, or to the Old Testament Yahweh," she said, slowly enough so she could take back a word in an instant if it felt like the wrong one, "and yet God was acting among them, then they'd have to find their own words and ways to explain what was happening, don't you think?"

"I'm certain you're right," he said, frowning. No doubt trying to understand how this fit with her previous discussion.

"So if that culture called the power they believed to be responsible by their own name of, say, George . . . then you or I might call them heathens, but wouldn't we be wrong? Wouldn't that mean they were only identifying God in the best way they knew how?"

Dayne was still frowning, but it looked more thoughtful than before. "God has worked through prophets to make sure we *do* know who He is."

"Yes, in the culture that we consider to be dominant," Brenna said. "But I should think God would be wise enough to choose a method that best suited the culture he was working within."

A slow smile spread across his face. "I'm not sure

I can agree with the fact that God isn't *wise enough*
be able to get his point across to anyone he wants
to," he said. "But this conversation truly does make
me wish I could entice you to the women's study
group. A fresh point of view would be most welcome.
It would give me time to consider the question more
thoroughly—in truth, I'm caught a little short here.
Maybe I've been a little too complacent lately, comfortable with counseling bereavements and divorce
issues."

"Well," Brenna said, "it's not like I called ahead.
And really, just being in a position where I had to
put the questions into words has helped." Because
no matter what the pastor's reaction had been to her
last comment, Brenna felt something inside her ease
as soon as her words came out. Differing labels wasn't
a complete resolution to her dilemma . . . but it felt
like it was close.

He reached for a fresh piece of paper, scrawled
down a couple of lines. "You might find these books
helpful, if you have a chance to get them. I don't
think the library has them, but they can borrow from
the city library."

Brenna took the paper from him. *Robin Lane Fox,
Ramsey MacMullen.*

"I don't remember the exact titles," he said, nodding at the paper. "The best Fox book is *Pagans and
Christians*, I believe. But go looking for those two
authors, and almost anything you find will be on the
subject."

"Thank you," she said, sticking the note in her back
pocket. Maybe when she returned this batch of books,
she'd ask about it. "Sorry to have interrupted."

Outside, she donned her helmet. The sun had
dropped low enough, behind her, that she stuck the
sunglasses in her pack before she shrugged it on. She
headed back for the road in a more thoughtful mood.
She was on the right track to reconciling her

relationships with two different belief systems—
supposing it was possible—but she hadn't gotten there
yet. And she needed to get there, because as a girl
she'd made a call to a very specific deity, and in
retrospect—knowing how impossible it was for the old
hound to have rallied, knowing what Masera had told
her and of all the recent events—it seemed obvious
that the . . . being . . . had responded. *If I'm going to
believe in the darkness, I darn well better believe Mars
Nodens*—or something—*was there first*. And Mars
Nodens—*or something*—had answered that specific
call when her early prayers had gotten her nowhere.

Which seemed very much to indicate a difference
in the beings involved. *The gods involved*.

It was hard to even think those last words. She
made herself face them, to linger on them. At least
Masera hadn't made any indication that he considered the darkness to be a devil analogy. Then
again . . . she wasn't certain he considered Mars
Nodens an actual god, either.

She groaned out loud with the awareness that she'd
have to ask him about these confusions, see if she
could pry more answers from his closemouthed self.
And also with the awareness that however she came
to peace within herself, it might never be on terms
that satisfied her own religious community.

She had nearly made it home, had reached the
long stretch of travel along the road that ran in front
of her house and had her pasture in sight, when a
vehicle came up behind her . . . and didn't pass her.
She hugged the shoulder, as close as she could come
without slipping off the pavement to the gravelly dirt,
and still it didn't pass her; she could hear the radio
blaring inside; then it cut off.

A man's voice yelled at her, incomprehensible over
the noise of the vehicle and the wind in her ears.
A trickle of uncertainty took up residence between
her shoulders; she found herself calculating how

quickly she could swap directions—faster than a car, that was for sure—and how long it would take her to reach the last house she'd passed.

Too long.

A glance behind showed her a small, square-fronted vehicle. She didn't recognize it, but at her look the shouting from within repeated itself. She bent over her handlebars, wondering if she should just ditch the bike and go cross-country, where the car couldn't follow—but as long as her legs were, they'd never been particularly swift. She pedaled hard. *I don't see you. You're not there. I'm just minding my own business. Almost home.*

If he wanted her, if he caught her anywhere, it would be going up that hill of a driveway. *Damn.*

Another car approached from the opposite direction; she thought about trying to catch the driver's attention—how? and say what?—and too late; it whooshed past.

As soon as it did, the car behind her accelerated; she heard the change in engine pitch. It pulled out and alongside her, with the driver still shouting, leaning over to the passenger window and steering with one extended arm. Great. If he didn't run her over on purpose, he'd do it by accident.

Brenna slowed, letting him pull ahead of her, getting her first good look at the vehicle—and suddenly it all fell together. A small, Jeep-like sport vehicle, the shouting—*Brenna*, he'd said, at least some of it—and the dark hair, the bold nose of the driver. She came to a dead stop; he pulled over to the shoulder just in front of her, and she dismounted the bike to walk with furious strides up to the passenger window.

"*Eztebe!*" she said, and hit his car for emphasis, "what the *hell* are you doing stalking me down the road? Don't you know any better than to scare a woman like that?" And she hit his car again, with the flat of her hand and making plenty of noise.

Enough to get him out of the car, looking at her over top of it, unable to reach her but stretching out his arms anyway, his hands spread against the roof. "Brenna!" he said. "*Ez dut ulertzen*—please, why are you upset? I done nothing!"

"Why do you *think* I'm upset?" Brenna said, but she didn't hit the car again. Her hand still stung from the last time. "How do the women in *your* country feel when a stranger lurks behind them?"

"But you know me," he said, true confusion apparent. "I'm Iban's brother, we talked at my door."

She hissed in irritation. "We talked *once*, Eztebe. We didn't do it with you on one side of your windshield and me on the other, moving down the road at thirty-five miles an hour!"

He took on an *uh-oh* look. Much easier to read than his brother. "The car," he said. "You did not remember it."

"No, not at first." She bit her lip, frowned through it. "You called me by name. I never gave that to you. And why did you stop me, anyway?"

"Iban pointed you out at the store," Eztebe said. That was bound to happen, she supposed.

"I stopped you because I am here on this road to see you, anyway. Your house is not far, I think."

That wasn't. She stared her most direct stare at him. "And you know where I live . . . how? Do you Masera brothers make me a habit or something? Haven't you got anything better to do?"

He scratched the back of his neck and said tentatively, "The phone book? Your address is right there."

"Meaning you didn't ask your brother."

"No, he doesn't know—" Eztebe stopped, scowled, and said, "This isn't going right."

"I don't suppose it is." She toed her bike's kickstand down, shifting the backpack. Too many books. "You've got about thirty seconds to *make* it go right. After that, I'm going home to call the police. That probably wouldn't do your visa any good, would it?"

That alarmed him, all right. "No, no—let me get some thoughts straight." He closed his eyes, fingertips massaging little circles at each temple. It didn't take him long, which was good for him as far as Brenna was concerned. He'd already used at least forty-five of his thirty seconds. "First, I apologize for scaring you. It was thoughtlessness of me." He hesitated as another car, too much in need of a muffler to talk over, passed them. "Iban speaks of you; I know he has been here. To your home, I mean, not this side of the road."

"I would think he goes to many homes," Brenna said, still without any understanding of what had prompted this visit, and getting impatient. *More* impatient. "Considering his line of work, I mean. What's the *point*?"

"The point." Eztebe shrugged suddenly, offering up his hands. "I worry about him. He keeps something from me, and it sits on him. He comes home with injuries all over his face. He buys young dogs not for himself, works with them, does not try to sell them. He does these things without sense."

"The pit bulls," Brenna said. "Fighting dogs."

"Yes," Eztebe said. "Not that I know things so well over here, but I see them on the TV."

"He said he wasn't going to fight the dogs." Brenna shifted the pack again, debated whether to shed it altogether.

"There, I was right. You *do* know things."

"No, I knew *a* thing. That was it. What on earth makes you think he talks to me?"

Eztebe shrugged again, a smaller response that revealed something of his despair over it all. "The truth is . . . I do not know that he does. If I were less worried, I would never bother you. But my brother is in trouble, I think, so I do everything I can think of. He has spent time with you. He points you out at the store. He mentions your name at home. So, I think of you."

"Is he in trouble so often?" Her shoulders won; Brenna slipped the pack to the ground and rested it against her leg.

Eztebe gave her a wry smile. "He is in trouble never. That is why it worries me so much to think that now, he is." He hesitated, and drummed his fingers on the top of the car. Finally he said, "And also, he tells me you have a place of power on your land." He glanced at her, a wary look, as though he thought Masera had betrayed a confidence to tell him and now he was betraying Masera to reveal that he knew.

And Brenna thought that Masera had, and that Eztebe was.

She took a deep breath, and forced the sudden tension from her body, right out her fingers and toes. It didn't work. With much effort, she unclenched her hands. Masera, she would yell at. She would let *him* take Eztebe to task, if he chose.

"I thought that might be part of it," Eztebe said, growing bold in her silence.

"I don't think so." Brenna couldn't help an involuntary glance at the pasture, the front part of which ran along the road, although the spring was not visible from here. "There *is* something going on. Frankly, Eztebe, there's a hell of a lot going on, and I'm not sure I can put any of it together. But I can tell you that he keeps things from me, too. Whatever he's up to, it's something else besides what he's found in my pasture and how he's helped me with my dog."

"Funny-looking dog," he said, and grinned at her, a woefully transparent—if earnest—attempt to earn back her good will. "But in a strange way, very handsome."

"He's a wonderful dog," Brenna said, having grown

used to Druid's short legs and long body and hardly even registering Eztebe's initial, poking-fun comment. It'd been good-natured enough, and a Corgi *was* an odd sight to those who'd never seen one before. Eztebe, she assumed, had seen Druid at the store. "But even the way he came to me is part of the strangeness." She shook her head. "Look, I'd tell you what I knew if I *knew* anything. But you know, Masera—"

"Iban," said Eztebe, eyebrows raised. "If he calls you Brenna, in this country, surely you are right to call him Iban."

"Only if I want to," Brenna said, pointedly enough to evince a flinch from Eztebe. "What I was saying was, he doesn't owe me anything. He has less reason to tell me any of his secrets than he has to tell his own brother. And he hasn't."

He raised an eyebrow at her. "You might think less of yourself than you should. Or maybe you think more of me. Iban and I have not been close. We care, but our lives have been spent apart since he left Euskal Herria. It is a funny thing, too. He had more time with our mother when she allowed herself to work; he had the time to learn of what she knew. He has the more feel for it. But it is he who went away, and I who stayed."

"Your mother doesn't . . . work . . . anymore?"

Eztebe glanced away. He was going to say something he was afraid she'd find offensive, then; she'd already learned that of him. Just the opposite of Masera, who deliberately looked you right in the eye. *Watching to see if you had the nerve to bite back at him*, she realized, and recalling that the first time, she'd all but chased him out of the room. For some reason it made her want to smile—but Eztebe wouldn't have understood, so she didn't. She listened to him instead. "My father wished not. She has her land, he says, but he is the one to work in the family.

She only ever wanted to help people, but . . . it is not always a safe thing, to be sorgin, and she agreed to his wishes. I was half-grown, then."

Brenna could feel nothing but the sadness of that, although Eztebe seemed oblivious enough, in his strange mix of Old World upbringing and New World awareness. "Maybe that's why Masera left," she said. "So he wouldn't have to watch her not do what sounds so important to her."

He jerked his gaze back to her, startled. "Maybe that is so."

"And what about you?" she said, turning the tables on him. He'd thought to get information from her; let him provide the same for her. She looked over to her pasture. "What do you think about the place of power by my spring? What do *you* think of whatever I connected with? Is it God? Is it *a* god? Is it blasphemy?"

At first it looked like he wasn't going to answer, that he'd just shrug her off. Then he said, "It bothers you."

Brenna said dryly, "Only intensely."

"You know," he said, still sounding reluctant—as though it were private. Or maybe that he didn't really expect her to truly understand, no matter what he said— "different people think different things. There are churches thinking Yainko commands smaller powers with personalities. That they act out His will on Earth. Angels, they say."

"Angels . . ." Brenna said. Angels. She'd never gone for the whole angel craze herself, not the cutesie ones or the New Age ones or the sappy ones on TV. But *angel* was just a term; the various modern perceptions sprang from the culture dealing with them. Angels were messengers and conduits . . . and if they'd been present in a culture not yet exposed to a One God, then what would keep people from considering the messengers to be gods themselves? To name them and discover their likes and their affinities . . . to touch them, and give them an easy way to touch back.

Mars Nodens, in her pasture.

Part of her wanted to weep with relief.

Eztebe looked like his brother then, watching her with tight scrutiny, his eyes even taking on the hooded gaze Masera took on when something struck him as significant—or when he was about to offer some subtle dare or challenge. Eztebe, she thought, was daring her to say something to belittle his comments, his people . . . his mother.

"Thank you," she said, her voice low and edged with the emotion he'd brought her. Given her, really, like a gift.

He looked away, once again nonconfrontational—and from his smile, gratified. "You should meet my ama—my mother—maybe."

Brenna grinned. "She should see my pasture, maybe."

"Maybe." He slid back inside the car, so she had to bend to the open passenger window to hear him. "I hope you'll tell me if you learn anything. Maybe with the two of us, we can stop Iban from his trouble."

"I don't think he'll ever tell me anything he doesn't quite specifically choose to tell me," Brenna said. "But I'll let you know. It'll be worth it, don't you think, to see the look on his face if I call and ask to speak to you?"

"I'll look forward to it. I promise to describe it to you."

Brenna stepped away from the car and watched it pull away, waiting until it was out of sight before reaching for her backpack. Eztebe had eased her mind on some counts . . . and roiled it on others.

Then again, where Masera was involved, there was nothing new about that.

❖   ❖   ❖

Life got quiet.

Almost too quiet, with such an absence of the strange events that had so bombarded her life that she began to doubt herself—what she'd experienced, the conclusions she'd been struggling toward. If it had all been real and true, would it suddenly have *stopped*?

On the other hand, with the grooming schedule she was holding down, having quiet in the rest of her life was undeniably a mercy. She arrived home from work each day exhausted in body, mind, and soul, and with nothing left over for inexplicable crises, though she rescheduled her dinner date with her mother, enjoyed her Aunt Ada's recent adventures in flirtation on a short bus tour of the Finger Lakes country, planted tomatoes in indoor flats, and put peas into the ground. Sunny's death receded to a poignant ache and Druid became her shadow. More importantly, he stopped having fits. He whined as he chewed his bones, he stood in the middle of the den and whined when there was nothing to whine about, but he didn't have fits.

At least, not when she didn't push him into it at the spring. Even then . . . he started to listen to her through his fear; the flinging and screaming and cursing shortened in duration each time. Then she'd put him downhill with the latest greasy basted shank bone she'd bought for just this purpose, and she'd sit by the spring and hope to touch something of that which she'd felt here before. It didn't happen, but the meditative time soothed her.

She never saw Parker. She didn't know if he'd taken her seriously or if he just came to the spring when he'd discovered she didn't. As Masera had pointed out, her work schedule was easy enough to divine, especially with Mickey in the loop.

And now that she'd come to recognize the darkness, it all but disappeared. Sometimes she thought she felt its brief touch . . . and sometimes she thought she'd been standing in a draft. Perhaps Emily felt her lack of urgency, for she apologetically mentioned that the girls were deeply buried in a 4-H project, and that unless Brenna was frantic for the information, it'd be a few more days before they could wield their Internet know-how on Brenna's request for information on Mars Nodens.

Brenna had to admit that she wasn't frantic for anything but more Pets! groomers.

Elizabeth visited the store a couple of times, and after a week and half started talking about returning to man the counter. Brenna narrowed the groomer applicants down and scheduled interviews, and the Pets! management, although typically failing to address the issue directly with her, kept their hands off the schedule book. She saw Masera at the store, and sometimes he stopped by the grooming room just in time to help her with an especially unruly creature. He didn't question her methods any longer—and that, she thought, spoke more to her about him than almost anything else he'd done. The fact of it dwelt inside her like something small and warm and waiting to hatch.

She kept his card in her wallet.

The thing that worried her most, that stuck in her mind as she carried the grooming workload and immersed herself in spring cleanup around the farm, finalizing another year of leasing out the ten back acres for corn, marking the barn leaks and sags and walking the fence line to fix what she could and make note of the rest, was the look that often settled on Sammi's face, whether she was in the store for supplies or to oversee an adoption day. She was no longer talking about the man's death, was no longer talking about rabies at all. Brenna had the distinct feeling that she'd been warned to silence by authorities who didn't want a panic, although the incident had been announced on the news, along with the fact that the dog had been put down and its brain tested—positive, no surprise to anyone. It answered the question about where Janean had gotten the rabies, and with the dog dead, also officially ended the threat.

Except that Brenna knew what Sammi knew, which was that the dog had gone through quarantine, and still hadn't been sick at the time of its new owner's death. The Centers for Disease Control knew it, too, because they had copies of all of PePP's records. But no one said anything about that part of it anymore, not even Sammi. *Especially* not Sammi.

A silence that said more to Brenna than any amount of normal questioning.

The day before Elizabeth's return, in the morning lull immediately after Brenna opened and with Gary in the back doing mysterious manager-type things, Brenna found herself savoring the quiet half-hour before the first scheduled customer, lining the day's index cards up on the lower counter and trying to come up with the best strategy for getting through them all. DeNise could brush and prep this one out, she decided, putting a card to the side, and could be counted on to bathe several medium-sized mixed-breeds without help or intervention; those cards went to the side as well.

She was startled when the door to the parking lot was yanked open—not a customer moseying in, but someone with great intent and no time to waste; Brenna could tell that even before she looked up. Still, she was entirely surprised to find Mickey there, looming over her from the other side of the counter. Not as though he had any particular intent to threaten her, but like it was simply his default mode although, in the first instant, Brenna couldn't be sure just why he was there—for work related reasons or because of Parker—and her confusion must have shown on her face.

Mickey didn't seem to care or even to notice. "I'm outta here," he said, rapping out the words. "You hang with Gil, I've seen you. Tell him this for me—" and Brenna almost lost his next words, so unused to thinking of Masera as Gil that she couldn't understand who Mickey meant. "Tell him it's been moved to Thursdays, same time."

"Tell him what?" Brenna said, still unable to understand what the whole thing was about.

"Heard me, didn't you? Tell him that. You don't gotta understand." He glanced inside and must have seen something he didn't like, because he reached for the exterior door. "You're his friend, you tell him that. Otherwise, like I said, he could be sorry. And you tell him to keep his mouth shut if he's stupid enough to get in that position."

And out he went, not straight out to the parking lot but directly off to the side; an instant later something out of sight peeled rubber—he'd either left the vehicle running or he'd jumped into the passenger side.

Before she'd even had time to process what had just happened, Gary came through the storeside door at what could only be called a run. "Was that Mickey Hefler?" he demanded.

Bemused, Brenna nodded; that was all for which she had time.

"What'd he want?"

That, she didn't answer right away, because Masera's business was none of Gary's business, no matter how little sense any of it made. "He asked me to deliver a message, that's all. What's the big deal?"

"What's the message?"

"Well," Brenna said, carefully neutral in tone, "it wasn't for you." Then, when she saw his response building, she shrugged. "It didn't involve the store," she said, in case that's what he wanted to hear, and then repeated, "What's the big deal?"

"There's been food product missing over the last couple of months," Gary said, and in that moment went from being ready to pull a manager-bully moment on her to venting *to* her. "We had a couple of stockboys in mind for it. Mickey was at the top of the list."

"I get the feeling someone tipped him," Brenna said, finding herself irritated to be holding a message from Mickey-in-trouble to Masera whose brother suspected he was in trouble. "I don't think he's coming back."

Gary stared at the empty parking lot for a moment and made a frustrated growling noise in his throat. "Fine," he said. "I'll bet whoever tipped him is still here." He went back into manager mode and gave Brenna a pointed look. "Don't tell anyone else about this."

Well, no. Except for Masera, who'd get his message when she saw him, along with a pointed question or two. But Brenna didn't remind Gary of that detail, just nodded. "Okay," she said, and went back to her schedule work.

Even with the odd Mickey incident, in the end the weeks added up to a seasonal normalcy, and Brenna allowed herself to be distracted by the normal routines of life, to fall into complacence. The day Elizabeth came back to work, dragging and grouching about the preventative antibiotics she'd been on, Brenna wasn't even thinking about the darkness or Druid's fits or even the way Masera had of catching her eye from the sales floor for just a moment of contact and the briefest of smiles, though she hadn't seen him for days. She was just working.

"The Damned Cat went home, I heard," she said, coming out to take a breather and assess the schedule for the rest of the day. Elizabeth had come in hours after Brenna and DeNise, once they were immersed in work and could use her help—handling the phone when things got crazy, intercepting the customer interaction, coming back to distract and beguile the wiggly dogs so Brenna could work quickly. In general, making Brenna's life a whole lot easier.

"I guess so," Elizabeth said. "No surprise. The damned Damned Cat ought to have been put down, if you ask me."

"You've got my vote there," Brenna said, which was all she *could* say without explaining about the darkness she was so sure had been involved. "Who's coming in next?"

Elizabeth smiled a wicked little smile, but her eyes looked tired. "Jeremy Cocker. In for a summer cut-down."

Brenna made a face. Nasty little biter, Jeremy was. Although . . . she'd noticed of late, that some of the less irredeemable dogs—the ones who simply hadn't ever been told they weren't the boss of the world—weren't as much of a problem for her as usual. As though she were somehow regaining a little of the feel she'd had as a child, the ability to touch them deeper than words or human dominance role-playing ever could.

Maybe Jeremy wouldn't be so bad today.

Though Elizabeth didn't look so good. Brenna said, "You okay? Maybe a full day the first time back was too much."

Rubbing her throat, Elizabeth scoffed. "A full day of *what*? Answering the phone? Copying over the customer cards that got too nasty?" She splayed her fingers. None of them were splinted anymore, but several were Vetrapped, and very few of them seemed to bend properly; they all bore scabs surrounded by angry red and shiny flesh. "I suppose I should feel lucky I'm doing this much so soon. It's those damned pills."

"Damned Cat's Damned Pills," Brenna muttered nonsensically.

Elizabeth burst into laughter; she shook her head when Brenna glanced at her, surprised. "You've been living alone too long, Bren," she said, reaching for her sports water bottle and rubbing her throat as she swallowed. Again.

Something in the oft-repeated gesture rooted Brenna to the spot, giving her chills from the base of her skull all the way to her heels.

Rabies. Wildly known as hydrophobia because its victims *couldn't swallow*. And the timing, though on the short end, was still right. From five days to as long as a year, with a couple of months average before the symptoms showed up. And then flulike symptoms for a week. More or less. And then the classic symptoms. The swallowing. The thickened saliva. Even as Brenna watched, Elizabeth took another sip, swished her mouth, and laboriously swallowed.

Ridiculous. The cat had had its shots, had gone through quarantine and returned home.

So had the dog Janean rescued.

She opened her mouth to say something and nothing came out. What could she possibly say? A suggestion that Elizabeth get checked for a disease she'd been inoculated against, a disease that meant certain death once it became symptomatic?

And yet Brenna had no doubt. And even as she couldn't bring herself to say anything, she couldn't stand the thought of one more moment of *not* saying anything, of watching Elizabeth struggle to swallow.

"Take Jeremy in if they get here, will you?" she said suddenly, her voice sounding a false note in her ears. "If I don't take this chance to run to the restroom, I might explode before I get another."

"Go," Elizabeth said, waving an imperious hand as she made some final notes on the card for the young Springer Spaniel Brenna had in the back.

Brenna fled to the bathroom at the rear of the store, beyond the looming shelves piled high with dog food. Slamming the stall closed behind her, she leaned against the door, covering her face with her hands, pressing her fingers against the instant sting of tears in her eyes. *Stop it,* she told herself. *Stop it, stop it,* stop it. *You can't be so sure. You're being ridiculous.*

She grabbed a wad of tissue, blew her nose, and made use of the facility. Stalling for time. By the time she reached the mirror at the sink, her nose was only mildly outrageous in its redness, and her cheeks residually shiny. Splashing cold water on her face helped; she blotted it dry with a rough paper towel and decided she could pass for overtired, which she was.

But when she left the bathroom, she found she couldn't bring herself to return to the grooming room. She found herself pacing back and forth in the short hallway that held the bathroom alcove, not even mindful of the fact that Roger's office was at the other end of it and that of all things, she didn't want to have to explain herself to him.

Masera's voice came to her ear, a cadenced rise and fall as he spoke to one of his clients, his words not audible but the effect somehow making his accent more obvious to her. Without even thinking, she followed it, bursting around the corner of a tall shelf and surprising them all when she nearly plowed through Masera, customer, and dog—a chronically happy Golden Retriever who flung himself at her with protestations of love.

"*That's* what I'm talking about," the customer said, as the dog planted one big foot in Brenna's gut and the other jammed her breast. Modest though it was, that body part still knew insult when it landed.

"My fault," Brenna said, trying not to squeak. "I wasn't watching—"

But Masera had intercepted the leash and stepped

on it, calmly asking the dog to go to a down position, removing his foot and repeating until the dog, all but bursting from its skin with the desire to express its exuberance to the world, stayed down. "That's what *I'm* talking about," he said. "Every time he gets out of hand. And you might want to think about making sure his food doesn't include corn. It's like feeding sugar to a child before bedtime."

The middle-aged man gave him a dubious look, running a hand over his bald pate as though to smooth hair that was no longer there—or maybe to check just in case something had grown back. "Corn? It matters?"

"It matters," Masera assured him, and stepped back just enough to make it clear he was moving on. "See you in class."

"Half an hour," the man said, perhaps confirming that he indeed knew when the class started. As soon as he stepped out, the Golden sprang to his feet and bounded away, taking the man with him.

"He'll figure it out," Masera said, watching him go—and then added thoughtfully, "Or else his chiropractor's going to make out." But despite his light words, when he turned to her, he had his serious face on. "What's wrong?"

She knew why she'd come to him, but those weren't the words she heard leaving her mouth. "Mickey stopped by early yesterday morning," she said. "He had a message for you."

"He did?" Masera evidently found the idea as startling as she had, the way his brows drew together.

"So he said. He wanted me to tell you that it was changed to Thursdays, same time. And not to go to the first time, or you'd be sorry, but if you were sorry, you'd better keep your mouth shut."

Well, it meant something to *him*. "Mickey's a fool," he muttered, anger shutting down his features.

"I don't suppose you'll tell me what that's all about."

"No." He looked right at her, captured her with the strength of it.

She felt like growling at him. She *did* growl at him. But she didn't pursue it—not now—and she had enough on her mind that she didn't even linger over it, nursing resentment. Standing there in front of him, with the flush of emotion still on her cheeks, her thoughts went straight back to the front of the store, drawn with the same horror that makes people gape at accident scenes.

"Maybe I should ask again," Masera said, pulled out of his anger by her disquieted distraction. "What's wrong?"

Brenna wrinkled her nose. "Nothing, I hope. I mean—" and she stopped, not even knowing where to go. "I don't even know why I'm here—"

"Because I'll understand," he said. For the first time she noticed that he had a new bruise and scuffle mark on his cheek, and a cut on his chin. Things might have been quiet for her, but it looked like whoever'd roughed him up the first time had come back for a small second helping.

"I think I'm being—" she hesitated. "That maybe the past month or so has gotten into my head. But I can't—I don't—"

"Brenna."

"I think," she said, squeezing the words out, "that Elizabeth has rabies."

But he didn't laugh, and he didn't say she was being ridiculous. He looked at her, his eyes hooding as he considered her words. "If she's showing signs—"

"Then it's too late," Brenna finished miserably. "I'm wrong. I have to be wrong."

"What you have to do," he said quietly, "is tell her."

"How can I? What can I say? It's a *feeling*, nothing more. Based on one day's observation by *me*, and I've never seen anyone with rabies."

"She's got a boyfriend. Unlike HIV, rabies *is*

passed in the saliva. If you're wrong, her doctor will say so."

Brenna closed her eyes. *It's not happening it's not happening it's not happening.* "She's my *friend*."

"That's the point," he said, and his hand brushed her shoulder, a brief reassurance. "And it's why you came to talk to me. Because you knew what I'd say."

At that she opened her eyes and scowled. "You think you know everything," she said, and spun away from him, stalking down the aisle and startling customers with her expression all the way back to the grooming room. Being angry at something made it just a little bit easier to live with what faced her there.

"Brenna," Elizabeth said in surprise, holding Jeremy Cocker's leash and his customer card. She wiped surreptitiously at a small gathering of thick saliva in the corner of her mouth. "What on earth's the matter?"

Brenna told her.

Chapter 14

I

ISA
Frustrations & Hindrances

Brenna pounded nails. Angry pounding, each impact banging out a word in her mind. *It's! Not! Fair!*

Not fair that she'd been right about Elizabeth. Not fair that her friend had gone downhill so quickly, and only a day later, was isolated in a hospital. Not fair that Brenna wasn't allowed to visit.

To say good-bye.

She slammed a final nail into place—*not-fair!*—and reached for the drill, aiming it at the holes she'd just marked for the replacement hinges of an interior barn gate. The barn itself was a hodgepodge of old and new, with huge main timbers and thick original boarding. One side served as a garage for small farm

235

machines and equipment storage, while the middle contained a grain area, a closed tack room, and a work space where horses could be fed, saddled, shod, and treated. The other side and along the back held run-ins for pastured horses—sections where horses from separate pastures could find shelter, and interior areas for isolation. There were no stalls; there had never been stalls. And try as she might, Brenna had never been able to conceive of a simple way to convert the barn—with its limited electricity and complete lack of plumbing—to a dog facility.

In its prime it had been an active, low-key boarding barn. And if she fixed a few important things—like this gate from one section of the horse runs to another—she might yet get a few co-op boarders in here. A few more dollars of income, though she'd likely eat it all with upkeep.

And in the meantime, worried about Elizabeth, she found it mightily satisfying to drill and hammer and bang things around with vigor, and then step back to find she had managed to construct something in the process.

The gate wasn't a thing of beauty. Weathered old boards, horse-nibbled and greyed, clashed with the stout new crosspieces. But it hung true enough to open and close easily, and the new latch snicked shut with a satisfying firmness. She'd add a chain; that would discourage horses who were clever with their tongues. She stood back, admired it, and looked around for something else into which she could pound nails.

And discovered that there, between the big double-sliding doors leading into the grain and tack area, stood her brother. Silhouetted against the early evening light, his shape—a little taller than her, arms a little akimbo, left shoulder slightly lower than the right, receding temples in his bushy hair evident even in outline from this angle—was too familiar to be obscured by such a thing as lack of three-dimensional detail.

"Russell," she said simply, a single word that encompassed both surprise and welcome, and hid the sigh she felt inside. Russell was not there to support her in her anger and sadness. He might think he was, but that's not the way it would turn out.

"Need some help?" he asked.

"I'm done, I guess." Fix-it puttering was a solitary chore, she'd always felt. She bent at the waist, limber enough to gather the tools without crouching down—but not quite endowed with enough hands.

"Here," he said, and came to take the drill and drill bit case from her so she could deal with the rest. "Sorry you didn't hear me drive up. Some fierce little watchdog you've got out there." *Not*, he meant, with that lightly sarcastic tone. "Odd little fellow. One of your strays?"

"Yes," she said, no longer rising to a jibe she might have lunged for as a teen. "He's a good dog."

"I figured as much. The kids are playing with him. Last I saw they'd taken him out to the old paddock to toss sticks for him."

Brenna stashed the tools in the old tack room and latched the door. "They won't have much luck. He's pretty clueless. He's good for a tussle with kids, though. They amuse him. Is Marie here, too?" She hoped. At five and seven, the boys were just a little too young to be left alone off home turf, and a little too wild to trust—they'd likely pull down one of the old fences and proudly present the results to her while Russell beamed.

"Nope," Russell said. "She's not feeling well tonight."

Wanted a well-deserved break from the boys, Brenna thought. Russell loved them dearly, but he counted his contribution to parenting as the sperm he'd donated and the hours he put into his flooring store to support the family. She took herself through the gate she'd just reinstalled, pausing to watch it click into place—*yesss*—and led Russell out the back way to discover that Druid had already learned an important lesson—Russell's boys did not equal Emily's girls. He was willing to romp, but he shadowed rather than interacted with them. That suited Brenna. She leaned against her stack of old, greyed hay and watched.

"Sorry about your friend," Russell said, shifting awkwardly and finally putting out an arm to lean against the hay.

"Thanks," Brenna said. "I guess it's made the news, then?" They'd wanted to stick a microphone in Brenna's face at the store, to ask questions like *what's it like to know it could have been you?* but Roger had forbidden it and for once she was just as glad for his Pets!-protective management.

They hadn't bothered her here. She guessed it wasn't the same without the store as background.

"Oh, yeah." Russell nodded, distracted, as he discovered her shooting targets jammed between the hay bales and pulled them out. "What's this?"

As if it weren't perfectly obvious, and as if he weren't really asking for an explanation—*justification*—of *why* she was target shooting.

"Targets," she said simply, taking them from him and putting them back where they'd been. "They stay dry in there."

"You know, you can always stay with Marie and me if you get worried about being out here alone."

That startled her into giving him a surprised look. "Worried? Are you here because Mom told you I was worried?"

"I'm here," he said, "because *Mom* is worried. About the dog packs, and she told me you'd lost your hound in some weird way."

"No one ever saw that dog pack," Brenna said. "A

lot of people assumed it. Could have been a particularly bad-acting coyote. You know they're in this area now." Words for Russell. She knew better than to believe either explanation.

"A coyote? Kill a dog the size of that red hound you had?" Russell gave her an annoyed big-brother look. "I haven't been living in town long enough for you to pull *that* one on me, Brenna."

She shrugged, rubbing her hands up and down her goose-bumping arms. Working, she'd been warm enough. Standing in the shadow of the barn, she wasn't.

"The point is, she's beginning to wonder if it was a mistake to let you have this place."

A prickle of alarm made the goose bumps bigger. "I've kept it up just fine. It's what I was doing when you got here, in case you didn't notice."

"That's not what I'm talking about. I'm talking about you out here alone all the time."

"I was *alone* when we decided I'd stay in the house," Brenna said, keeping her tone even only with the greatest of determination. *I don't need this. I don't need this* now. Sensitive brother Russell, coming to stomp all over her when she just needed someone to accept her and feel with her. *Masera wouldn't stand for this shit.*

That last thought startled her enough that she almost didn't hear Russell say, "We didn't think you'd *stay* alone." But *nothing* could have blocked out the implications of that one, as belatedly as they came to her.

"What? You thought I'd find myself a man? Settle down like you did and start a family? Give up work and stay at home to raise kids? That's *bullshit*, Russell."

"Shhh," he said, giving the boys a hasty look and evidently deciding they were out of earshot. Still, he kept his voice lowered. "It's not *bullshit*, Brenna. It's my life. It's a good life."

"That's not *your* life, it's *Marie's* life. And you don't know anything about it!"

The boys stopped running at that, looked back at them with questioning faces. Redheads, both of them, with profuse freckles and Marie's fair skin, and no more understanding of their Aunt Brenna than their father had. Russell gestured them out and they ran to the hand pump by the water trough, where they discovered the well in perfect working order. Brenna doubted that Marie would share their delight when they slopped into the house.

Then again, she'd resigned herself to *kids will be kids* long ago and truly seemed happy with it. Brenna could understand that, even envy it a little. She only wished Marie and Russell were capable of doing the same for her. "Listen, Russell," she said. "I don't live my life to suit you. I don't even live it to suit Mom. I'm sorry if that's some big disappointment to you both, but you might try being glad that there's someone who *is* willing to live here and keep the place up—keep it in the family."

"Quit thinking only of yourself," Russell said, once again managing to startle her. "It's Mom who has to worry about you. And me."

"But I'm *fine*—"

"And I'm telling you, we've been talking. The deed was never transferred to your name, you know. Mom might decide to sell the place."

Fury booted aside any common sense she might have had. "And whose idea was this, Russell? Hers, or *yours*? Has someone made you an offer on this place, is that it?"

Parker, ohmygod, Rob Parker.

He'd said he had ways. He'd apparently meant it. She knew her brother too well to think this was coming from nowhere, or from any sudden concern about her life. And at that she did lower her voice, though she couldn't stop it from shaking, and she couldn't keep from closing on him, forcing him to back up as she pointed him through the run-in opening. "Get out,

Russell. Get out *now*. No one's selling *anything*, you can count on that. This is my *home*."

He looked like he wanted to protest, his mouth open, his head primed to shake at her.

He didn't. He called the boys, and though they gave her innocent and heartbreakingly cheerful farewells, she could only bring herself to return a brief wave. Druid stood by her side, his happy tail slowly lowering as he looked up at her and divined her mood.

"*Hwoo?*" he said, in one of his weird little whining questions. Brenna knelt to rub his ears and kiss the neat white forehead splot that ended his broad blaze.

"I wish you really *could* understand," she said. "You'd probably have the answers."

She'd call her mother. Russell was slick, was the consummate salesman with years of experience in deals and dealing, but he probably hadn't told Rhona about the buyer. Probably didn't know it was the same person who'd trashed the land while Brenna's father lay dying, probably hadn't bothered to find out that Parker, behind his good old farmboy talk and his charming smile and his disarming conservative-looking mustache, was police-blotter material.

Beyond police-blotter material.

Her mother would listen to that, would hear it over Russell's talk of money and his patronizing *for Brenna's own good* words.

She had to.

Druid sighed, a mighty sigh of the sort that only a world-weary dog can make, and Brenna kissed his head again, a loud exaggerated smack of a kiss. "There," she said. "All better."

As if.

"Brenna?"

Emily? Inside the barn? Brenna called back to her and jogged inside, finding herself surprised and thrown off guard once more. As much as Brenna tromped a path through the modest fallow field and the small stand of trees between her place and the upscale housing development that held Emily's home, Emily never came the opposite way. Sometimes she showed up in the family van, the girls in tow and begging to explore Brenna's crammed attic while Emily and Brenna shared a soda and news, but never on foot. Rarely alone.

"Everything all right?" Brenna asked, her eyes adjusting to the dim interior and not able to see much besides the blob of Emily and the particularly pink appliqued vest she wore. Brenna suspected Emily would consider herself undressed if she left the house without at least one homemade item of apparel on her body.

"I should be asking *you*," Emily said. "I saw Russell leaving. As if you needed *him* on top of what's happened to Elizabeth." .

"Yes," Brenna said, leaning on the repaired gate. "He was a treasure, as usual."

Emily looked away; Brenna could see her well enough, now, to note the strained look around her eyes, the tension at the corners of her mouth. She said, "What?"

"What do you mean, *what*?"

"Oh, don't even try. Here you are in the middle of my barn, come over on foot without the girls. And with that look on your face. As if you could hide that look from *me*."

Emily gave her a small smile. A very small smile. She offered a sheaf of rolled-up papers she'd been holding quietly at her side. "I brought these," she said. "More information on rabies, for one. Thought you might like to have it, though from what I hear . . . I'm not sure it'll apply to what's going on now. And there's some stuff on Mars Nodens. I didn't look at it; I'm not sure how carefully the girls screened it, to tell you the truth."

"It's probably not quite in their interest range," Brenna said, blowing her bangs out of her eyes and reaching for the roll of paper, squashing it flat and stuffing it in her back pocket beside her braid. "I'm not sure it'll be in *my* interest range."

"They did ask why you wanted it," Emily admitted. "I told them you were a unique and strange individual, and we should treasure you as such."

Brenna laughed out loud. "Thank you *so* much." She dropped one hand to the latch, clicking it open, easing the gate back, and snicking it closed again, waiting for what Emily *really* had to say.

"There," Emily added, looking meaningfully at the gate. "You prove my point entirely."

"I heed my inner child," Brenna said with a theatrical haughtiness. "And you still haven't answered my question."

Emily sighed. Now they'd get to it, Brenna knew, and she was right. "Well, three things," Emily said. "One is, can you come over for a cookout this weekend, and two is . . . we'd rather you didn't bring Druid around just now." She smiled apologetically, but it looked a little sad, as if the request were really an odd, sad focal point to everything that had happened in Brenna's life . . . and that now seemed to be spreading to encompass the rest of the community.

"*That's* what you're worried about?" Brenna said, shocked; inside she felt it, a rejection that didn't make a whit of practical sense but existed all the same. "I suppose I can't blame you for that. I hope you've told them" —for they both knew this was for the girls— "to keep their hands off stray dogs, too."

Emily scoffed affectionately. "You're a fine one to be saying *that*, Brenna Lynn Fallon." And Druid whined, as if he agreed, and they both laughed, though Emily's was strained.

"Don't worry about it," Brenna said. "I'll crate him

up. I won't be able to stay as long, but you can bet I'll stay long enough to eat plenty of your food."

"Of that I have no doubt." Emily smiled, a real smile this time. "Thanks for understanding. We know Druid's okay, but—"

"Hey, until someone figures out what's going on, none of them is *okay*," Brenna said. "You know, Roger doesn't know it yet, but I'm not going to book any known biters any more. It's one thing to risk a roughed-up knuckle or two . . ."

"You shouldn't be grooming at all," Emily said. "It doesn't take a mauling like poor Elizabeth got. It only takes a scratch, and if the animal's got it and has been licking his paws—"

"If people were dropping right and left, I *wouldn't* be grooming," Brenna said. "But it's not like I didn't take the plunge and get inoculated this year. And if I'm not working, I'm not getting paid. And right now . . ." She looked away, to where the driveway was if she'd had X-ray vision and could look right through the barn. To where her oh-so-solicitous brother had recently been. "Right now, I can't afford to ask favors of family."

"What *is* he up to?" Emily asked, crossing her arms over her chest in a most suspicious posture and giving Brenna a *fess up* look.

Brenna only laughed. "You're not *my* mother," she said. "Save that face for the girls. And whatever that third thing is that you're holding on to, give it up."

"Ah," Emily said. "The *really* awkward one."

Brenna made an impatient come-hither gesture. "Just give."

"It's that fellow from the store. The one I've seen talking to you? The really—okay, I'm a married woman. I won't go there. But you know how Sam hears things . . ."

"As if I could *not* know," Brenna said. But she didn't like where this one was going.

"Well, he's heard things, all right. And he won't tell me what, because it's just mutterings, expressions, and reactions more than anything. But it could be that this guy's getting in with a bad crowd, Brenna. So just . . . be careful."

Brenna hunted down her annoyance and decided it wasn't because of the warning, but what she'd been warned about. "He works at the store," she said, and the annoyance slipped out. "That's all."

"That's all I thought." Emily gave her a puzzled look, a silent *what else*? "But if *I* worked at the same store with him—well, forewarned is forearmed, don't you think?"

Brenna sighed, already sorry for snapping, or coming close to it, and trying to look at Masera from Emily's eyes—Emily, who would be astonished if Brenna said *he's only spent one night here* with the wicked impulse she barely suppressed. "Yeah. You're right. Best to know." Even if she'd already known. The clues couldn't be hitting her any harder, one after the other. "So I'll see you this weekend, and I'll leave Druid here. I even promise not to lick the girls myself."

"Oh, now that *does* put my mind at ease," Emily said as she headed for the door. "It truly does."

Brenna grinned at the empty space she'd left behind, and yelled after Emily, "Oh, and hey—now that you've figured out how to get here, maybe you should come over more often!"

"Shut up!" Emily shouted back at her, words flung over her shoulder from the sound of it. Brenna looked at Druid and decided he was in complete agreement with her own perspective, but her smile faded quickly enough.

"Nuadha's Silver Druid," she said. "Kind of ironic, isn't it, Mister Dog with the Strange Rabies Tag? I get the feeling you're probably the only dog around that *is* safe for the girls to play with. Not that I understand one damn bit of it."

He cocked his head at her. Clueless. Of course.
She might as well be making strange flying saucer
noises through her lips. Which, on second thought,
she decided to do, and found that it not only made
him cock his head from side to side and back again,
but his big ears somehow perked so intently that they
looked bigger than ever. "Okay," she said. "That earns
you dinner. Let's go."

That, he understood. Five minutes later she was
dumping food into his dish and scraping Spaghetti-Os
out of a can for herself, not particularly interested
in anything that took longer than three minutes to
prepare no matter how wholesome it was. She slid
the bowl into the microwave as she called her mother
and listened to the phone ring, only belatedly realizing it was bingo night at Sunset Village. Right.
Rhona and Ada cleaning up in the dining hall, faster
on the draw than half the people there. When the
machine clicked on, she left only a brief message, and
then poured herself some soda. Druid was done
eating by then, and he came into the kitchen through
the half-open door from the dog room and looked
at her quite expectantly, as though he hadn't been
fed for weeks and she had the only food in the house.
Brenna looked back at him.

He belched resoundingly.

"You know," she said, smirking, "that really does
ruin the hungry-dog effect. Back to the drawing board
for you. Better yet," she added, pouring herself a soda
over lots of ice, "come into the den with me. We can
watch the news. Maybe they'll even say something
about the rude Pets! manager who won't talk to
them."

The microwave dinged, presenting her with over-
heated Spaghetti-Os—she'd never found the *just right*
setting for that particular comfort food, and had
resigned herself to blowing endlessly on steaming
spoons of pasta and burning her tongue at least once

anyway—and she took them and the soda out into
the den, knowing Druid would follow. Faced with full
hands, she poked the television power button with
her toe and plunked down into the couch, freezing
at the unexpected crinkling she heard.

Emily's papers. "You touch, you die," she warned
Druid, putting her bowl on the floor so she could lean
forward and yank the papers from her pocket. "There.
Uplifting television, educational reading, and a
repaired barn gate. What more could a woman ask
for?"

New headlines, for one. There they were, still
leading off with the story about Elizabeth. *Wait. No.*
Someone else.

"This man, recently found dead in the northwest
area of the city, has been identified as a known felon."
Cue mug shot, replacing the face of the mature,
perfectly coifed anchor woman.

Mr. Cocky.

"Alarmingly, the cause of his death has been identified as rabies. Centers for Disease Control officers
have no official comment on the unheard-of number
of rabies cases in humans recently, although they're
still unwilling to consider it an 'outbreak.' " The
anchor woman reappeared, with a clever graphic on
the screen to the upper left of her head shot, a big
red block *R* with a hypodermic crossing it and a
jagged, Batman-like *KA-POW* outline around it. "Nor
have they pinned down the primary source of these
infections, originally thought to be a stray dog—a
theory recently dismissed when a local woman came
down with the disease."

Cut to a reporter standing outside Pets!, apparently oblivious that directly behind him, a large
Malamute was lifting his leg on the fake fire hydrant
provided especially for that purpose—although as the
seconds passed, he moved to block the view, no
doubt directed by the cameraman. Brenna, dizzily

overcome with the portent of Mr. Cocky's death, imagined the cameraman's thoughts. *Note to self: Avoid fire hydrant backdrop*.

And then he started talking, and things got worse.

"We're saddened to report that local groomer Elizabeth Reed succumbed today to rabies—only moments ago, in fact—contracted through injuries sustained at this Pets! store—"

Brenna dropped the spoon back into her Spaghetti-Os, dropped the bowl into her lap. Stared at the screen, unheeding of the reporter's words, unable to hear anything but the voice in her head, the memory of a voice that had once sneaked inside her thoughts over Emily's kitchen table—

. . . local groomer Brenna Lynn Fallon succumbed today . . .

It was supposed to have been her. It truly was supposed to have been *her*.

And then Druid was staring at her with searing intensity. Whining his whine, so impossibly earnest—

Crowded shelters, dead pets piling up faster than they could be cremated, live ones impossibly crammed together—

On-site reporter: "Officials are suggesting that animal lovers keep their pets indoors or under supervision at all times out of doors."

Closed schools. Special hospital wards. Children chanting rhymes over double-scotch. Emily crying. Druid whining. "*Shedding Rabies* is the term being used for the mutated virus, an illness which incubates more quickly in humans than the well-known counterpart, but slowly in the common carrier animals . . ."

Cut to animal control building exterior with voice-over. "The dog and cat drop-off rate has already doubled. Humane Society spokesperson Sarah Monscour suggests that this is an overreaction, and could lead to the needless deaths of beloved pets."

Conditioned pit bulls in training, ravaging a small dog, clamping down long after the victim went limp in death, blood coating its face and chest. Emily crying. Emily crying.

Sarah Monscour: "Please, unless you know your pet has been in contact with a wild or stray animal, don't abandon or give them up. If you're concerned, there's a test available through your veterinarian. It's called the Rapid Fluorescent Focus Inhibition Test and can allay any concerns you might have about your pet and rabies."

Druid whining.

Almost a bark and almost words, warm brown eyes pinned to hers, his front feet on her knees. Not caring about the pungent pasta before him—the smell of which suddenly made Brenna ill. Truly ill, and she realized it just in time to plunge for the bathroom and flip the toilet lid up.

After she'd been sick, when she slid back on the tile floor and up against the tub, her arms wrapped around her knees, Druid crept in—he'd always been wary of the toilet—and whined a different whine. An ordinary sound, a dog confused and worried. He squeezed in under her arm and licked her face.

"They say not to let dogs do that," she told him solemnly. "But it can't be any worse than sticking your head in the toilet."

So they sat together, and she tried to put her thoughts together. Well, *her* thoughts . . . and thoughts she was certain weren't hers at all.

Parker and Mr. Cocky. Rabies.

Parker's girlfriend and her cat. Rabies.

Parker's barn and Parker's dogs. *Dogfighting.* Small animals ravaged in training. Small animals found by the roadside.

The Sheltie mix, found mauled by the roadside and taken through quarantine, through Janean's hands and into the home of a man now also dead.

Parker and his fighting dogs and the animals he'd touched and they'd touched and rabies.

Shedding rabies.

Parker's barn and Parker's dogs and shedding rabies and the darkness-feeding force that had come from the very spring she loved so much.

And it would only get worse. She knew that from the things she'd seen . . . things somehow connected with Druid, that upset him as much as they upset her, though she couldn't fathom why or how. Maybe she never would.

Fine. She'd created that place of power; *she'd* started this.

She knew how to finish it.

Only then did she notice that Druid's white muzzle had an inconspicuous rim of tomato red, and that his breath smelled familiar, though that smell no longer sent her for the toilet. She gave a shaky laugh, and squeezed him in a hug until he protested. "Maybe you're a normal dog at that," she said, and wiped the corner of his mouth, coming up with a single forlorn pasta *O*.

But she had a feeling that was only wishful thinking.

Call animal control.

That's what she needed to do.

Masera had said they knew about it. He hadn't wanted her to call, though he hadn't come right out and said it; he hadn't needed to.

More pieces of the puzzle whirled in on her. Parker's girlfriend and Mickey the stockboy, missing dog food, Masera and Mickey, arguing, exchanging cash for dogs . . . Mickey's message to Masera about something that was happening . . . *tonight.*

He'd said he wasn't going to fight those dogs. He'd meant it, she knew that, and when he'd said it she'd interpreted his comment to mean he wasn't involved. But she should have known better, should have remembered how good he was at sliding past things he didn't want to reveal or discuss. Somehow, in some way, Masera was mixed up with the fighting. Even Eztebe knew of it—he just didn't know what *it* was.

But Brenna did.

Wherever tonight's action was, Masera was there. Now.

Mixed up with Parker and his dogs *and his rabies*. Right now.

Brenna lunged up from the bathroom, leaving one very surprised Corgi in her wake, and went tearing through her beat-up purse, hunting her wallet and the card with Masera's cell phone number. She didn't think about what she'd say, or marshal her arguments. She fumbled with phone and card until she'd gotten the number dialed and then listened to his line ring. And ring.

Answer it, you idiot, she thought fiercely at him. "I don't care where you are, answer the damn—"

"Masera," he snapped, not sounding at all glad about it. Shouts and catcalls and curses filled in the background noise, swelling suddenly to a frenzied cacophony, making her sure she'd been right.

"It's Brenna," she said, and didn't wait for a response. "Get out of there."

"Brenna, I don't have time for this—"

"You *do*," she said. "You *take* the time, and you listen to me. Get out of there! It's not safe."

That, for some reason, amused him. He *knew* it wasn't safe, she realized, even as he said, "I know what I'm doing." But the noise in the background diminished; he must have been moving away from it. She at least had that much of his attention.

"You think so?" she snapped. "Did you know Mr. Cocky died from rabies?"

"Mr. *Who*?" And then, barely muffled, he shouted to someone, "Yeah, *yeah*, I'll be right there."

"That guy who chased us off Parker's driveway—

you know, the guy with the I'm-hip walk and the sleazy attempt at a beard."

"He's dead?" Masera asked, checking to make sure he'd gotten it right; the background noise faded a little more.

"He's really dead. And they say it was rabies. Listen, every animal and person who's gotten rabies has a connection to Parker. And you're there at a dogfight, aren't you?"

"Don't be—"

"No, *you* 'don't be.' Parker's running dogfights and he's got his own dogs and at least one of them is spreading a new variation of rabies. I don't *care* what you're doing there, just get out! With all the blood and dog spit being slung around at a fight, you think you're not in danger?"

"I've been inoculated," he said, and she could tell she was losing his interest, could hear someone calling his name in the background, rising above the general hubbub of the place.

"Well whoop-di-do, and so have I. So had his girlfriend's cat, and Elizabeth's dead. And the Sheltie mix made it through quarantine and still wasn't showing signs of rabies after passing it to two people who are also now dead. Aren't you *listening?* It's a *new strain.*"

There was a pause; in the background she heard a purely human scuffle break out and quickly subside, and she hated to think of the men who could quell such a thing so quickly in that charged atmosphere. What they'd do to Masera if they even guessed what he was talking about. Then Masera said, "She's dead? Elizabeth died?"

"Yes," Brenna said in misery. "I'd really rather you didn't die, too."

His voice got quiet and intent; she could tell he was holding the phone close to his mouth, and probably had his hand cupped around the receiver. She could also tell immediately that he was going to do his own thing no matter what she said. "Okay, Brenna. I hear you. I'm not in that sort of danger here. I'm strictly back row right now. But I can't leave. And I damn sure can't spend time on the phone and then leave. Parker's tight, and he's careful. I'll never get back in."

She didn't ask why the hell he wanted to get back in, and she didn't care. "You want to talk trouble?" she said, her voice dropping low and shaking a little from the very nature of the exchange, from what she knew she was about to say—knowing that deep down, no matter what she called him, no matter how he alternately hid himself from her and shoved himself into her life and annoyed the hell out of her, she didn't want to push him away for good. "Here's trouble for you—you have this nice long talk on the phone and fifteen minutes later the cops arrive and break up the party."

"The hell you will," he said, and every bit of the anger she expected was there. "You stay out of this, Brenna. You have no idea what you're meddling with."

"And I don't care. It's your choice. I see you here within ten minutes, or I call the cops. I don't even care if you're *not* at Parker's. It'll mess up your secret little plans just as much if they storm his training barn."

He reacted with such utter silence that she knew he didn't even trust himself to respond to her. Then he muttered—no doubt through clenched teeth— "It'll take me more than ten minutes. Fifteen."

"Fifteen," she agreed.

He hung up on her.

She wasn't surprised. She couldn't even blame him. She put the phone down on the cradle and looked at Druid, ever attentive Druid. "He's mad."

Druid, well-ensconced in normal-dog mode, cocked his head, and his intent was plain enough; he might

as well have spoken English. *I really liked that bowl
of round things. I'd like more.*

Brenna laughed, a shaky laugh, and crouched to
put her cheek against his gently domed head. Then
she looked him in the eye and said, "Not a chance."

Sixteen minutes had passed when she heard a
vehicle turn up her driveway. At seventeen minutes
she would have called him again, another warning.
And then she would have called the cops.

Her relief upon hearing the car, upon knowing she
wouldn't have to make either call, was immense. It
lasted only long enough for her to realize she was
now going to have to face Masera in his anger. She
went to the back door and waited, the screen propped
open with one foot, the porch light beckoning.

The SUV came to a hard stop before the barn; she
could hear him yank on the parking brake through
the open window. He closed the door with a solid
swing, though not with a slam—she supposed that was
good—and walked toward the house with big angry
strides, coming right up to the door, right up to *her.*

They stared at one another a moment. He didn't
look as furious as she'd expected, but definitely brim-
ming with frustration; beside himself, as if besieged
by so many strong emotions he didn't know where
to turn first.

Boy, could she relate.

So he did nothing, just latched his eyes onto hers
and stood there on the verge of something, while
Brenna herself didn't know whether to say *I'm sorry*
or *I'm not sorry* and ended up, to her great surprise,
reaching out to touch the side of his face.

It changed something between them. For the first
time, Brenna felt like she had given him something
that no one else could, and that for the first time
she'd chosen to give. And he relaxed, as though she
had released something within him, although his

manner was no less grave. "We have things to talk about," he said. "We have a *lot* of things to talk about. But not now."

Rabies, Parker buying her land, visions from a dog and the death of a friend. Lots of things to talk about, all right. But not now. Brenna said, "Okay," and stepped back from the door in invitation. "Want a bagel? I've got that great black cherry butter, and Druid ate my dinner so I'm having one anyway."

He grinned, giving a helpless shake of his head. "Yeah," he said. "I'd love a bagel."

So they had bagels, and they didn't talk, and when he was leaving he said, "Tomorrow. I'll come over tomorrow after my early evening class."

"I'll be here," she said simply, and they left it at that.

Chapter 15

OTHILA
Connection to Heritage & Kin

Brenna couldn't remember the last time she'd gone to her mother's unannounced, but the next day she found herself hunting a parking spot in the upscale retirement community, cruising around banks of immaculately tended landscaping as she navigated the maze to the correct clump of apartments. Her day off, with the world going weird around her and last night's conflict still unresolved, and she walked through the reception and sitting areas where the world was nothing *but* normal, with elderly women comparing knitting projects made painstaking by their arthritis and an elderly man snoozing through his friends' conversation while the single visiting family tried to control the small child ping-ponging from chair to chair and raising affectionate smiles from strangers.

Not only couldn't she remember the last time she'd come here without calling ahead—though she knew her mother's habits well enough to be comfortably sure Rhona would be at home, and probably Aunt Ada, too—she couldn't at all place the last time her mother had been to the farmhouse. All she knew of it lately was what Brenna told her; Rhona had no feel for the recent changes Brenna had made, for the ways she'd made it her own. For the obvious ways she'd loved and cared for the place.

Maybe it was time for that to change. Maybe if it *did* change, her mother would be less susceptible to any old idea Russell decided to plant.

Or maybe not. In any event, this was one old idea she wasn't going to let reach fruition.

"Brenna!" her aunt said, opening the door at Brenna's knock, as surprised as Brenna would have expected but welcoming. They exchanged a quick hug—Brenna was always careful with her aunt, a light-boned and thin-skinned woman in her seventies—and Ada called back over her shoulder, "Rhona! Your girl is here, so tear yourself away from that soap opera and come out here!" She gave Brenna a wink, wrinkling her crepe-papery skin. "I never let her watch those things in the sitting room. Those commercials drive me up a wall!"

"More power to you," Brenna said, grinning.

"Go in and sit on the couch, dear. Your mother'll be out directly, I'm sure. Would you like some tea?"

"Water would be nice." Brenna took a spot on the couch, the same spot she took every time she visited here. Her mother would take the recliner, and Aunt Ada would drift in with refreshments and sit on the other end of the couch if she pleased. Ada, Brenna's mother had always said, was an *individual*—as if being an individual were not entirely a good thing. Brenna had been surprised when the sisters had decided to live together after her father's death and had been even more surprised when the arrangement endured—but glad that it had. This community gave her mother a secure place next to a medical facility, and was engineered with hand grips, wide hallways, high toilets, and showers with built-in seats. And with all of that the apartments still looked more like luxury living than anything else. Which was all a great relief, because Brenna couldn't imagine life if her mother had stayed at the farmhouse.

Although unless she did something, it didn't look like she'd have a life at the farmhouse to imagine.

Brenna's mother came out from the hallway, using her cane today; must have been a bad bone day, as Ada called them. It made Brenna reflexively check her old injuries to see if she felt any aches, and then sigh with relief when she didn't. Not yet. She got up from the couch to greet her mother with a kiss, and waited for her to settle in the recliner before sinking to the couch again.

"I can't remember the last time you came by without calling," Rhona said.

"I was thinking the same as I drove in," Brenna admitted. "But if it was a bad time, it wouldn't have been a big deal to turn around and go home. It was a nice day for a drive, anyway."

"Nonsense!" said Ada from the kitchen. "It's never a bad time to see you, Brenna."

"But I can't imagine you came all this way for no reason," her mother added.

Brenna couldn't help a grin, though there wasn't much mirth behind it. "It's not that far," she said. "Maybe you should come out and visit me sometime, refresh your memory."

"I remember the old place well enough, I suppose."

"You remember the way it was," Brenna said. "It's been my home for a while now. Things have changed."

"Don't tell me that old hulk of a barn has changed."

"Not so much," Brenna said. "But I don't live in the barn. I live in the house. And you're right, I'm not here for no reason. I'm here because of some things Russell said to me last night."

"Goodness," her mother said. "I stopped interfering in your quarrels a long time ago."

Brenna took a deep breath. A very deep breath. *Don't give up. Don't escalate.* "I wouldn't call this a quarrel . . . it's much more significant than that. And it involves you."

"He talked to you about the house," her mother said flatly.

"Yes. He talked to me about the house." She looked at her mother, who sat motionless in the chair, not a gesture or twitch giving away how she might feel about the subject although there was an innate disapproval in her unbending posture. Her cane rested beside her, and her delicate pink sweater and close-weave, off-white linen slacks seemed at odds with the rest of her. The pension from Brenna's father had done well by her, supplemented by Social Security—but mostly by Ada, who picked up all the household expenses. And somehow Rhona had never seemed truly to enjoy it—to allow herself to enjoy it. Nothing except the community restaurant outings; she'd picked up a taste for fine food in the last four or five years. Other than that, it was difficult to get a conversation of substance out of her.

This time, Brenna wasn't leaving until they'd had one. "He talked to me about the house, all right. And he had no right to go behind my back with whatever offer he's been made."

"I wasn't aware there was a firm offer."

"If there isn't, there will be. This is pure Russell, Mom—he came here and made a grand speech about poor little Brenna living all alone out in the country, didn't he? Got you to wondering if you'd made the right decision in not selling when Dad died after I said I'd stay there and take care of it, didn't he? When you said I could stay as long as I wanted to be there?"

Her mother had gone disapproving. "I'm not sure I like your tone."

She kept that tone carefully modulated. "How did you *think* I'd feel, after all these years of caring for the place on my own, and neither of you showing an interest? I've paid the taxes, I've repaired the fences and the barn and the roof. And I helped Dad hold it together for years before he died—Russell sure never put a hand to it."

"Your brother had a good job, and a career."

"That doesn't change what *I* did. What *I* put into the place. That I'm the one who's always loved it, and I'm the only one who's kept it up or even spent time there at all. You don't visit, and Russell doesn't visit. If there's to be any conversation about selling it, then I'm the *first* one who should have known about it."

"I'm sure Russell did as he thought was right."

Anger crept out. "That doesn't mean it *was* right. Do you even know who he's talking to? Rob Parker, that's who. The very same jerk who tore up the pasture the month Dad died. He's only been back in town a little while and he's already got a reputation for picking up his dead friend's drug business. Did Russell tell you *that*?"

Ada brought water and tea on a tray, setting it on the low coffee table that centered the conversation area, and sitting quietly on the other end of the couch, watching her sister thoughtfully. Brenna gratefully took the tall glass of ice water, glad to have something to do with her hands.

"He didn't say anything about that." Her mother smoothed the front of her sweater and leaned to reach her tea, resting the saucer carefully in her lap and leaving unspoken the implication that Brenna was therefore wrong.

"He wouldn't have, would he? And I'll tell you what else—I'll lay odds that Parker's paying him to engineer this sale—something on top of whatever Russell figures he's got coming to himself from the house."

"Brenna," her mother said sharply. "Russell would do no such thing."

"Russell *would*." Brenna said it without hesitation, but without any edge, either. Just the certainty, the hard-earned, painfully won certainty of what her brother could justify when he wanted to.

Ada cleared her throat. "Rhona, listen to your girl. She's the one who's there, and I daresay she knows Russell better than you think. Even I know Russell well enough to know he'll do as he sees fit when he thinks he can get away with it. What do you think happened to that lovely silver platter of yours that you thought was lost in the move?"

"Ada," Brenna's mother said, stiffening, "I think this is a private conversation."

"Not as far as I'm concerned," Brenna said. She'd never heard her aunt offer an opinion about Russell one way or the other, and she didn't have any illusions that Ada wouldn't say similarly astute things about Brenna herself during the conversation, if she saw fit. But a third person made things easier—made it more than just Brenna talking and her mother never quite listening.

"I saw Russell looking at that platter while we were packing your things," Ada said, unperturbed by her sister's rejection.

"You never mentioned it." She said it as though Ada had taken the platter herself. Finally real, honest emotion—and it was misdirected.

Ada shrugged and took a sip of her tea. The delicate, silver-edged teacups were left over from her days of entertaining her long-deceased husband's business associates; when it came to difficult social situations, Ada could hold her own with aplomb. "What would have been the point? The platter was gone, and it wasn't like Russell was coming here on a weekly basis to plunder things. He saw an opportunity and he took it. He's always done that; he always will. I doubt he would be half so successful in his business if he didn't think on those terms. He just goes a little too far now and then."

Brenna left the moment to her mother and aunt, but her mother didn't seem likely to take it anywhere. Not while she stared at the tea sitting in her lap, a bit of it spilled over into the saucer with her last, nearly vehement words to her sister. But then she pulled herself together and took a breath and, as if Ada hadn't said anything, told Brenna, "I'm sure your brother is thinking of you, Brenna Lynn. He's not the only one who's wondered if it's best for you to stay alone in that big old house, away from town and the social opportunities it offers you."

"Mom, it's *Parma Hill*! What social—" Brenna shook her head, cutting herself off. "No. That's not the point. The point is, it's up to me where I want to live. If it's a mistake for me to be away from town, then that's a mistake I'll have to live with. *My* problem, not yours. It's not up to you and Russell to decide what I should or shouldn't do with my life!" Especially not when Russell probably didn't truly have an opinion about it one way or the other, but had chosen the most expedient way to get what he really wanted. "You want to know something? You can take the house away, but it won't get me into town. I'll find another place out in the country. I heard about an apartment over the Sawyers' barn—I can probably even get a reduced rent in exchange for barn chores." *But it wouldn't have my spring.*

"Brenna Lynn!" her mother said, shocked past her shell of prim-lipped propriety. "You'll do no such thing!"

"I will," Brenna said. "If you take the house away, you'd better believe I will."

"Don't think you can manipulate me into doing what you want."

"Why not?" Brenna said quietly, knowing it would be a blow no matter how she said it. "Russell's done very well at it."

Her mother's lips pressed tightly together even as Ada's eyebrows rose. Her skin, always fair and now paler than ever with her age, bloomed with her flush—two red, fake-looking spots high on her cheeks. But her eyes were rimmed in instant red, and none of it was artifice or drama. Inside, something of Brenna folded and faltered, never able to hold her own past this point of any rare confrontation with her mother that made it this far. She felt her own cheeks grow hot, and no matter how she tried, her gaze slid away from her mother's face. To her hands, to the inlaid wood of the coffee table, to her aunt's knees; to the glass of water she sipped not because she was thirsty, but because it was an alternative to running away.

She wondered again what happened to the Brenna she could be at work, facing down snarling dogs, shrugging off unreasonably irate customers. Or what about the Brenna who'd ordered Parker off what she'd then considered *her* property? That Brenna knew what was fair, and what was right, and stood up for herself.

This one didn't seem to know a thing.

Brenna's mother put her tea on the coffee table in jerky motions. When she straightened, she said, "I don't like this conversation. I don't like it at all. But it does seem like the best thing to do is to table the idea of selling the house for now. I need time to think about all of this."

Brenna's mouth said, "I want you to sign the deed over to me."

It was, she thought, a good thing that the saucer and cup were safely aside on the coffee table; they'd have slid right off her mother's lap and onto the floor. Ada gave her an astonished look—not at all disapproving, just as though she'd never thought to hear such a thing come from her niece. Brenna's mother herself seemed speechless. Brenna didn't wait for her to gather any words; she barreled on with her own. "You once told me I could live in the house for as long as I wanted. Now I know you're willing to go back on those words, and if I stay there without the deed, I'll always wonder *when* it's going to happen—when you'll change your mind. I'm not going to live like that."

"I don't," her mother said faintly, "think that would be fair to Russell. Just giving the house to you."

Ada snorted, a most un-little-old-lady sound. "And *I* think it would serve Russell exactly right. He's the one who initiated the whole thing."

Brenna smiled, a little tremulous but with true humor. "It would, wouldn't it?"

"I have to think about it." Her mother's voice gained strength. "I really have to think about it."

"Think about it without talking to Russell," Brenna said. "He's already had his say; he's had it plenty. And I'll ask you about it in a week. Because I'm not waiting around forever. I'm not leaving my future in your hands, or his—not even if it means I have to walk away from here to go make my own."

And her mother would have spoken in protest, working to regain her untouched equilibrium, but Ada said firmly, "That's only right, Rhona. You said she could stay in the house—put your actions where your mouth is. You of all people should know how important it is to be able to trust someone on a matter like this." And coming from Ada, it wasn't an insignificant statement. Not in that tone, and not with that eyebrow arched as it was. Not here in Ada's more-than-comfortable apartment, where her sister Rhona had two rooms to call her own. Brenna truly felt sorry for her mother at that moment, had the sudden impulse to go over and hug her.

But wasn't quite brave enough to face the rejection of those stiff shoulders.

So she put her glass on the tray and said, "I hope the next time I stop by, we can talk about something like what was on television the night before or where you two went gallivanting off for dinner over the weekend. But I didn't start this. I'm just doing my best to end it." She stood, awkward for a moment, and then headed for the door, hesitating by her mother's chair to put a hand on her shoulder.

Just as stiff as she'd imagined. But at least she'd done it.

Ada followed her to the door, and once they were there, Brenna turned to apologize to her. At the least she'd ruined her aunt's afternoon; at the worst Ada would have to deal with the fallout for days. But Ada put up a finger, hushing her before she'd even gotten started. Then she put a hand on either side of Brenna's head to draw her down and kiss her cheek, murmuring an astonishing, *"You go, girl."*

Brenna left sad and smiling to herself at the same time.

And feeling strangely lighter than she had for a long, long time.

Chapter 16

TEIWAZ
Protection for the Warrior

Brenna turned her truck up the driveway and stopped at the bottom of it, just out of the insignificant traffic flow. The farmhouse looked down at her from the top of the hill; the barn was set back just far enough so only the roof was visible. Beside her spread the front pasture and the creek, which ran under the road bridge before snaking boldly through the pasture. Though the spring was out of sight, she could envision its presence strongly enough that she could almost feel it—just as she knew the cultivated acres behind the barn, the individual character and idiosyncratic placement of each custom-sized gate in the fence, which boards squeaked and sagged in the loft, and where the drafts always seemed to bring in snow each winter.

266

The place was hers, had always *been* hers.

Until now.

Now, as she looked up at the farmhouse, noting for the first time the signs of peeling paint near the eaves and the slight sag along the roofline, it suddenly didn't feel like *hers* any more. Not in the least. And she didn't know whether she should go up the driveway and inventory her painting supplies or if she should start packing instead.

She heard a faint bark through the open truck window; Druid had heard the familiar engine, and couldn't understand what was taking her so long to get up the driveway. No doubt he had to go out, and he was ever impatient to see her. She eased the clutch up and took the hill, thinking as she did that she heard the faintest indication of muffler distress and deciding that she just didn't care. Not today.

In the house, Druid flung himself upon her with unusual abandon—she'd taken to leaving him out of the crate, and hadn't yet been sorry—patting his broad round paws against her thigh until she crouched to rub her cheek against the white spot at top of his head. He hooked his paws over her arm and groaned happily until she stood and ushered him out the door. His freedoms were growing; she stood at the door with her arms crossed and thought about how only a month ago she'd never have trusted him outside.

Of course, a month ago, she'd been naive enough to believe that there was a dog pack churning through the area leaving mangled animals in its wake, instead of the more sinister truth—the dead and injured animals were the results of fighting dogs in training, and once someone cried *dog pack*, Parker had no longer bothered to hide the remains in the woods. No threat to her or Druid or even Emily's goats, at least not from any dog pack.

The darkness, now, that was another story. It had

been the touch of darkness that had so frightened Druid the night Sunny died, and hungry, angry darkness that had rent her body to the winds—the very day after she'd caught Parker's attention, bracing him at the spring for the first time.

No coincidence, that.

But the darkness didn't usually come in the day, and of late had not landed heavily upon her or Druid at all. Brenna had the sudden sense, intuition blooming to life, that Parker had found a way to sate it with the dogfights, that it was hanging back, snacking on unwitting sacrifices of blood and honor, pleased to spread chaos with its twisted strain of rabies along the way. That before it had been young and hungry and hunting, striking out in snakelike blows; now it had its ready sustenance, and gathered strength for a more profound hunt.

Intuition unbidden and unsettling.

She wished she thought she'd have nothing to do with that more profound hunt, that she could ignore what she knew and go on with her insulated life. But even if the rabies threat didn't loom—if she hadn't *seen* that possible future—she had a feeling that what she knew was simply too much. And that what the darkness really wanted—what drew Parker back to the spring time after time, and inspired him to reach out to Russell about selling the house—was access to her spring. She'd taken it back, unwittingly rededicated it to a godly power; now she'd strengthened her tie to that power, returning to the spring day after day.

The darkness must think of it as home. She'd closed the door and barred the gate, not even truly understanding the significance or ramifications of her actions, and twice Parker had gone for her. Through a rabid cat. Through Russell.

She had the feeling he'd be more direct the next time.

So no packing. No repairing gates or looking for paintbrushes. No, there were only two things of importance left to do in this day. One was to visit the spring, to attempt deliberately what she'd unwittingly started—to strengthen her ties to Mars Nodens. The god. The angel. The being of power that existed in her God's universe. Whatever.

The other was to talk to Masera.

The day had turned warm; she watched as Druid settled in on a sunny patch on the lawn and moved inside to pour herself a glass of orange juice, which she left behind on the table after only one gulp as she headed for the bedroom, shedding her jeans on the way. Inside her bedroom—a bright east-facing room that caught the morning light—she hesitated with the jeans in hand, unable to stop herself from running her gaze over the two antique dressers and the wardrobe that held her handful of seldom-used dresses in lieu of the closet the room didn't have. With much relief she realized that the room still felt like *hers*, no matter what happened with her mother and Russell and the deed. She'd grown up here; she'd stripped the old layers of wallpaper and repainted, she'd bought and refinished the furniture, she'd chosen the watercolors—bold, colorful images of baroque-style horses—and she'd found the nubbly area rug in an estate sale. For however long she was here, this room was fully hers.

Thus fortified, she slipped on a pair of cut-offs, did the ritual spring examination of the old scar on her thigh from the time she'd taken the driveway descent too fast on her bike and landed on a broken bottle, and went back into the kitchen to gulp down the rest of the orange juice. Then she sat on the porch and cleaned and loaded the rifle while Druid rolled belly-up in the sun and stretched his legs to the four winds, not even twitching when she told him he looked like a pig ready for roasting.

Finished, she gathered the Hoppes cleaner and patches and returned them to the dog room, and would have headed for the spring if she hadn't had a second thought, a twinge of remembrance. A gift, that's what she needed. Just like before. Although this time she wasn't asking for anything—just trying to reach out. Which was just as well, because offhand she couldn't think of anything equivalent to a nine-year-old sacrificing her hard-grown hair to a damp spot on the side of a hill. After a moment she grabbed a carefully hoarded Ghirardelli dark chocolate bar from the freezer, and grinned all the way out of the house.

She suspected that Mars Nodens had never been introduced to chocolate.

Druid sat on the hillside and looked over the pasture, happy enough with his ritual of waiting in a down-stay just below the spring while Brenna went the rest of the way—not that there was far to go anymore, after weeks of working with him. If she stayed here long enough this afternoon, she might even get him all the way up. But she didn't particularly feel like either pushing him or putting up with the results.

So she kicked off her sneakers and pulled her hair free of its binding and finger-combed it as she sat by the spring, easily falling into a contemplative reverie. The sun warmed her shoulders, and her dark hair soaked up its heat; with the unusually mild breeze and temperatures in the seventies, it was easy to forget this was only late April. Almost May.

When she remembered the chocolate, she first set it next to the spring, and then decided that Mars Nodens would probably prefer it unwrapped. Tightly balling the paper and foil and tucking it into her pocket, she put the bar right into the ooze of water, where it would eventually melt and soak into the ground.

Chocolate for the gods. At least it was *good* chocolate. Masera's mother would probably laugh herself silly, Brenna thought, and that notion made its way to her face in a wry expression. She sobered quickly enough, wishing for the expertise of this woman she'd never even met, truly wondering what she'd have to say about the chocolate, about the whole situation.

And wondered what else the woman would be able to tell her, what lifesaving little tidbits Brenna didn't even know enough to ask about, and then wished again that she'd run into this entire mess during the winter, when she didn't have the spring grooming rush to deal with and so would have had the energy—emotional and physical—to do proper research. Not only about Mars Nodens—and here Brenna suddenly remembered Emily's papers sitting on her couch, unread—but maybe into other ancient ways, so she'd have some idea what she was dealing with, and how to go about it.

Then again, what she needed to know probably wasn't the sort of thing she'd find in a book. Probably it hadn't ever been written down at all.

She wondered if any of it were lurking in Masera's experience, or if it had stopped with his mother.

But she *knew*, sitting there staring at the forlorn candy bar in its mushy bed of slowly oozing water, that she was in way over her head. That she didn't have the faintest grain of true knowledge on which to base her actions. How absurd to think that such a person was the only one who stood between her world and a twisted rabies epidemic. How ridiculous to expect that somehow, *she* could be the one to stop the darkness.

Then again . . .

As a girl she'd set out to contact Mars Nodens, and she'd done it.

Why not this?

Below her, Druid whined; one of his thinking whines, the kind she suspected he didn't even realize he'd made. But it served a purpose anyway . . . a reminder. She *wasn't* alone. She had Druid, a dog who'd somehow shown up at this spring and who offered her tidbits of information and someone else's memories—*his* memories?—and enough mysterious clues so if nothing else, she'd been able to pull Masera from that dogfight the evening before.

He discovered her watching him, and gave her a doggy smile—dropping his jaw in a relaxed pant, letting his ears tilt back in happiness—as his tail wagged briefly. He'd given her that, too—companionship, and a quickly deepening partnership that had gone past words and existed almost entirely in the realm of body language and expression.

Not alone.

And then there was Masera, feeding her tidbits about older powers and opening her eyes to possibilities of this world, possibilities that she hadn't even imagined—and still didn't even begin to understand. Latching on to her. Watching over her whether she asked him to or not.

Caring.

Whether she asked him to or not.

No, not alone.

Brenna took a deep breath, deep enough so it triggered a yawn and stretch, although that hadn't been her intent at all. It didn't seem solemn enough for the moment.

Then again, neither did chocolate. And maybe Mars Nodens would appreciate a unique approach. After all, for the very first time since her childhood, Brenna was here to talk to Mars Nodens—not in a confused muddle of very Presbyterian prayer and guilt over religious conflict, but with a comfortable notion of how the pagan god fit into her own theologies. "Hey," she said, not having meant to speak out loud but not stopping now that she'd started. "Mars Nodens. I just came by to say hello and bring you something. I'm glad you're here."

And oddly enough, that seemed sufficient.

Brenna lay back on the hill and spread her arms to the sunshine and fell asleep.

Goose bumps woke her; she didn't know if they were from the cooling air or Druid's whiskers grazing against the sole of her foot. "Oh, stop," she said, twitching her foot away from him. She didn't bother to open her eyes, but gestured, crooking her arm into an invitation of a waiting hug before she remembered how close she lay to the spring.

But before she could change her mind, she felt him creep into place by her side, almost belly-crawling. He tucked his nose under her arm and burrowed into the hug, and she crooned praise for his act of bravery while one of those big Cardi ears twitched against her arm, tickling her.

He couldn't bring himself to do anything else, to turn around and sit with the breeze in his face or even to lift his head. So she had no idea what had warned him when he startled her with a muted woof, but when she sat up, she knew immediately what had triggered it.

Parker.

A glance at her watch showed her she'd slept longer than she'd ever intended to be out here, and a look at the sky confirmed it—the sun hung low, and the rising breeze held the chill of impending twilight.

And now here came Parker, still a small figure in the far corner of the pasture, but undeniably Parker. She knew that casual swagger, that particular shade of gold-laced blond hair. Hair that belonged on an angel, and not on the head of someone who could call up a darkness to threaten the world.

She sat, uncertain what to do—to go or to stay, to pretend his enmity and attacks hadn't affected her. Or that she'd been too dense to puzzle out who lay behind them. In the end she decided to do nothing but sit. Not to turn tail and run, not to throw out angry words or drive him off the land. Not to tip her hand in any way.

Just sit there. A woman next to a spring with her dog, the rifle at her side.

She could see the moment he realized she was there, the way his body stiffened and the brief hesitation in his stride. But he, like she, was not about to run away. They'd bluff this one out together, she thought, each pretending more innocence than they had.

To her relief, he didn't come to the footbridge. He went straight to the creek, opposite her spot on the hill and with the little island between them. The water ran lower today, down from its earlier spring swell, quieter and easier to speak over.

"Does this mean·you've changed your mind about having visitors at your place?" she asked him, an oblique reminder of her declaration of closed boundaries on her side until he opened them on his.

He shrugged, smiled that charming smile. "Not to speak of." Then he tilted his head slightly, another charming maneuver. It let him look at her from angled and shadowed eyes, but she suspected there was no warmth in those eyes. There certainly wasn't any in his voice. "Seems to me you've found ways to step into my business anyway."

That took her right off guard, baffling her. He couldn't have had any news from Russell about the house sale yet; even if her mother had immediately called Russell, her brother simply wasn't that easy to get hold of during the workday.

"I told you I had ways," he said. "You might be a little easier to get along with."

What did he know? Her conversation with her mother, her phone call to Masera the night before, her awareness of the rabies? About his *ways*, she didn't even want to think. He certainly seemed to have obtained a comfortable relationship with the powers he'd helped call up years earlier, unlike her own blundering ignorance.

In an attempt to avoid revealing that blundering ignorance, she kept her silence. Beside her, Druid's throat vibrated in a barely audible growl.

Parker seemed unperturbed by her lack of response. "You were here earlier," he said.

He must have seen her while she was sleeping, and deeply enough so any response Druid might have had to his presence didn't rouse her. *While she was sleeping.* The very notion made her shudder.

Not that Parker appeared to notice her reaction; he tossed a stick into the creek and watched it float away. "Not your usual day off."

He'd been keeping track, all right.

"Nothing's usual at work these days," Brenna said, unable to keep the edge from her voice. *Elizabeth, dead.* "How's your girlfriend feeling? I hear she had that cat put down. Too bad they didn't do any advanced testing on it."

He gave her a sharp look, completely distracted from his twig-throwing. "Those close to me are safe," he said. "I can't say the same for you and yours."

"Don't underestimate me and mine." So much for pretending innocence. So much for avoiding angry words.

His expression came alive, his body alert and intent and all but leaping out of its skin. The gloves were off, the battle joined . . . and he liked it. "I want this land," he said. "I'll get it, too. And by the time I have it, you won't really be in a position to care any more."

"Or maybe not," she said, but she didn't like that

shift in his posture, the way his shoulders seemed to fill, and how his slanted gaze grew full of condescending confidence. Only years of standing down aggressive dogs allowed her to look back at him without evidence of the fear that tickled between her stomach and spine. To even look back at him with her own disdain.

But beside her, Druid's growling rose in pitch and intensity, and beneath her, she felt a responsive tingle between herself and the ground—as if it felt her fear and responded to it, rippling outward like pebbles thrown in a pond.

"Oh, please," Parker said, and she wasn't entirely sure to what he reacted. "Don't even try. You think I don't know you haven't got a clue?"

"I'd come back with some equally clever response if I even knew what you were talking about," Brenna told him. Casually, she felt for the rifle by her side.

"That's the whole point, isn't it? And don't bother with that rifle. We know you won't use it."

"Do we?" Brenna said, lashing out at him with the very fear of how right he was. She couldn't even bring herself to *point* the thing at him. "Do you really want to find out? Why don't you just run home instead? Go back to whatever socially responsible thing you've been up to. Or do you plan to stand there and try to intimidate me all night?"

She knew the words—their challenge—were a mistake the moment they came out of her mouth, even before she saw Parker's sudden dangerous grin, before Druid whined . . .

Before she felt the surge of darkness.

A sharp spike of fear stabbed through her and right into the ground, and again triggered the strange tremble of response. Parker gave her a knowing look, one that said he'd seen her fear, and he shook his head with that frightening grin still in place beneath the mustache—that good-old-boy mustache that she'd never be able to reconcile with his nature. He should at least have some sort of pretentious mustache-goatee combo.

Fine, she told herself numbly. *When he gets here, maybe you can talk to him about that.*

For he was coming, and she had the feeling it wouldn't be for conversation. As he eyed the bank and the shallow, navigable water between himself and the island and then Brenna's side of the creek, she had the feeling he fully planned to haul her away, back to his place—where he'd hold her, or feed her to the dogs, or give her to his boys, or simply keep her out of the way while he did as he pleased on her land, watching the rabies problem grow out of control.

She could shoot him.

She couldn't.

Not so coldly, so brutally. Not with a rifle she'd started carrying against feral dogs.

She could run.

Yes. She could outrun him, surely—

But not the darkness. Not whatever the darkness had done to Sunny. And she'd felt that darkness hovering moments earlier, she and Druid both. Druid still, the way he'd gone to crouching against the ground, frozen in fear, utterly unable to decide which direction might be the safest.

None of them.

That's when she found her hands shaking, her knees shaking, her whole body trembling with fear—

No, not her body. Not shaking *that* hard. That came from the outside, not the in. And Parker felt it too; she saw it in him, his condescending confidence interrupted by the inexplicable; it was his redirected stare that aimed Brenna's attention to the right place, that and the way he hesitated on his way down the sheer-cut bank to the stepping stones of the creek.

Down where the water had flowed away without being replaced, trickling away to leave nothing but tiny pools caught between rocks, the spring peepers along the banks caught startled and out in the open, a few cold crawdads crawling in befuddlement around what should have been their watery domain and quickly scuttling backward into rocky crannies when they realized how they'd been exposed.

Exposed, like Brenna sitting on the hillside, clutching Druid's collar in one hand and a rifle she couldn't bring herself to use in the other.

Parker's smile renewed itself. "Looks like someone's going to make this easy for me."

The darkness, he thought, as did Brenna, so gapingly astonished at the sight of the drained creek bed that she could barely think. *Use the rifle. Pick it up and point it and pull the damn trigger.*

She didn't have to kill him. She didn't even have to hit him. She only had to drive him off. It didn't even matter how mad she made him in the process—they'd gone beyond stopping whatever he'd started between them, it was only a matter of when they'd finish it. Now . . . or later. Later, when she knew more. When she was ready.

As if she'd ever be ready.

But Parker was ready. Parker was about to set foot in the exposed creek bed. If she saw correctly, he was deliberately aiming for one of the unhappy crawdads.

She pulled Druid into her lap and wrapped the leash around her leg. Then she picked up the rifle and sighted on the ground at Parker's feet. The smell of gun oil struck her nose like an acrid punctuation.

"Ooh," he said. "Scary. So convincing. Your finger's got to be on the trigger to have any real threat behind it, Brenna."

She didn't like the way he said her name. She moved her finger to the trigger.

Still undecided.

But saved, then, as they both heard the new rumble of sound in the earth. She lifted her head from the smooth cool wood of the rifle stock as he halted in mid-stride; for all his previous snide confidence he now looked just as baffled as she felt, and nearly as alarmed. Druid gave several sharp barks . . . and they held no fear. They were an announcement of some importance, and he was on his feet now, braced against the reverberations in the earth but not with that look of crouching panic. His ears pricked forward and alert and very intent, and he stared up the creek—which remained empty of water as far as Brenna could see.

Maybe because he stood in the creek bed, Parker understood first; maybe his connections with the darkness gave him some advantage when it came to puzzling out things that couldn't possibly be happening in the first place. But Brenna had done no more than rise to her knees, the rifle drooping, looking right and left and even behind, when Parker lunged for the bank from which he'd come. He clawed his way up, digging fingers and toes and knees into the mucky soil, and as he threw himself over the top Brenna finally saw it—a high wall of water, tumbling toward them at amazing speed.

It filled the creek banks to the top and overflowed along the way, spilling over with the force of a tidal wave. Parker didn't even try to get up in his flight from the creek once he reached the pasture; he rolled, gained quick ground before finding his feet and sprinting another fifty yards away. The water rushed by them, completely overtaking the small island as Parker stopped and turned and glared.

The roar of it obliterated his words but couldn't obscure the acrimony with which he shouted them, or the way his face distorted with the enormity of his rage.

Rage at Brenna. For it wasn't the astonishingly flooded creek at which he screamed and gestured, but at Brenna herself, as if she had somehow created this event she couldn't even bring herself to comprehend.

Cold water sprayed Brenna's face; only a few drops, but enough to jar her mind from utter vacancy and into denial. This wasn't the Red Sea rushing into place after Charlton Heston for pity's sake, it was her *pasture*, where horses had quietly grazed, where Brenna had romped and played through her childhood. And the creek was that same in which she'd spent humid summer days, splashing and wet from head to toe with cool water. Had she been down there a moment ago, she'd have been washed clear to Lake Ontario. Had *Parker* been there a moment ago . . .

He'd been so sure it was his darkness, making life easy for him—and moments ago, Brenna had thought so as well. Thought herself cornered by the man and his dark ally. Or the darkness and its human ally—she wasn't sure which. He'd been wrong. *She'd* been wrong.

Druid nudged her arm, his nose wet and cold; she put the arm around his shoulders, glad for his presence. Glad beyond belief that he hadn't flipped, hadn't added one of his fear fits to her already overwhelmed senses.

Beyond belief. That was the text of all of this. Beyond belief. For it hadn't been darkness coming to Parker's aid . . . it had been Mars Nodens coming to Brenna's. No longer just a theory, a vague tingle, a confluence of hints and clues and things that defied other explanation.

Mars Nodens in action.

Here.

Right in front of her.

The creek slowed and swirled and began to settle;

the island brush reappeared, bent and stripped of leaves, shiny wet. Dismally muddied, Parker approached the scoured bank; he made a few steps toward the footbridge and halted. Two long tree trunks it had been, with spaced crosspieces of wood—some old, some newly replaced and bright in contrast to the others—and laid across the width of the creek, high above the water. Heavy, sturdy . . . not going anywhere.

Or so Brenna would have said.

Except it was no longer there; it wasn't even in sight.

Brenna wiped the dripping water from her face and sat back on her heels, knees pointed downhill, to make a rag of her shirt hem and run it around the rifle barrel. She swiped a hand down each side of Druid's face, muzzle to ears, and removed the water sparkling there. There was no haste to her movements; she was here, Parker was there, and never the twain to meet. She didn't have to make the decision to pull the trigger; she didn't have to try to run. And if there was something of a dazed shock in the quality of her movement . . . then well there ought be.

She had to tell Masera. Forget the dogfights, forget what she'd done to him the night before and how they'd stared at one another at the threshold of her house. Never mind the things it had stirred in her, the feelings she didn't recognize and didn't know what to do about. He was the one who could put this into perspective, and who could tell her what to do next. How to protect them from the darkness.

If anyone could.

Silence slowly overtook the roar of the flash flood, leaving them in unnatural quiet—though not for long.

"You shouldn't have done that." Parker stood across from her again. Just as miraculously as it had overflowed, the water was back to normal, gurgling along in altered creek channels. The island, scrubbed clean to the dirt between what brush had remained rooted, was as bare as she'd ever seen it. The upstream edge had seined out an accumulation of debris—sticks, leaves, an old horseshoe, the proverbial old shoe. The stepping stones between it and the bank on either side were clearly exposed, but Parker made no attempt to descend to them. No, he stood there and glowered at her from beneath lowered brows, and repeated, "You shouldn't have done that."

Brenna said simply, "I didn't."

He laughed, as dark and low as the forces that now shaped his life. "You did," he said, and his gold hair glinted ruddy in the light from the setting sun; it felt like more of an omen than anything she'd seen so far—as if she, in the presence of one miracle, was suddenly able to read omens. "Whether you know it or not, you did it. You and whatever puny little god you first called to this place. Did you even know what you were doing, way back when?"

"No," Brenna said, almost a whisper, though she suspected he somehow heard it anyway. "Do you know what you're doing *now*?"

A strange, conflicted look passed over his features, so quickly that she wasn't even sure what she'd seen. Hesitation. Doubt. As if in that moment, he actually *thought* about what he'd gotten into, what he was aiding and abetting and causing. As if she'd managed to touch something of him that had once been more human than what lived in him now.

And then the anger and hatred returned tenfold, and she had the feeling he'd make her pay for that moment.

"I know exactly what I'm doing," he said. "Which means that you haven't got a chance. I want this spring, Brenna Fallon. *Honey*. I want the land it's on. I'm even willing to pay for it."

Money, she thought, probably wasn't what mattered to him anymore, anyway. Why *not* pay for it?

"And you'd best take me up on that offer."

For that instant, she found herself tempted. He was right; she had no idea what she was doing and she had about as much chance of getting through any escalation of power—*where did one go from* instant flood? *Fire? Tornado? Fast-moving glacier?*—as she had of controlling his darkness. So why not give him the land, that which she'd so recently contemplated leaving behind by choice, simply so she could make her own choices? Why not walk away, when the rabies and the chaos had already taken hold?

Because you can't outrun a plague, you idiot.

And because she simply couldn't bear to be the one who handed Parker's darkness its anchor point of power. If it was strong and restless now, what would it become with a god's well of power to feed it?

"You're right," she said, hearing her own voice grow steadier, louder. *Enjoy it while it lasts.* "I'd *best take you up* on your offer. But you know I won't."

He grinned at her. A nasty grin, the sky fading behind him. Oh, Lord, she was going to get caught out here after dark. He said, "I *hoped* you wouldn't. It wouldn't have been as much fun. You know, lately I've imagined ripping that hair out of your head fistful by fistful. I should thank you for the opportunity."

Not the same man she'd first met out here weeks ago. Not at all. That man had been an easy liar, not much concerned with things like honor and truth, but not malevolent, either.

This man was malevolent. Changed. And he had something hungry in his expression.

Hungry for her.

Druid growled.

"You've got that right," Brenna muttered at him, smoothing down the hackles he'd raised. She glanced again at the sky—could she get home before dark?— and at Parker, trying to gauge him. What he might do if she simply got to her feet and left him there.

What *could* he do? He was stuck on the other side.

And that's when Druid whined. His fearful whine, the warning whine. Reminding her that while she was out of Parker's reach, the darkness had no such boundaries. And that she couldn't depend on another miracle, when she had no idea how or even if she'd called the last one. "Shhh," she said, nonsensically enough, even as she dreaded what she feared would come next.

That trickle of breath-sucking dread she'd finally come to recognize. The hair standing up on the back of her neck, goosebumping down her already chilled arms. The breeze rising, lifting the strands of her long thick hair, black in this light and without the chestnut streaks that spoke of sunshine and light-hearted days in this very pasture.

Sunny's bloody collar tossed aside by her barn.

What would remain of her?

Nothing, if she just swayed here on her knees waiting for the inevitable.

But the inevitable was here.

Roaring across the bottom of the pasture like a directional tornado, it tore up chunks of sod and sticks and debris, a blotch of midnight in the twilight air, heading straight for her.

Parker only grinned. Fearless. In control.

Brenna didn't think. There was no time for *thinking*. She did the only thing left to her. She threw herself over the spring, over the grave of her old companion. And as darkness thundered up the hill for her, ripping through the creek, shredding what brush remained on the island, churning a wide path up the hill, she dropped the rifle and yanked Druid's leash, jerking him right off his feet and into the area she'd always considered part of the spring.

Too much for a sturdy little dog who'd already pushed his limits for the day. Druid landed already shrieking, not that Brenna could hear him above the

maelstrom that churned around them—*around*
them—not touching them. It deafened her, oppressive enough that her ears popped and she, too,
screamed, a mindless, gut-level scream of protest and
fear. But within the sphere of the spring the air barely
stirred, and when Druid's struggles took him to the
edge of that calm, Brenna hauled him in close, throwing herself atop him and squinching her eyes shut
against the onslaught from without and within—and
now from beneath. For Druid flipped and flung
himself, whacking his solid skull against her mouth,
her nose, her forehead—

No, Druid—no!

Someone else's familiar voice in her head and she
held him tighter, heedless of the claws that gouged
her arms and legs—

*Wails of grief, wails of fear and loss and Emily's
voice moaning Jill's name over and over and unfamiliar voices crying their own sorrow, a deep and
gibbering laughter underlying it all—*

And Druid shrieked and Brenna screamed and held
him tight and the darkness tightened in around them
until her ears were agony and her head felt like it
would implode and it seemed like this was all her
world had ever been and ever would be—

And then it stopped.

Then there was utter silence, and Druid went
quiescent beneath her, so flaccid she thought she'd
smothered him to death and held her own breath
until she felt the jerk of his chest as he panted.

She couldn't hear it yet. All she could hear was
a ringing in her ears, and then her own harsh, gulping
breaths through a throat raw and abused. "Shhh,
shhh," she told Druid, and couldn't hear that, either.

But as she lifted her head and shoved her hair
aside, she saw star- and moonlight, and as she straightened her cramped back and looked out over the lower
pasture, she found Parker on his knees, his shoulders

slumped, his head dropped. Sounds started to trickle back in—her own breathing and Druid's, both easing, and even Parker's, sounding as exhausted as she felt.

Exhausted, and in no shape to chase after her in any manner.

Brenna grabbed Druid's leash and ran.

Chapter 17

ᛗ

EHWAZ
A Partnership in Effort

When she reached the barn, Brenna staggered up to the target-shooting bales and threw herself against them, thumping the stack against the barn. Druid sat on her feet, clinging to her like a Velcro dog while she caught her breath and took stock of herself—and first and foremost was the fact that she'd made it at all, sprinting like a woman possessed all the way from the spring.

Which maybe wasn't far from the mark.

But her tremulous legs berated her for such effort, and her arms and thighs throbbed from the claw scrapes they'd endured while a painful fat lower lip swelled at the corner of her mouth. Her hair hung against her bottom in a solid snarl—hair that had been

outside the spring's protected area. Just from the
heavy feel of it, she doubted she'd ever manage to
comb it out.

You're a mess, Brenna Lynn Fallon.

Which is what she got for not paying attention. For
falling asleep by the spring with so much conflict
focused on that very spot. The anchor point. The
place of power.

Brenna snorted softly to herself. "You are so, *so*
in over your head," she said softly, suddenly wondering if returning here was the right thing at all. Maybe
she should have stayed at the spring, where she at
least knew she had an area of safety.

A small one.

No kitchen at the spring. No bathroom. Not even
any water to speak of, at least not for drinking pur-
poses. And boy, did she want a tall glass of ice water
right this very moment.

Druid still leaned against her, stress-panting—but
he managed to pause long enough growl, his ears
canted back at a wary angle, his attention toward the
house.

"Oh, no," Brenna groaned, tipping her head back
so the barn overhang loomed dark in her vision. *No
more. Not tonight.* Please.

Russell, maybe. It was just about the right timing,
if their mother had reached him after work. She
groaned again.

On the other hand, after what had just happened,
facing Russell didn't feel like such a big deal. Why
hadn't she ever told him he could call ahead if he
wanted to talk to her? And another new concept
bloomed, suddenly obvious—*this is a bad time, you'll
have to come back when it's convenient for me*—as
she abruptly realized all the times it had been true
and she'd never even considered sending him off.
Never even thought of inconveniencing *him*.

But Druid only growled once, and then dismissed

whatever he'd detected, returning his worried attention to Brenna.

Someone he knew, then. She didn't think that would include Russell. She found herself almost disappointed she wouldn't get to act out her new concept—and then dreading the effort of dealing with whoever it really was.

Brenna pushed away from the hay bales and went through the barn on wobbly knees, not bothering to admire her newly hung gate this time. And when she rounded the corner and saw the pale, becoming-familiar lines of Masera's SUV, she could have sobbed with relief.

When she saw him sitting against the front hood, one heel propped against the bumper, his dark form relaxed and waiting, she did. "Iban!"

His head whipped around; he'd been looking across the yard, as though she might have been off at Emily's. She didn't think about it; she dropped Druid's leash and ran for him, so full of relief she was no longer alone in this suddenly terrifying journey that she didn't even hesitate. Not caring that he was startled, not caring that there was anger left unresolved between them. Not caring that he'd never held her before—and knowing that his arms would close around her just as they did, firm but careful. Warm. As if for that instant, she could let herself believe she was safe here. No matter what. Darkness be damned.

But the instant was bound to end.

He stood, moving to the side, maintaining contact. And when he said, "Brenna?" it was as much a statement, an affirmation, as a question. He said it again, lower this time.

She didn't respond; she suddenly didn't know what to say, how to explain what had happened. How to admit how much she needed his help when she'd never even resolved for herself whether she trusted him at all. How to ask him to hold her for just a few moments longer before she had to face the world again. And while she was thinking about it, he changed—stiffening a little, growing somehow more focused. She felt it in his hands, the way they rested against her back, how they followed the curve of her spine. And she felt it in the set of his shoulders, how he took himself back just far enough to look at her in the darkness—though he could see no more than she, not with the moon easing from quarter down to new.

Some part of her had seen this coming, even knew the look on his face through the darkness. Intent, as usual. She shouldn't have been surprised, but somehow—since her brain had evidently ceased to function—when he buried his hands in the hair at the nape of her neck and kissed her mouth, it *did* surprise her.

So much for common sense. So much for *do I trust you or don't I.* So much for *we've got things to talk about.*

At the moment, she couldn't think of a single thing she wanted to say.

At least, not until he tipped his head to kiss her more deeply and she tipped her head the other way to say *yes, let's* and her fat lip came between them.

"Mmm!" she said, the best she could manage at the moment.

"Hmm?" He drew back enough so she could say, "Ouch!" but not so far that she didn't brush his mouth when she did it, and replied, "I don't think *ouch* is the appropriate response." But he must have seen something, because he took her face and tipped it to catch what little of the moonlight there was, and then he pulled her unresisting to the porch and flipped on the light.

One glance at her face and he swore heartily, causing Druid to give a prim bark. At Masera's tone, no doubt, but Brenna couldn't help but laugh, in spite of all that had happened to her within the past few hours. *From supernatural attack to a dark assignation in the driveway.*

Or maybe *because* of all that happened. A nice little hysteria.

He swore again, not amused. "You should have said something, Brenna. What the hell happened?"

"I didn't have the *chance* to say anything," she told him. "*I'm* not complaining, so you'd better not."

He gave that a double thought, even had the grace to look a little sheepish. "No," he said. "But let's get a cold washcloth on some of those bruises." He opened the door for her, let her precede him inside, and held it open long enough so Druid could come through trailing his leash. She flicked the light switches on her way in, blazing a trail to the bathroom.

Where she looked in the mirror and swore.

"I told you," Masera said, sounding satisfied. "Now you tell me—what *happened*?"

Brenna stared at the blood streaking her upper lip and dried down the side of her face; the slight normal bump in her nose now swollen and reddened off to the side; she gingerly touched it and made a face when—*surprise*—pain shot through it. Similar swellings marked her brow and cheek, and she had another cut on her chin. Welts dotted with blood raked her arms in neat claw lines, and a glance down at her thighs revealed the same.

"Parker," he said, unable to refrain from guessing and now lurking by the closed bathroom door. "You came from the pasture. I heard the noise out there—thought it was a town truck somewhere with the jake brake on. But it was Parker, wasn't it?" His voice darkened. "*Parker* did this to you."

"In a way." Brenna fished a washcloth from the linen closet and ran cold water over it, raising her voice. "It was Druid. I pulled him on top of the spring, and what with the wind and—" Well, that wouldn't make any sense. Not told inside out like that. "Wait a minute. I'll be right out."

She looked much better with her face clean and her arms and legs washed down. She came out of the bathroom with purpose—almost knocking him down, he stood so close—and marched to her bedroom, where she pulled off her shirt and replaced it with a soft old cotton sweater, one with little horseshoes marching around the cuffs, bottom, and neckline. Warm and soft. She'd left the windows open and the heat off, and the house was no longer pulling in sunshine . . . and besides, she wanted it around her, snug and comforting, like an old blanket. Pulling her hair out from the neck of it, she found again the horrifying snarls near the end and wandered back into the kitchen where Masera now waited, examining them with resignation. "I'll have to cut it, I think."

"You will *not*," Masera said, rising from the chair in which he'd finally settled, coming to face her and do what he'd probably wanted to do all along—put a hand over either shoulder and lift her hair, running his fingers through it as far as they could go before encountering tangles. "Do you know how hard it's been to keep my hands out of this hair? Get a comb."

She laughed. "You think it's that easy, do you, you with your hair that can be measured in inches?"

He raised an eyebrow, acceptance of a challenge. "My mother has long hair."

She really didn't want to cut it. Not that much of it. She went to the bathroom and returned with two combs and a bottle of horse finishing spray.

"This is for *horses*," he said, taking it from her. "Just how hard did that dog hit you?"

She gave him a warning look, one brow quirked up. "It'll make the hair slick. I use it all the time." She took the bottle back and went to the den, where she plunked herself in the couch, draping the snarls around to lie across her thighs. Druid put himself at her feet. "Come on, then."

He came in with a glass of water for each of them, anticipating what she'd forgotten to ask. Sitting on the floor beside her, he picked up a section of hair, mulling the extent of the tangles, running his fingers over it as though it were a strange Braille that only he could read.

"Here," she said, handing him the finishing spray. "What happened was, I was at the spring, giving Mars Nodens a candy bar. And then I fell asleep, and Parker came, and we had an argument."

"Giving Mars Nodens a candy bar," Masera repeated, looking up at her with disbelief.

He sounded as bemused as she'd probably feel if she stopped to think about all the things that had happened since she woke from her nap, and having him sitting beside her working gently at her hair was hardly the least of it. So she somehow didn't snap at him in the sudden embarrassment of the absurdity of what she'd said. "I didn't want to go empty-handed. And you know what, I think he liked it."

Masera looked down at his work, frowning over a particularly tight witch's knot. "You might be right about this."

"Giving up so easily?"

That got his attention all right. He gazed at her with those blue eyes hooded, long enough to see if she'd back down or ease up—very much the look he'd given her in the break room that first day—and said, "You should know better than that."

She just smiled. Then she told him the rest of what had happened at the spring, and by the time she was done he had come up on his knees to take her into his arms again, holding her tight—only this time she felt it was for him more than for her, a fierce reaction to the thought of the things that might have happened but hadn't. And it was she who stroked his ruffled hair back and rubbed her thumb along the evening stubble on his cheek and gave him the moment he needed.

But not much more.

"Now," she said. "You tell *me*."

"Tell you—?"

"*We have things to talk about*," she said, repeating his words from the night before. *Only the night before*. She moved aside a small section of hair they'd actually managed to untangle; it was soaked with the coat finisher but drying fast, as sleek and shiny as ever. Not normal hair, she thought, not for the first time in her life . . . only now she knew why. "I could have called animal control a long time ago. I didn't, because you dropped a few vague comments. I didn't do it . . . because you didn't want me to, even if you never said so in so many words. *Now* . . . I want to know."

He grew distant, then, without ever moving a muscle that she could see. A distinct vibration in the air around him, complete with little *no trespassing* signs. Brenna ceased working on her hair, let her hands rest in her lap, and looked at him. Whether he knew it or not, he hovered at a point of no return.

He must have known it.

He still hadn't moved, he still watched her with as much tight concentration as ever, but something inside had relaxed, and she knew it without having to know how she knew it. She went back to work on her hair.

"We were trying to build a connection to Parker's cocaine source," he said, apparently starting right in the middle of the story.

"We, who?"

He looked up, mildly startled. "Me, animal control, the cops . . . who else?"

Brenna shrugged.

"No," he said, and then laughed, short but truly amused. "You didn't think—"

"You tried hard to make sure I didn't know what to think, didn't you? Me *or* Eztebe. Do you know how worried he is? And since when do the cops go to civilians to solve their problems?"

Masera sobered. He ran his fingers through the hair he'd freed up, letting it slide through his fingers like heavy silk. "I was walking a line, Brenna. I didn't intend to get involved at all. Before I even started working at the store, Mickey spotted me there and asked me about the best food for performance dogs."

"The same brand he ended up stealing, I suppose."

"He was walking away with merchandise from the start. He only worked there so he'd have access to what he could take, and a discount on what he couldn't. Parker's supply man. Happens I saw him in a dogfight photo my friend in animal control was showing around. By then Mickey knew me . . . I started asking around and ended up in the middle of it. The cops wanted me out, especially after Parker's boys pulled their little initiation stunt on me. Lots of shouting over that, believe me."

Brenna thought back to their first real conversation, when he'd barely been able to move and the bruises had obscured the well-defined features with which she'd since become familiar. "That day in the break room? The first of many times you pissed me off?"

Grinning, he glanced up; the light reflected from his eyes in translucent indigo. A rare humor, and she thought it was just as well; it was nigh to irresistible. "The day you got my attention."

"I was trying to get your *goat*," she said, and wrinkled her nose at him. "That *beating* was their little initiation stunt?"

He snorted; instead of working on her hair he'd transferred his attention to scraping a blob of mud from the fringe of her cut-offs. "As far as I can tell, it was a transparent attempt to gauge my determination. Parker's minions; they came and went, except for Mickey and a few others. Didn't matter. It was Parker I wanted, the son of a bitch." He scowled and reached up, using a knuckle on her chin to tilt her head to the light; she let him. Whatever he saw satisfied him, for he let it go without comment. Her nose, probably. It still throbbed, but with less fervor. "There was no way . . . not once I knew Parker had blundered through akelarre and had a fast-growing power at his back . . . that he would do anything to gain access to your spring—" He shrugged, and quit trying to put it into words. "It wasn't something I could leave to the cops."

"What about those dogs you bought?"

He didn't answer at first. Then he said, "What do you think?"

What did she think? She knew he'd been working with them; Eztebe had cheerfully told her so. He'd said he didn't intend to fight them. He'd also said he didn't currently consider himself as having his own dog. "I think you're trying to rehab them, find them homes."

He smiled a private little smile, not looking at her. "You'd be right."

"Can you?"

"If they'd ever been fought . . . no. But they were just pups, not even in training. They'll be fine. I've just been waiting till this was over."

"And is it?" she demanded. "You're *not* going back to that barn." Worried by her tone, Druid got to his feet and put his front feet against her leg, balancing lightly on his haunches to whine at her. She rubbed the base of his speckled ear and watched Masera.

He shook his head, frustrated. "We hadn't gotten to the bottom of it."

"It doesn't sound like it *has* a bottom, if you ask me."

"You may be right, given what Parker's got going for him." He shook his head again. "Whatever. It's over. I suppose it was over as soon as you told me about the rabies. I told Rick—my friend in animal control—and they're going to shut it all down; I don't know exactly when. They'll get the training barn you saw, the fight rings, two or three breeding barns—Parker's been pretty methodical about it all. Not a hobbyist, a pro. Breeding carefully, taking good care of the dogs, training them with all the tricks—in it for the long haul, and running a nice little drug-distribution scheme alongside it. You saw the cat mill out behind his barn while you were there? That's probably where most of the dead animals came from."

"I saw it. I didn't understand it."

"It's like a horse walker," he said, trying to keep his voice even. "Put a dog at the end of one arm of it; put a cat in front of it. The cat runs, the dog chases. After a while, the dog catches. It builds fitness in the dogs, and bloods them at the same time."

Brenna made a choked noise, opened her mouth to respond, and couldn't find any words strong enough. Not to respond to this new image of the cat mill, with blood in the dried winter grass, the smell she couldn't quite locate or identify, the worn rut of dirt—she grimaced, and took a deep breath, and moved the conversation forward. "The drugs came from his dead pal Gary, I suppose," Brenna said, and then, unable to let go of the cat mill, added, "I hope they turn that thing into scrap metal."

"It doesn't matter," Masera said darkly. "It doesn't matter, because Parker will get away, and his cocaine source is still unknown. He'll just start it up again somewhere else."

"No," Brenna said. "He won't. He's got to be near

this spring. He might start up with some*thing* else, but he won't leave this place."

"Whatever. Dammit, if I'd just had a few more days—" He got to his feet, unaware of the comb he clenched in his hand, frustrated to find that the den wasn't big enough for any sustained movement.

"Iban," she said gently, "Iban, you stopped the rabies. They'll put down every single one of those dogs, knowing there's rabies among them. They'll test them—and I swear I think CDC already knows this is a new strain." She thought of Sammi's constrained and unnatural silence. "They'll work up a new vaccine in case anything slipped through the cracks. Damn, *this* is what it's all about, what it's *been* about."

"What?" he said, as his eyebrows pinched in on his nose. It made her want to reach up and erase the resultant line with her finger, though she could do it just as well with words.

"For weeks I've had those weird visions. I can't explain it . . . I know they're connected to Druid."

"Visions?" he said.

"Impressions . . . memories. Only not *my* memories. I know it sounds crazy—"

And it did. Too crazy. She hesitated, would have stopped.

Masera said, "Tell me."

Still hesitant, she did. She started at the beginning, at Emily's kitchen table with Druid asleep at her feet and dreaming, and took Masera all the way up to the stark moments she'd envisioned only the night before. "I felt like I was looking at the days of the black death. All caused for—and *by*—Parker's dark power, and by its new rabies." She stopped to look at him, aware she'd gotten sidetracked. "It would have killed *so many* people . . . it would have killed *me*. It would have changed *everything*. But it won't, not now. Maybe you didn't get the drug dealer, but you stopped *the rabies*." Even if Parker didn't know it yet. And if he'd been angry during their recent confrontation, then he'd be utterly beside himself when the raids went down.

And he'd blame her. He knew enough to do that.

"*We* stopped the rabies," he murmured. "One of us had to figure it out, first, and then have the stones to call the other in the middle of a dogfight."

"Stones?" she said, and grinned, sliding the comb through the last of the tangles and gathering her hair up in one section again, feeling, despite its natural resilience, the loss of some bulk, the broken ends in the affected area. "Is that what I have, Iban?"

"Say that again," he told her.

"About the stones, or—"

"My name," he said.

"Iban," she said, drawing it out.

"I'm coming over there," he said. "Now."

How they ended up on the floor a short time later, she wasn't sure, but Druid wasn't slow to take advantage; he walked right over them and whisker-inspected Brenna's face, then Masera's, then back to Brenna, paying particular attention to the cuts and bumps. And while Brenna was altogether focused on how nice it felt to run her hands over—well, to have him run his hands over—well, maybe she wasn't altogether focused, maybe she was altogether *un*focused. But the whisker inspection didn't work for her at all. She relinquished Masera's lower lip and looked over at Druid. "What," she said, breathing unreasonably fast, "What in this picture doesn't belong, Druid?"

He whined. A reminder whine. A doggy nudge. Brenna let her head rest on the carpet, which gave her an appalling view of the dog hair she needed to vacuum up. "He's right, though," she said. "We've got a lot of other things to—what?"

For Masera was laughing. He was trying to hide it, lying on his side with his head propped on his arm and one nice strong hand resting on her hip, but she

felt it through that connection, the slight jostling it
gave her. "He's *right*?" he said, and let some of the
laughter slip out. "The *dog's right*?"

Brenna gave him a little shove; he didn't resist so
he ended up on his back. Then she conceded, "Maybe
I've been living alone too long." But, leaning closely
over him and his amusement, she added, "Or maybe
he's just *right*." She climbed to her feet and plunked
back down in the couch, but since she hadn't been
careful enough, she sat on her hair and had to bounce
up to free it. By then he sat opposite her, fiddling
with a folded piece of paper and not objecting when
she invited herself to put her feet across his thighs.
"Seriously," she said. "That cat was meant for me;
whether it was Parker's idea or—I mean, how much
can he communicate with that . . . thing, anyway?" It
would seem unfair that the darkness would be so
willing to communicate with Parker when she was still
leaving voice mail with Mars Nodens.

"At this point, I suspect quite a bit. Parker's the
perfect point man for something like that, trying to
gain a foothold in this world. He's a first-come, first-
served kind of guy, even if it means eating off other
people's plates, and he's smart enough to carry his
end of it without messing up—unlike his two friends
before him. That's why it doesn't mean much in the
long run, that we've stopped the rabies. He'll start
up with something else."

"No," Brenna said, still stuck on that point.
"Parker's come at me a couple of different ways
already. He won't give up yet. He—*they*—need this
place, the access to the spring. We've got to do
something to protect it. That's where you come in."

"Me," he said blankly.

"You know about this stuff! You and Eztebe, but
he says you more than he."

Masera shook his head. "Nothing like this. I know
runes you can use. I know this is a bad phase of the

moon to brace darkness—Medusa Moon, like when you lost Sunny. I know we're better off for having made it past the vernal equinox before reaching this point. But how to go up against this darkness? This is way outta my league, Brenna. Way out."

"Then call your mother. Ask *her*."

He seemed to think about it. In the end, he didn't outright reject it. He just said, "It would take time to reach her. They don't have a phone and don't want one; I have to call the neighbors and arrange a time."

"I gather the nearest neighbors aren't exactly within shouting distance," Brenna said. Not altogether surprising; neither were hers.

"About as far as from here to that housing tract north of you," he said. "If it's a local call and the timing's good, it works out. Eztebe and I generally stick to a schedule; we've had it for years. But I'll put a call in when we hit the right time period."

"It's worth a try," she said. "But until we get through, we've got to do something. Masera—*Iban*—he's going to come for me. As soon as he figures out you were in on the dogfighting, he's going to come for you, too, but right now he wants that spring. And I pretty much figure if he gets it—if he changes it so his darkness can use it again—we don't have a chance. Am I right about that?" And Druid, sitting beside her again, gave Masera his most earnest look and whined.

Masera said most dryly, "One of you is."

"Take it from him, then. And what's that paper?"

He shrugged, unfolding it. "It's your paper—*papers*—from your couch."

Emily's printout. "The Mars Nodens research!" Brenna said. "Anything interesting?"

He smoothed the papers out against his leg and pulled the top one off, handing it to her. "Rabies information," he said, and she scanned it while he read the other page.

They reacted at virtually the same moment, as he stiffened, muttering, "I'll be a son of a bitch!" and she waved her paper at him and said, "I get it, I get it!"

They looked at each other for a heartbeat and he lifted his chin, a gesture of interest, as though he could read her rabies information from there. She said, "Okay, listen to this," and looked back at the paper, where all the strange bits and pieces she'd been hearing—from Sammi, from her Druid-memories—coalesced to make sense. "Rabies incubates in the animal before it becomes active, right? Incubation periods vary, but the animal's not contagious until the virus kicks in. That's when it sheds virus in its saliva."

"Not news so far," he said, but his attention remained fixed on her, waiting for the rest of it.

"The thing is, with regular rabies, once the animal starts shedding the virus, it becomes symptomatic within ten days. So if you're bitten, and the animal makes it through quarantine, then you *know* it didn't have rabies. Which is what everyone assumed with the cat, and with the stray dog that killed Janean and its new owner." She waved the paper at him again, so caught up in the new concept she had a hard time putting the words together. "In those visions . . . I kept hearing the term *shedding rabies*. And I couldn't understand it, because *all* rabies is shedding rabies. But what if this new rabies allows the animal to shed the virus in its saliva for a long time before it gets sick? It could infect people, go through quarantine, and be released . . . no one would ever know it was carrying the disease!"

Masera just stared at her a moment, working it through, until he closed his eyes with the impact of it. "Parker's darkness took away our safety check. Every assumption health-care professionals have made about the prevention and treatment of rabies would be invalid."

"*Is* invalid," Brenna said. "There's no way to tell

how many animals have the new rabies by now, not if Parker's been spreading it with his dogs. And not without new detection tests—all the current ones assume the animal has viral damage to the brain by the time it's shedding the disease."

"God*damn*," Masera said with enough quiet vehemence to make Brenna wince.

"I think you should be careful with that one around here," she said, and rolled her eyes toward the pasture. "We don't want to get on anyone's bad side."

He gave a rueful grin. "Good point. But the ramifications—"

"Will your friends in animal control listen to you? Or we could go straight to the CDC—" She cut herself off, thought about Sammi and her sudden reticence after the CDC had contacted her. "On the other hand, I think they already know they've got something new on their hands. The question is whether they know just what. We might be able to save them some time. . . ."

"I don't know who'll listen to us," Masera said. "We'll have to try them all."

"We could go to the media," Brenna suggested reluctantly. "We'd probably just look like crackpots."

"Maybe we would. We'll do what we have to." He had that look again—the one she'd noticed in their first conversation and many times since. The one that meant he had things to do and no intention of being dissuaded or interrupted. The one that said *join me or get out of my way*. Focus.

Only this time, she was part of it. "We'll do what we have to do," she agreed. "Your turn."

"My—" He gave her a puzzled look, then remembered the paper in his hand. "Hard to believe this information's just been sitting here on your couch."

"Not for that long," Brenna said. "Yesterday evening . . . I was sitting down with it when I—well, when I saw the things that made me call you."

"Remind me to thank you for that sometime."

"I'll put it on my list of things to do," Brenna said. "Now hand over that paper or get your tongue in gear."

He glanced at the page and shook his head. "Mars Nodens," he said, "is associated with Lydney Spring, which you knew. And he has an affinity for dogs, which you knew. What you probably didn't know is that the gods of that time went by a whole collection of different names, depending on the region in question. Throughout Ireland, Wales, and England, Mars Nodens is also known as Ludd, Nudd, Nuadu, and—" he looked up her "—Nuadha."

Nuadha's Silver Druid. It hit her like a physical blow; she literally felt the blood drain from her face as she whispered it out loud. "Nuadha's Silver Druid."

Druid put his paws on the edge of the couch, alert to his name. Druid, the dog whose footprints came from nowhere. *From out of the spring.* Druid, with his strange fits at strange times and memories he kept passing to her. Fits that occurred when he confronted a conjunction of things future and past, things from the memories conflicting with things as they were now. Dangers she hadn't yet realized were dangers.

Druid, with his ID and rabies tags that had led her nowhere.

Rabies I/II.

"He's been vaccinated," she blurted, still breathless in reaction. "He's been vaccinated against the shedding rabies!" Much to Druid's surprise, she pulled his collar over his head and shoved it at Masera. "Look—the local phone exchange that doesn't exist— *yet.* Five numbers instead of six on the rabies tag, a new cycle of vaccine—Rabies I & *II.* He's been vaccinated, and it's right here in his blood, *right now.* What could CDC do with *that?*"

"Arrest us, probably," Masera said absently—though his gaze on Druid was anything *but* absent.

"He came from the spring," she reminded him. "With memories of things that haven't happened yet, and a vaccine that doesn't exist yet. He came from Mars Nodens. Nuadha. From the—" and then she couldn't say it. Not quite. It was too absurd when put into words.

Masera was never so shy of such things. "The future," he said, but then even he looked surprised at what he'd said.

Brenna shook her head. "No. No way."

Masera said nothing. He looked at Druid and said nothing, although his mouth opened as he hunted for words. Finally he swore, a single emphatic word.

"Anyway," Brenna said, nonsensically enough, "Nuadha liked hounds. All his statues at his Lydney shrine are hounds. So if he was going to send a dog back from . . . if he was going to send a dog, he'd have sent a hound."

"Gaze hounds," Masera said, and shook his head, waving the printouts at her. "They were all gaze hounds. Aloof dogs. Laid-back, except for those moments they're on their prey. Cardigans are people-oriented herding dogs. Intensely loyal. The kind of dog who could connect with you so strongly, so quickly, that you'd put up with his problems."

"The future." She said it out loud, trying it on for size. And then realized, "A world where no one stopped the rabies," more horrified than ever to put the borrowed memories into perspective.

"*Or* Parker," Masera said. He reached over her legs to give Druid a gentle scritch, as much full of awe as affection. "He's here to change that. With your help."

"*Our* help, I hope," Brenna said. "We. Us. I don't think I can do this alone."

"We and us. Oh, yes." He gave her lower leg a squeeze, still looking at Druid. "*Nuadha of the Silver Hand*," he added. "That's what they called him."

He dropped the paper in his lap, through with it. "He had a prosthetic hand made of silver, and an invincible sword that could not fail to slay his enemy. Looks like Druid here is one package meant to be all of it. No wonder he's nuts."

"I don't know," Brenna said, realizing that to Druid, even being in the Pets! parking lot for the first time—seeing Masera for the first time—could pull up conflicting memories of his own past. His own past . . . in the future. "I'd like to think I'd have done half as well under the same circumstances. Though that *does* explain why he's Nuadha's *Silver* Druid. I'd thought maybe it was for the speckling on his ears."

"Maybe it is," Masera said. "We could go nuts, too, if we give too much meaning to every little thing. There are enough meaning-laden things going on here as it is." He rubbed a hand along his jaw, looking speculative, still watching Druid. "Hold on," he said, carefully lifting her legs so he could get up, and not explaining further as he left the house. She heard his vehicle door close a few moments later and when he returned he had a hypodermic and packaged alcohol pad. She watched without questioning as he scrubbed the inside of Druid's front leg, held his thumb over the vein, and withdrew a full syringe of blood. Druid allowed it with a much put-upon sigh, his ears planing down to indicate his displeasure. Masera capped the needle and left again, just long enough to deposit the collection in Brenna's refrigerator.

She didn't ask why, as he returned a final time and reclaimed his seat beside her. She didn't have to. Instead, she asked, "What next?"

He gingerly rubbed his eyes. "Next? Are you hungry? I am."

"I missed dinner," Brenna admitted. "Not that I ever have what you might call a real dinner, but I missed it all the same. That's not what I meant, though." She put her hands over her face, covering her eyes with the sweater cuffs. Thinking, suddenly, that she had to return to work the next day, and that she had a groomer interview along with all the customer appointments. And she had the distinct feeling their work was far from done tonight.

"I know," he said. "Thought I'd fit it in while we still could. Because I don't think we have any choice—we've got to figure out a way to reinforce that spring anchor to Nuadha, and we've got to do it tonight. If Parker gets to it, if he reorients it back to the darkness, we'll lose anything you might have gained today."

"The darkness," Brenna said, suddenly overcome by a moment of great silliness, just peeking out from above her fingers and cuffs. "Let's just call it Harvey. Or Fred."

"Parker Junior," Masera suggested.

"Parker Senior," Brenna said. "It's bigger than him, I think. And wild. He just doesn't know it." She dropped her hands, struck by a sudden thought. "You know, as long as old Fred doesn't have access to the spring, I think it's working through Parker. After it went for us at the spring, Parker looked beat. Just as bad as me and Druid. That's how I got out of there. *He* might actually be its weak point right now." Then she grimaced. "I don't really want to take that thought to its natural conclusion." *She should have pulled that trigger.*

She still knew she couldn't.

"Then let's not," Masera said quietly. "Let's get something to eat."

She opened her mouth to protest, thinking of Parker and the darkness and the spring, but Masera shook his head. "I know," he said. "I don't want to wait, either. But we'd better not be hungry and exhausted when we go out there. It doesn't mean we have to wait till morning."

She still didn't want to wait . . . but she *was* hungry.

And exhausted. She leaned her head back on the couch and sighed out some of that exhaustion. "It's dark now already," she said. "It's not going to be any darker later on."

"No," he agreed. "Not under this moon."

"Medusa Moon," she said.

"Not great for us," he said, rubbing a hand over his face. "Be better if we could put off any more confrontation with Parker until Beltane and after the new moon." He glanced at his watch. "Going on nine, now. That pizza place on Main Street should still be open."

It was. They split a large pizza between them, eating enough to make Brenna waddle back into the house when they returned. Masera disappeared into the bathroom and reappeared wearing glasses, classic and unobtrusive frames that somehow turned his generally ruffled appearance into something more refined . . . if at the tail end of its day. By then Brenna was on the couch, trying to turn her mind to ways of strengthening her connection with Mars Nodens.

Nuadha.

When Masera sat next to her, she pulled the afghan over herself and curled up against him without saying a word.

And with the fate of the world riding on her shoulders, she did something so mundane as to fall asleep.

Chapter 18

ᚢ

URUZ
Strength & Endurance

Something pushed her leg, gently. Something cold. Brenna muttered in irritation and swatted at it, connecting with nothing—but there it came again. Slowly she woke enough to recognize the nudge of Druid's nose. Had she forgotten to let him out? No, he'd gone when they were returning from pizza. Then . . . ?

Then maybe he most of all of them still had Parker and the darkness on his mind. Or maybe he was still dog enough not to know what bothered him, but had some link to Nuadha, urging him on.

Nuadha. It was hard to think of Mars Nodens by that name. But if that's how Druid had come to her . . .

She realized, then, that her generally pliable but

firm sleeping surface wasn't the sagging couch to which she'd grown accustomed. No, it was flat muscle and bone and gently rising ribs.

Masera.

No, *Iban*.

How strange, she thought, that things between them had coalesced so suddenly. How strange that they needed to say so little about it.

But then, that was Masera.

The living room lamp was on its lowest setting, and Brenna carefully moved back from him, far enough so she didn't think she'd wake him, and still close enough to watch him—the glasses slightly askew on his face as he leaned back against the arm of the couch with his head tipping to the side in a way that he would surely rue once he woke. She considered waking him with a kiss, and then reconsidered the old-pizza taste fermenting in her mouth and moved away instead. She padded to the bathroom to brush her teeth, plait her hair into a quick braid, and wash her face.

The bruises looked both better and worse—already less swollen, but the red parts turning dark and more obvious. She'd spend the next few days inventing excuses for that, no doubt. *I walked into a door. An elephant used me for mortar and pestle. An ancient source of angry power got pissed with me and tried to kill me.*

They all sounded about equally plausible to her.

She rummaged on the bedroom floor for a pair of jeans that wasn't too dirty. Shoving her cold feet into slippers, she moved quietly to the kitchen, turning on only the light over the stove.

There was a particular feeling to creeping around one's own house while trying not to wake a guest who needed to sleep a little longer. A caring thing, almost like a conspiracy between her and the house, and something that made the quiet time special. Even

Druid seemed to be in on it; he'd curled up on the part of the afghan that draped onto the floor, and though he followed her with those big chocolate brown eyes when she passed by the entryway, they were the only things about him that moved.

Chocolate.

Masera had laughed, but now she found what chocolate she had left in the house—a giant economy bag of chocolate chips, bought at the bulk warehouse and meant for cookies. Chocolate. But she needed more. What else did she know about Mars Nodens? About the spring?

There'd been a roughly circular area of protection. Not a big one . . . encompassing the rocks of the old gravesite, the spring itself, and the small area she'd kept clean. So if they wanted to strengthen the connection, maybe she needed an official way to make that area larger, the perimeter stronger. Boundaries of stone, maybe—it seemed to have worked with the gravesite. Or of another material that meant something to Mars Nodens. Nuadha.

Silver?

She had a sudden image of her mother's old silverware sticking into the ground in a big circle around the spring, little marching soldiers holding their border. With chocolate chips spread all around the interior.

God fertilizer.

She clapped her hand over her mouth to hold in her laugh and avoid waking Masera, but even in her laughter she liked the notion.

After all, what did a god care about? That it came from the heart, that's what. Like the little drummer boy, giving his gift of music. Brenna would give something of her family's, and offer a bit of her own quirky self to go along with it. It was how she would have approached things at nine years of age, trying to solve this particular puzzle.

After all, the last time she'd gone at this, she'd been nine. And she'd gotten it right.

Which was how she explained it to Masera when he woke, no more a middle-of-the-night person—for it was just going on 4 A.M.—than he'd been an early morning person. She brewed him coffee while he stuck his head under the sink faucet—literally, for he returned from the bathroom with a triangle of wetness down the front of his dark T-shirt and his hair slicked back and already getting unruly in spots. They faced each other over the kitchen table and the left-over pizza she'd forgotten to put in the refrigerator.

"You think we should mark a border with your family silverware and then toss out chocolate chips," he repeated, still bleary—but not so bleary he couldn't convey his skepticism.

"*Strengthen the anchor point,* you said. Well, I think this will do it." That plus a little heart-to-heart expression of appreciation. Prayer, she couldn't bring herself to think of it as.

He tilted one eyebrow up behind the large coffee mug—*I love dogs!* it proclaimed, in loud colors and surrounded by cutesy hearts, a gift—and said nothing. Just looked at her that way.

"Go ahead, give me that face. It may come as a surprise to you, but sometimes I have my own ideas—I don't need you to jump up and down about this one. I just need you to *go along* with it—because I don't want to go out there by myself to do this."

"Don't worry about that," he said, rubbing a hand over his face and starting to look a little more alert. "I'm with you. I think it'd be a good idea for you to take that rifle, too."

"Oh!" *Damn!* "Damn!" she repeated out loud. "I *had* the rifle. At the spring, this evening. When the winds stopped—when I saw Parker was whipped—I just grabbed Druid's leash and ran. I left it there!"

"Then bring extra rounds for it," Masera said

evenly. "It'll still be there. We're in the late Pylgaint *aetiir*. Not the best time—" He stopped short at her suddenly deadpan expression and said, "Tides of the day, Brenna. Think of this one as the PMS tide, if it helps." He gave a mild roll of his eyes, muttering, "My mother would pinch my ear for saying that, but . . . as it applies to this situation, it's good enough."

Ohh-kay. But she didn't voice the comment; she went out into the dog room and dumped some shells into her hand. Extra grain, hollow-point. The kind she used for shooting up dead stumps when she wanted to watch the splinters fly. She slid them into her front jeans pocket. She stuffed the chips bag into her knapsack and then dumped the silverware on top, hoping her mother would never find out. "My heirloom silver!" she'd say. Well, it *wasn't*, it was just your average silverware, and if it had been all that important to Rhona, her mother could have taken it when she'd moved out. Brenna had never considered herself the Keeper of the Silverware.

Although she seemed to have turned into the Keeper of the Spring.

She slipped her vest on and hooked up Druid's leash, and by then Masera was truly awake and was out there with her, standing close, coming up behind her to wrap his hands around her waist and pull her back against him. He rested his chin on her shoulder and then pressed his lips to her neck, and said, "We'll be okay."

She wanted to stay that way forever.

But she grabbed the big halogen flashlight from the dryer and led him out into the yard.

It seemed immensely silly.

Even upon reflection, a gathering of all the reasons she was here on her knees jamming forks and spoons and knives into the ground with her .22 just within reach, it still seemed immensely silly. "I'm thinking," she said out loud, "of how terrifying it was when Parker and his darkness attacked me this evening. I mean, yesterday evening." She sighed and admitted, "It's not helping very much. Why did this seem like such a good idea back at the house?"

Masera, uphill from her and working a little faster, said, "I'm thinking about what it felt like when I got a good look at your face, and it's helping a *lot*." She couldn't see his shrug in the darkness—they were saving the battery flashlights—but she could hear it in his voice. "Don't worry about it, Brenna. I have to admit you took me by surprise with silverware and chocolate, but you were right—it's a good first step." He'd added another detail to their ritual, teaching her the rune Teiwaz—protection for the warrior—that she now carved into the earth every few inches as the circle formed.

"Let's just get in touch with your mother as soon as you can, okay?" Although it did feel better to be doing something—*anything*—other than just waiting to be acted upon. Even with a day of Pets! ahead.

She sat back to survey what she could of the spring. The silver gleamed dully in the night; her knapsack with the chocolate sat in the middle of the enlarged area. It was somewhat surprising to see how many individual utensils marched around the ground, and that's when it occurred to her that maybe it didn't really matter *what* she used to reach out to Nuadha, as long as it was done with care and thought, and that maybe she ought to be thinking more about Nuadha than how silly she felt.

We need you. Into the ground went a knife, an easy one. *We know what you've done for us already.* She reached for the pile of utensils, came up with a fork. *I'm sorry it took so long to figure out what you'd sent me in Druid.* Druid, leashed but unattached to anything, wandered over to brush his whiskers over her hand, whining softly. *We're doing our best to make sure the darkness doesn't win.*

It occurred to her, then, what would happen to Nuadha's beloved dogs if she and Masera didn't stop the darkness, and stop the rabies it had chosen to wield. *Strays and lost dogs, killed on sight. Pets limited to those dogs who could stay indoors their entire lives, foxes and raccoons hunted down, their populations devastated . . .*

She realized she'd quit working, that she was staring blindly into the early morning darkness; she had the distant awareness that Masera had called her name not once but several times. She looked at the utensils beside her, the ones already sticking in the ground. Druid eyed them, his ears perked forward with utmost interest. She reached out to brush her fingers along the top of the line—

And jerked her hand back when she received a sharp tingle in response, an electric shock but at a lower pitch. To her mortification, she also gave a quick squeal of surprise, and by then Masera was beside her, his hand on her shoulder. And by then, too, she felt it in the ground, thrumming up through her knees and the tops of her feet where her sneakers rested against the ground, humming through her bones and vibrating in her lungs like distant drums. She looked over to him, his face so close to hers, and whispered, "Do you feel it?"

He looked at Druid—standing on his toes, looking like a dog who expects a rabbit to break from the brush before his nose—and back to Brenna, and shook his head. But before she could suggest it, he, too, reached out to the standing silver.

He didn't quite snatch his hand away. But Brenna felt his entire body tighten, and he eased back to sit on one heel. After a moment he shook his head. "Not unless I touch them," he said. "You're definitely the *Mari* here." And at her look, he grinned. "Basque myth. A tall, beautiful, and kindly woman with magical powers."

"I think you need to have a talk with my family," Brenna muttered, but held tight to the startled little warmth in her chest. *Tall, beautiful.* He thought that. He said it without hesitation.

She glanced around, saw they'd almost closed the circle. Another foot or so right where she'd been working and they'd be done. "You want to do the rest?" she asked. "I'll get the chocolate." She'd already noticed the Ghirardelli was gone; she only hoped it had gone to Nuadha instead of a coyote. Masera squeezed her shoulder in assent and she went for the knapsack.

Spreading the chips was like sewing seed by hand; she scattered it in the circle, feeling the tingle that fed up through her soles and spread through her body. Done. She rinsed her hand in the damp spot at the spring. When she turned back she found Masera feeling around the ground, reaching for the flashlight and flicking it on to peer closely at the spring grass.

"Hunting worms?" she said.

His reply held none of her light tone. "Take a look for yourself."

Grass. Verdant green washed out by the bright, close light, growing but not yet thick; the resilient ground peeked through, almost covered by last year's thatch. "No chocolate," she said, taken unaware by a sudden shiver. "There's *nothing.*"

He held a hand over the curving line of utensils, hovering above it without actually touching the silver. "No chocolate. And this. You've done well here, Brenna."

She sighed in deep relief. "Do you think . . . do you think Parker can get in?"

He stared over the circle for a moment, then got to his feet, holding out his hand to her. "I don't know. But I think we've done what we can."

She didn't need the hand up; she took it anyway. And she let him pull her in close, to stand together long enough for her to become aware that his heart beating against her own chest held a curiously similar rhythm to the pulse of the earth at her feet. When she told Masera he just laughed and held her a little tighter. "The pagan gods are generally like that," he said, and then, when she pulled back in question, he added, "They enjoy all celebrations of life, including the one where I hold you." And he held her tighter for a moment, his face against hers, with pulses beating around and through them, until she felt him smile. "There," he said, murmuring. "Now I feel it. It's nothing that will suffer Parker's presence here."

A soft paw landed lightly against Brenna's knee—Druid, sitting on his haunches. "Silly," she told him, reaching down to caress his head. "Yes, you too."

Masera glanced at his watch, a glow-in-the-dark bright from recent contact with the flashlight beam. "Not quite enough time to be worth catching any more sleep," he said. "But time to get cleaned up and go out for breakfast, if you want."

"I want," Brenna declared. "That pizza last night feels like it was two days ago." She bent to retrieve the limp and empty knapsack, taking a moment to run her hand across the ground in a caress much like that she'd just given Druid. "I'll be back," she told it.

And Druid growled.

"Druid," she said, surprised. "What's up with you?" She followed his alert-eared gaze out over the pasture, but saw nothing in the darkness. Not surprising; she wouldn't have been able to see an elephant in the pasture bottom, not unless it glowed in the dark like Masera's watch.

But Druid stood like a statue, growling steadily, no doubt apparent in his hot glare out over the field. Masera thumbed the flashlight on, swept it over the field, though at that distance, the beam dissipated too much to show anything but—

Eyes.

Off to the right, on this side of the creek. Eyes reflecting back at them, green, winking in and out with the movement of the attached animal, never steady enough to get a feel for just how many there were.

"Oh, man," Brenna said softly. "Oh, *man*."

"Stay inside the circle," Masera said, his voice just as low. The grim quality in his words made her wish she was anywhere else but here, *inside the circle*. Two giant targets inside a bullseye and one small, quickly moving target—for Druid had stopped growling, had skipped back a few steps—and when she went for his leash he bolted, kicking off his run with a sudden yip of fear and clawing up sod with the vigor of his retreat. She lunged after him, but spun abruptly around with the implacable force of Masera's hand grabbing her arm. "Stay in the circle," he said. "You can't catch a dog that doesn't want to be caught."

"I know, dammit, but—" She stopped just before her voice cracked with frustration, jerking free of his grasp and turning away, reeling inside with the sudden change of atmosphere—although she could still feel the pulse of the earth against her feet, and wondered if Masera could, too. A faster beat, a stronger tingle, a feel of urgency and danger. She didn't know if it was a warning or merely a reflection of her own turmoil. "If only we could see," she muttered, taking a long step to the center of the circle, where she'd left the rifle. Still loaded. Still armed.

She closed her eyes and took a deep breath, steeling herself to turn around.

That's when she heard Masera's quick intake of breath, and she whirled around, opening her eyes to—

Light.

Soft, silver-colored light, washing out over the hill,

growing to reach across the creek, trickling out over the pasture below. Baffled, she turned a circle, hunting the source.

She didn't have to look far.

The oak looming over the spring, barely leafed out in that slow, taking-things-on-its-own-schedule way that oaks had. A perfectly normal oak.

Glowing moon-silver, growing steadily in strength. Illuminating the field of battle.

She let her own breath hiss through her teeth and exchanged a quick, wide-eyed glance with Masera. "You know what?" she said. "We're not in Kansas anymore."

"No, Dorothy, we're not." He looked out over the pasture. "Let's just hope Toto is safe at home." And he nodded, taking her attention back to the field.

Of course it was Parker. Parker, striding toward them with all the assurance back in his walk and a pack of pit bulls spread out around him. He'd bypassed the creek at the road bridge along the house frontage, probably cut through her fence as soon as he was across it. Seven dogs, she thought—no, eight. Eight, when one would have done the job. One powerfully jawed dog, trained to kill.

She had wondered if she could kill a dog. She suddenly knew the answer.

Parker himself carried a bat.

"A bat?" she murmured out loud, moving close to Masera again. "He knows I have the rifle."

"Think like the darkness," Masera murmured back; she could barely hear him for the thrum of pulses— earth pulses, her own racing heart—in her ear. "It wants the experience close and personal. It wants to crush and maim and feel the results."

"And how reassuring *you* are," she muttered. She gestured with the rifle. "This is what we've got. Do you want it?"

He shook his head without taking his eyes from

Parker—halfway across the pasture now. "As much as I'd like to leave you free to . . . communicate . . . with Nuadha, I have no doubt which of us can handle the shooting best. But there shouldn't be any. Don't start anything. Just *stay in the circle*—"

"No kidding," she said. "But just what makes you so sure they can't get to us here?"

"It's stronger than it was before. He couldn't reach you then."

"That's just the point," she said. "He *couldn't* reach me. He was stuck on the other side of the creek. It was the *darkness* that got repelled by the circle. I have no idea whether Parker himself will care the least about our silver marching men."

His response was silence, while Parker grew close enough so the glow of light painted his gold hair silver, sparking off it like bright sunshine. Then he swore a low curse, accepting her argument . . . but not, Brenna was glad to hear, with the *goddamit* against which she'd cautioned him.

"Yeah," she said. "So I'd rather—Iban, if they get any closer and they start running, I won't get them all in time. I'm not used to a moving target."

He nodded. "Start something, then."

Brenna raised the rifle to her shoulder, finding the old ball and notch sight, settling it on a broad white chest. "I'm sorry," she whispered, following the approach of that chest, shifting the ball just to the left of the notch to account for the quirky sight . . . she held her breath and gently squeezed the trigger.

Never a loud weapon, the rifle shot seemed somehow muted by the pounding of the earth, the subtle pulsing of the oak's glow. And the dog didn't flinch. Didn't hesitate. Still sighting in, Brenna quickly pumped in a new shell and took the shot again.

Nothing.

"Buck fever?" Masera asked, suspicion in his voice.

Not suspicion aimed at her, as he looked out over the field to Parker's big grin.

"No," Brenna said miserably. "He's protecting them, somehow."

"Don't waste the bullets, then."

"I can't just sit here and wait." On an impulse, she spun away from the edge of the circle, took the rifle back to the center, right next to the spring, and thrust it flat against the ground. "Please," she said to the spring. "We've got to fight the darkness." She jammed her hand into her pocket, fishing out the fresh shells, and scattered them in the ooze of the spring—a crazier thing she'd probably never done. *Wet ammo.* But they weren't any use to her as they were . . .

She jacked the old shells out of the gun, scooped up the wet ones, and pulled the rod out for a hasty reload. "Here goes," she said, and gave the firing chamber a quick kiss of a blessing.

When she returned to Masera's side, Parker was just below them. Waiting. For her, evidently, considering the way his congenially self-pleased expression darkened as she took up a shooting stance.

"You were in on this together," he said. "I should have known. It explains a number of things."

"We're together now," Masera said. "No doubt there are others who have their sights on you."

"Apt way of putting it." Parker tipped the bat at Brenna and the rifle. "Except surely you've figured out that won't do you any good."

"Let's pretend I'm slow," Brenna suggested. "Slow enough so I'm going to give you the chance to turn around and walk away."

Parker laughed out loud. "Not much chance of that at all."

"This isn't really *you*, Parker. This is whatever you raised here four years ago. Following it got your friends killed, and it'll kill you, too." But he'd hear the desperation in her voice. Could he also hear the hurried thrum of the earth, that reflection of her fear? But the rifle, half-raised, remained steady. Masera, at her side, remained steady. She realized that he held one of the silver knives, a dull but slightly serrated knife that could do plenty of damage with enough strength behind it.

"I understand more than they did," Parker told her. "I *listened* better. And I'm not going anywhere." He scowled, tapped the bat against the ground at his feet. "You think I couldn't feel what you're up to? I can't allow that." He hit the ground again, harder this time, and looked at Masera. "Not that I'd let you live, anyway, after the raids tonight. Mickey's already dead, did you know it? Nothing less than what he deserved, for bringing you into my life."

"The darkness," Masera observed wryly to Brenna, "seems to be somewhat egocentric."

It probably shouldn't have struck her as funny, not at that moment. But she couldn't quite muffle her laugh of response, and Parker jerked his head back, eyes narrowed, stung and angered.

Brenna reacted instantly to his expression, seeing in it the imminence of action. She lifted the rifle and squeezed the trigger, and the pit bull next to Parker—huge of chest, huge of head and jaw, powerful in every hard-trained muscle—gave a childlike cry and collapsed where it stood. Heart-shot.

The tree flared with light, and the world turned suddenly slow around her, even as everything happened at once—the dogs, Parker, the bat, Masera—all in motion. She targeted a second dog, missing the killing shot but stunning it into aimless wandering, nothing more than a dog in shock. By then the rest of them were moving, surging up the hill with Parker in their midst, and Brenna deliberately side-walked away from Masera even while sighting in a third dog—grazing its flank, pumping in a new shell, taking it down. "Over here!" she yelled at them, thinking only that she had the weapon and that she couldn't allow even one of them to close its jaws on Masera. *Rabies*. Parker's finest tools, these dogs, Parker and the darkness. *Rabies*. She whooped at them, an aggravating incitement. *Prey noises.* "C'mon, dogs! Over here!" She took another shot, took another dog down, astonished at her efficiency, her smooth reactions, the way the tingling power of the earth had turned to energy and strength in her body.

"Brenna!" Masera's uncertainty laced the word, and then he had no time to question her; Brenna saw from the corner of her eye as Parker headed for her, laying low a section of standing silver with one sweep of his bat, and Masera leapt before him and went into a crouch, trying to be ready for anything—a duck, a dodge, to grab the bat—

It slammed into his shoulders and took him off his feet.

"Iban!" she cried, even as she put a shot down the throat of the dog who'd gone for her, blowing out the juncture of skull and spine. *Five.*

And the sixth dog, changing course to run along the hill from the other side of Parker, eyeing her with more intent and intelligence than a dog ought to have—*more than dog, dog with darkness*—and she heard the bat land again, heard Masera's grunt of undeniable pain, saw him roll away from the blow and then twist himself around to drive the silver knife into Parker's leg, taking another, more awkwardly aimed blow even as the blade sank in and Parker howled and Brenna took a shot at number six—

And the pin tapped dully against the shell. Dud. Too wet, too old, too *something*. Brenna pumped it out but it got stuck in the chamber, stuck enough that she'd never work it free in time.

And then the drumming grew loud in her body, so loud she couldn't hear the snarls, hear Parker's wail as the silver knife—Nuadha-blessed—did more damage than any single small blade ought, so loud she couldn't even hear her own harsh breathing and frantic heartbeat anymore. The world slowed and went silent, bathed in the silver light of Nuadha's oak.

Silent, but for the determined gallop of a short-legged dog, launching himself over the crest of the hill. Silent but for his snarling cry of challenge, his fear overcome by fierce and deep devotion. Silent but for the sound of Brenna's own cry, her suddenly far-too-familiar shout of emotional agony as the Cardigan threw himself against a dog more than twice his weight, a dog bred for duck-and-dodge herding offering himself up to a killer. "No, Druid—*no!*"

The world skidded into motion. Druid tumbled downhill, taking the pit bull with him; Brenna frantically worked the pump, freeing the dud shell and jacking in a new one. And when the pit bull's nature betrayed it, when it hung onto Druid's snowy throat, turning the silvery white fur red and dark, when it clung to Druid's limp and unresisting body, its jaws clamped by instinct and training, Brenna shot it down. Crying so hard she could barely sight in on the dog, she still took it down with one steady shot, and found herself halfway down the hill to Druid before remembering there were two more pit bulls. She whirled around, pumping in another shell even as she brought the gun up, but she knew she'd be too late.

She ought to have been. With Parker sprawled on the ground, dragging himself away from Masera, with Masera staggering, barely on his feet, as the last two dogs leapt over their master to charge Brenna—

She ought to have been.

She couldn't see how Masera did it. How he had the chance. How he set himself up in front of the lead dog, jamming his forearm at its open jaws, bracing himself, throwing his other arm behind the dog's neck and shoving with one arm, jerking in with the other—

She heard the crack of its spine from there. And she lost herself entirely, screaming his name, thinking only of the rabies even as the second dog hit him from the side, knocking him back into the circle as it ravaged his neck. Screaming his name as she sighted the rifle, the dog so close to his head, too close for a safe shot. Masera flailed at the animal, reaching for Parker's abandoned bat, his struggles determined but fading, his fingers closing over the handle as all the fight seemed to drain from him *and it's got to be now*—

Brenna slid the ball just to left of the sweet spot on the dog's chest, so close to Masera's head from this angle, *too* close—

And pulled the trigger.

The dog jerked back, gave Brenna a puzzled stare, and folded to the ground with the faintest of whimpers.

"It doesn't matter." Parker's voice was jarring, his harsh laugh even more so. He'd gotten himself halfway down the hill, trailing blood that turned the grass black in Nuadha's light. "It's too late. If he's not dead yet, give him a few days. And then I'll be back for you."

Brenna pumped another round in the chamber. One of the last, most likely; she'd lost count, but knew she'd started with twelve on hold and one in the chamber.

He laughed again. "You won't do it. You know you won't do it. Don't even try to play that game."

She hefted the rifle, then lowered it. He was right about that. He'd always been right. But . . . around her, the ground thrummed with a different song, one she'd heard only the night before, and this time she didn't think it was of Parker's doing. *The darkness.*

She wouldn't have to do it.

The darkness would use him. It would use him up. A feral darkness, never under his control.

"You're right," she said. "We'll play another game instead." And she tossed the rifle inside the circle. Then she stumbled down the hill to Druid, moving as fast as her suddenly wobbly legs could take her without risking a fall.

She didn't think she could get up if she fell.

There he was. His head lolled back, his sightless eyes half open and already glazing. Sweet Druid, dog of her heart. Quirky Druid, overcoming his fears long enough to sacrifice himself for her. Courageous Druid, sent through time to give his spirit to her.

She pulled off her vest and wrapped him in it, avoiding the blood, moving as quickly as she could, her body operating independently of her stunned and ravaged emotions. His long body hung flaccid in her arms; the hanging brush of his tail grazed her knee at each steep stride back up the hill.

And all the while the darkness gathered around them, angry and building up to power, with Parker just beginning to realize it.

To see that he didn't have control this time.

He scrabbled his way down the hill, stopping short of the bank as he saw he couldn't navigate it, tried to rise and failed.

Brenna had no eyes for him. Inside the circle, the warmth of Nuadha's earth and light enfolded her, showed her just the right spot to lay Druid. And grieving, fearful, she turned to Masera, where he lay limply, one foot twitching, his uninjured arm moving aimlessly, its goal some purpose she couldn't fathom. Maybe just to move. To prove to himself he was still alive.

She sank to her knees as she reached him, taking that groping hand in hers, and felt new pain tear across her chest when he didn't return the squeeze she gave it. "Iban," she whispered, close enough to see that his other arm, flopped across his stomach and badly ravaged, was too obviously crooked not to be badly broken. Close enough to see his shattered glasses bent beneath the body of the dog beside him.

Close enough to see that his neck pumped steady blood into the earth, that his eyes had rolled back in his head, that his breath was no more than a shallow gasp. "Iban," she said, brushing his cheek with her fingers, unable to stop herself from threading her fingers through his thick and ever-ruffled hair. "Don't go, Iban."

Rabies. Better this death than that. But still— "Don't go, Iban," she pleaded, while the darkness rose around them, raging against the circle, desperate to break through and gain access to the spring and its unlimited power.

Willing and able to use up every last bit of Parker in the doing of it.

Brenna saw it all, silent beyond the shelter of the circle, and yet saw none of it. Dark whirling winds, buffeting black power, raging anger spinning out its stored chaos. It didn't touch her—not its fear or its power or its violence. Only one thing held her now, this face with its expression she'd never seen before. Faded. Without the force of personality Masera had brought to every word he'd exchanged with her. Every touch.

"Please don't go," she said, so close she could feel his faltering breath on her cheek. "Not yet. *Not yet.*"

With impossible effort he brought his eyes into focus, and then his hand did tighten down on hers, somehow the trigger for tears to spill over her eyelids, one after another and each holding unvoiced misery. He said something—a few words, but no sound behind them, and she had no idea what they were. "I know," she told him anyway. "I'm here." She kissed him, carefully, and said into his mouth over and over again, "I'm here. I'm with you. I'm here," and at some point his breathing grew strange and erratic and then suddenly eased.

Gone.

She looked up, blinked, looked around. *Gone.* All of them. No sign of the pit bulls. No evidence that Parker had lived a last few frantic moments by the side of the creek, trying to escape his own darkness. Druid, gone; no sign of his furry body anywhere. And the shining silver of Nuadha's light had been replaced by the wash of a gentle rose dawn.

Nothing but Brenna and a knapsack and a bloody vest, surrounded by a circle of marching silver—some lurching, some flattened, all gleaming with an odd sheen in the morning light.

It was as she sat numbly, contemplating what do to next, coming to terms with the fact that there was no sturdy little Cardigan to bury, to say good-bye to, that she realized the implications of it all.

The dead, gone.

Masera, by her side.

Nuadha, the healing god.

She threw herself back down beside Masera, frantic for signs of life. *Let me be right, oh please let me be right*—running her hands up and down his chest, seeing for the first time that the horrifying wounds at his throat were closed and healed, the scars there shiny but already fading to white, the broken arm still mangled but not bleeding as it once had been. And his good hand, twitching around a fistful of air as though he expected to find something else there.

She slid her own hand into it, and neither of them were alone anymore.

Chapter 19

ᚱ

RAIDO
Union & Reunion

From the crest of the hill under the oak, the pasture presented an interesting sight. On the other side of the creek, the bottom, lush and green and crying out for horses, looked virtually untouched by the events of the past week.

This side of the creek was a different story.

The hillside around the spring was scoured clear of grass and thatch; barren, Brenna would have called it, if the persistent green tips of recovering grasses weren't already poking their way into the light. The time since their struggle on the hill didn't lessen the impact of what had happened here. Nor had it eliminated the thrum of life that came up through her bare soles and through her bottom planted firmly on the ground.

Just below marched the disrupted circle of silverware, looking more like a strange child's game than the crucial border of safety it had been. Brenna had already determined to replace the silver with rocks, and to replace the rocks with gradually acquired but more seriously interesting rocks and mineral chunks.

Supposing she still lived here. She'd given her mother a week, and most of those days had tumbled by; she might let it go to two. And then she'd leave. After all, it wasn't as if she had a job here, holding her down. Not anymore.

Just this spring. And the circle, within which the grass was as green and happy as that below, and showed no signs of the dark blood that had soaked the ground. As hard as it would be to leave the farm, it would be even harder to leave this circle.

But she could make another. Somewhere.

And, she hoped, not alone.

She leaned over to rub her nose on Masera's shoulder. The good one, the right one, although the padded sling straps passed over it, holding his arm with its cast and its wrappings up at a high angle. Hours and hours in the emergency room, that's what that cast represented. Another day in the hospital, recovering from surgery as they all tried to understand how he'd lost so much blood from the arm injury. Brenna kept the truth to herself; when they asked about the silvered scars on his neck, she said airily, "Oh, old dog bite," and left it at that. She stayed by his bed with Eztebe, who wormed the whole story out of her in bits and pieces and now treated her like one of the family. Especially since they'd finally reached Masera's mother, who had clapped with delight at Brenna's use of chocolate and—although neither Masera or Eztebe would tell her exactly—seemed to have put a stamp of approval on Brenna's overall handling of the situation.

As well she might, considering that her son had survived it.

Masera rested his cheek against the top of her head, which of course was what she'd wanted. He had new glasses, matched to the old ones as closely as she'd been able. They still softened his face, easing its hard edges and changing the scruffiness to appear urbanely ruffled. The rest of him was hard to fix— bones and bruises, wrought by Parker's bat as well as pit bull jaws; that, too, showed in his face—as well as a certain muzziness wrought by painkillers.

"You okay?" she said, now that she had his attention.

"Just thinking," he said. "Still have a few brain cells up to the task. Just then, for instance, I was being grateful that you chose the only safe place to rub your nose on. Just an itch, right? I've got a handkerchief if you need it."

"I *will* smack you," she warned him, though of course she wouldn't. Not on his first day out and about, on Beltane no less—or so Masera called May Day, and seemed to think it was a big deal—with Eztebe waiting for them at Masera's place.

It just seemed right to come here first.

Besides, she knew what he was thinking, and it wasn't about her nose. "You're not still worried about the rabies, are you?"

He gave her the barest of shrugs.

"I'm not," she told him.

"That's quite some confidence."

She smiled serenely, knowing it would annoy him enough so he'd really listen to her instead of barging ahead with his own thoughts. "Maybe I have inside information."

He snorted, then stiffened. "Ow. Don't do that to me. So old Nuadha's dropping messages at your door now, is he?"

"It's not a difficult code," she said. "Look at you. You're a mess. You're not going to work for months—"

"—*Weeks*—"

"—and maybe in a week or so you might even put on a shirt without help. But the injury that would have killed you" —and she traced a finger down the scars on his neck— "is so completely healed that no one can tell it was more than a surface wound."

He caught her finger with his good hand. "Kindly don't do that until I can do something *about* it, would you?"

"Don't duck the point. Druid sacrificed himself for me. Nuadha took that gift, and gave me one in return. *You*. That bite on your neck didn't just *go away*, it was *healed*. You may have had the shedding rabies in your system, but it was healed before I ever got you to the hospital."

He didn't answer. Looking out over the hill, his face drawn and his eyes confused, he didn't answer. She thought maybe it was simply a little too much, too intense to deal with. After all, she'd had days to think about it. He'd spent that time drugged and just trying to muddle through.

But he surprised her, because once he worked it all through, he said, "If you're right . . . my blood . . ."

"Just like Druid's!" Brenna said, sitting straight up. One of her greatest regrets of the past days was that she hadn't done anything with that blood sample, hadn't even thought about it until it had spent far too much time sitting in her anything-but-sterile refrigerator. "But there's no way we could explain it."

"Maybe we don't even try," Masera said. "I'll use the contacts I made when I was working with animal control. The authorities take anonymous tips all the time."

"I doubt they get many with blood samples attached," Brenna said, but not in argument. "Still . . . if only one person took it seriously . . ."

"We'll try," Masera said, which was about all that could be said. It left them sitting in the afternoon sunshine again, while Brenna tried to think of all the pleasant times she'd shared this hill with Druid, instead of the last few moments of his life.

Russell to the rescue.

She heard him calling from quite a distance, though he'd never quite gotten the knack of bellowing across pasture distances. Not enough time spent calling in the boarding horses, just like he'd never spent much time with chores on the farm. What he wanted, she knew, was for her to come to him so he wouldn't have to walk all the way out to the oak. She just twisted around to wave to him.

He was puffing by the time he reached them, and whatever greeting he might have had was lost in his shock. "What the hell happened here? What—is that Mother's *silver*?"

"No," Brenna said, having decided that indeed her mother had abandoned it. Which didn't exactly make it Brenna's silver, but neither, strictly, was it her mother's.

Though at that moment she suddenly realized she would have lied to him without qualm, just so she wouldn't have to deal with his reaction. It was a surprising revelation.

"You must be Russell," Masera said, a distinctly cold note in his voice—though not one Russell was likely to notice. It surprised Brenna, who had said little about her family, good or bad. Then again, Masera had never been one to restrict his knowledge of her to what she told him. "Have a seat?"

I'm not getting up, that's what that meant. Brenna brushed Masera's shoulder with hers and said, "It's a nice day, Russell, and the ground's dry." She patted the grass beside her.

After a hesitation, he realized that she wasn't going to get up to talk to him, but he couldn't bring himself to sit; instead he came down the hill to stand before her, more or less at eye level. It was then she saw his fury, and his irritation at having to suppress it for a stranger. But it showed, to one who knew him—the high color on his cheeks and throat, the set of his shoulders, the way his full eyebrows somehow looked even thicker.

And hope flickered in her throat, fluttering all the way down through her chest and legs and through the soles of her feet into Nuadha's earth.

"I just spoke to Mother," he said, somehow making it a demand. "What have you said to her?"

"Nothing, recently." It was his stage; let him play it out. "I've been busy. Gil Masera, this is my brother Russell. Russell—Gil."

Russell nodded at Masera, a token thing meant to look polite but not the least so; Brenna felt Masera shift into predatory mode, through the drugs and the pain and his distraction. She brushed against him again, murmuring, "It's okay."

So Masera only said, "Brenna's been helping me since I was hurt."

"That would explain why you didn't bother to return my calls from this morning." Russell's hands landed at his hips, and he said bluntly, "Mother's signed the deed to this place over to you. She told me this morning, said she wanted to surprise you with it. What I want to know is what the hell you've been up to behind my back."

Masera spoke first, while Brenna let the flutter of hope settle firmly into place and blossom into happiness, hidden from Russell . . . but not from Nuadha's earth, which fluttered back at her. "I don't suppose it'll be a surprise, now."

"This is family business," Russell said.

"If you don't want Masera in on the conversation, then you'll have to come back another time," Brenna told him, smiling inwardly at the memory of her mother saying something similar to Aunt Ada, in the same evasive tactic. "Once you started talking about selling the place out from under me, I asked Mother for the deed. That's all there is to it." Well, perhaps a little more than that. But nothing Russell needed to know.

"This isn't right, Brenna. It's not fair."

"I had always thought that in *your* book, *fair* meant whoever thought of it first," she told him, and was surprised to see how much redder his face grew, though it faded as he regained control. "Besides, Russell, haven't you read the paper lately?" For that was one thing she *had* done these past days, while sitting around in the hospital or passing time with Eztebe while Masera slept. "The raids that took place around here? Whose property they took place on? I don't think you'll be hearing from your buyer."

"I never told you—" he started, but stopped short of *who it was*, as though it was finally sinking in that Brenna was no longer someone who was just letting life—letting *Russell*—happen to her, but that she knew more than he'd ever thought she did. He made a sudden change in tactics. "I want the chance to go through the house, Brenna. There are things there that I want."

If they meant that much to you, you'd have asked for them long before now. "Okay," she said. "I'm sure I'll be cleaning some stuff out, anyway. Give me a call after a few days, and we'll arrange a time for you to take a look." *And don't bother coming by when you think I'm out, because I'll have the locks changed before the end of the day.* But she didn't say it. Let him discover it for himself.

And he hesitated a moment more, as if there were something else he wanted to say, but he couldn't quite find the words . . . or use them in front of Masera. Finally he muttered in excessively bad grace, "I'll call you. Soon," and stalked away.

Masera waited only until Russell was barely out of earshot. "I always knew you had that in you."

"How could you even wonder, considering our

first conversation? And our second, and our third. . . ."

"You work at Pets!, that's how I could wonder. You think I didn't know what that place was like before I started with them? Being there was part of the cover, Brenna, so I could stick close to Mickey, see if anyone else there was part of it all. I'll find somewhere else to hold my classes now."

She threw herself back on the grass, leaving the conversation behind, staring up at the roving clouds. Fluffy white ones, the fun kind. "Happy happy!" she said, and then couldn't stand it, but jumped to her feet, wanting to pull him up, too, but resisting and skipping around him instead. "It's mine, now, I don't have to go anywhere!" She wanted to throw her arms around him, too, but threw them around the deeply fissured bark of the oak instead, which bore no wounds from the night of battling darkness. "Happy me!"

He'd gotten to his feet anyway; one arm closed around her from behind. "Happy us."

But for all her happy, Brenna couldn't quite forget. There should have been three of them.

"Look," she said, as they headed back to the house at a leisurely pace. She pointed to the back end of the barn. "Don't you think kennel runs would fit perfectly there? Not straight off the back, but meeting corners at the northeast of the barn?"

"Are you building kennels?"

"And a grooming room. But maybe I'll just run the kennels and hire out a groomer for a while. Take a break from it while I take some classes. And oh, did I mention I quit my job?"

That, she saw, truly stunned him. Took him by surprise, as she'd never managed to do before. He stopped walking, put all his attention into looking at her. She smiled beatifically at him as he said, "I thought you were on vacation, or sick days. You didn't quit your job for—"

"I quit my job," she said firmly, "because when I told Roger I'd had a family emergency and needed to take a week of my extensively accrued vacation time, he said no."

"No notice?"

"I gave him plenty of notice," she said, and snorted. "I told them any number of times in any number of ways that they'd lose me if they didn't change how they managed the grooming department. How they managed *me*."

He smiled, and held out his hand to her; they started walking again, and she started up with the plans. "And I definitely want another horse or two in here, maybe even one of my own. The barn's just about ready for it. And you know, don't you think the loft is big enough to hold obedience classes in? If we kept all the hay on one side, and used electric heaters in the winter?"

"It might be," he said, still sounding bemused as they reached the barn.

"Lydney Hill," she said. "Good name for a kennel and training facility, don't you think?"

"Are you making this up as you go along?"

"I am," she said, stopping him in front of the gate from the innermost run-in section to the plank-floored middle part of the barn, just before the gate she'd fixed on the day Russell sprang what he had thought was a successfully manipulated deal on her. "But I like it." She put a hand on the gate, not about to let him go through just yet. "Listen to me. I need to be with someone who likes the way I think, who I am. Someone who brings me alive, not someone who tries to change me into who they think I should be. That's you, Iban." This, she thought, was as bold as she'd ever been in her entire life. A little too bold; she couldn't just let it hang there, as he looked back at her, unreadable. "Besides, didn't you tell me once that you wanted this place?"

"That's not what I *really* wanted," he said, and gave her one of those intent looks. And who knows where it might have gone, had not Emily's voice echoed across the yard.

"Brenna!" she called, slightly breathless.

Brenna sighed. "Hold that thought," she said, and turned her head away to holler, "In here!"

"Busy around here today," Masera said, not looking away from her.

"Too busy." Another sigh, but she smiled, too. "I can guarantee Emily will be much more pleasant than our last visitor. You've probably seen her at the store."

Emily appeared at the open double sliding doors, definitely breathless—her face flushed, her eyes wide with worry—but already talking. "Brenna! Where have you been? I haven't heard from you for days and Pets! says you quit and I've been so worried—"

Brenna opened the gate, let Masera precede her through. "I'm sorry," she said. "We had some trouble, but things are okay now."

Emily hesitated a moment, looking at the two of them, and relaxed a little, tucking a strand of blond hair back into her ponytail as she came into the barn. "So I see," she said, eyeing Masera—if not with approval, with an understanding of how things stood—although as her gaze traveled his well-packaged arm, the look turned quickly to sympathy. "I hope that's not too bad."

"Better than it could have been," Masera told her with a dryness she couldn't and didn't understand. "Gil Masera."

"Emily Brecken," Emily said. "Brenna, did you see that big storm a few nights past? That's when I first tried to check on you. The whole sky lit up—it was the strangest thing—" she cut herself off, looking around the barn. "Where's Druid?"

Amazing how two little words could change the world, kicking her mood out from under her, closing her throat up painfully tight. Brenna tried to answer, but could only manage, "He's—" before finding herself without words or the wherewithal to say them.

"The storm caused some damage over here," Masera said, taking her hand. After another moment, when it became clear she couldn't say it herself, he added, "We were out in it, and Druid was killed. One of those freak things."

Emily gasped, and covered it with a hand over her mouth. "Oh, Brenna! I'm so sorry! What happened? No, never mind—forget I asked. You can tell me when you feel like talking about it." She stuck a hand in her pocket, pulling out a folded paper and giving it a doubtful look. "I don't know if you want this, now . . ."

Brenna ran a finger under each eye, sighed deeply, and pulled herself together. "What is it?"

"The girls were playing on the Web, as usual. They found a new site under their Nuadha search—they still run one for you every time they go on. Look, there's a brand-new kennel not twenty minutes from here." Emily held out the paper.

A new kennel. Brenna took the paper, unfolded it and held it so both she and Masera could see; it was the printout of the Web site's home page, complete with photos of a striking merle Cardigan and contact information.

"Look at the phone number," Masera said.

"I see it," Brenna said, and the paper trembled in her hands.

He took it from her and said, "I'll be back in a moment," as he left the barn.

Emily looked after him, looked back at Brenna, and raised an eyebrow. "Niiice," she said, which was exactly what she'd said the very first time she'd spotted Masera, the day he'd been making arrangements to work with Pets!. Then she sobered, and added, "Are you really okay, Brenna? And did you hear about the raid at Parker's—" She stopped short, narrowing her eyes at Brenna, her thoughts moving so fast Brenna could practically hear them churning away. "You were involved, weren't you? You and Mister Busted-Up? I take it he turned out to be one of the Good Guys?"

Brenna laughed, tremulous though it sounded. "Later, Emily. I need to get things sorted out for myself." And she did, because she only now realized that there would be talk, and similar questions from other people. She and Masera would have to come up with a simple all-purpose response, although Emily . . . Emily alone might get the whole story. "And yeah, he's one of the good guys, and yeah, I'll be okay."

"Okay," Emily said, accepting the short version. She spent a few moments with deliberately changed subjects—the girls, her recent needlepoint-pattern sale to a craft catalog, Sam's latest gossip. "We were going to get together for dinner last weekend . . . maybe this next one? And . . . maybe the two of you?"

"Me, for sure," Brenna said. "Him, I'll ask."

And *him* walked back into the barn. "Sure," he said to Emily. "Just make it something a man can eat with one hand," and held out his car keys to Brenna. "Wanna go for a drive? Just twenty minutes or so."

"You called them," Brenna said, and put her hands over her eyes, not knowing what else to do with herself, and not quite understanding why she felt like she was about to step off the edge of a cliff and walk on thin air. "You called them."

"And they said *come*. Eztebe knows we'll be late for dinner. Your choice."

She took the car keys.

"Call me," Emily said, standing in the doorway with

her arms crossed and a knowing smile on her face as they headed for Masera's SUV.

Brenna had become accustomed to driving it these past days—it purred along like a luxury car, and didn't jolt Masera around as her truck would have. Now she drove it in a daze, and when she found the right address, pulling in the driveway to sit next to the spanking-new NUADHA KENNEL sign, she just sat there with her hands on the wheel. The house stood before them on a large rural lot with lots of grass and carefully landscaped trees; the realtor sign still leaned against the garage. A newer home than Brenna's, but old enough to have charm instead of a cookie-cutter look. The back was entirely fenced, and several adult Cardigans appeared at a side gate to announce their arrival in tones of great importance.

Masera reached over and removed the keys from the ignition. "It's all right, Brenna. You don't have to explain anything to them. I told them I was in the market for Cardigans—and I am. I wasn't just spinning words way back when."

"Okay," Brenna said, her voice low. She nodded to herself, and repeated it. "Okay." Then she slid out of the car, tucked her braid into her back pocket, and went around to the passenger side to help him ease the long step to the ground. He was getting tired; she could tell from just how hard he leaned on her, and she only then realized how long she'd kept him out on this first day of full mobility.

"I'll last," he said, which was the first she knew how much of her thoughts had made it to her face; she wrinkled her nose at him and he grinned. "Let's go."

So she took his hand and walked up to the front door, where she would have hesitated if he hadn't been there, but because he was she punched the doorbell with her finger even as they stepped onto the landing.

The middle-aged woman who answered the door greeted them with a smile and a thick Irish brogue. " 'Twas you who called us, then? I'm Kathleen O'Meara. Please come in." And she opened the door wide, leading the way through to the back of the house without preamble, taking them past moving boxes both empty and full and to a set of wide sliding glass doors and an enclosed porch. "I was telling the young man, we've just got a litter ready to go, but they're mostly show prospects, and I really do want to place them in show homes. We need to establish a presence here in the States—" Through the porch they went, a brightly lit place full of crates and water bowls and a folded exercise pen.

"Showing's not a problem," Masera said. "I'll be showing obedience in any event."

She gave them a second glance, one with interest and more intent appraisal. "Is that so, then?" she said as she led them through another sliding door and into the backyard, where they were immediately accosted by five Cardigans, tails wagging. But Brenna had eyes only for the second exercise pen, a portable enclosure of wire panels set up in the far corner of the yard where the grass was thick and the sun was bright. She only vaguely heard Kathleen O'Meara usher the dogs into the house, or the comments she made to Masera as they headed for the ex-pen, where Kathleen unhooked one of the panels and let the puppies spill out. Six of them, a couple of months old and still floppy-eared, aside from one or two oddball exceptions and a single brindle pup with both enormous ears already pricked upright.

"The brindle is already placed," Kathleen said, and that was the last Brenna heard, for her gaze fell on a stout-legged little tricolor, his jagged white collar gleaming and his struggling ears charmingly speckled, running straight to her feet as if he knew he belonged there. She clutched Masera's arm, unable to say a word. And then she fell to her knees and gathered him up to find familiar love-me eyes framing a white muzzle and a perfectly symmetrical white blaze.

"We just lost one," Masera was saying, as Kathleen murmured an understanding, "Yes, I know the look." And they went on to talk about the things a good breeder asks any prospective owner—their facilities, their background, the family members, their sched-ules—while Brenna buried her face in the puppy's ruff and cried in disbelieving joy. Until at last the woman said, with some apology, that while their normal policy was to let the new owners choose a registered name, for this first litter in the states they'd decided to name the pups ahead of time. "This particular puppy hasn't ever taken to anyone like this before. We call him Nuadha's Silver—"

"Druid," Brenna whispered, resting her cheek against the top of his puppy-soft head. "Druid," she said again, while the rest of the puppies clamored for her attention, climbing her legs and licking the exposed skin of her arms as Masera's hand grazed the top of her head in a comforting caress. Druid brushed his whiskers against her face, inspecting her.

Not the same. It couldn't be the same.

She looked up at Masera, found him grinning as broadly and foolishly as she'd ever seen.

It could be *better*.

Doranna's Backstory

After obtaining a degree in wildlife illustration and environmental education, Doranna spent a number of years deep in the Appalachian Mountains, where she knew several Redbones just as deeply brain-challenged as Sunny. When she emerged, it was as a writer who found herself irrevocably tied to the natural world and its creatures.

Doranna, who isn't sure if she lives in New York or Arizona, hangs around with three Cardigan Welsh Corgis—Carbon Unit (Kacey), Jean-Luc Picardigan, and Belle—and drags her saddle wherever she goes.

You can contact her at:
dmd@doranna.net
or
PMB 207
2532 North 4th St.
Flagstaff, AZ 86004
(SASE please)

or visit http://www.doranna.net/